DETECTIVE QUINN ISAACS:

THE EARLY MORNING CRIME

JACQUE JACOBS

An imprint of
Drellag Press, LLC

Acknowledgements

Thanks is never enough for the people who encourage you in life and in writing. Dr. Dondra Maney and Susan Lovelace continue to read every word I write and generously share their insights and comments. Thank you for being my friends. Ivy King, talented and gifted human and professional, is the inspiration for a critical character in this story. We worked with an amazing team of professionals and staff at Highlands Elementary School in Indian River County, Florida, in the 1990s. Collectively we created, as Ivy pointed out, our own "Camelot."

Thanks to my friend and neighbor, Debbie McDaniel, for her interest and support in my writing. As in all my stories, names of characters are often prompted by names of friends over my lifetime. Dr. Reg Laughton, friend and former colleague, is observant and analytical, but not an FBI man. I hope he gets a kick out of this young character in my story.

As mentioned in other works of mine, I am proud of my grandsons, Kris and Michael, and deeply appreciate their interest in their Choctaw heritage. As members of the Choctaw tribe of Oklahoma, they have a commitment to learning and honoring that aspect of their heritage. Over the years, I have tried to learn about American tribes and learn from their recorded wisdom. I hope I honor that heritage in the words I share in various books.

Last, but certainly not least, I am grateful for the many writers in the Laura (Riding) Jackson Foundation who inspire me by their writings and who willingly give feedback to help me improve mine.

The final steps in bringing this book to print and e-book could not have happened without the amazing photographic work of Bill Johnston, awesome cover design by PixelSudio at http://www.Fiverr.com, and book formatting by Arkonna at http://www.Fiverr.com

Dedication

To all who write and all who read—I dedicate this book.

As Samuel Johnson (1709-1784) said, "A writer only begins a book. A reader finishes it."

Other Works of Fiction by Jacque Jacobs

Love is a Cabin Series

High on a Mountain – Book 1

Life on a Mountain – Book 2

Settled on a Mountain – Book 3

New Beginnings on a Mountain – Book 4

Community Unites on a Mountain – Book 5

Holidays on a Mountain – Book 6

Detective Quinn Isaacs Series

The (Almost) Perfect Crime – Book 1

The (Imperfect) Web of Crime – Book 2

Table of Contents

Part I: Crime Comes in Many Forms 1

Part II: Follow the Clues 147

Part I
Crime Comes in Many Forms

Chapter 1

Be patient and tough; someday this pain will be useful to you.

Ovid

Not an Ordinary Morning

"Detective Isaacs..." Chief Hansen of the Round City Police kept her eyes focused on Quinn.

Quinn Isaacs, lead detective, looked at her boss. "Yes, ma'am?" Her eyes darted around the room. *It's okay, Eliza, they can't hear the drip outside.* Then she focused on the large analog clock on the wall in the Chief's office—hearing the quiet tick, tick, tick. *It's not the faucet in the science lab. I'm not back in a high school shooting. This shooting just happened—didn't it?* It was eight thirty-five on a warm spring morning in the mountains of east Tennessee.

The Chief waited a beat.

Sitting where he could see both women, Captain Brown slowly moved his eyes from the Chief to their lead detective.

Chief Jill Hansen's voice was clear and crisp. "Do you understand you're on administrative leave pending the completion of the investigation in this matter by the State Bureau of Investigation?"

"Yes, ma'am."

"You will need to sign this document for the surrender of your badge, ID, service weapon, secure phone, and all keys including the ones to your official vehicle. You are not to leave town, is that understood?"

"Ma'am?" Quinn looked from the Chief to Captain Brown. "Sorry, yes, ma'am, I know the protocol for an officer involved shooting." She reached for her service weapon to hand to the Chief—only to remember it had been taken from her at the scene. Her badge, still clipped to her belt, clicked as she took it off and placed it on the table. She slid it toward Chief Hansen along with her ID, phone, and keys.

Wee Hours of the Morning

Off a remote road near Round City, Phillip Young's day started like all the others—with his main goal in life to escape the screeching voice of his unemployed mother. The black walls in his teen-age room and the music blaring in his headphones took him to places in his head he just couldn't explain to anyone. He slid deeper under the covers, pulling the black duvet over his head—as if it would stop the psychedelic colors swirling before his eyes. *Bitch, who does she think she is?* He sighed. *She'd say, "I'm your mother, that's who. Blah, blah, blah."* He tightened his hands over the earphones amplifying the sounds inside his head even more. *Then she'd say, "Get a job. Do you think I'm made of money?" No, Bitch, I think you're a...* He'd call her a bitch in his head but never out loud and for sure he wasn't going to call her a whore—even though he was pretty sure she met the definition of one. *She takes money and gifts from those old men, doesn't she? She doesn't have a job either, unless you call...*he let the thought drop. *How'd you expect me to learn about getting a job? Answer that one, Bitch.*

The cover was snatched off his face and a flashlight shone in his eyes.

His blood-curdling yell bounced off the walls.

Tall and thin, like her son, Sonia Young glared at him. "Get up, Phillip Anthony Young. You're not going to sleep the day away. I have a temp job today in Maryville and you can ride with me and go look for work. Get showered and be dressed decent in fifteen minutes—and I mean it." At the knock on the front door, she stomped out of the room.

He raised up on his elbow and glared at her slender back. *Oh, I'll get up alright, Mama. You might not be ready for what this morning...* He plopped back down and pulled the cover over his head.

An Unusual Start to Quinn's Day

Quinn's normal drive to the Station at six-thirty was greeted by the pale, early, light of morning as the glow revealed the full bloom of spring: the white and yellow trillium in abundance, and the "drink your tea" chirp of the Eastern Towhee floating in the air. She had spotted an officer in what appeared to be a routine stop standing beside a red sports car with the top down. She slowed to see if he needed assistance. As she lowered her window, she heard his command—clear and crisp, but polite: "Put your hands on the steering wheel." Quinn listened for sirens from any approaching backup vehicles. Hearing none, she stopped several car lengths behind the sports car. She checked the position of the convertible and noticed the police SUV was facing her and very close to the front left bumper of the convertible. *That's a strange position.* She scanned the park and saw no one. The driver's head was turned toward Officer Simmons and Quinn made note of the oversized sunglasses with a paisley blue scarf wrapped like a 1960's movie star. Later, like a video stuck in a repeating loop, Quinn would replay the incident in her head trying to figure out how things turned so horrible—so fast.

Now, though, in the quiet tick of the clock on the wall, she was across the conference table from Chief Hansen

"Quinn..." Jill Hansen's voice was softer now—compassionate.

Quinn stared at her boss. "Ma'am?"

"I expect the SBI to have this matter cleared up in forty-eight to seventy-two hours. During that time, you'll need to meet with the psychologist who does our fitness evaluations. She will contact you and arrange your first meeting."

"First meeting? Will there be more than one?" Quinn felt her brain flip—from her emotional reaction to the events of the morning—to the competent detective she was. "I've never..."

"Quinn, I know you've never been in this situation before. It will be over soon. Is there someone I can call to come be with you?"

Quinn tipped her head up slightly and looked toward the ceiling. *How can this no-nonsense chief be such a by-the-book cop and at the same time a kind and caring person?* "No. I'll be fine. Can someone take me home?" *Guess I could walk.*

"Detective Marshall is waiting to take you."

George Marshall was the senior detective in the Round City Police. Quinn, as lead detective, was officially George's boss but Jill knew they had become friends. Confident in her own competence, Jill had also invited Quinn to use her first-name when they were alone or away from the job. Jill valued the importance of community—at work and in the town.

Jill studied Quinn as she tried to tame her own flashback to the first time she had surrendered her credentials and her weapon. It was a police officer's nightmare—no matter what the circumstances.

Quinn nodded. "Thank you." She stood, looked at the Chief, then the Captain, and promptly sat down again. "May I go?"

Jill smiled at Quinn and nodded. *You'll get through this. The wait is the worst.* "Take care of yourself, Quinn. This will be behind you soon." Jill extended her hand to Quinn.

Quinn stood to her full five-feet-nine inches, squared her shoulders, looked her Chief directly in the eyes and shook her hand. She turned and shook hands with Captain Brown, and walked toward the outer door as the Chief opened it. Before she walked through the door into the hall, she heard the normal buzz of chatter stop as the officers came to attention. Quinn glanced back at the Chief. *They respect Chief Hansen. That's good.*

The Chief nodded at the officers because she knew they were respecting a fellow officer who was involved in the death of another officer. She kept her face somber. *Some will be cheering silently for Quinn—hoping she's the one responsible for the death of the suspected killer of their fellow officer.*

George Marshall was standing by the front desk and walked toward Quinn. "This way, boss. My car's out back." He gently touched her elbow and turned her away from the hall toward her office.

The Chief nodded and walked back into her office.

"Right. Sure. Don't know what I was thinking." She gave him a wan smile. "Thanks, George." *Of course I can't go to my office; it's not mine anymore.*

George saw there was no one in the hall—as if they had silently slipped into a doorway in a well-choreographed dance. He wondered if Quinn noticed. He spoke softly. "I've got you covered, Quinn."

Boss? Quinn? Got you covered? She looked at him and then jumped as the sounds of the early morning echoed in her head: *Pop! Slam! Pop! Help…*The pop of gunfire was unmistakable—even in her memory.

A Cup of Tea

George pulled into the driveway at 1211 Sunrise in the older part of Round City where large lots were common and elegant homes hid behind large oaks and maples. He knew Quinn's grandmother had given her the house and paid to remodel it a decade ago. He turned off the engine.

"Won't you come in?" Quinn's southern drawl seemed accentuated at the moment.

"I'll make you some tea and then I need to head back." George was out his door and around the vehicle before Quinn realized he was out of the car.

"Okay. Sure, George, I understand." *Do I? Is this how a criminal feels? Am I a criminal?* She jumped when George opened the passenger door for her.

"Normal reaction, boss. Want me to call Billy?" George had considered calling Billy Williams, Quinn's friend and the lead detective in the Valley Sheriff's Office, the next county over. He suspected most of the area, if not the state, had already heard what had happened. *They wouldn't know Quinn was involved.* He was trying to be careful, for Quinn's sake, as he balanced his responsibility as a police officer and his personal friendship with her.

"No. I'm fine. I've got some reports to catch up on, so I'll…" She trailed off. She took her hand off the door knob to her front door and turned to look at him. "Guess I don't have access to my files, do I?"

His downturned mouth told her all she needed to know. He gave a slight shake of his head. "Might be a good time to catch up on some of those projects you've put off—well, if you're like the rest of us. You know…clean the closets, put away the winter clothes…that kind of stuff."

"Yeah. Right on the top of my list for a great way to pass the day." She turned back and entered her code and heard the whirr of the lock. She stepped to the side once she walked in. "Welcome." She bowed like a butler in a B-rated movie.

George tried to keep his face impassive. "Go put on some comfortable clothes. I'll put on the water for tea." He hesitated. "If that's alright?" His eyes showed the pain he felt for her.

Something in Quinn seemed to click—like a light switch that hadn't worked for days. "That's would be great. Thanks. I'll be right out." She headed down the hall to her bedroom.

George had been in Quinn's home several times. He and his wife had supper here with her and Billy just last week. He walked to the kitchen but realized he had no idea where anything was. He scanned the counters and his eyes stopped on the stove top. *Ah, a tea kettle. Of course.* He filled it with water and turned on the stove. He looked around to see if there was some obvious place the tea bags would be. *A bear canister? Really, Quinn?* He lifted the lid to find short bread cookies. Then next to it he saw a wooden box decoupaged with the word "TEA" on the face of it and a dragonfly on top. He opened it to see compartments with different types of tea. He picked it up and put it on the island. *She can choose her poison. Mugs? Where would she keep the mugs?* He jerked his head when she spoke.

"In the upper cupboard to the left of the stove." Quinn pointed.

"Okay, mind reader, too?"

"No, just next logical step in making me tea. Thanks, George." She felt herself flinch when her personal phone vibrated. She reached into the pocket of the jeans.

The text was brief: "U OK?"

She clutched the phone tightly and slipped it back in her pocket. *You'll have to wait, Billy Williams. I don't know what I can say yet.*

"None of my business," George spoke in a soft well-modulated tone, "but if it's Detective Williams, you can talk to him. I'm headed out." He saw her hands flat on the island countertop and reached across and lightly tapped the top of one of them. "It'll be okay, Quinn. Call if you need me." He turned and walked to the front of the house and out the door.

Quinn grabbed the tea kettle as it started to whistle. She opened the cupboard and took out the teapot, filled it with hot water, and let it sit for a minute. Then she poured out the water, refilled it, and added two bags of chamomile tea and let it steep. She pulled out the stool at the counter—then pushed it back in. On autopilot, she took the tray from the shelf, put the tea pot and tea cup on it, walked over to the bear canister and took out two shortbread cookies. *Why not? Seems like a good time for a pity party.* She walked into the great room off the kitchen which overlooked her large and very private back yard. She set the tray down and opened the French doors, turned back to pick it up, and felt her phone vibrate again.

"Pls call when u can." There was a heart emoji, too.

She put the phone back in her jeans and picked up the tray, walked out on the expansive brick terrace, and put the tray on the table next to her favorite rocker. She poured a cup of tea and sat down. She was totally on autopilot. She rocked gently as her eyes scanned the white and pink blooms on the dogwood trees. An image of her grandmother rocking in this chair caused the corners of her mouth to turn up in a smile—then she choked—and a tear ran down her face.

Well, Granny. This is one story you wouldn't believe...and one you wouldn't want to hear. I miss you. You always understood, even if you didn't like it, why I had to be in law enforcement—after seeing Eliza die from the shooter at our high school. She shivered and wrapped her arms tightly across her chest. Slowly she pulled out her phone and entered a text: "Time to talk?" *Please don't ask me anything, Billy. Just let me talk.*

The response was not a text; it was her phone ringing.

"Hey, Billy." Her voice was soft.

Billy heard the sorrow in her voice. "Hey, yourself. Where are you?"

She found some solace in the tenderness of his slow southern drawl. "On my back terrace." *Wonder if he'll still love me? Will you, Billy?* Trying to clear her thoughts, she blinked and shook her head causing the ponytail of her golden blond hair to brush against her neck.

"Want company?" Billy had heard there was an officer-involved shooting, but no details. He knew there was likely only one reason she was home.

Her tone was flat. "Not very good company at the moment."

"Hey, I'm not the best company, but I'm better than 'not very good.'" He hoped the quip would make her laugh. There was no response. "Quinn, I'll be there in about ten minutes."

"Okay. Not going anywhere."

Billy couldn't decide if he should hang up the phone and floor it—or keep her talking while he drove sanely.

Things Are Not Always What They Appear

The A-team of the forensic experts at the Round City Police were combing the scene around the red convertible to make sure they had all evidence around the shootout that resulted in the death of the sports car driver and a police officer. They had three guns and knew for sure the owners of two of them: Detective Quinn Issacs and Officer Albert Simmons.

"Hey, Sarge, look at this."

Sergeant Steve Clark stepped away from the police cruiser and moved over to the convertible where a technician was searching the trunk. He saw the mat over the spare tire well flipped back. He let out a long slow whistle.

"Yeah, right boss?"

"How many?"

"I haven't moved them yet, need to get photos, but I count at least six guns."

"Step back a minute, please." Sarge moved in without touching any part of the 2011 Saab convertible. "I count six, too, but there also appears to be something black under them."

"I saw that, too. Ammunition?" The tech looked at Sarge.

"Could be." He stepped away and looked at the back end of the vehicle.

"What's up, Sarge?"

"The box isn't heavy enough to weigh down the back end. There could be a booby trap to some explosives, too. Get your photos as quickly as you can. Then move away. I need to make a call before we touch anything."

"Sure, Sarge."

Steve moved over to the sidewalk and hit send on his phone.

"Marshall."

"Hey, George. Clark here. Are you lead on the shooting?"

"Local lead. SBI folks are coming in. You know—objectivity and all that."

"When do you expect them?"

"Walking through the door momentarily, I think." Out the window, George saw a sedan and black van, which had the State Bureau of Investigation decal, pull into the parking lot. He watched as folks who could only be law enforcement got out.

"Any look familiar?"

"Yep. I recognize Agents Davis and Lawton. Don't know who the others are. What's up?"

"Might have some explosives here. I'd feel better if we could get the SBI dog in here."

"Got it. I'm sure the Chief will meet with them, but I'll head up the hall to meet them. I'll call you back." He was about to end the call when he said, "Hey, Steve."

"Yeah?" Steve sounded distracted.

"Be careful."

"10-4."

"10-4." George ended the call and headed out into the hall.

"Detective." Chief Hansen was in the hall headed toward him.

George who had been lost in thought looked up. "Ma'am?"

"SBI is here. Please join us in the conference room."

"Yes, ma'am." He wondered if she would have invited him if he hadn't been in the hall. *Stop it. She's not the late Chief. Much as I liked him, he had a divide and conquer view of the world.* He opened the door to the conference room and stepped back for the Chief to enter. *Nah, he had more of a silo mentality. Need to know and all that.* He sighed. *New boss in town.*

"Are you alright, Detective Marshall?"

"Yes, ma'am. Never an easy day when we lose one of our own."

"Exactly. Now let's figure out why we did."

They turned as five SBI agents crossed the lobby toward the conference room. "I'll get coffee ready, ma'am."

"Good idea. Thanks."

George moved to the back counter. *Well, Carrie, it's my day to be the barista. Thanks for teaching me.* He smiled as he thought of his wife at her bakery and coffee shop. *Wish I had some of your croissants to offer them. Tea for Quinn and coffee for the SBI agents.* He looked around the empty room, stopped, blinked his eyes, and sighed as it settled on him that Quinn wouldn't be sitting at the table today.

He turned to see the agents entering the conference room. He walked up to Agent Sandy Davis. "Nice to see you again."

"Sorry it's under these circumstances." Sandy extended her hand.

"Me, too." He wasn't aware that he reached for his own badge with the black band on it as he looked at the SBI agents' black bands. It was then that he noticed the Chief had her badge with the black band on her jacket. She normally didn't have her badge showing. The somberness of the moment hit him. He exchanged greetings with the other agents and stood until the Chief spoke.

"Looks like everyone has coffee. Please, let's get started." She moved her hand indicating they should sit.

"Thank you for coming, Agents. Detective Marshall will be point-person for our team. I, of course, am available as you need."

All heads nodded.

"I'll get you up to speed with what I know at the moment, then Detective Marshall can work with you to decide next steps." She spoke with quiet efficiency as she recounted what was currently known around the events in the officer-involved shooting. "So, we have the officer and the driver in our morgue. Officer Simmons was single and his parents live out in the country. I'm headed out to speak to them as soon as I've answered any questions you have. The driver had no license, but she is also in the morgue and…" She saw George lift his finger indicating he had something to say. "Yes, Detective."

"Ma'am, I just got a text from the Medical Examiner and the driver is a male."

"Oh?"

"Yes, ma'am."

"Agents, we assumed the driver was female due to the clothes, sunglasses, and headscarf."

No one spoke or commented.

"Thank you, Detective. I've summed up what I have so far. Anything to add, Detective Marshall?"

"Sergeant Clark has requested a dog search."

"Based on?" The Chief raised her left eyebrow almost imperceptibly, but George knew it meant she was probably running scenarios through her head.

George spoke with a clear, clipped voice. "There are six guns, appear to be Glock G-18s, and something in a black box under them in the wheel well."

Agent Davis looked at the Chief. "With your permission, ma'am, I'll request one immediately."

Jill looked at Agent Davis. "Please do. I will be out of the station for the next few hours." The Chief stood.

George and the SBI agents stood in a show of respect.

As the door closed behind Jill Hansen, George and the others sat.

"Thanks for coming, folks. As you were told by the Chief, our lead detective, Quinn Isaacs was involved in the shooting."

They all nodded but none looked him in the eye.

Chapter 2

We're each of us alone, to be sure.
What can you do but hold your hand out in the dark?
Ursula K. Le Guin

The Stillness of Quiet

"I've almost finished my special project in my woodshop." Billy continued to talk while he drove. He brought up whatever popped into his head as long as it wasn't related to either of their jobs. There was no response from Quinn. "I can't wait for you to see it."

"Me, either." Her response was flat—almost robotic.

He pulled into her driveway. "I'm at your home, Quinn. I'm going to let myself in."

"Okay."

She was either involved in the morning incident or knew the officer who was. On the police broadcast of an officer-involved shooting, Billy had not seen any identifying information, nor would he have expected any. There had simply been an "all clear" which was notification to surrounding jurisdictions that there was no imminent danger to their communities. He took the front steps two-at-a-time, punched the code on the door, and shut and locked it behind him. He took long strides as he crossed the great room and stopped in his tracks when he reached the French doors to the back of the house. Quinn was staring off into the back garden with her hands clinched on the arms of the rocking chair. His heart dropped in his chest. He straightened his shoulders and opened the doors making as little noise as possible.

"I'm here." His voice was low and warm. He didn't want to startle her. He pulled up a rocker next to her and sat down without saying anything else. He put his hand on top of hers.

Without shifting her gaze, she turned her hand over, laced her fingers through his, and squeezed tightly.

He gave a quick squeeze and let his fingers rest with hers. They rocked silently.

After a minute or two she spoke. "I can't say anything."

"Okay. You don't have to." He leaned over and kissed her on the cheek.

She turned her head toward him.

His heart ached. The pain was so deep in her hazel eyes he thought he might drown in it. "Okay. Thanks." She turned her gaze back to the garden.

"Are you drinking that tea?"

Quinn jerked her hand from his. "Oh, my. I haven't offered you anything." She jumped up.

Billy stood up as fast as she did and pulled her to him. "Shhh...I don't need anything but you. If I do, I can get it myself." He held her and stroked his hand down her back. "Shhh, shhh, it'll be okay." He felt her rock gently against him and then felt her go slack. He thought she was going to slide to the floor. He felt her hand jerk away when she hit his service weapon. "Shhh, we'll get through this."

"Thanks...for...coming." She choked back tears. "I needed you."

"I'm glad. I'm here for as long as you need." He turned her back toward her rocker.

She sat. Her voice was barely a whisper. "Do you want some tea?"

"Think I'll get some iced tea. Anything you want from the kitchen?"

"Just for you to come back."

"In two shakes of a lamb's tail."

She chuckled—it was almost inaudible. She managed to grab breaths through her words. "My grandmother...would...have loved...to hear that." She looked up at him and her voice went soft. "I haven't heard it in years."

He leaned in and kissed her on the forehead. "Be right back."

Quinn rocked in silence trying to keep her mind from the events of the early morning. She jumped when her phone rang. She answered without looking at the screen. "Yes."

"Detective Isaacs?"

"Yes."

"This is Ivy Kingston; I am a psychologist…"

"I've been expecting your call, Dr. Kingston."

Billy stopped just outside the door. *Dr. Kingston? This is not good.* He knew she was a psychologist on contract with several of the rural policing agencies. He waited.

Quinn's head was nodding. "Sure, that's fine." She looked down at her watch. "I'll be there at eleven." She paused. "Yes, I can find your office. I'll see you then." She ended the call and stared at her phone screen.

Billy walked toward her and sat down. He sipped his tea with his left hand and put his right one on hers again.

She kept her gaze on the garden. "I have to go in a few minutes."

"Sure. What can I do for you?"

She turned and looked at him. Her breathing was slow and steady. "I wish I knew. Are you working today?"

"Nope. Took leave."

"Why?"

"Sixth sense that the love of my life might need me closer than the Valley."

She smiled. "I do. I just can't talk right now."

"No need." *How can I tell you I understand? I'm pretty sure where you are at the moment and I've been there.* He didn't say a word as he squeezed his fingers gently on the top of her hand. "May I drive you to your appointment?"

She stared at him.

He smiled at her. "It's entirely up to you, but I'd like to be there for you. You don't have to tell me anything. I think it might help to know I'm outside waiting for you." *I wish someone had been outside waiting for me when I…* He knew to let the thought drop.

"Okay. I'm going to go change clothes. She's at her office here in town, not the one in Maryville."

"I know where it is, Quinn."

She looked over at him. "You do?"

He nodded.

"Okay. I'll be ready in fifteen minutes." She stood and started to pick up the tray.

"Leave it. I'll take care of it. You go do what you need to do."

The Morgue

Three of the SBI agents headed to the scene of the shooting with Kevin Millwood, another Round City detective. George Marshall stayed in the station with Agents Davis and Lawton.

George stood and took his cup to the sink and washed it out. "Let's head down to the morgue and then we can set up a board."

"Agent Davis, finished with your coffee?" Lawton lifted his and held out his hand for Sandy Davis's cup.

"Thanks." She handed him her cup as she stood. She looked at George. "Mind if we stop down the hall on our way?"

"By all means. Should have offered our facilities when you arrived."

"No problem." She looked at the text on her secure phone. "Dog handler just arrived at the scene."

George let out a sigh. "Good news. Lots of tension when you can't visually assess the risk at a scene."

Agent Lawton slapped George on the back. "You got that right."

George ignored the unexpected familiarity which almost caused him to reach for his weapon. *Yeah, I was young once, too. You'll learn.* "This way." He opened the door.

They walked into the hall and George pointed to the sign for the women's restroom for Agent Davis. "This way, Lawton." He headed for the men's room.

Back out in the hall, George led them down then hall, stopped at the door to the stairs, and opened it. "Doc's expecting us. Follow me."

"Morning, folks." Dr. Walters looked up from the body he was working on.

"Dr. Walters, meet Agent Davis and Agent Lawton of the SBI."

"Agent Davis and I have met. Thanks for coming. Nice to meet you, Agent Lawton."

"Hey, Doc. Sorry for your loss." Agent Davis stood back waiting for an invitation from the medical examiner to step forward.

Dr. Walters leaned his head toward his assistant. "Don't think you've met Sue. She's my assistant." He pointed to the metal stools at the top end of the table. "Pull up a stool." His eyes glanced at the three shields all with the black band signifying a fallen officer.

The three sat on the stools.

The medical examiner pointed to the body on his stainless steel table. "This is Officer Albert Simmons. Officer Simmons, these fine folks are going to find out what happened today. You're in good hands."

George knew that the ME spoke to the bodies on his table. *Not sure I believe they speak to him...well, not in the true sense of speaking. Guess their remains do need to speak to him to figure out what happened.*

"Hard to tell how many hits the body took." The ME's tone was flat and matter of fact. "No chance of surviving the assault. God rest his soul." He never looked at the visitors.

"The John Doe?" Detective Marshall watched the ME's face.

"Our officer is my priority at the moment, but a cursory overview indicates definitely male, multiple bullets—bullet to side of head likely COD."

George turned to the SBI agents. "Questions at this point?"

Agent Lawson started to speak and then didn't.

George stood up. "Doc will let us know when he's finished a thorough exam and can determine the cause of death. Anything else we need at this point, Doc?"

"I'll let you know as soon as I have something to share."

"Thanks for taking care of Officer Simmons, Doc." He turned to the assistant. "Thanks, Sue. We'll leave you to it."

George turned and walked toward the elevator. The two SBI agents followed.

A Seemingly Casual Drive

"The flowers on the trees are beautiful, Billy."

"So, I see."

"I wonder why we don't take more time to appreciate the beauty of nature." Quinn kept her gaze out the passenger window of his SUV.

"We should."

"But we don't." It was a simple statement—flat of emotion.

"Then let's see that we do better about taking walks and hikes. I noticed the pink and white blossoms on the dogwoods in your back yard. Does it take a lot to care for them?" He knew the distraction of a simple conversation was the best thing for her right now.

She turned to look at him. "Billy Williams, how would I know? All I do is sign the check to pay the gardener. I assume he fertilizes them—I don't even know that. Pretty pathetic, isn't it?"

"Normal, I'd say—not pathetic—normal. I think most of us hope there are enough nutrients in the soil to take care of the plants around our homes. I sure do." He chuckled. He glanced over and saw a brief smile on her face. "I do manage to cut the grass from time to time."

"Don't overdo it." She chuckled.

Billy loosened the grip he had on the wheel. *She's settling into herself. That's good.* He turned on the blinker to turn onto the downtown square. He had been trying to time it so Quinn would be able to walk in the door of the psychologist's office just before eleven. He drove three blocks and turned into the parking lot of the two-story office building. He'd been here before. He parked and left the engine running.

"I have no idea how long I'll be." Quinn stared out the windshield. She reached over and took his hand. "Is that okay?" She turned to look at him.

"I'll be right here. Your phone is in your pocket and I have mine. Call or text if you need me for anything. I'm not going anywhere." He leaned over and kissed her lightly on the lips.

She responded with a long desperate kiss. "I love you, Billy."

"I know." He smiled at her. "Do you want me to walk you to the door?"

"No. I'll be okay. Knowing you're waiting for me will help."

"Then head-on in so you're not late. I love you, Quinn."

"Back atcha." She made an effort to put on a smile, opened the door, and her long stride carried her to the door in eight steps.

Billy admired the way her low heels and tailored black suit accentuated her height. He watched her hair brush her shoulders with each step. He leaned back. *That's my Quinn. Keep that confidence. You'll come out of this okay—maybe a little worse for wear, but okay.* He lowered his window an inch, turned off the engine, and leaned his head against the head rest. *I'm here for you, no matter what.*

At the Scene

Sergeant Clark stepped forward as the dog handler exited the SBI van. "Steve Clark." He extended his hand. "We've met."

"Right. I'm Sid Brown. Give me a minute and I'll get Millie out and see what we have here."

Steve watched the van door open and saw the dog sitting obediently waiting for a command. "Expecting some of your folks from Knoxville any minute." Both men turned as a black sedan stopped at the crime scene tape at the end of the block and people exited.

Steve saw them show their credentials to the officer posted there.

Sid was scanning the area of the town park beyond the yellow tape. "Hope you've had some time to sweep the scene."

"Mostly bullet recovery—but good photos of everything. We're good for you to do what you need to do."

Detective Millwood approached with the four agents. "Sergeant Clark, these folks are from the SBI." Introductions were made and handshakes exchanged.

"Thanks for coming. We've done an initial sweep and collected everything we can see within the perimeter of the scene. We can see at least six Glocks, probably G-18s, in the trunk under the spare tire mat. There's something black under it and it may simply be ammunition, but prefer to have this gal check it out." Steve pointed to the dog.

Sid Brown had the dog's lead in his right hand. "Assume you know those G-18s are illegal?"

"Known and noted."

"Millie will pick up the powder in ammunition, too. With the firing of guns, we may still end up having to suit up to remove what's there to be sure what we have." He saw Steve nod. "Any evidence of anyone in this park?" He pointed toward the large park to their left.

Steve spoke up immediately. "No. We've had it secured for a couple of hours. Closest house on the other side of the street is unoccupied." All eyes turned to the "for sale" sign. "We verified with the realtor and did a perimeter check. Traffic on either cross street has been diverted."

Sam nodded and pointed to the park. "Good. If you folks will step over there, we'll get to work."

Steve led his team, the SBI agents, and Detective Millwood into the park area, ensuring they had a line of sight to the rear of the convertible.

The Visit

Quinn opened the door to the office building and started down the hall. Dr. Kingston had said her office was the third door on the left. Quinn looked at the sign: *Ivy Kingston, PhD - Please enter and be seated.* Quinn opened the door into a sedate reception area. The walls were pale blue with paintings of the surrounding mountains. There were three chairs upholstered in pale blue with soft yellow and white geometric lines and a two seater sofa in a dark blue leather with yellow pillows. Quinn let out a sigh. She walked over to one of the paintings which she recognized as Clingman's Dome. She saw the artist's name in the corner and recognized the name of a well-respected regional painter. She turned to sit just as the door opened.

"Come in, Detective Isaacs." Ivy's blond hair softly framed her face highlighting blue eyes which conveyed compassion.

"Thank you. Dr. Kingston?"

"I am." Ivy Kingston extended her hand. "Please come in."

Quinn shook it. "Thanks." She walked into the interior office which was similarly appointed with the addition of a long cherry table used as a desk.

Dr. Kingston pointed to the sitting area. "Sit wherever you like."

Quinn chose a blue patterned wingback chair, sat, and crossed her ankles—an automatic posture taught by her wealthy and well-educated mother and grandmother: *A lady never crosses her knees.* She saw the carafe of water and the closed white carafe which she assumed had coffee.

"Would you like some water or coffee?"

"I'm fine at the moment, thank you."

"Then you won't mind if I have some coffee?"

"By all means." She watched as Ivy Kingston poured coffee and took a sip—no cream or sugar.

"In my review of your personnel file, I see you are from Knoxville." It was a simple, neutral comment.

"Yes." Quinn was not surprised the psychologist would have reviewed her file. She judged that Dr. Kingston was close to her own age—mid-to-late thirties.

"How long have you lived in Round City?"

"Just over ten years."

"Fortunate for our community." Ivy looked directly at Quinn.

Quinn did not respond.

"May I call you, Quinn?"

"Of course."

"Thanks. Feel free to call me, Ivy."

Quinn nodded.

"I'm aware as a detective you're accustomed to asking the questions. I have no doubt I could learn techniques from you to enhance my own questioning skills. That said, in our respective roles, we have an obligation to determine fact from speculation and to the best of our abilities get to the truth of what happened in this situation and its aftermath."

Quinn studied the woman's face. She let out a slow sigh. "I apologize. It's a turn of the tables, for sure." *Turn of the tables*: she felt the smile creep on her lips thinking of her grandmother using this old saying. *Oh, Grandmother, I miss you so much.*

"Not a problem. We may just have to figure out how to navigate together."

"Sure. What do you want to know?"

"First, and most of all, how are you feeling?"

"At this moment?" Quinn's eyes squinted.

Ivy Kingston nodded.

"Confused. I left for work at my usual early hour in the small rural town in the Smokies which I call home. Now I'm sitting with a psychologist to explain my reaction to being involved in a shoot-out which resulted in two people dying."

"I know you've already been debriefed at your station and..."

"I'll be debriefed again by the State Bureau of Investigation."

Ivy nodded. "Yes. Yes you will."

"I also know the more I tell what happened, the better the chance I'll remember some detail I omitted, and the better the chance I'll question what the real details are."

"From an investigative point of view, your initial recording, as you know, will be used as a baseline for the continuity of your statements." Ivy sipped her coffee. "For our purposes, you're aware my responsibility is to assess your emotional response to the incident."

"And my fitness for duty."

"Yes, that will come at some point, too."

Quinn turned her gaze from the painting above the desk to look at Ivy. "At some point?"

"Yes, Quinn. That point may be in a day or two or it may be longer. As you know, I'm just one element of the process."

Quinn leaned forward. "May I?" She reached for the carafe of water.

"Please, help yourself."

Quinn poured the water, took a sip. and sat back in the chair. "I'm accustomed to recording my observations to crime and reviewing the recordings of my interrogations. I'm very analytical and...and..."

Ivy waited. She watched Quinn's face as she seemed to settle into herself.

Quinn took another drink of water and continued. "And I'm my own worst critic."

Ivy smiled. "Is that a problem?"

"Sometimes. I'm not very good at cutting myself much slack."

"Might be a good trait."

"Most of the time."

"Have you cut yourself any slack today?"

"Only in as much as I knew I was better off not to drive myself here."

"Oh? Who brought you?'

"My friend, Billy Williams."

"Does he live here?"

"No. He lives in the Valley." She looked Ivy in the eyes. "He's lead detective there and we've been dating for a while now." Quinn continued. "I haven't said anything to him about what happened and he has not asked. I assume he saw an officer-involved shooting bulletin, but other than whatever deductions he has made by my presence here in your office, he does not know I was involved."

"Why?"

"Why, what?"

"Why didn't you tell him?"

"Because I know my responsibility to my oath, my code of conduct, and I haven't been interviewed by you or the SBI."

"Did he ask you what happened."

"No. And if he had, I would have been surprised."

"Will it bother you if he asks?"

"No...yes...maybe..." Quinn took a sip of water. "Honestly, I haven't even thought about it, because I wouldn't expect him to ask and he didn't. I also know when—if—I tell him at some point, it will go no further and he will consider the detail in light of its impact on me and the details of solving a case."

"Sounds like you do have a clear view of what would happen if you told him. Relax, Quinn. I'm not the enemy."

Quinn gave a wan smile and lifted her glass—as if in a toast. Then she took a drink of water and proceeded to recount the events of the morning.

Chapter 3

We could never learn to be brave and patient, if there were only joy in the world.
Helen Keller

The Crime Scene

Kevin Millwood stood with Steve Clark and the SBI agents and the Round City forensic techs near the middle of the park while keeping his line of sight to the convertible clear.

Kevin kept his eyes on the vehicle. "Steve, I assume there was no evidence of a timer or an explosive device."

"Not an audible one or one with any visible light. Challenge is there could be one that is activated by a phone."

Millwood turned to look at him. "Do you have the driver's phone?"

"Bagged and tagged. Doesn't mean there isn't another person involved in whatever is represented by those G-18 Glocks in the trunk."

"True."

Both men saw the wave from Sid Brown as he and Millie walked away from the red car and moved toward them.

Sid signaled Millie to halt. "Best guess is it's ammunition, but I'd rather we use caution and get the bomb disposal truck here."

Steve nodded. "Good by me. That work, Millwood?"

"Let's get it done." Millwood pulled out his secure phone and sent a text to Detective Marshall to update him and request the bomb disposal team from the SBI.

"Go ahead." Marshall texted back.

"10-4." Kevin Millwood responded. He turned to Sid not realizing he was on the phone. "How long do you think it will take?"

He held up a finger. "Hold on." He put his phone on his belt. "They'll be here within forty-fifty minutes. I suggest keeping the area clear just to be sure."

"No problem. I'll speak to the officers on patrol. Steve, if you're covered here, I'll take our SBI agents back to the station and be back shortly."

"We're good. If you'll update the officer down by your car, I'll get the other perimeters."

"Thanks. Appreciate it." Kevin Millwood stepped to the side and spoke to the SBI agents. The four followed him toward the street where they had left the car.

So Much to Consider

"Quinn, is this your first officer-involved shooting?" Ivy was watching Quinn carefully as she spoke.

"Depends on whether you're asking if it's my first time seeing a fellow officer shot or my first where I fired the shots at another person."

"Either."

Quinn looked up at the ceiling, off to the right, and then directly at Ivy. "In Immigration Enforcement, I was on scene at three shootings, but none involved the death of a fellow officer—although one was injured. I have aimed my weapon in a hostile situation, but not fired..." she paused, took a deep breath, and let it out slowly, "until today."

"Tell me how you feel about what happened today."

"The fact that I likely killed a person or that a fellow officer was killed in a hostile situation where I fired my weapon?"

"Just tell me whatever you're thinking. Don't feel you have to measure every statement before you say it. Just tell me what you're thinking—feeling."

Quinn's face went pale. "The good and bad news in law enforcement is you get lots of practice at suppressing your feelings." She sipped her water. "I suppose that's true in other professions, too–like yours, physicians, hmmm… ." She looked at Ivy. "I told you I'm prone to over analyzing, didn't I?"

"You did. Go on."

"I don't think I've ever considered what it would feel like to have to wait—on all we do in forensic work before we know anything about the sequence of events and ability to assign responsibility at a crime scene." She realized she was gently tapping her toe on the oriental carpet. "It seems different on this side of things." She paused. "I will accept my responsibility however it plays out… ." She stopped, turned toward the window, and stared at the large maple tree. She saw a bright red cardinal and was sure he was looking at her. "I… ." She stopped again.

Ivy waited without saying a word. She knew all too well the struggles of law enforcement officers to talk about any shooting, much less one which resulted in the death of one of their own.

"When I'm at the firing range, I try to be fully aware that I'm preparing to fire at another human being. It's part of the job. I have to believe I can handle knowing my bullet took the life of a perpetrator—that I am being judge and jury." She took another sip of water and her voice was barely audible. "I've had someone die right next to me…" She looked away. *Does she know about the school shooting when I was in high school?* She straightened her shoulders. "I've now realized I have never considered I might take the life of a fellow officer; it will be a struggle if I took Albert Simmons's life."

Ivy studied Quinn's posture and facial expressions. Both women knew arms could move when firing and bullets could land in unintended places and they wouldn't know until after the forensic analyses were completed which bullets took lives. Both also knew the waiting had psychological tolls on those involved.

"Tell me what you like to do in your off-duty hours."

Quinn all but guffawed. "Off-duty? Hard to go off duty in this profession. I like to hike, I occasionally get to cook which I enjoy, and Billy is teaching me to turn wood…" She paused and smiled. "I visit my parents in Knoxville when I can and...well, once I settle into this position I suppose I'll figure out what normal might look like."

"You've been lead detective for about four...five months, right?"

"Something like that. Never been one much for counting the days. I like being in law enforcement, and I'm generally pretty good at it." Quinn's tone was calm and steady.

"Your record corroborates that. I'm glad you know you're good at it."

"Are there specific things you want to know?" Quinn looked directly at the psychologist.

"Only if you want to talk about them. We'll meet again in a couple of days, sooner if you want."

"Right now, I don't think things that happened today have settled in my brain enough for me to know what I might need or want."

"That's not unusual, Quinn."

"Good." She placed the glass of water on the table and put her hands on the arms of the chair.

"Let's plan to talk day after tomorrow. This time work for you?"

"Sure. That's fine." Quinn stood.

"Quinn, you have my number. Feel free to call anytime. If I'm with someone, I won't be able to answer immediately. So if it's urgent, please text me. I'll respond right away. That work for you?"

"Sounds fine." Quinn extended her hand. "Thanks, Ivy. I'll see you soon."

"Take care of yourself, Quinn. Go clean out a closet or read a book."

Quinn emitted a soft chuckle. "You're the second person today to tell me to clean out my closets. Must be a lot of closets that need cleaning in the world." *And a lot of cobwebs in my brain.*

"Most of them." Ivy smiled and opened the door. "See you soon."

"Thanks." Quinn walked down the hall.

Crime Scene

The barrier was moved and the large white bomb disposal truck drove slowly toward the parked convertible. The vehicles Officer Simmons and Detective

Isaacs had been driving were still in their original positions. Kevin Millwood drove up right behind them and walked toward the group.

Agent Sid Brown and Millie, followed by Sergeant Steve Clark, moved toward the vehicle. The driver jumped out.

"Hey, Sid."

"Hey, Marian. This is Sergeant Steve Clark of the local police."

Handshakes were exchanged and Steve turned back to the two SBI agents in the bomb disposal team. "Thanks for coming. Sid can give you his assessment."

Sid described the guns and the black box under them stored in the wheel well of the convertible's trunk. Then he gave her the basics of the exchange of gunfire earlier in the day.

Kevin trotted down the hill and joined them.

Marian looked at Steve. "Sorry for your loss, Sergeant." She looked at Kevin as he stopped beside them.

"Thanks." Steve turned to Kevin. "This is Detective Kevin Millwood from our shop."

"Nice to meet you. Sorry for the circumstances."

"Thanks for coming. Chief Hansen asked to extend her thanks."

"Here to serve." Marian's head turned toward the truck.

All heads turned at a loud whirring noise and the rumble of heavy tires along the pavement. The SBI agent who had been the passenger had exited and deployed the robot they would use to check the black box.

Marian pointed toward the SBI agent and the robot. "Meet Lola."

Steve looked from the agent guiding the robot to the robot. "Which one?"

"The robot. The Agent is Debbie McDaniel."

Debbie, dressed in what looked like a cross between body armor and a space suit, stepped closer to the assembled group. "Hey, y'all." Her grin behind the thick glass on her helmet was clownish. She knew her voice through the helmet sounded as strange as she looked. "Meet my partner, Lola."

"Thanks for coming." Detective Millwood looked from Marian, to Debbie, to Lola. "What do you need from us?"

"Mostly for y'all to get back to a safe zone. Lola will take the guns and box out of the trunk and put them in that box you see under her head. Then we'll put Lola back in the truck and she'll take the box out and put it on the floor. Then another robot with finer grip, his name is Waldo, will open the box. If it explodes, well, we'll only know what was in it after forensics examines the remains. If it doesn't explode, we should be able to see what's inside from our cameras and know how safe it is to get it out so we can examine it." Her head seemed to swivel inside the helmet as she looked from one to the other.

"Questions, anyone?" Millwood looked from Steve, to Sid, to Marian, back to Debbie.

All shook their heads.

"Okie dokie. Time for me and Lola to go have some fun." Using the remote buttons on the pack around her waist, Debbie moved Lola toward the convertible.

The others moved back into the park where the forensic techs were watching. As the group approached, one of the younger techs turned to the other and said, "Well, if it goes off when it's picked up, might be quite a few openings on the police force and SBI."

All eyes turned toward him. He shrunk next to his buddy and gave an apologetic look at Sergeant Clark and Detective Millwood. "Sorry."

They ignored him, turned around, and watched as the robot arm went into the trunk.

Lunch Time

Billy sat up when he saw the outside door of the office building open. As soon as Quinn stepped out, he got out, and had her door open before she got there.

"Thanks." Quinn got in the SUV and stared out the front window.

"My pleasure." Billy closed her door.

"Thanks, Billy. Really, I mean it. Thanks for bringing me, thanks for opening the door..." she turned to look at him as she turned in the driver's seat to look at her, "...even though you knew I might react to it."

He kissed his index finger and reached over and touched her lips. "Shhh, it's okay."

"If only it were."

He knew by her meeting with the psychologist that she knew the officer involved or was involved herself. He suspected the latter. "It's a little after noon. Want to get some lunch or want to take your chances with me whipping something up at your place? We can eat out, or get something, and eat out in your garden."

She continued to look at him. *Did you fall out of the sky, Billy Williams? There can be no other explanation for your patience, kindness, and intuitiveness.* She leaned her head back against the headrest.

Billy watched her.

She turned to look at him. "I think I'd like to see people—at a distance. Could we order sandwiches from Carrie's bakery and go sit in the park?"

"Your wish is my command." He took out his phone and pulled up the app for Carrie's bakery. "What would you like?"

"Ham and Swiss cheese with mustard, lettuce, and tomato on a croissant."

"Drink?"

"Iced tea."

"Dessert?"

She turned her head toward him. "Dessert? Oh, Billy, you *are* an angel." She smiled at him. "A macaron. Strawberry."

"Done." He tapped the screen of his phone and she heard the double click as he paid for it. "Ready?"

"Ready as I'll be—for now."

He leaned over and gave her a soft, gentle kiss.

She returned it just as softly. Then she rolled her head back on the headrest and closed her eyes.

Billy headed for Sweet Creations. He pulled into a parking space facing the park and spoke in a soft voice. "I'm going to get our food. You decide where in this lovely park you'd like to sit." He was out the door and across the street before she realized it.

Quinn looked out the windshield and saw an empty picnic table under a large oak. There was nothing else close to it, but it gave a nice view of the children's play area where several moms and dads were pushing their children on swings or the merry-go-round. She opened the door and almost hit Billy. She jumped back.

"Oh, Quinn. I'm so sorry. I didn't mean to startle you." Billy stood back against the passenger door.

"My mistake. I didn't look." She opened the door fully. "Here, I can help with that." She reached to take the bag of food from his right hand. "Good thing the drinks are in a carrier." She tried to laugh but it came out like a snort.

"Find a spot?" Billy wanted to keep her distracted.

"Over there." She pointed to the picnic table.

"Then let's go." He took her hand and they headed toward the table.

Just as they approached the table, a little boy about four-years-old ran toward the same table. "Mommy, look. Here's a table."

"Billy, stop." The mother called out.

Both the man and the boy stopped.

"Yes, Mommy?"

"That table is for those nice people." She pointed toward Quinn and Billy.

Quinn stepped toward the table. "You can sit here, too. Or, we can go to another table."

The little boy looked at his mother. "Can we, Mommy? Can we sit here? I'm hungry."

The woman approached. "I'm sorry. He's been very patient waiting for his lunch while I did a little shopping." A red blush rose on her face. "Honest, I'm a good mom. Just time got away from me."

Billy stepped up beside Quinn. "Hey, little guy. My name is Billy, too."

The younger Billy looked at him with wide eyes. "Really? Are you teasing?"

Without thinking, Billy took out his ID and showed him.

"Mr. Billy, I can't read. Mommy, does it say his name is Billy?"

The woman stepped forward and reached out her hand. "I'm so sorry to bother you."

Billy held up his ID. "It says I'm Billy, right?"

"Well, son, it actually says his name is William, just like yours. So if he goes by Billy, it's just like us calling you Billy."

"Okay. That's fine then." The little boy had climbed up onto the bench of the picnic table. "Have a seat Mr. Billy." He turned to Quinn. "What's your name?"

"I'm Quinn. Nice to meet you, Billy."

"Thanks. Nice to meet you, too." He turned to his mother. "Sit, Mommy. They're safe I saw his badge. He's a cop just like Uncle Tom."

"Police officer, Billy. I've told you before, please don't say, 'cop'."

"Are you a cop...uh, police officer, Mr. Billy?"

"I am. I'm a detective over in the Valley."

"Are you a police officer, Ms. Quinn?"

Quinn almost dropped the bag of food on the table. *Am I? I can't act like one. I have no authority.*

"Billy, that's enough questions. Let Ms. Quinn and Mr. Billy have their lunch. If you keep talking, we'll have to move to another table."

The younger Billy lowered his head. "Okay, Mommy, I'll be good."

Quinn took out their sandwiches as she looked across the table at the little boy. "Billy, I am a detective here in Round City. Where is your Uncle Tom a police officer?"

Billy looked at his mom. "Mary-ville. Right, Mommy?" He said it as two words.

"Yes. Maryville. Now, please let the officers eat."

Billy sat across from Quinn at one end of the table and the mother and son were at the other end. They all ate in silence for some minutes.

"Ms. Quinn? Do you know how to play, 'I spy.'"

"I do. How many guesses do I get?"

"Five." He said it with all the authority of a four-year-old.

"Then let's play." She looked at him as he stared off toward the children's playground.

"I spy something black."

Quinn looked around and put a serious look on her face. "Is it the slacks on that man?" She pointed toward a man pushing his child on a swing.

"No. That's one."

"Is it...?" Quinn tried to choose something that would not be what he had identified. "Is it letters on the sign on the corner?"

"No. That's two."

Quinn guessed three more things and the young Billy looked triumph.

"No. That's five. Give up?"

"The rules of the game say I lost, right? I guessed five times and didn't guess it. So, you have to tell me."

"It's the bird." He pointed toward the top of the tree where a jet black crow cocked his head as if he knew they were talking about him.

"Good job, Billy. I never even saw the bird."

"Okay, it's your turn."

"Billy, honey, I'm glad you've had fun with Miss Quinn and Mr. Billy, but it's time for us to go. So please eat your last carrot. Maybe we'll run into our new friends again one day and then you can play."

Billy frowned and picked up the carrot. "Sure, Mommy." He bit into his carrot.

Quinn took another bite of her sandwich while Billy watched her and the younger Billy.

As they stood to leave, the mother turned to Quinn. "Thanks for being such a good sport to play with him. My brother is Tom Kent if you ever run into him in Maryville."

Quinn swallowed her bite. "Officer Kent?"

"Yes, he's an officer."

"I have met him. He's about thirty or so?"

"Thirty-eight but looks much younger. What is your last name? I want to tell him I met you."

"Quinn Isaacs. Detective Quinn Isaacs." Quinn smiled and extended her hand to shake. "Please tell him 'hey' for me. I appreciated his professionalism on a recent case we worked together."

The younger Billy walked up to Quinn. He put out his hand. "Nice to meet you."

Quinn smiled at him and took his hand. "Nice to meet you, too. We'll have a game of 'I Spy' another day. Have a nice afternoon."

"You, too." Mother and son said in unison as they walked away.

Billy watched Quinn as she watched them walk away.

She turned to look at him. "Well, Mr. Billy, how's that for coincidence?"

"Good reminder."

"Of what?" She cocked her head.

"That we really are lucky to live in a part of the world where the chances of having a person in common with a stranger you meet is pretty good. It's one of the things I like about living in these mountains."

"What else do you like?" Quinn put her elbows on the table and rested her chin on her hands as she looked at him. They had finished their sandwiches and were drinking their teas.

"The woman across the table from me."

"I mean about the mountains."

"I do, too. If we lived in an urban area, I may never have met you."

She chuckled. "Fair enough. Do you remember how you met me?" She wiggled her eyebrows.

"From the first call." Billy wiggled his eyebrows, too.

"First call?" Now she knitted her eyebrows trying to remember a call.

"Sheriff Oliver called you on our return to the Valley after finding the immigrant family up on the mountain. I was smitten when you held your own with the Sheriff's banter."

"I was on speaker phone?" She stopped. "Smitten? You were smitten?" She laughed a deep belly laugh.

"Yep. Smitten. And yes, it was on speaker." He reached over and tapped her nose. "You didn't know that?"

"No. Shame on him for not telling me." She tried to feign anger.

"Well, you have to realize neither of us expected a woman to answer when he called someone named Quinn."

"Disappointed?"

"Not then or now."

"I'm glad to know the first time you heard my voice."

"And I hear it every night in my dreams."

"Schmoozer."

"That's right. Been trying ever since to schmooze my way right into your heart."

She dropped her hands on top of his resting on the table. "You have." She squeezed his arms. "Look. It must be naptime. No one left in the children's park. Shall we try the seesaw?"

"Dressed in that gorgeous suit?"

"You bet. I've got more than one." She stood up and put the papers in the bag and headed for the trash can at the edge of the playground. "Come on. What are you waiting for?"

Billy stood up, ran past her throwing his empty paper cup in the trash as he passed her, and stopped at the seesaw. "Do you know why we call this a seesaw and others call it a teeter-totter?"

"No, kind sir. Do enlighten me!"

"Because we live in the south and our language is heavily influenced by the French and English. The English took the French, *ci-ça,* which means 'this and that' and said 'seesaw.'" He grinned. "Impressed?"

"Only if you can tell me why others call it teeter-totter." She grinned back at him as she swung her long leg over the seat of the metal seesaw.

Billy sat on the other end and they slowly moved up and down on the board that was much too close to the ground for their long legs. *This, my love, is exactly the distraction you need.*

"Well, I'm waiting. Need to make up something or searching that file cabinet in your brain?" Quinn threw her head back and almost laughed. She planted her feet solidly on the ground and stopped. "What is wrong with me, Billy Williams? I should not be here riding a seesaw and laughing. Let's go." She stood up straight and headed toward his SUV.

Billy was right behind her. She stood beside the door waiting for him to unlock it. He decided it was best to use his key. As soon as she heard the click Quinn was in the passenger seat. As he headed for the driver's door, he heard his name.

"Billy. Billy." Carrie was waving to him from across the street.

"Carrie, what's up?"

"You forgot the macarons. I was waiting on you to return to your SUV. Here, I've added a few more. Quinn can have her choice."

Billy realized they had totally forgotten about the macarons. "Thanks, Carrie. Sandwiches were great. We'll enjoy these, for sure."

As she got up close to him, Carrie whispered, "I don't know what happened today, but I know something isn't right. There's lots of talk from folks in the shop and George isn't available. I hope Quinn's okay."

"Thanks, Carrie. She'll be fine." He lifted the turquoise box with the macarons. "This will help, I'm sure."

"Take care of her."

"You bet. Thanks, Carrie." Billy got in the SUV and put the box in Quinn's lap.

She stared down at it and a tear dropped right in the middle of the box top.

Billy started the SUV. "Let's go home." He slowly backed out of the parking space.

Chapter 4

The only thing we can do is honestly learn from our falls.
Ai Weiwei

Round City Police Station

The conference room table was not large in the first place but six SBI agents, two local detectives, and two local forensic specialists put them elbow to elbow.

George Marshall lightly tapped the table with his pen. "If I may have your attention, please."

The murmuring subsided and all eyes turned to George. "Thanks. Agent Davis and I have conferred and she will take the lead on this case."

Millwood was annoyed at having been called in from the crime scene. He wanted to watch the work of the robots. George's declaration added to his frustration. George wasn't the lead detective in the force, but since Quinn was relieved of duty for the time being, his position as senior detective should have given him the lead in Millwood's view. He tried to keep his emotions in check but blurted, "But, Detective, we lost one of our own."

George looked at Kevin. "Yes. Yes, we did. And, one of our own has been relieved of duty pending the outcome of the investigation as to her specific role in the death of that officer and a civilian." He took a breath. *This is exactly why I never wanted to be lead detective.* "Everyone at this table knows it is in the best interest of Detective Isaacs and our local police force that we bring total objectivity to the case." He saw Kevin look down at the table.

"Detective, may I?" Agent Sandy Davis waited.

"By all means." George nodded to her.

"As you already know, we are here at the invitation of your Chief. We want this matter solved as quickly as you do and it may well be that once the immediate facts of the events today are known, there will be much about this case that will fall back in your hands. We will work as a team where we can, and I will take the lead on the interview by the SBI with Detective Isaacs."

Kevin started to speak but bit his tongue. He nodded.

"Now," Sandy looked around the table. "These four agents will return to Knoxville and will be available if the need arises. Do any of you have any observations to share at this time?"

One SBI agent raised his hand. "Ma'am, I'd just like to say that our time out at the scene suggests there was thorough attention to protocols. When we left, the bomb team was there to remove the things found in the trunk. I suspect what they learn from that will lead to important next steps."

"Thank you, Agent. Anyone else?" Sandy looked around the table again. "Okay, then, safe travels and thanks for your time. We'll let you know if we need to expand the team."

The four agents stood and extended hands to shake with the locals. The locals stood, shook hands, and thanked them for coming.

Down to six people at the table, George felt more comfortable and he noticed Kevin relaxed a bit, too.

Agent Davis cleared her throat. "For the expediency of moving forward is everyone okay with first names?"

"Yes."

"Sure."

"No problem."

"I know my ID says, Sandra, but Sandy is my preference. And Agent Lawton prefers, Reg." Everyone nodded.

"Okay, let's divide and conquer. Reg and George will set up a crime board in your workroom. Chuck, as forensic tech lead, you'll work with the medical examiner and the team at the scene once they have evidence to run."

"Yes, ma'am." Chuck was polite but struggling with their real boss, Quinn, being excluded from the investigation.

"Appreciate the respect, but no need for the ma'am." Sandy smiled at him. "Kevin, I'm sorry to have called you in from the scene, but I just need a few minutes with you so when you return we've agreed on protocol."

"Sure. No problem." Kevin settled into his chair.

"Anyone have any questions?"

No one spoke.

"Then let's get this investigation set up." George, Reg, Chuck, and the other forensic tech stood and left the room.

"Coffee, Kevin?"

"I'm good. Thanks."

"Anything you want to say to me about this investigation? Concerns you have about the SBI role in it?" She smiled at him.

"No." He paused. "Well, yes. No disrespect to you as an SBI agent, ma'am—Sandy, but we can be objective. We want the truth as much as anyone."

"I understand. You recently lost your Chief in a tragic case. Was there a problem with the SBI role in that investigation?"

Kevin sat back and looked at her. *Should have thought about that. The SBI folks were fine, it was our old lead detective, Albright, who was the problem.* "Nope. They were very professional."

"Was that case resolved to your satisfaction?"

He nodded. "It took more time than it should have, but that wasn't on the SBI."

"Oh? Something I need to be aware of now?"

"Nope. Problem left town."

Sandy was aware the former lead detective had abruptly resigned. "Okay, then. Let me hear your plan for handling the scene from this point."

Kevin sat up in his chair. He outlined his thinking and emphasized they had a good local team and the SBI agents seemed top-notch. "I worked with Sid on a case a few months back and he's really good with that dog."

Sandy chuckled. "Yes, Sid and Millie are quite the team. Glad to hear it was a good experience."

"I need to check with George to see the plan for the forensic on the vehicles. Not sure our shop can handle three of them. Is the SBI an option?"

"Of course. Let me know when you have a decision."

Kevin sat up a little straighter as he outlined the rest of his plan. "That about sums it up."

"Sounds like you've covered all the bases. If you have no questions for me, head on back, and let's see what more we can learn at the scene. I'm sure Chief Hansen wants the vehicles moved as soon as practical."

"Yes, ma'a…Sandy, I'm sure she does. I'll be in touch."

Sandy stood. "Thanks, Kevin. See you this afternoon, I'm sure."

"Right. I'm on it." Kevin walked to the door. "I apologize for my outburst earlier."

"No need, Kevin. Rough day all around. See you soon."

What's Next?

While he'd been waiting for Quinn in Dr. Kingston's office, Billy had checked the location of the crime scene so he could avoid it on the way back to Quinn's house. He turned onto Maple Street and Quinn sat up.

"Billy, it's shorter to go down Orchid…" she trailed off. *Of course he checked to see where the crime scene was.* She closed her eyes and took a deep breath and let it out slowly. "Hard to remember I'm not in charge."

"No problem. We'll be home shortly." He turned the next corner and half way down the block pulled into Quinn's driveway. He opened the garage door with the remote she had given him weeks ago and was surprised to see she had actually cleaned out the third bay in her garage. "Well, well. Guess my idea that we clean out the garage was preempted by some good fairy."

"Don't *you* tell me I can spend my time cleaning closets." She glanced over at him as she was opening the door. "I guess I better go look at them. Maybe they do need to be cleaned." She headed for the kitchen door.

Billy took his time getting out and let her enter the house. He closed the garage door and reached the kitchen door in time to stop it as she closed it.

"Oh, Billy. I'm so sorry." She pulled the door open. "I'm just so distracted." She kept walking.

He stepped in, put his sidearm and badge in the gun safe by the kitchen door, and followed her into the great room. He stopped in the doorway and watched her staring out the French doors.

In an almost inaudible whisper, Quinn said, "You never did tell me why some people say teeter-totter."

He walked up behind her hoping not to startle her. He put his arms around her and pulled her to him putting his face next to hers as they looked out at the back garden. "I have no idea. When I find out I'll let you know." They stood gently rocking.

She turned and kissed him deeply and hugged him with all the desperation of a drowning person clinging to a life ring.

He continued to rock her gently. Then he stepped back, took her hand and walked to the sofa. He sat down and patted the cushion beside him. "Come on, sit down."

She sat and stared at the wall with the fireplace. "I'm sitting."

He put his arm around her shoulders. "Quinn Isaacs, I love you. I am here for you and we'll get through whatever this is."

She pulled away from him. "Whatever this is?! Don't you know what this is? You're the long-time detective." She was all but shouting at him.

He didn't move. *Go ahead. Get it out. You are scared, angry, upset. I get it. I can also take it.*

"Well, haven't you figured it out? Tell me." She glared at him with feral eyes.

"Fact: I heard the bulletin of an officer-involved shooting in Round City. Fact: I heard the all-clear for surrounding communities. Fact: The love of my life, lead detective in said community, is home on a day when there was an officer-involved shooting." He paused.

Quinn leaned back into the sofa.

Billy continued. "Fact: the lead detective met with the psychologist who assesses all area law enforcement officers involved in a shooting…" He stopped as she turned to look at him. "whether or not they were they shooter. Fact: I love you."

Quinn wiped tears as they ran down her face.

In a slow and deliberate tone, Billy continued. "Report: text received from one of my colleagues said an officer had died in said shooting. Fact: It was not you. Thank, God." He took her hand and squeezed it.

Quinn did not pull her hand away as she muttered, "Fact: an officer was killed as well as a civilian." She turned to look at him. "It's probably already on every news channel in East Tennessee if not the nation." She wiped away her tears and used the hem of her shirt to dry her cheeks.

"Listen, Quinn." He waited.

She turned to look at him. "I'm listening."

"You know there is a process. You're just not accustomed to *not* being in control of the process. Maybe you could think about this in terms of the confidence you have in your team to sort it out. I'm pretty sure they're going to want you back on the job as soon as possible."

Quinn let out a long slow breath. "Thanks, Billy. That helps. I don't want to talk to you about it—yet." Her phone rang in her pocket. She pulled it out. "Quinn Isaacs."

"Detective Isaacs, this is Sandy Davis with the SBI. Is this a good time?"

"Good afternoon, Agent." Quinn stood, walked over the fireplace, and leaned against the mantel. "Thank you for coming to Round City, Agent."

"Here to serve, ma'am. As you are aware, I need to take your statement."

"I know."

"You can come to the station, I can come to your home, or we can identify a neutral place if you prefer."

Quinn took a quiet breath. "You're welcome to come to my home. Do you need the address?"

"No. I've got it. Will two o'clock work?"

"That's fine. I'll see you then." She ended the call and studied the picture on the mantel with her parents and grandmother beside her. It was at her graduation from the University of Tennessee. *How naïve I was in those days. All I wanted was to do some good in the world.* She turned back to Billy.

He smiled at her.

"Agent Davis is coming at two." She looked at the time on her phone. It was one-fifteen.

"How about I go get some groceries and I'll make you a surprise supper tonight?"

"Don't you want to stay?"

He stood and went over to her. "Trust me, there is nothing I would rather do than stay by your side." He kissed her lightly on the lips. "This isn't the time. You'll be fine and I'll be back."

She kissed him. "I know it's the right thing to do." She paused. "Has your cooking improved?"

"Ouch."

"I deserved that. Maybe." She took his hand and walked toward the kitchen. "Let's see what might actually be in my larder."

"Are the cupboards bare?"

"Most of the time." She chuckled. "Maybe it's my cupboards I need to clean out."

The list completed, Billy gave her a kiss, took out his service weapon and badge and headed out the door. *I hope it didn't upset her to see me take out my weapon.*

"Drive carefully, Billy. See you when you get back." She closed the kitchen door, heard the garage door open and close, and slid to the floor. She sat there and wept trying to keep the images of the shooting when she was in high school from doubling down on her now.

The Crime Scene

All eyes were on the robot as it put the materials in the box under its head.

"Well, nothing went boom when Lola picked it up." Kevin looked around at the others.

Agent Newberry spoke. "So far, so good."

Agent McDaniel maneuvered the robot toward the big white bomb truck and up the ramp at the back and once it was inside she closed and bolted the large doors. She moved to the sidewalk.

Marian waved. "Good work, Debbie." She turned to Steve and Kevin. "Should be easy enough for the three of us to look over Debbie's shoulder at the video monitor. You can send the rest of these folks to wherever you need them."

Kevin, relieved to have made it back for this part, turned to Steve. "Makes sense for the techs to wait here, don't you think?"

"Fine with me." Steve nodded.

Marian, Steve, and Kevin walked toward Debbie on the sidewalk.

Debbie smiled and pointed into the park. "Let's go over to that bench. It'll make it easier to look over my shoulder." She sat down, adjusted the device on her waist, angled the eight by eight video screen, and started pushing buttons. The box under Lola's head was about the size of a picnic cooler. Lola put the small black box from the trunk of the car, which was about twelve by eight inches and six inches deep, on the top of the work cabinet. Debbie pushed more buttons and a robotic arm appeared from the side wall as she maneuvered it to the black box. The arm picked up the small black box. Debbie kept her eyes on the screen when she spoke. "Pretty simple clasp on the box. Good not to have to try and open a locked box." She moved the arm in closer and the mechanical hand, shaped like the bones of three fingers and a thumb, flipped the latch on the clasp with no trouble. "No apparent triggers there." Her running commentary was as succinct and clear as a top-rate professor. "Now the real test." She had the robotic hand lift the lid. She let out a long slow whistle. "Come closer, folks."

Marian let Steve and Kevin move in closer. Kevin also let out a whistle. "Can we see it in person?"

Debbie nodded to Marian. "She's the boss. She makes the big bucks to make decisions. I just get to play." She grinned.

"How about we have Waldo put everything on the table first?" Marian looked at the two men.

"No problem." Debbie started lifting the items out of the box with the mechanical arm and set them on the table.

"Excuse us a moment, Marian." Kevin nodded to Steve. They stepped to one side. "Do you have everything you need from the vehicles?"

"Everything we can do on-site. Can I give you my two cents?" Steve waited to see how Kevin might react.

"Anytime."

"I think we can handle Isaacs's vehicle in house. There's no damage to it, no evidence of anyone but her in it, but we'll do a thorough breakdown and dusting. That said, I think we should send the other two to Knoxville. They have more people, can make quick work of them, and…"

Kevin nodded understanding. "It can expedite getting our lead detective back on the job. Give me a minute." Kevin pulled out his phone.

"Davis here."

"Agent, uh, Sandy, we're clear on the items in the trunk of the convertible, but have yet to assess the contents of the box. However, to expedite clearing the crime scene we'd like to move the vehicles." He told her Steve's recommendation and said he concurred. He smiled. *It felt good to give Steve credit for his idea.* He couldn't help but think of the changes in how things functioned in their department since Quinn had become lead detective—and he thought they were good changes.

"Good plan. I'll notify Knoxville to expect the vehicles. Do you want to send someone from here with them?"

"That's up to Detective Marshall."

Sandy smiled. "I'll talk with him. Good work, Kevin. Get 'em rolling. Think we can regroup later this afternoon for an update on the contents of the box? Say—four-thirty?"

Kevin looked at his watch. It was one-thirty. "Four-thirty should work fine. See you then."

"10-4." Sandy ended the call. She walked from the conference room to the detectives work room to update George Marshall and Reg, the junior SBI agent.

Kevin updated the folks on scene. They walked toward the back of the white bomb truck and up the ramp into the open doors toward Debbie.

Billy

As soon as he was away from Quinn's house, Billy hit the button on the steering wheel to dial the Valley Sheriff's Office.

Billy was relieved when Chad Oliver, the Valley Sheriff, answered his phone. "Hey, boss."

"Hey, Billy. What's up?"

"Assume you saw my emergency request for leave?"

"Yes. And approved it. Thought Cecelia had told you."

"She did text me. Just needed to know you knew."

"What's going on, Billy?"

"Assume you saw the officer-involved shooting in Round City."

"Yes, we now know there was an officer killed. No name has been released." Chad paused. "Billy, is Quinn alright?" The concern in his voice reflected his friendship and his respect for Quinn and Billy.

"She will be. Just needed you to know she's going to be."

"Okay. Take whatever time you need. Need any help from our shop, just say the word. You okay?"

"I'm doing better than I might have thought—if I'd ever thought Quinn might need me in this way. I'm trying to stick to the personal and help her not get sidetracked by this. I don't know any more than you do—except Quinn is home."

"Got it. Stay in touch and let Quinn know we're here for her. Here for you, too, Billy."

"Thanks, Sheriff—Chad." Billy ended the call.

He drove toward the grocery store out on the highway so as to avoid any gossip downtown and to give Quinn and the SBI agent plenty of time to talk.

Chapter 5

You must do the thing you think you cannot do.
Eleanor Roosevelt

Quinn's Statement

Quinn pushed herself up from the kitchen floor and walked to her bedroom. She put on a pair of Eileen Fisher natural-color, organic-linen capris and a side-slit tunic in Amalfi green. She slipped on a pair of Antonio Melani thong sandals. *Comfortable but not over the top. Mother, would you approve? Ha. Wonder if I'll ever tell you what I'm going through at the moment?* She jumped when the doorbell rang. She had completely lost track of time.

Walking toward the front door she glanced at her watch and saw it was only ten minutes until two. She looked out the front window and saw a news van. She promptly turned around and went to the kitchen. The doorbell rang again. She ignored it. She took iced tea out of her refrigerator, a pitcher from the cabinet, and filled it with ice. She poured in the tea, sliced some lemons, and put some of the short bread cookies on a plate. She put everything on the tray Billy had left on the table earlier and took it to the great room. She had planned to be in the living room with the SBI agent, but she didn't want to deal with seeing reporters or with having the heavy drapes drawn over the sheers. She sat down to wait.

She picked up a magazine and was flipping the pages when her phone rang. She looked at the number. "Isaacs."

"Quinn, it's Sandy. May I have your permission to put a deputy on duty at your property?"

"What?" Quinn sounded confused. "Sure. I guess. Why?"

"I could order these reporters off the premises, but it would be better if we had someone to enforce that."

"Won't that make things worse? Couldn't I just make a 'no comment' statement?"

"We can talk about that. For now, I think the prudent thing is to put them on public property and tell them your house is off-limits."

"Okay." Quinn disconnected the call without thinking. A minute later her phone rang again. She saw it was Sandy.

"I'm about to ring your doorbell."

"Thanks for letting me know." Quinn stood and walked to the front door. She looked out the peep hole, saw Sandy, and stood behind the door as she opened it.

Sandy extended her hand. "Hey, Quinn."

Quinn shook it. "Welcome to my home. Please come in." She walked toward the great room. "Please have a seat. Would you like some iced tea? Water?"

"Tea would be great. I can get it." Sandy reached for the pitcher. "May I pour you some?"

Quinn lifted her glass. "Already have some." She hoped her smile looked more relaxed than she felt.

"Sorry to be here under these circumstances, Quinn." She set a recording device on the coffee table. "I find it's easier if we just get this done and then we can chat. That work for you?"

"Sure."

Sandy started the recorder. "This is SBI Agent Sandra Davis of the Knoxville Division at the home of Detective Quinn Isaacs of the Round City Police at 1211 Sunrise in Round City, Tennessee." She nodded to Quinn.

"I am Quinn Isaacs of 1211 Sunrise in Round City. I am on leave from the Round City Police where I am employed as a detective and I am voluntarily providing this statement to Agent Davis at my home. It is five minutes after two on Monday." Quinn's voice sounded as routine as if she were the one conducting the interview.

Sandy nodded and gave Quinn a smile. "Detective Isaacs…"

Quinn held up her hand. "Can you please just call me Quinn?"

"Sure."

"Thanks. Go ahead."

"I am here to take your statement regarding the shooting this morning here in Round City at approximately six-forty. If you will, please tell me your actions from the time you left home this morning."

Quinn took a sip of tea. "I routinely leave home around six-thirty each morning and today was no different. As I drove across the intersection at Orchid and Park, I saw an officer in what appeared to be a routine stop of a vehicle; it was a red Saab convertible with the top down. Although I could have turned around, I stopped several car lengths behind the convertible and lowered my window to see if the officer needed assistance. I didn't hear sirens indicating any other officers had been called and assumed it was a routine stop. Officer Simmons—" Her voice caught, she stopped, took a sip of tea, and looked at Sandy. "Officer Simmons was polite and clear in his direction to the driver to put her hands on the steering wheel." She paused. "The top was down, as I said, and the driver had on large sunglasses and a blue paisley scarf tied around the neck like an old fashioned movie star." Quinn's eyes searched the room ceiling to floor, wall to wall. *Is what happened next correct? Am I sure?*

Sandy kept her pencil poised on her notepad and her eyes discreetly watching Quinn.

"Then it happened so fast..." she choked on the word.

"What happened, Quinn?"

"Officer Simmons was stepping out of his vehicle—the left arm of the driver swung out and I thought I saw a weapon. Officer Simmons drew his weapon and I opened my door with my left hand while pulling my service weapon with my right. I crouched in the shelter of my door and aimed my weapon. I heard Officer Simmons yell, 'Drop the weapon.' He was using his door as a shield." Quinn shook her head slightly. "Then gunfire seemed to erupt all around. I tried to focus my weapon on the arm of the driver of the convertible to cause her to drop the gun. I know I fired multiple shots, but I don't know how many." Quinn stood up and started to pace and then remembered the recording. She sat back down. "Agent...Sandy, it happened so fast. I don't know how many times I fired my weapon. I saw the head of the driver fall to her shoulder and...and I saw Officer Simmons slump to the ground. I kept my weapon aimed at the driver but ran to the officer. There was no movement from either one. I checked Officer Simmons and found no pulse, just like Eliza." Her tone was flat and devoid of emotion.

Sandy made a note: "just like Eliza." *Do you even know you thought of the girl killed beside you in high school?*

"Then I moved toward the driver and the pool of blood on the ground from her left arm told me there was no way she was alive. I moved around the car to reach in and check her right arm for a pulse and there was none."

Quinn sat rigid with her feet flat on the floor. "I've been trying to remember how long all that could have taken. I think I called for back-up as soon as I saw the driver's arm extended but I don't know. I keep trying to remember. Did I call it in before I checked for a pulse on Officer Simmons? My mind feels like I was in motion the whole time and was calling it in at the same time as I opened my door—or was it when I checked Officer Simmons. I just don't know." She lowered her head. "I just don't know."

Sandy didn't say anything.

Quinn seemed to blurt out. "I didn't see a gun on the ground. I just realized I didn't see a gun on the ground beneath the arm of the driver. Was there a gun? Where was it? Did it go under the car?"

Sandy had watched the video from Quinn's vehicle, which Quinn had not mentioned activating, and the footage from Officer Simmons's body camera. She, too, was waiting on the answer about a gun from the convertible driver.

"I stood by my vehicle waiting for the other officers who I knew were on their way because I could hear the sirens." Quinn looked around the room again. "I surrendered my weapon to the first officer who arrived and stayed by my vehicle until I was taken to the station where I met with Chief Hansen. I recorded my statement there." She looked at Sandy.

"Thank you, Quinn. Are there any other details at this time you would like to add?"

Quinn shook her head. "No, nothing specific to the event." She picked up her tea and leaned back in her chair.

"If you're up to it, I have a few questions."

"Ask away." Quinn lifted her glass in a mock salute that looked like surrender.

"Have you spoken with anyone other than the officers at the scene and Chief Hansen today?"

"Yes. Detective George Marshall brought me home. My personal friend, Billy Williams, came to check on me. At eleven this morning, I met with Dr. Ivy Kingston."

Sandy nodded. "Anyone else?"

"No."

"Have you told anyone other than the officers on the scene and Chief Hansen what occurred this morning?"

"Yes. Captain Brown was with the Chief." She paused. "And I told Dr. Kingston. That's all." She watched Sandy's face. "And in case you're wondering neither George Marshall or...oh, wait. I've spoken with someone else today."

"Oh?"

"Not about what happened." Quinn shook her head. "Billy and I had a picnic lunch in the park at the square. We sat with a woman and her young son and talked with them." Quinn smiled. "I played 'I Spy' with Billy."

Sandy furrowed her eyebrows.

Quinn chuckled. "The little boy's name was Billy, too. Quite a coincidence. Even more than that his uncle, the mom's brother, is an officer I worked with on a case in Maryville."

"Small world."

"Yeah, that's what Billy—the big one—said, too. Anyway, I haven't given any information about the shootings to anyone other than the officers on the scene, Chief Hansen and Captain Brown, Dr. Kingston, and now you." Quinn seemed to sink into the chair.

"Thanks for the information."

"Sandy, may I ask a question?"

"You may ask. I may not be able to answer."

"Will I lose my badge?"

"Why do you think you would?"

"I can't think of a reason, but I have so many emotions. I feel hollow; a fellow officer is dead and a civilian is dead and I don't know why or if by my gun. I feel stripped—honestly of everything: my role, my responsibilities, my badge, my gun. All of it."

"Quinn, every law enforcement officer who has been in your position knows the turmoil of emotion. I know that isn't very comforting at the moment. Your responsibility is to keep your wits about you, let the system work, and you'll have plenty of time to sort out what you'll have learned from this. Be prepared—some of it will actually be good."

"How can you say that?"

"Experience." She nodded her head. "Now anything you want to add to your statement?"

"Not that I can think of at the moment." Quinn sat up straighter in the chair. She picked up her glass of tea and sipped.

"This is SBI Agent Sandra Davis ending the recording of interview with Detective Quinn Isaacs. Time is two-twenty-two in the afternoon." Sandy closed her notebook, pushed the button on the recorder and sat back.

"Am I still allowed to ask you any questions?"

"Again, you may ask. I may not be able to answer."

"Should I give a statement to the press?" Quinn studied the face of the other woman.

"What do you think?"

"I don't think I should. I think it's up to Chief Hansen how to handle the press."

"Smart woman. Now what else?"

"How long does it normally take to get clearance?"

"I've seen them take forty-eight hours and I've seen them take months." Quinn slumped her shoulders again.

"Quinn, the reasons behind the incident this morning may be much more than the surface appearance, but the actions are likely to be much more straight forward. Stay busy, let the system work."

"Are you going to tell me to clean my closets?"

"Are you kidding? One look around this home tells me I need to go home and clean my whole house." She smiled at Quinn. "Besides who would waste some uninterrupted time cleaning closets? It's beautiful spring weather. Sit outside, read a good book, visit with friends you don't have time to see normally. Hell, shock your parents, call and invite them for a visit."

Quinn started laughing. "That would be a shock. In fact it might cause them to faint. For sure they'd be convinced I was dying or totally off my rocker."

"Then keep them guessing." Sandy smiled. "You'll be up and down emotionally for some days. Call Dr. Kingston if you need to. She's really smart and she's got really good experience helping people navigate what you've just been through. I'll be at your station if you need me."

"Are you in charge?"

"Of this part, yes. Your team is sharp and top-notch professionals. They won't leave one stone unturned—and they will not mess this up."

Quinn nodded.

"They care about you and want you back on the job. So, keep yourself busy and let us do our jobs." Sandy stood.

Quinn stood with her. "Thanks, Sandy. I appreciate your professionalism and your humanity. Be safe."

"By the way, Chief Hansen has put round-the-clock surveillance on your home. The press will be handled from her office. So ignore them. Talk to you soon."

Quinn opened the door and stood behind it as Sandy walked out. She locked the door, drew the heavy drapes and walked back to the great room. *Why do I need round the clock protection from the press?* Her phone buzzed.

It was text from Billy: "All clear?"

She entered: "Yes." She tapped his number.

"Hey, lovely lady. I'll be there in about fifteen minutes. Need anything?"

"Just you to get back. There is an officer out front who will likely stop you, but opening the garage door will help verify you have the right to be here."

"Got it. No worries. See you in a few. I love you."

The Robotic Find

Kevin, Steve, and Marian pulled on gloves as they walked up to the table where the robotic arm had stacked the material from the box. They had seen the wrapped bills on the monitor, but couldn't tell the denomination as they were stacked on their sides—the length of a bill the same height as the inside of the box: 6 1/4" Now, they were stacked on the table and the "$100" on the bills was clear as day. The bills filled about two-thirds of the box

Marian spoke first. "Much experience with money, gentlemen?"

Steve chuckled. "Just in trying to make the paycheck stretch as far as possible."

"Did some work on a counterfeit ring in my early detective days," Kevin said.

Marian counted down the three stacks of bills on the table. "Forty-eight bundles at ten thousand a piece is pretty close to a half-million if my math is correct."

"Once we get them to the lab…" Steve looked up and down the stacks, "we can tell if they are real or counterfeit."

Kevin pointed to the three small open boxes. "Those are safety-deposit box keys. Guess it would be too much to expect they would have left them in the envelope the bank issues."

Marian nodded. "With any luck they'll have the bank routing code. Many of them do these days."

Kevin pointed to the largest box which contained a white powder securely wrapped in plastic. "Looks like a kilo there easily. Depending on whether that's fentanyl or heroin, that block could be worth twice what that money is."

Steve nodded. "Guess you'll be calling in the drug boys?"

Kevin shook his head. "Not me. But I have no doubt Sandy will. George will concur."

Steve looked at the six guns on the table. "Rather not pick them up, even with gloves, until they can be dusted. Any visible markings?"

"None that I see." Kevin tilted his head to one side looking at the bottom ends of the guns.

"Okay, then," Steve stepped back, "I'll get my team in here and we'll get all this photographed and to the lab."

For the first time Debbie spoke. "I've already sent my video to Agent Davis."

"Thanks, Debbie." Marian stretched her hand to shake Debbie's. "Nice work on maneuvering all this."

"Good job." Kevin said.

"Top notch." Steve echoed. "Okay, my folks are coming up the ramp."

Kevin looked at his phone. "Text says two tow trucks are here. Let's get this place cleaned up." He headed for the ramp and over toward the two tow trucks drivers. "Hey guys, thanks for coming. This SUV goes to the Round City Police garage." He pointed to Quinn's official vehicle. "Keys are on the dash. Guess that one's yours." The driver who could only take one vehicle nodded. "Those two go to the State Bureau in Knoxville—must be your lucky day."

The driver extended his hand. "Frank's the name. Thanks for the work."

"Hey, didn't you pull that detective's car out of the side of the mountain last fall?"

"One and the same."

"Name's Kevin Millwood, Round City Police. Heard it was some pretty neat maneuvering." Kevin slapped Frank on the back.

"Then let's see if I can get these two where you need them to be." Frank walked toward Officer Simmons's vehicle. He made a low whistle when he saw the bullet holes. "Guess you're going to want me to put tarps on these, eh Kevin?"

"Perfect. Know where the SBI lab is?"

"Been there a few times. They expecting these cars?"

"Yep. So, let's get them out of here and on the way."

Frank looked at the blood caked on the ground. "I'll try not to mess up your scene."

Kevin looked at Steve who had just walked up. "Problem here, Steve?"

"Nope. All photographed. We'll get more when the vehicles are pulled out, but let's get them on the road."

Frank headed back to his tow truck and pulled around the police vehicle and started loading it.

Marian and Debbie walked up and Marian turned to Steve. "We're headed back to Knoxville. You got everything you need, right Steve?"

"Yes, ma'am. Fine work, both of you. Thanks for all your help." Steve shook each woman's hand.

"Wish I could tell you there'd be a little something in your paycheck for such awesome work." Kevin had his hand extended. "Best I can do is tell Agent Davis you did fine work."

Debbie laughed. "Are you kidding? I get to play with these cool toys *and* I get paid. That's all I need."

Marian grinned. "Appreciate the compliments. We're off." The two women jogged back to the white bomb truck.

"Kevin, my team will get these last photographs of moving the vehicles and the ground under them. Need anything else?"

"Nope. Thanks for the good work by you and your team, Steve. See you at the station."

Kevin headed toward the end of the block where the area had been closed off and spoke to the officer in charge. "Evans, I've called for a fire truck to come do some water work and clean up the street once they vehicles are moved. When that's finished, you can clear the area."

"Yes, sir." Officer Evans nodded her head.

"I'm headed to the station." Kevin walked toward his vehicle, got in and let out a long sigh. "Lost one of our own today," he said to no one.

Chapter 6

You don't luck into integrity, you work at it.

Betty White

Passing Time

Quinn stepped into the kitchen and took out her phone. She sent a text to Billy: "Billy Williams has permission to enter my garage and my home. Call 865-555-1212 to verify." *Might be the longest text I ever sent.*

Billy saw the text pop up on his phone. He grinned. *That's my Quinn. Thinking like a detective.* He pulled up in front of her house and had his ID ready. "Afternoon, Officer."

"Afternoon, Sir. May I ask your business." The tall trim officer turned as the garage door opened and then looked back at Billy.

"Friend of Detective Isaacs." He held out his ID from the Valley Sheriff's Office.

"Detective Williams, we've met. You probably don't remember."

"Face looks familiar. Sorry can't remember the circumstances."

"Not important. Detective Isaacs expecting you?" The officer pointed toward the garage.

Billy showed him the text on his phone.

"No offense, sir. You'll understand I need to call."

"Expect nothing less."

Quinn's phone buzzed. "Isaacs."

"Detective Isaacs, this is Officer Jamison."

"Good afternoon, Jamison. Thanks for being out front. Hope you won't have to be there for too long."

"Ma'am, Detective Williams says you're expecting him. Just needed to verify."

"I assume you verified his identification?"

"Yes, ma'am."

"Relax, Jamison. Just a joke. Please let him pass. He has already opened the garage. Thanks, again, for being here."

"Yes, ma'am." The call ended.

"Have a nice day, Detective Williams." Jamison pointed toward the garage and walked back to the front walkway.

Billy closed the garage door before taking out the groceries. He heard the kitchen door open.

"Need help?"

"Sure. An extra pair of hands will get this all in one load."

Quinn walked behind her own SUV to his.

He kissed her and handed her the turquoise box from the bakery. "I think you left these on the front seat. I've got the rest."

Quinn looked at the top of the box and saw the tear stain. She felt a lump in her throat. "Surprised you didn't eat them all."

He heard the strain of her choked voice. "Ha. And take the wrath of Isaacs? Not on your life—well, for sure not if I want to keep mine." He nodded his head toward the door. "Into the house, fair maiden. The ice cream will melt."

"Ice cream? What flavor?"

"Flavors!"

"More than one?" She started opening the bags Billy sat on the kitchen counter. "Where is it?" She stopped when she opened the bag with the ice cream. "*Häagen-Dazs Jerry Garcia!*" She ran around the counter, hugged Billy, and gave him a kiss that almost took both of them to their knees. She pulled her head back. "You're the best!"

Billy feigned panting like a dog out of breath and said, "Wow! Wish I'd known that a pint of *Jerry Garcia* ice cream was all it takes."

Quinn planted her hands on her hips. "Takes for what?"

He pulled her into an embrace and kissed her even more passionately than she had kissed him.

She pulled back and this time she was gasping for breath. "Well, now I know what a little gratitude can bring." She reached behind him and opened the silverware drawer. "And, now, I'm going to have a spoonful of ice cream."

"Only one. Don't want to spoil your supper."

"Oh, do tell." She pulled the plastic seal off the ice cream and scooped out a spoonful of ice cream. She put the lid on and walked to the freezer. She turned around and Billy was staring at her. "What's the matter?"

"Seriously? You ate one spoonful? How is that possible?"

She shrugged. "You told me not to spoil my dinner. I listen."

He laughed and laughed. "I love you, Quinn Isaacs."

She whispered to him. "I love you, too." Then her eyes appeared to change like a shade being pulled down on a sunlit window.

He stepped over to her, stood in front of her, and gently took her hands in his. "Quinn, these highs and lows will happen for a while. You know what you know from this morning, but you don't know what's known since then. It's hard not to know. You've lost a fellow officer. Someone you've worked alongside. Others are able to support each other in this loss. You aren't part of that. It will change you forever—just don't let it take you down with it." He stopped talking and looked at her. "I love you."

She moved in and rested her head on his shoulder. "Hold me. Just hold me."

He put his arms around her as they swayed back and forth like a gentle breeze on the shore.

Almost as abruptly as she had leaned on him she pulled back. "What's for supper? Need help?"

"I actually make a pretty decent Alfredo sauce and they had fresh shrimp at the store. Want to peel some shrimp?"

"Sure." She put on an apron and took the package of shrimp from him. She looked at the clock. "Oh, my. It's only a little after three. Isn't that too early to start all this?"

"Tell you what. Let's peel the shrimp, put them in the fridge, and then go walk in your backyard."

"Good idea. Then I can tell you what happened with Sandy Davis."

Billy didn't look at her or say anything. He took a shrimp and pulled off the tail and shell.

Round City Police Station

Sandy Davis stopped at the door labeled "Detectives Workroom." She knocked on the locked door.

George Marshall opened it. "Hey, Sandy. How'd it go with Quinn?"

"Good. How are things here?" She looked around the room. "Looks like you're getting the board set up."

"Reg has a good eye for layout. Just got a text from Kevin. Said he requested to bring in the DEA."

"Already requested. Sam Nations is in the area, so he'll be here at four. I told Kevin we'd do a team meeting at four-thirty. Does that work for you?"

"Sounds like a plan." George pointed to the screen on the wall behind the door. "Here's the video you forwarded of the contents of the box from the convertible."

Sandy stepped back and looked. "Well, well. Glad it's not a bomb, but that's a pretty expensive haul from what I can see."

"Chain of custody was signed off by your agents to Steve Clark. He and his techs are bringing it in as we speak."

"Yes, Kevin and I discussed it. Isaacs's SUV is headed in here and the other two vehicles are on their way to Knoxville. Do you want to send someone from here to work it with them?"

Without thinking, George said, "Up to Quinn." He looked at Sandy. "Well, guess it's up to me. I think we need to keep Chuck here—he's the best. He can lead the technicians on figuring out who the civilian is. Okay if I check with him and see who he'd suggest sending? Seems to me it's good for our folks to get exposure to the labs at SBI. Just want to send someone who can contribute and benefit from it."

"Fair enough. Just send me the name when you have it. I'll let the folks at headquarters know who to expect." She turned to leave. "Oh, and George, whoever goes should plan to stay over at least a few days. There's a bunk room there."

"Got it. Thanks." George followed her out the door and entered the lab across the hall. It was also the same space that housed Quinn's office. He entered the code and tried not to look at Quinn's darkened door as he walked to the lab area. "Chuck, you here?"

"In the corner, George. Running DNA on the civilian from this morning."

"Any hits?"

"Just started. Doc took care of Simmons first. Tough to lose one of our own."

"That's the truth." George felt his hand involuntarily go to his badge with the black band on it. "Tell me when you can talk."

"Sure. Give me two minutes."

George pulled out a stool and stared at Quinn's door. *It's going to be okay, boss. Honest. You'll be back in here soon.*

"George!" Chuck stared at George. "Hey, buddy, said your name three times."

"Oh, sorry. Lost in thought."

Chuck nodded toward Quinn's door. "Try working in here right now. Think she'll be back soon?"

"Damn sure will if we can get things moving."

"Working on it. Working on it. Now what do you need?"

George explained about the items found in the convertible, the things collected at the scene, and the disposition of the vehicles. "I think we need you here to head the team on all this stuff coming in. Someone you think could help out and benefit from going to SBI headquarters lab?"

Chuck stayed quiet for several seconds. "Senior tech after me is Larry Swanson. There's a pretty good team downstairs and they can handle the routine stuff. I'd say he's our best bet."

"Okay. Done and done. Thanks, Chuck." George stood and walked to the door. *Would Quinn tell Larry or would she have Chuck do it as senior tech? He is part of the supervisory team.* He turned around. "Hey, Chuck. Not so sure on protocol on this, but seems to me it's in your shop. You good with letting Larry know?"

Chuck grinned. "Sure, I'll take care of it. Do you have an estimated time of arrival for the vehicles in Knoxville?"

"On their way. Tell him to plan to bunk over at the lab for a few days. Text Sandy Davis and me once you talk to Larry."

"On it." Chuck picked up his phone. "Hey, George. Think Quinn would be proud of us? You know, trying to make things work like she does?"

"Yes, Chuck. I'm sure she will be." He opened the door and reentered the workroom.

"Hey, George," Reg tapped the white board. "See what you think."

George walked over and saw the color photographs of the crime scene and the diagram Reg had drawn of the actual position of the vehicles. "Looks good. Something tells me this is only the beginning."

Marking Time

The last of the shrimp peeled and deveined, Quinn covered the top of the bowl and put it in the fridge. She took out a two wedges of lemon from the container she kept for her tea. "This will help with the shrimp smell." She held out a wedge to Billy.

"Really?"

"Really?" She squeezed her wedge so the juice dropped in one palm and then she rubbed her hands together until they dried. Then she put them under Billy's nose. "See? No fishy smell."

"Aren't you the clever one." He followed her lead. "Ouch!"

"Ouch? Oh, do you have a cut on your hand? Sorry, should have warned you."

"Just a paper cut. No big deal. Just needed a little sympathy." He winked at her.

"Don't look here for it."

"Got it. Okay, about that walk. Ready?"

"Ready for a walk for sure but not in my back yard."

"Okay, where?"

"Let's go walk on the beach."

"Well, as much as I'd love to whisk you away, I don't think that's very realistic at the moment."

"Sure it is." She took his hand and headed toward to the great room. Her phone buzzed. She started to ignore it and then pulled it out of her pocket. "Isaacs."

"Quinn, it's Jill Hansen."

"Yes, ma'am. Good afternoon."

"Afternoon to you, too. I just returned from visiting with Officer Simmons parents."

Quinn went rigid. "Yes, ma'am."

"They asked me to tell you that they are deeply appreciative that you were on the scene and are comforted knowing their son had a fellow officer by his side."

"But, ma'am...."

"No, buts, Quinn. The investigation is ongoing. That does not negate the fact that you stopped to help a fellow officer. I wanted you to know his parents appreciate it."

"Yes, ma'am."

"Stay strong, Quinn. You'll get through this. We're all here for you and doing our part to move things with as much thoroughness and speed as we can. Stay busy. It'll help."

"Yes, ma'am. Thank you."

"Call if you need anything."

"Thank you. Chief...Jill...thanks."

"Take care. Talk to you later."

"Yes, ma'am."

Quinn stared at the phone in her hand. She realized Billy had moved over by the French doors. She walked over beside him. "When can I talk to you about all this?"

"When you think it's right." He put his arm around her and pulled her close to his side. "You'll know—I always have."

She looked at him. "More than once?"

"More than once. Anytime you discharge your weapon there is an investigation. The system will work, Quinn. Trust it."

"I do." She leaned her head on his shoulder. "I don't want to go to the beach anymore."

"Okay, I didn't want to have to pack anyway."

"You know I meant on my virtual reality exercise equipment."

"I do. Just wanted to see if I could make you smile."

"Almost. His parents thanked me."

He just pulled her in closer.

"What if I…" she slumped against him.

He steered her over toward the sofa and they sat. "It's mostly impossible not to question your actions or your split-second decisions, but they are done. The evidence will help your folks figure out, to the greatest likelihood anyone can after the fact, what actually happened. The waiting is the worst. No matter whose bullet landed where, you will carry this the rest of your life. The secret comes in trusting your training, trusting your decision making in the heat of the moment, and trusting your team and the SBI to get to the bottom of it. Then you talk about it when you need to—with Dr. Kingston, with the Chief, and if or when you are ready, with me."

"I told Sandy that I feel hollow. Is that normal?"

"Good word for it."

She stood and took his hand. "Come on. I do want to go to the beach. Let's go change and hit the treadmill and bike. I call dibs on the treadmill."

"Your wish is my command."

Ten minutes later they were in her exercise room with the beach stretching out in front of them on her large screen and she felt like she was running for her life.

Mystery of the Driver

"Well, Doc. No fingerprints in the system and no hits yet on DNA." Chuck leaned against the stool at the end of the examining table where the civilian driver from the morning was being stitched back together.

"Pretty young fellow. I'd guess fifteen to twenty-five at the outside. Will run the dentin on the intact tooth which should give us age of this fellow. I've called the sketch artist to see what he can come up with. Lots of damage to the face and bones, so likely be hard to get a good image."

"Yeah, hope we don't find family who wants to see him."

"We'll deal with that if it comes to it. For now, let's hope we get a DNA hit. Any word on the car ownership?"

"Nope. They took it to Knoxville, so they'll pull the vehicle ID off the frame. The one on the dash is destroyed."

"Everything in due time, Chuck. Everything in due time."

"I want it faster than that. We need our lead detective back."

"Working on it. That's all we can do. Now go check your DNA run. You never know what a few minutes will yield."

"True that. I'll let you know." Chuck turned to the door and ran up the stairs. He was opening the door to the lab when Sandy Davis walked up.

"How's the DNA run going?"

"Just came from the morgue. Nothing on fingerprints, but hoping the DNA will yield us something. Welcome to come in and see if we've had anything hit."

"I'll be in the conference room. Let me know. Thanks, Chuck."

"Sure." He entered the lab and headed for the data run on the DNA. He sat down in front of the screen and found two familial matches: Parent 1 and Parent 2. He quickly looked for identifying information. Parent 1: Anthony

Young, Parent 2: Sonia Phillips Young. Chuck ran a report for any current address and criminal record and captured it.

"Davis."

"Sandy, We've got a parental hit on the civilian in the morgue."

"Would you please transfer to Detective Marshall in the Detectives Work-room? I'll be there momentarily."

"Yes, ma'am. Do you want me to meet you there?"

"Sure. That'd be great."

"10-4." Chuck disconnected the call and sent the information through an encrypted file to George. Then he took a quick walk down the hall to the men's room. He passed Agent Davis on the way.

"Be right there, ma'am."

"Give us time to catch up on what you've already read. Good work, Chuck."

Agent Davis knocked on the workroom door and George opened it.

"Sandy, can't I just give you the code?"

"Nope. Thanks for the courtesy, but let's keep this clean."

"You're right. Come on in. I just ordered some fresh coffee and my wife is sending over some treats for our four-thirty meeting."

"Ohhh. Sweet Creations, right? Name of her shop and her delightful baking?"

"One and the same. I've just pulled up the files Chuck sent. I thought he was joining us?"

"Passed him in the hall. He'll be here."

The door lock clicked and Chuck entered.

Sandy looked around the group. "Okay, let's see what we have." Each started reading the information on the screen.

Reg stood and drew lines under the unknown civilian in the morgue and put: (F) Anthony Young (M) Sonia Phillips Young. "Okay, we know the parents. Now where are they."

George let out a low whistle. "Look at the rap sheet on the father." They all scanned down the sheet.

Sandy stood up and walked to the screen. "Here's his address."

The other three looked where she pointed. "Riverbend Maximum Security Prison Cemetery."

"Well, I bet there's a story there." Reg stopped as abruptly as he had spoken.

"Always is, Reg. Always is." Sandy gave a small shake of her head. "So, he's no immediate help. Chuck did you find a birth certificate for any offspring of these two?"

"Yes, ma'am. Found a Tennessee birth certificate on Phillip Anthony Young born August 17...." He wrote the date of birth on the white board.

George spoke softly. "Hmmm. Not quite nineteen years old. No record on him?"

Chuck shook his head. "Nope. No arrests, no prints, no DNA. Haven't looked for school records. Want me to do a deeper dive on him?"

Sandy put up her hand. "Let's see if we can find the mother first." She looked and saw a rural address just inside the city limits of Round City. "Look up the property records, Reg."

Reg was sitting at one of the computers and searched the property appraiser's website. "Property is listed to Sonia Phillips Young."

"Bingo. Let's go." Sonia looked at George. "Come on, you're the local lead on this case."

"Yeah. Yeah, I am." George stood up and headed for the door.

"We'll take my vehicle. Reg, get the conference room set up for our four-thirty meeting. Let Millwood know to meet DEA Agent Sam Nations and let Sam know I may be late for our four o'clock." Sandy turned to Chuck. "Fast work and now go dig up anything you can find on the two parents and the young man: divorce, schooling, you know—the works."

"On it." Chuck was out the door and across the hall almost as fast as she finished talking.

"I'll call your Chief as we head out the door, George. You call for backup, please."

"10-4." George pulled out his phone and kept pace with Sandy as they walked out the door to her SBI SUV.

Chapter 7

Great things are not done by impulse, but by a series
of small things brought together.
Vincent van Gogh

Quinn's Home

"Hey, Billy." Quinn raised her voice as she slowed her pace on the treadmill to start cooling down.

"Yes?" Billy adjusted his pace to slow down on the bike and looked at her. "What's up?"

"I'm going to take a shower. Stay as long as you want. I'll figure out a vegetable to go with the pasta. Okay?" She watched his face knowing he was disappointed she didn't ask him to shower with her. *Not today, Billy. I hope you understand.*

"Sounds like a plan. I'll be up in fifteen-twenty minutes. Take your time. Love you."

"Love you, too." She gave him a wan smile.

Fifteen minutes later, Billy's hand was raised to tap on Quinn's bedroom door when it opened. He kissed her on the forehead. "If I may slip past you, I'll shower, and then put together some hors d'oeuvres before supper." He stepped into the room as she moved to the side.

"I can put together something."

"No rush, it's only four-thirty. I'll be there in a few minutes."

"Okay."

Billy heard the flatness he knew signaled she was drifting to memories. *This shooting? The school shooting when she was senior? Both? Others?*

He stopped his thoughts. He'd been there. "Hey, on second thought. If you don't mind doing it, it would give us a little more time to sit out on the back terrace before the mosquitos join us."

"Always thinking, Billy." She walked through the door. "You're always thinking."

"Mostly. Now scoot. I'm headed to the shower."

Quinn had dressed in jean capris and a lightly flowered pale blue top. She had dried her hair and found herself now wishing she had pulled it back in a ponytail. When she got to the kitchen she opened her junk drawer to see if she could find a rubber band. *Aha! Here's a space I could definitely spend time cleaning.* She shuffled papers, pens, paperclips, scissors, and reached into the back of the drawer. She found a small plastic cup with three rubber bands—one of them coated. She tied the band around her hair as she walked to the fridge.

A soft whistle caused her to look up from the kitchen counter.

"We're going to have supper, you know. This is a spread for an army."

"Right, an army of two: you and me. I'm famished."

Billy walked around the counter, stepped up behind her, and put his arms around her waist. He kissed her cheek and rested his face against hers. "You smell lovely."

"Just soap and water, kind sir." She pressed her cheek against his. "Come on, you get the drinks. I want iced tea, please. See you on the terrace." She gently pushed back against him, picked up the tray, and moved toward the great room.

Well, Daddy, you always said, "When you find the right woman you'll know it." You didn't tell me how hard it would be to navigate my desire for her and the pain she is currently experiencing. Any advice? Billy put crushed ice in a glass and filled it with sweet tea from the pitcher in the fridge. He took out a Sierra Nevada Pale Ale and slipped it in the beer koozie Quinn had given him. He looked at the wording on it: "Life Happens." He took the beer out of the koozie and walked out to the terrace with the glass of tea in one hand and the beer in the other.

Quinn was sitting at the round table on the far side of the terrace.

"Your tea, lovely lady."

She reached up to take it from him. "Thanks."

"My pleasure." He turned his head toward a tree. "Do you know what that bird song is?"

"Which one? There are several."

"I only hear one."

Quinn picked up her phone off of the table. "Do you know this app?" She turned the phone toward him.

"Nope."

"It's the Merlin Bird ID from the Cornell Ornithology Labs. All you do is start recording with it and it will identify the birds in your area." She handed him the phone.

He tapped the "Start New Recording" tab. "Like this?"

"Shhh...." Quinn put her finger to her lips.

Billy was quiet and after about thirty seconds he stopped the recording. He tapped the play tab. "Wow! That's really amazing." He turned the phone to her. "Look there's a hooded warbler, a northern cardinal, and a Carolina chickadee." He grinned like a school boy.

Quinn clapped her hands. "Never a day wasted when you learn something new. Right?"

"Absolutely." He pushed the record button again.

Quinn rolled her eyes. "You're hooked."

"Shh..." Billy put his finger to his lips.

Quinn smiled, looked at this man she now knew she loved, and leaned back in her chair. *Help me through this, Billy. I'm sinking into unknown territory. I'm afraid if I sink back to the shooting in high school I may never resurface. Please...*

Rural Roads

Sandy turned off the main road onto a narrow paved road marked Sunset Lane. "How well do you know these roads, George?"

"Better now with GPS. Most of the roads are mapped thanks to the technology, but the signals not always good enough to get you where you want to go."

"GPS is showing this address about another mile down this road."

"No houses between here and there and probably not much beyond it."

"Meaning not many houses or not much of anything."

"Both."

Sandy laughed. "Lots of that in these mountains."

"Yeah, between state and federal land and the sheer challenge of building on some of this land, most of the old settlers opted for the flatter grounds."

"GPS says the house is on the left."

"Let's drive past it and scope it out."

"Good idea." Sandy had thought of it herself but didn't feel any need to claim having the same idea. She maintained the slow twenty MPH speed she'd been driving due to the potholes.

George started reciting. "Pretty typical house. Wood frame, probably built sometime between the 1940s and 1960. Paint peeling off, phone line running to the house, pump house off to the north side."

"Good observations, Detective."

"Comes with the job."

"Better observations than most, I'd say."

"Thanks." He continued without further comment. "No garage unless it's around back, but no evidence of tires in the grass along the side. There's an old Chevy truck parked under that oak tree by the south side of the house—not sure it could be moved without pushing it."

"Any sign of movement around the house?"

"None. Looks like there's a light on in the living room window."

"After four in the afternoon in the late spring? Hmmm…"

George shrugged. "No figuring what makes folks tick."

"Looks like a place to turn around up here. No sign of houses beyond here."

"I didn't see any on the aerial map."

"What aerial map?"

"The one I looked at on my phone with Google Earth."

Sandy glanced over at him. *Why do so many people think that people who live in small isolated areas are less intelligent than city folks?* "I should have expected you'd have looked."

"Detective. Remember?"

She laughed. "Okay, Detective, let's go knock on a door."

They pulled into the rutted lane on the property and quietly closed their doors.

George looked around. "No dog barking. Unusual out in the country like this."

"Good to know. I'll take point." Sandy headed for the front door and knocked.

George stood back and to the side away from the front window holding his service weapon by his side.

"Hello?" Sandy called out as she knocked the third time.

"Could be no one home. Could also be someone in need of help. Back me up and I'll try to look in that window where the light is on."

"Got you covered."

George moved toward the ragged shrubs, if you could call them that, under the front window. He peered in from the lower left corner of the window. He stepped back. "Body on the floor. Pool of blood. No movement." He had his secure radio out calling the station.

Sandy moved quickly. "I'm headed to the back of the house."

"Let's wait for back up—they should be here momentarily."

"I'll stay at the corner. You cover the opposite side."

George moved toward the far corner of the house. *If there's anyone alive in there, we would have heard them leave already.* "Got an apparent DB at…" He took a breath. *What if someone else is in there and injured?* He moved back to the side Sandy was on. "Back up turning down this road, ordered a wagon. Could be someone inside who needs help." He waited for her reaction.

"Agreed. Let's go in from the back."

George realized she had calculated that if someone were trying to get out, they would exit from the opposite door. Sending them out the front would put them on the road. They could each take a door but given the circumstances knew backing each other up was paramount. "I'll take point." He stepped around her at the corner, climbed the rickety wooden steps to the back door, and touched the door handle. It wasn't locked. He pushed it open causing it to bang against something. *No surprise entry on this one.* He called out. "Police entering this house." He called it twice. He listened. No sound or movement. Then he heard a chirping noise. He looked over his shoulder at Sandy. "Chirping noise. Like an alarm or a bird."

"Let's go."

George heard the sirens coming from the main road. "Okay, backup is right behind us." He held his service weapon in front of him and entered. He nodded to Sandy to go to the right. He turned down the hall. All three doors off the hall were open. The first was a bathroom, the one across from it was a bedroom and the chirping noise was accompanied by a flashing light on an alarm clock. The door next to the bathroom was also open. The black walls and blackout curtains made it hard to see. He turned on the light on his phone and he saw a body on the bed. It didn't move. He pulled on a glove and checked for a pulse. There was none.

"DB in here." He called to Sandy.

"Opening front door to backup."

George walked to the front of the house and leaned down to check for a pulse on the woman on the floor. He hadn't expected one. He stepped around the body and to the front door, pulled the glove off, turned it inside out, and held it in his hand. Both he and Sandy waited on the doorstep for the others getting out of vehicles.

George walked toward the officers. They huddled beside the SBI SUV. "Two DBs. One appears to be female. The other unrecognizable and I didn't check further."

Sergeant Steve Clark stepped up. "Understand this could be related to the morning."

"Appears to be familial—not sure the events in here are related." George turned toward Sandy.

"George," Steve moved in closer to them. "Give me the details on your access."

George was recounting their actions when his secure phone beeped. "Just a minute." He lifted his finger to Steve. "Marshall."

"Detective, you have a warrant. Have the A-team do a thorough job."

"Thanks, Chief. Two DBs here. About to brief Sergeant Clark."

"Two?"

"Yes, ma'am."

"Okay. Anything you need here at the station?"

"Don't think so. I'll let you know, Chief."

"10-4." She ended the call.

George turned back to Steve. Sandy was standing with him. "We have a warrant. So, it's all yours." He finished giving the details of their arrival and entry into the premises. "We entered to render aid."

Steve just nodded. *A judge may or may not agree.* He looked at George. "Got it. Unless you need anything, we'll get started. Could be a long night."

"Steve, we were careful. Only contamination was our footsteps and we'll hope they didn't obliterate those of whoever did this."

"Always a challenge, George. No doubt. Could also be a murder/suicide."

George looked at Steve. "True. I honestly hadn't thought of that."

"Yet—I'm sure you would have."

"Hey, Steve. You guys were on the scene pretty early this morning. Don't you want the other team to take this?"

"Not on your life. DNA here likely connected to this morning. This is ours. We'll survive." He turned to his team. "You know what to do."

"Okay. Looks like you have perimeter cover and the tech support. If you don't need us, Sandy has a meeting that we've already moved from four to four-thirty pushing back another meeting. We need some time with the DEA agent so we're outta here."

Steve nodded. "You've had a long day already, too."

"Gonna get longer. Be safe out here. Call if you need me."

"10-4." Steve headed toward the house.

George and Sandy turned toward her SUV without speaking. They were backing out of the driveway when a loud bang rocked their vehicle and the house.

Round City Police Station

"Thanks for coming, Sam." Kevin Millwood shook hands with the DEA agent as he walked through the door from the front lobby into the secured area of the station. "What's new in your world?"

Sam shook hands. "Seems I should be asking that of you. Good to see you, Kevin. Been a while."

"Guess that's a good thing, right?"

"Given what I do, it is."

Kevin noticed Sam had a black band around his badge. "Appreciate your time and your support. Rough day here." Kevin walked toward the conference room. "Coffee?"

"Anytime. I can get it." Sam headed toward the back counter.

Both men turned at the voice behind them.

"Gentlemen," Chief Hansen stepped toward Sam. "Thanks for coming, Agent Nations."

"Here to serve, ma'am. Sorry for your loss."

"Thank you." She pointed to the chairs. They all three sat. "I just got word there was an explosion at the Young house where Agent Davis and Detective Marshall are with our A-team."

"What?" Kevin moved to stand.

She signaled him to sit. "They're assessing damage, but none of our team is hurt."

Sam jumped in. "That's a relief. Is the Young house related to what happened this morning?"

"We believe it is the mother of the civilian involved in this morning's incident. Davis and Marshall found two bodies in the house—deceased. Cause unknown at this time. Anyway, I came to update you and suggest you get Sam read in on the crime board. Agent Lawton from the SBI is in the Detectives Workroom. He can bring you both up to speed. Obviously the meeting pushed back has now been postponed until we assess these new developments. Any questions for me?"

Kevin shook his head. "No, ma'am."

Sam sat quietly for a moment. "I'm assuming there are drugs involved in this morning's incident?"

"Yes. And firearms. We've got the SBI on scene and we'll take their lead on calling in the DAF."

Both men knew she meant the Department of Alcohol and Firearms. Kevin suppressed his temptation to say, "Alphabet soup."

Jill Hansen stood and extended her hand to Sam. "Thanks, again, for coming. By the way, George Marshall is the lead on this."

Sam stood to shake. "Oh? Is Detective Isaacs on leave?"

"Yes. As of this morning." The Chief left the room.

Sam turned to Kevin. "Is she okay?"

Kevin had no knowledge that Quinn and Sam had been a couple in college. "Yes, Quinn is physically okay unless there's something I haven't been told. Come on, Sam. Let's go look at the board."

Sam walked behind Kevin down the hall. *Quinn, are you okay?* He knew he wasn't first on her call list anymore, but it didn't negate his concern for her—professionally and personally.

Supper on Sunrise

"The chill is creeping in as the sun moves behind the mountains." Quinn's tone was conversational and relatively normal. "Thanks for getting groceries. The brie and grapes were perfect."

"Glad you like them. I'm going to go start the water boiling for the fettuccini. Want to join me or enjoy the dimming of the evening light?"

"I'll be in shortly." They were sitting side-by-side at the round table. She reached over and touched his cheek. "Thank you for being here, Billy. The events of the day are difficult for me and you are being very patient with me."

He took her hand in his and kissed it. "Quinn, I love you. Simple as that. I love you. We'll get through this together."

"But you don't even know what 'this' is!" Her voice was raspy and curt.

"And, my love, you only know part of it. That is one of the hardest parts of what your trying to sort out; *You* don't know either."

She stared at him. She pulled her hand away, put her elbows on the table, and buried her face in them. *There's the truth, Billy Williams. I'm not in control.* As quickly as she had put her face in her hands she sat up straight. "Control. Life is all about control, isn't it?"

"Or lack thereof."

"Oh, God, do you have to be so smart?"

"Yes. You wouldn't love me otherwise."

"See, there you go again."

He knew the banter, although tainted with sadness and fear, was important. "I can go on all night. Want to try?"

She shook her head. "No, I want this to be over. I want the day to start again and Officer Simmons's stop to be a routine traffic violation—one that didn't..."

Billy didn't speak. He had some understanding of the process emotions and knowledge take you through when you've witnessed a shooting, much less when you've been part of it. He knew she'd be all right. He stood, picked up the tray of the hors d'oeuvres, and went in the house.

Quinn picked up her glass and his beer bottle. She turned the bottle in her hand as she looked at the green and yellow of the label. She focused on the mountains in the background. *The Sierra Nevada Mountains. Lovely. Not my mountains—not my beautiful Smoky Mountains.* She closed the French doors and walked into the kitchen.

"I smell garlic."

"Yes, ma'am. First ingredient."

She rinsed out the bottle and put it in the recycle bin, then filled up her tea glass. "Want another beer?"

"No, thanks." He lifted his own glass of tea. "Pull up a stool and keep me company."

"I wouldn't miss this for the world—Billy Williams cooking." She sat down and stared at Billy stirring the garlic in the frying pan. She jumped up. "I forgot to get the asparagus out."

"Relax. You prepped it and it's already in the oven."

"Billy, have you been taking cooking lessons?" She stared at him.

"I can read." He turned from the garlic and winked at her. "And, to be fair, I've been watching some cooking shows. Wanted to try and impress a certain lovely woman I know."

"Oh?" She pouted. "And who might that be?"

"If I have to tell you…" he hesitated.

"Okay, okay. I'm off my banter game and besides you are the master of it. I couldn't win if I wanted to." She smiled at him. "Did I ever tell you that you're good for me?"

"Maybe—but you could tell me again just to be sure." He pulled the frying pan off the stove and kissed her on the nose. "Now, if you'll get plates ready, we'll eat in less than five minutes."

"Okay with you if we sit here at the counter?"

"My kind of meal."

Quinn seemed to perk up as she took out place mats, cutlery, and plates and put them on the counter. "Did you find the strainer for the pasta?"

"I did. Very organized kitchen you have here."

"Thanks. Smells great. Let's eat."

They talked about food and the weather as they ate. They were putting away the last of the pans which Billy said wasted space in a dishwasher.

"Thanks for dinner, Billy."

"Loved doing it. Don't count on it becoming a habit."

"Okay." She jumped when her phone rang. She grabbed it and looked at the screen. "Isaacs."

"Quinn, it's George."

"Hey, George. Should you be calling me?"

"Chief asked me to call you."

"Oh?"

"This case has just gotten more complicated. We're doing everything we can to get this morning worked so you can come back. Just needed you to know it may take a day or two longer."

"Are you okay, George?"

"I'll be fine once you're back."

"Thanks, George. You've got this. Thanks for letting me know. Tell Carrie I sent my regards."

"Will do. Take care, Quinn."

"10-4." It slipped off her tongue before she realized it. She looked at Billy who was watching her. She set the phone on the counter, then put it in her pocket, took his hand and walked into the great room.

They sat on the couch and she leaned on his shoulder. "Are there still reporters outside?"

"Don't know. Want me to check?"

"Not really. I know they can't get around to the back, so it's okay. Just hate that an officer has to be on duty to keep them from hassling me."

Billy let her talk.

"I want to be part of the solution, not part of the problem. Why do things have to be so complicated?" She lost energy on each of the last few words and was totally unaware as she fell asleep.

Billy leaned back against the corner of the sofa, pulled her close to him, and held her.

Chapter 8

If your determination is fixed, I do not counsel you to despair.
Few things are impossible to diligence and skill.
Samuel Johnson

Tuesday Morning

Quinn rolled over and looked at the clock face on her night stand. It was five-thirty. She sat up and threw the covers toward the center of the bed. Her hand hit Billy's back. She jerked her head around.

Billy rolled over and looked at her. "Morning."

"What is today?"

"Tuesday."

"What are you doing here?" Her voice was raspy.

"I was sleeping."

"Cut it out, Billy. Why are you here on a workday?"

"Every day's a work..." He put his hand up to stop the pillow she had picked up to throw at him. He sat up. "Okay. Sorry. I'm here because..."

"I'm on leave." Her shoulders sagged. She slipped back under the covers and moved close to Billy. "I'm sorry I was so rude."

"Shh...no apologies needed." He stroked her hair.

She turned to him and kissed him with such passion he didn't know if he could control himself. He pulled his head back and looked into her eyes. He knew that hunger. The need for intimacy that is so primal—that comes in times of trauma and fear—when one should least expect it. He pulled her to him and answered the desire in the way only two people who deeply love each other can—with lust, and passion, and tenderness.

The Place That Never Sleeps

Sandy Davis rolled over in the single bed in the Round City Police Station sleeping quarters. Rarely did more than one officer need to stay overnight so the rooms with multiple bunks were hardly used. The nicer rooms with the private bath and single bed which she had were generally left for visiting law officers. She smelled the coffee from outside the room, showered and dressed, and headed into the dining area.

"I smell coffee."

"Yes, ma'am." The local officer smiled at her. "DeLoach, ma'am. We didn't get a chance to talk last night but we met on the Wilkie house earlier in the year. Coffee?" She held up a mug.

"Oh, yes. Thanks for reminding me. Sandy Davis, SBI." She reached for the mug. "Thanks."

"Yes, ma'am."

"Please call me Sandy."

"I'm Ruth."

"You're lead on the A-Team, right?"

"That I am. We got in pretty late, so just decided it was easier to bunk here. One of these yahoos will appear shortly and make breakfast. Good news is none of them can mess that up." She laughed.

"I can fry an egg and make toast. Point me in the right direction."

"Relax. You've got a long day ahead." She looked toward to the far side of the room. "Why look, you're in luck. Best cook we have."

The older officer looked at Sandy. "Don't believe everything you hear, ma'am. Wilson's the name." He extended his hand.

"Sandy Davis, SBI."

"Word travels fast around these parts. Already knew your name and pedigree. Pleased to have you on board. Eggs? Grits? Bacon? Pancakes? Name your poison—so to speak." He guffawed.

"Not funny, Wilson." Ruth DeLoach shook her head.

"No disrespect, ma'am, to you or to our fellow officer." His eyes turned toward the kitchen area.

"I can help. Toast and an egg is good for me."

"Poached, scrambled, fried?" Wilson was relieved for the quick response from Sandy.

"Scrambled is fine."

Their plates in front of them, Ruth and Sandy sat across from each other. Ruth saw that Sandy had a black band on her badge.

"Mind if I ask the SBI protocol for wearing the band?"

"Basically until after the funeral for another agency—thirty days for one of our own."

"Same here. Guess I was really wondering if you only wear it for a case you're on or for any officer in the state of Tennessee."

Sandy looked at her. The death of a law enforcement officer brought out random thoughts for most officers. This question didn't surprise her. "For the most part, if it's an SBI agent anywhere in Tennessee, we wear it thirty days. If we're helping with a local officer, or we've worked with or knew the officer, until after the funeral."

"Thanks. Guess it's a bizarre question."

"Bizarre situations tend to bring out lots of questions. Are you joining the briefing this morning?"

"Not yours. We'll have one in about twenty minutes then we're headed back out to the Young house. Daylight will help with the outside part of the scene."

"I'm sure. I'm also sure the update from Sergeant Clark this morning will help the rest of us get focused on next steps."

"He's the best."

"I can see that. Good team you have—along with the rest of the department I've met."

"Thanks." Ruth pushed her chair back. "If you'll excuse me, I need to head upstairs. Thanks for coming to help."

"Here to serve. Thanks for your service. Good luck putting the puzzle together today."

"We'll solve it if it can be solved."

"I have no doubt of that." She watched Ruth walk off. She had seen the precision in the team on the case earlier in the year. *Yep. No country bumpkins on your team, Ruth DeLoach.*

"Ma'am?" Officer Wilson stood beside Sandy.

"Oh, sorry. Lost in thought."

"Yes, ma'am. I could see that. Want anything else?"

"No. That was perfect." She stood and lifted her plate.

"I've got it. Need you to go figure out what happened to Simmons." His eyes held a plea. "Please."

"We're on it. Thanks for breakfast."

"Anytime."

Sandy decided to climb the stairs to the first floor. She forgot to put workout clothes back in her "go bag" and didn't have time to go buy any. *Ha! No time to work out either. Maybe tomorrow.* She took the stairs two at a time and at the top opened the door almost hitting someone. She stepped back and the door opened. Chief Hansen was standing there.

"Sorry, Sandy. Been meaning to put an 'Open with Caution' sign on the door."

"My fault. I'm bad about moving too fast."

"Sounds like a good trait to me."

"Mostly. How are you this morning, Chief?"

"Like most folks in this station are today—waiting so we can help a family bury one of our own."

"We'll try to get that part wrapped up so a funeral can happen. The rest—well, it may be a lot more than meets the eye."

Chief Hansen nodded. "I need to step in my office and get briefed before our meeting at seven-thirty. Need anything from me?"

"Not at the moment, ma'am. See you shortly." Sandy continued to the conference room and was surprised to see George setting things up on the counter. "Morning, George."

He turned. "Morning, Sandy. Just getting us set up for the meeting. By my count there will be seven of us."

"Seven?"

"You, me, the Chief, Chuck, Steve, Reg, and Sam Nations."

"Problem for you if we include Kevin?"

George shook his head and looked at her. "Not a problem for me. Something I should know?"

"Seems to me he's pretty committed to making sure I do my job right. I'm okay with that. I can respect someone who contributes to a straight forward approach to getting at the truth."

George chuckled. "We've all grown pretty protective of our new lead detective. She's a good leader and a really sharp mind."

"Seems to me she sets a pretty high bar."

"Ha. That's the truth—mostly for herself, but it makes us want to reach for it, too."

"That's a good leader in my book. I work for one of those, too."

"Then let's figure this out so we can get ours back."

Sandy walked back to the counter and saw the croissants in the teal boxes marked "Sweet Creations." *I knew I shouldn't have eaten the other half of that toast.* "Looks fabulous. Tell your wife thanks."

"She loves doing this for us. I encourage it." He smiled.

"It's our good fortune." She turned as the door to the conference room opened. "Morning, Lawton."

"Morning. Okay if I get coffee?" He walked to the back.

"Back in a few." Sandy left the room and walked to the front of the station. She didn't recognize the young woman on the front desk. She showed her ID. "Just want some fresh air."

"No problem, Agent Davis. We have plenty of it here." She pushed the buzzer to release the lock on the door.

Sandy walked out the main door and onto the sidewalk in front. She looked out to see the pale light which creeps over the mountains in the early morning before the full sun joins it around ten o'clock this time of year. She took in a deep breath of cool spring air and walked briskly around the mostly empty parking lot. *Will Quinn Isaacs be back to work some part of this case? It's shaping up to be a lot more than just an officer-involved shooting.* She shook her head as if to clear the cobwebs and walked ten laps around the parking lot. As she entered the outside door of the police station she thought of her father who had been a sheriff in middle Tennessee. *He often said, "This sheriff's office and the hospital are the public buildings which never sleep." True in this small town police station, too.*

Start of a Long Day

Quinn had fallen back asleep and Billy slipped quietly out of bed and into the shower. Coffee made and a mug in his hand, he walked to the front window and pulled back the heavy drapes. An officer was still on duty and there were two news vans out front. He closed the drapes and walked to the back terrace. He sat down on a chair without thinking about the morning dew. *Dammit, wet slacks.* He took out his phone, saw it was five after seven, and made his call.

"Whitehorse."

"Billy here."

"Hey, Billy. How's Quinn?"

"About what you'd expect. Any word on that side of the mountain?"

"About our side of the mountain or hers?"

"Well, either I guess."

"Joke, Billy. Joke. Boy, you can dish them out but you sure can't take 'em."

"Not always true."

"Fair enough." Sylvia Whitehorse was the Chief of the local native tribe and the second-in-command at the Valley Sheriff's Office. Most folks suspected if Chad could convince Sylvia to run for sheriff, he'd gladly step down. If he ran, he'd win against anyone.

"Well?"

"What do you know, Billy?"

"Nothing. I haven't asked and I won't. Quinn's not ready to talk and doesn't have to in any event."

"Good man. Here's what we know officially: the deceased officer was Albert Simmons. A civilian was killed and the shooting involved another law enforcement officer whose name has not been officially released. The Maryville paper said it was Detective Quinn Isaacs."

"So it would seem." Billy's voice was soft and somber. "Simmons was a good officer. Dealt with him on another case that crossed jurisdictions."

"That's the nature of a small rural area, isn't it? We're either kin or we've worked together."

Billy chuckled. "Yeah, that's about the truth of it."

"How are you holding up?" Sylvia knew Billy had dealt with his own officer-involved shootings and more recently a near death escape in the fall.

"Good. Just wish I could make it go away for Quinn."

"Make what go away for Quinn?" The voice was not on the phone. He turned to see Quinn standing there with a mug of coffee. She came toward him.

Sylvia had heard her. "Billy, hand her the phone this minute. Do not hesitate. Hand it to her."

Billy reached the phone out to Quinn.

She mouthed, "Who is it?"

"Sylvia."

She took the phone. "Morning, Sylvia."

"Morning, Quinn. I was checking on you and Billy. I'm sorry for the loss of Officer Simmons. Is there anything I can do for you?"

"Yes." She looked at Billy as she spoke. "I need to talk to a woman officer I know. Do you have any time?"

"You name the time. I'll be there."

"There might be news vans out front. Maybe Billy could drive me to meet you somewhere. I can't leave the county."

"Give Billy the phone. I'll tell him where and when. Hang in there, Quinn."

Quinn handed Billy the phone.

"Meet me at..." He listened and he watched Quinn stare out at the trees. Sylvia was very specific in her directions. "You know where that is?"

"I do. What time?"

"I'm off today, so whatever works."

"The sooner the better." He looked at his watch. "Eight-thirty?"

"Eight-thirty. See you then."

"Thanks, Sylvia." He ended the call.

"Did she call you or did you call her?" Quinn studied his face.

"I called her."

"She distinctly said she was checking on me and you."

"She was. I asked her what she knew officially. She asked me about you and me."

Quinn let out a breath. "Fair enough. Fair enough." The mountain double speak was a sign of acceptance.

"We're going to meet her at the picnic benches by the parkway. That way the two of you can be alone. Okay?" He looked in her eyes. "I'll keep my distance."

A tear slid down Quinn's face. She reached over and put her hand on top of Billy's. "Don't you think I want to tell you? I do, in the worst way, but I need you not to know. Not yet. Not 'til we know what happened."

"It's okay, Quinn. It'll be good for you to talk to Sylvia."

She barely whispered. "I need you to be my safe haven."

"I am. Now go put on long pants and socks. The chiggers are fierce this time of year."

She shook her head and chuckled. "Only you would think of chiggers. I heard you say eight-thirty. So can we eat first?"

"French toast and ham coming up." He headed to the kitchen.

She patted him on the bottom as he walked by. "Ugh, you're wet." She stood up and touched the bottom of her pants. "So am I? Ugh. Morning dew."

"I'll dry. Go put on long pants and socks. Breakfast in ten minutes." He kept walking.

Quinn went to her bedroom, changed into a pair of designer jeans, tennis shoes and socks, and a plaid shirt over her sleeveless top. She took a big brimmed hat off the shelf and her Maui Jim's sunglasses out of the drawer.

Billy had opened the gun safe and retrieved his weapon and badge as soon as he entered the kitchen. He just hoped Quinn wouldn't reach for him and hit his sidearm. He decided to microwave the bacon like he did at home. He had the syrup warmed and the French toast soaking in the egg and milk mixture. He heard her coming down the hall and put the French toast in the skillet.

By eight o'clock they had finished eating, cleaned up the kitchen, and were ready to head out the door.

"Billy, let's take my SUV."

"Okay. Reason?" He just wanted her to tap into her logic. He knew why.

"One, you're in your official vehicle. Two, they can get my license plate anyway. Three, my windows are tinted darker than yours..." she saw his raised eyebrows, "within the legal limit and the sticker is between the tinting and the window on the driver's side."

"That's my cop."

"So you're okay to drive my car?"

"Your wish is my command." He picked up a basket and a cooler bag. "Let's go."

"What's in there?"

"Lunch. Let's go."

He headed out the door.

She stopped in the doorway as he put the basket and cooler bag in the back. "Billy, you didn't get your sidearm."

"Never leave home without them. Let's go." He winked at her.

You will never know how good you are for me, and to me, Billy Williams. "Thanks, Billy."

"Love you." He held her door open as she came around the back of the car.

"Do we need to let the officer on duty know we're going out?"

"Good thinking, ma'am. Already done."

"Might be good thinking but not fast enough."

"Fast enough for the circumstances. We won't be bothered or followed." *I won't tell you Sandy Davis knows where we're going. Can't be too careful.*

"This I have to see."

Billy opened the garage door and backed the car around on her large driveway so they were facing out.

"Funny, I park my official vehicle facing out, but didn't park my personal car that way. Wonder why?"

"In a hurry?"

"Who knows. Doesn't matter anyway." She slid down in the seat, turned her face toward Billy so the brim of her hat covered the side of her face toward the front windshield.

They were headed down Sunrise and Billy said, "Not one camera that was visible."

"Ha. Don't believe someone didn't figure out a way to get a photo."

"Okay, madam, I now need you to be another set of eyes for any remote vehicles a snooping reporter may have alerted."

"On it."

"But hold on. I've got some pretty slick maneuvers." He turned at the end of her block and did a loop around a park that was not on the normal route to the Round City Police Station or shopping.

A few minutes later they were on a country road with no cars in sight.

"Detective Williams, it seems to me that you gave me some grief a few months back for those kinds of maneuvers on a back road."

"Guilty. Don't you think that was pretty slick, though?"

"Sure, you win the prize for craziest driving by a law enforcement officer not in pursuit of a criminal."

"As far as we know." He laughed.

It made her laugh. "True, that."

Billy slowed and took another side road that was unpaved.

"Where to now?"

"This is a rough road, but your SUV can handle it. It will bring us out on the other side of the place we're meeting Sylvia. I promise I'll wash your car when we get home."

Quinn leaned the back in her seat and looked at the window toward the tops of the trees. She sighed and watched them move by in shades of yellow-green, emerald green, and the deep green of pine. Her eyes drifted shut.

The A-Team

Sergeant Steve Clark and his A-Team were in the conference room to have a briefing before they headed out to the Young house.

"Good job, folks. Yesterday started early and ended late, but you stepped up and did your jobs. Glad you're all safe and hope you got some sleep."

One of the younger forensic techs raised his hand. "Sarge, any word from Doc Walters on the DBs?"

"Not yet. He'll be thorough; you know that." *I also know you were pretty rattled by the body in the bedroom.* "Doing okay, Carl?"

"Yes, sir. Just curious to know the COD."

"That's what the ME does—finds the cause of death. Hang tight. Now, on the explosion."

Another member of the team jumped in. "Sarge, I think we need to do a shoulder-to-shoulder search and see if we can find what took that truck out."

"Good observation. We have some officers joining us and we'll do just that."

"DeLoach, run through the plan for today."

"Yes, sir. First order of the day...." She outlined the work the team would do and answered questions. She turned to Steve. "That's it, sir."

"Need anything from me?"

DeLoach shook her head. "Not at this time. Daylight will help, but should be good by the time we get out there."

Steve stood. "Then, head 'em up. I'll be there after my briefing with the Chief. Thanks for your good work." He walked out the door.

"Van's loaded, let's go." DeLoach headed out the door and the others followed. *Let's go see what almost took our lives last night.* She tried not to think of those things—sometimes it just happened.

Chapter 9

Don't be afraid to cry. It will free your mind of sorrowful thoughts.
Hopi

Conference Room

Chief Hansen spoke first. "Thank you all for being here, and especially for the support of the SBI and DEA. Agent Nations, I'm particularly sorry we got you here yesterday and couldn't meet until this morning."

"No problem, ma'am. Chuck and I had some quality time pouring over the evidence you found."

"Good to hear. Agent Davis will take over and I will stay to be briefed and then I will leave it to all of you. All of our resources are at your disposal and I will bring in any other support you think you need. Questions for me?" She looked around the table. No one moved. "They're all yours, Agent."

Sandy Davis looked around the table. "Morning, folks. No need to hang on formalities if you need coffee or temptation. Thanks to Ms. Marshall, we have croissants that will melt in your mouth. Okay. We'll start with local updates on forensics from the morning incident from George, then the evening from Steve. I have a preliminary report from the SBI labs. Let's start with an update from George."

"Thanks, Sandy. I believe everyone was up-to-date as of five pm yesterday. Sandy and I left here in hopes of verifying identity of the civilian killed yesterday whose DNA identifies him as off-spring of one Anthony Young and Sonia Young. As you will learn in more detail from the team at the Young residence, we arrived to find two DBs. Both are in the morgue. That's all I have."

"Questions for George?"

Head shakes moved around the table.

Sandy nodded to Chuck. "What updates do you have?"

"We only found one certificate of live-birth in Tennessee to Anthony and Sonia Young, so we assume the DB from yesterday morning to be Phillip Anthony Young. I have run, and am still running, searches trying to learn anything I can about Phillip. He graduated from our high school and I have requested his records. There is nothing else about him at this time. As for the DBs from the Young residence, I'm still waiting on specimens from the ME so I can run them. He expected to have them to me early this morning. That's all I have on the humans."

"Other?" Sandy looked at him.

"The white powder in the black box retrieved from the convertible is fentanyl. It's also got Xylazine in it. Everyone know what that is? Agent Nations can best speak to it."

"Thanks, Chuck." Sam looked at Sandy who nodded. "A new twist in the fentanyl distribution is a deadly combination created by the addition of Xylazine which is an animal tranquilizer. Over 150 people a day are dying from these synthetic opioids. There was enough in that black box to kill a million people." He looked across the table. "Kevin?"

"What is that figure based on?" Kevin was steady and intense.

"We know that two milligrams can cause death—depending on body weight. There are almost half-a-million milligrams in a pound and that package was just under five pounds." The room was absolutely silent. "Most forms of the drug are from two milligrams to five. So, no matter how you count it—lots of lives at risk. Distribution is most prevalent in cities and on college campuses. However, we're not immune to it in rural areas." Sam leaned back in his chair.

"Anything else, Chuck?"

"No, ma'am. I'll let you know as soon as I have DNA on the new bodies."

"One more question." Eyes turned back to Kevin.

"For me or Sam?" Sandy raised an eyebrow.

"Sam, what's the street value of that amount?"

"As you already know, location and demand are factors, but somewhere between $500,000 and a million."

Kevin whistled. "So that box had up to two million dollars of money and drugs—and keys to bank boxes which hold who knows what. Where did it come from?"

"That's part of what we have to find out, Kevin." Sandy smiled at him as she nodded her head affirming the importance of his question. "Let's move on to Sergeant Clark. Steve?"

Solace on a Mountain

As they approached the area Sylvia had designated, Billy woke Quinn. He reached over and touched her hand. She pulled her left arm toward her right.

"Quinn. Time to wake up." His voice was slow and carried the love he felt for her.

She turned her head toward him and her voice was sleepy. "Hey." Then she turned her head again and saw the trees lining the road. "Oh, Billy, I fell asleep."

"Good for you to rest. Now, you might want a couple of minutes to wake up before you see Sylvia."

"Thanks, Billy." She touched his arm. "I don't know what I'd do without you."

"Don't need to find out. I'm here—for whatever you need." He handed her a bottle of water. "Now drink."

Quinn took the bottle and was sipping water when she saw the picnic area ahead. There was only one vehicle and she recognized it as Sylvia's. She let out a long, slow breath. *Perspective. Female cop perspective. I need it.*

Billy parked at the opposite end of the parking area from Sylvia and turned the SUV so he could see them and have his mirrors to pick up anyone coming from the other direction. On a weekday this time of year there were not many tourists. Any locals were likely headed to or from town. Caution was foremost on his mind. "Okay if I walk with you to Sylvia?"

"Sure. I'd like that." Both of them opened their doors. They met in front of the SUV and Billy took her hand. She let him. They waved and called out to Sylvia like any friends meeting up.

"Hey, Sylvia." As if on cue, they were in unison.

"Hey, to you two, too." She waved.

Long strides had them at the table in seconds. Sylvia hugged each of them.

Billy hugged her back. *I think the last time you hugged me is when you came to check on me after I was hauled out of the side of a mountain.* He smiled at her. "Thanks for coming."

"Any time." Sylvia smiled back.

"I'm going to go sit in the car. Wave or holler if you need me." He hugged Quinn and whispered in her ear. "You're in good hands and I'm right over there. I love you." He turned and jogged to the SUV.

Quinn set the bottle of water Billy had handed her on the table. "Thanks for meeting with me, Sylvia."

"Whatever you need, Quinn. I'm here for you."

"Is that a motto in the Valley Sheriff's Office?"

Sylvia cocked her head. "Hmm…No, but maybe it should be. I'll tuck it away. Tell me how you're doing."

Quinn looked past Sylvia toward the tree. "Up, down, turned around, confident, scared, relieved of my professional identity, how much more do you want?"

Sylvia looked at her with compassion. "Quinn, I want you to put your hands flat on this table." Quinn did. "It is made from the wood of these forests. I know because my tribe helped build them. You are grounded here. That's what the earth does for us—if we allow." She put her hands on top of Quinn's. Quinn didn't move. "Human touch is the other grounding for us. To remind us that we are living, breathing, animals endowed with a brain." She gently squeezed the tops of Quinn's hands then moved hers onto the table, too.

Quinn took Sylvia's hands and held them. "I need perspective. Perspective from a woman who knows what it is to function in a still predominantly male profession; a profession that is about service and at the same time presents the potential to lose your life—or take one—every day."

Sylvia let her talk.

Quinn let go of Sylvia's hands and took a drink of water. She watched as Sylvia drank from her water bottle. "How do you remain so calm all the time?"

A slow smile spread across Sylvia's face. "Because I know the love of a good man who is my husband, the heart of a sage mother, and the enlightenment from a very wise father." Her smile lit her face. "All three have allowed me the space to be me: temper flares when they arise, sadness when it overwhelms me, celebrations of joy, and each has given me unconditional love."

Quinn sat without a word. Then with the slow meter of a waltz, she started. "My parents are wise and loving. My work is not part of the world they have known. I think you're already aware they're highly educated people, teach at the university, and both come from long lines of wealth and privilege." She stopped and studied a brilliant red cardinal calling across the wind. "Mother grew up in the world of private education and debutantes in Knoxville." She sighed. "She didn't make me do the debutante thing—I think she knew I wasn't interested. Maybe I've *always* kept that part of our family life at a distance." *That's it. I've shut them out.* "Maybe that's what I'm doing now—keeping them at a distance. I think I've allowed myself to believe I'm protecting them from the seamier side of life." Quinn stepped up and over the seat of the picnic table and walked toward the trees. She turned around and came back. She leaned in with her hands on the table. "Sylvia, I *have* kept them at a distance."

In the soft voice of the new Chief of the native tribe, Sylvia Whitehorse said, "They are waiting for you, Quinn. They always will."

The tears ran down Quinn's face. She sat down on the bench as if straddling a horse. She nodded her head. She took a sip of water. "I haven't told Billy what happened yesterday. I know he would keep my confidence, but I need him to be my safe haven right now. Does that make sense?"

"It does."

Quinn drank more water.

Sylvia said, "Do you trust your fellow officers?"

"Ha! The question is, 'Do they trust me?' I may have taken the life of one of our own yesterday."

"Do you trust your fellow officers?" Sylvia repeated the question.

"Absolutely."

"Then let them do their jobs. Stop second guessing them and use the time to think about what it means to step back and let others lead. Word I hear is that you are already pretty good at doing that, so trust it—and trust them. If I were a betting woman, I'd put a pretty good wager that they're doing everything they can to get you back with them."

"Do you ever feel scared, Sylvia?"

"Every day when I put on my badge and my service weapon. I know the power I have because of them. I never want to abuse it, and I pray I am never the officer my family has to grieve over. Then I straighten my shoulders, enjoy breakfast with my husband whenever we can, and go to work in a profession I love."

"Do you ever want to be in a different place doing what you do?"

"Never. This is my home."

"Yeah. Round City is mine. I'm so grateful I could move from Immigration to the police. It anchors me in Round City. The Director at Immigration was my boss for ten years. I learned some things from him that are useful, but I also figured out a lot about what is not useful in a leadership role. I learned more about good leadership from your sheriff...Chad...in the few months I worked with your team than I could have imagined." Quinn's eyes strolled the edge of the forest.

Sylvia watched her. "Chad is a good man and a great sheriff, Quinn. I think he would tell you he has learned from you. He has always been willing to learn what it takes to build a team."

Quinn laughed. "Yes, he has told me that he learned from your tribal traditions how to lead as a member of the team and not the head of the team."

"Then my father would be pleased. I'm sure he is smiling from the great beyond."

"I wish I had known your father. I only met him briefly. I'm truly sorry for your loss."

"It is the way of life."

"Yes. Yes, it is." She sat without speaking.

So did Sylvia.

Quinn swung her legs over the picnic bench. She reached out and took Sylvia's hands. "Thank you for taking the time to be with me. You have done more in this short time than I can ever repay."

Sylvia squeezed Quinn's hands. "Payment is the loss Europeans brought to these mountains—no offense to you. We are sharers of this land and this time and place. I have no doubt you will someday be beside me in grief or someone else who needs it. That is our responsibility."

Quinn nodded. "Wise woman."

"Now, there is a very special man waiting for you. If I'm any judge of people, and remember I know him pretty well, he will be by your side as long as you let him."

"Sylvia, I can only hope to be worthy of his love."

Sylvia lifted their hands. "Come now, let's go see what this man has planned to help you enjoy this beautiful day." She handed Quinn a card. "My personal cell is on the back. Call me anytime."

Quinn walked around the table and hugged Sylvia. "Thank you."

"It is I who thank you. We are a better community for having you in it." Sylvia took Quinn's hand and they walked toward Billy.

He opened the door and stepped out of the SUV. "Ladies."

"Hope you have something planned to enjoy this beautiful day, Detective Williams."

"I do, Sergeant Whitehorse. If Quinn is agreeable, we're going on a short hike in these woods and then sit here and have a picnic lunch."

Sylvia nodded. "I approve—mostly."

Quinn frowned. "Mostly?"

"The hike here is easy enough in tennis shoes. But drive up to the lake for the picnic."

Quinn clapped her hands. "Great idea. That work, Billy?"

"Perfect." He hugged Sylvia. "Thanks, Sylvia."

"Anytime. Now go." Sylvia turned and walked back to her SUV.

"Ready?" Billy took Quinn's hand.

"Lead the way."

Round City Police Conference Room

Sergeant Steve Clark, head of the A-team, pulled up pictures on the screen. "As you can see here, when we arrived, the pickup truck was approximately three feet from the house. Although we weren't focused on the foundation of the house, you can see the house appears to be secure and the brick pillars a little the worse for wear—but stable." He moved to the next picture. "Here is the what's left of the truck and pictures of the house after the explosion. Our preliminary assessment is it was an amateur explosive device, not well placed in the vehicle with a timing device—yet to be found—which was likely amateurish, too. The A-team is out doing a shoulder-to-shoulder search as we speak. If you look at the pictures of the house, you'll see there was enough force to shift the house a bit and put some of the old mortar on the ground. The explosion was not enough to put *us* on the ground and we were inside the house when it happened." He pointed to what little debris they could see in the fading light. "Our best estimate is that there had not been fuel in the tank of the truck for a very long time. We may find that there was no gas cap which would have ensured any fumes would have dissipated long ago. Given our victims inside the house, we may never know." Steve looked around the table.

"Go on." Sandy nodded.

"Our priority last night was removal of the remains of the two DBs inside the house. We are back there today with additional officers and our night lights, so we will be there as long as necessary to comb every inch of the place. Questions?" He saw the slight nods from each of the team.

Sandy jumped in. "Good work by you and your team, Steve. Hearing no questions, let's get coffee refills and I'll bring you up to date on what we know at this time from the SBI lab on the convertible and Officer Simmons's vehicle."

Chairs scraped and folks headed out the door to the restrooms or to the back of the room for coffee and croissants.

Climbing the Mountain

The early part of the trail was wide enough for Quinn and Billy to walk side-by-side. They held hands and swung their arms like third graders on the playground. Billy started a soft whistle of "Climb Every Mountain."

Quinn stopped, turned him toward her, and kissed him. "You never cease to amaze me. You could have whistled 'On Top of Ole Smoky.'"

"No way. I don't plan to lose the gal." He kissed her back. "Now, let's see who gets to the top of this little hill first."

"If memory serves, the last time we did this race it didn't end so well—for you." She took off running.

He watched her and walked leisurely behind her. *That was too easy, Quinn.* He chuckled softly. *Run it out. That's what you need to do.* He saw her look over her shoulder and he started running. *Can't always lose to her.*

Quinn stood at the top of the hill, put her hands on her knees, and was panting. "Come on, slow poke. Show me what you've got."

He covered the last fifty yards and stopped right in front of her. "Winded are you?" He imitated her panting.

"Okay, I am. Glad you're not."

He turned around. "I'll beat you to the bottom."

She grabbed his shirt as he turned around to head down. "Slow down, fella." She plopped onto the ground and took her water bottle off her waist carrier. "Water?"

He lifted his own. "Got it covered."

"Good run, Billy. Let's sit a spell."

"Whewee, I love it when mountain talk creeps into that city girl's words." He kissed her on the cheek.

"I may be from the city but it's a city in the mountains, don't forget."

"So it is. So it is."

"And I can do the double-speak of the mountains, too."

"Not a competition, Quinn." He was glad she was settling some. "If we take a leisurely stroll down the hill, and drive to the lake, it will be time for some lunch. What do you say?"

"In a minute." She turned to look at him. Her tone became serious. "Billy, I needed that time with Sylvia. When we left home, I thought I would tell her what happened. I didn't. I realized the details will be sorted out by the investigators—what you and I do every day. What I got from her was the grounding I needed to let the system work, trust the love of you and my parents, and believe in myself in this circumstance."

Billy had put his arm around her. He leaned his head to hers. "That, my love, is wisdom."

"I'm going to call my parents and ask them to come for supper. That work for you?"

"Anytime."

"I don't know their schedule and I really don't want them to come as long as there are reporters and police officers outside my house."

"You'll figure it out."

She stood. "*We* will." She winked at him. "Now, let's get to the lake. I'm hungry."

"Okay. Let's run. The workout is good for us." He took off and she watched him go.

Nice moves, Williams. Nice moves.

Chapter 10

The song you heard singing in the leaf when you were a child is singing still.
Mary Oliver

Morning Updates

"Everyone ready?" Sandy noticed Chief Hansen had returned but was sitting near the door this time. "At this time there is no evidence that Officer Simmons stopped the convertible for anything other than a routine traffic stop. His call-in indicated the driver failed to stop at a stop sign. Anything changed on that?" She looked around the table. "Okay. If you'll draw your attention to the photos on the screen." She stood and walked toward the screen. "This is the police SUV. You can see Officer Simmons was driving toward the intersection where the driver ran a stop sign. He turned toward the oncoming car but we can assume the driver stopped upon seeing the flashing lights. Simmons door was opposite the driver. You can see the shell casings on the ground and holes in the side of the vehicle." She pointed to the pattern of holes. "The only shell casings are from the Glock G-18 used by the driver and all casings, except one, of the thirty-three round magazine were recovered in the doors, floor, and trunk of the vehicle or on the ground. For the record, Sergeant Clark transferred the shell casings to the SBI lab with the chain of custody going through Larry Swanson, the Round City Police tech who is working with the SBI. There are no other casings and no other holes." She stopped and looked at the group knowing the implications would have already dawned on each of them.

"Praise God." The whispered words came from Kevin Millwood.

There were others who echoed, "Amen."

Sandy continued. "This suggests that death of Officer Simmons was caused by the driver of the convertible. Of course, final analysis to match shell casings to the gun, fingerprints to the driver, etc. are ongoing. This is a priority case at the SBI labs and Assistant Director Nelson has informed me all necessary resources are at the disposal of the team. Questions?"

Quiet hung over the room for several seconds.

Chief Hansen stood. "Thank you for the current updates. Let me know when you plan to meet again." She left the conference room. Her phone out, she sent two texts as she walked: "See me ASAP. JH."

Sandy decided to continue. "Here is the convertible." Even the seasoned officers turned pale at the first picture of the driver in the convertible which was taken shortly after the incident. Sandy quickly moved past it and had the pictures in the SBI lab. "We'll post these on the board in the workroom, but for now, suffice it to say that bullets hit the civilian's car from the side and the rear. This suggests both officers fired at the vehicle. Examination of the convertible is ongoing."

Chuck raised his hand.

"Yes, Chuck."

"Ma'am. May I be excused? I just got a text from the ME and he has specimens from both victims at the Young house. I need to run DNA."

"By all means. Any immediate questions for Chuck?" She nodded to Chuck who stood and left.

"Sandy?"

"Yes, George?"

"I think we need to figure out how to divide up the work ahead of us. While the SBI folks are figuring out what they can about the evidence related to the vehicles, we appear to have confirmation of the identity of the driver, the contents of the vehicle, and the scene at the Young house."

Sandy returned to her seat. "We know the relationship of the driver of the civilian vehicle by parental DNA, but not specific identity, is that right?"

George paled. "Yes, Sandy. Sorry. I should have been clear. Finding out if he is Phillip Anthony Young is our priority and also who the DB is in the bedroom at the Young house."

"No problem, George. No problem."

George relaxed at the use of the mountain double statements.

They spent the next few minutes working through details and Sandy made assignments in consultation with George. "Okay, folks. Thanks for your thoughtful insights and planning. Questions?"

Kevin raised his hand. "Yeah, when will we get our lead detective back?"

"Not my call, Kevin, but soon, I suspect." She smiled at him. "Gentlemen, let's get this moving."

Chief Hansen's Office

Sandy stopped at the women's restroom and then headed to the Chief's office. She stepped into the outer office.

"Good morning, Ms. Leonard."

"Good morning, Agent Davis. Chief Hansen asked me to let her know when you arrived. Please have a seat."

Chief Hansen's assistant sent a pink slip note by computer to tell the Chief that Sandy was in the outer office. Several seconds later the door to the inner office opened. "Sandy, join us, please."

Sandy walked in and saw Captain Brown standing at the table. She walked over and shook his hand. "Good morning, Captain."

"Agent Davis."

"Please sit." Jill pointed to the chairs. "I need to move quickly on this. Captain Brown and I have spoken with our District Attorney Peggy O'Haire who is in contact with the State District Attorney General. We agree that we are comfortable, based on the preliminary SBI report, to inform Detective Isaacs that the evidence suggests the driver of the convertible is responsible for the death of Officer Simmons. Additionally, once I have done that, I will inform the ME that as soon as he has his final autopsy report on Officer Simmons, which I believe is imminent, we will notify his family they can make arrangements. Do you see any reason to take another course of action?"

"Ma'am, I appreciate being asked, but my training and my skill is in investigation. Perhaps Director Nelson would have some perspective. I would concur that the preliminary evidence on Officer Simmons vehicle supports the conclusion. However, as you would have noticed, no one asked about the thirty-third casing from the Glock G-18."

There was a soft knock on the door.

Chief Hansen stood. "That may be our answer." She opened the door. "Dr. Walters, thanks for joining us."

The medical examiner walked in and shook hands with the others. They all sat when the Chief did.

"Do you have a final report on Officer Simmons?"

"Yes, ma'am. Here's a printout. It's also in your secure E-folder." He handed her the report.

"I'll read it in detail, Dr. Walters, but the immediate question is whether you may have retrieved a shell casing from the remains of either Officer Simmons or the civilian? Unlikely we understand, but so you know only thirty-two of the potential thirty-three casings from what is assumed to be the civilian's weapon were recovered at the scene. Of course, we don't know if there were thirty-three in the clip."

Dr. Walters spoke immediately. "Just to be sure we are all on the same page, in fully automatic position the Glock G-18 has a rate of fire at twenty rounds per second. It is likely Officer Simmons never knew what hit him. To specifically answer your question, Simmons had a metal plate in his skull from childhood and it stopped one of the bullets. The lab now has what I assume is your thirty-third bullet."

"For the record, Dr. Walters, is it your determination that Officer Simmons was killed by the Glock G-18 bullet?"

"The official cause of death is brain trauma from a gunshot wound likely caused by a Glock G-18—9 mm bullet." The ME stopped. "It's in the report."

"Thanks, Doc. Anything else you want to share?"

"Not at this time, ma'am. Still working on the other two I received last night."

"We appreciate your time and due diligence. I will inform the family they can make arrangements for Officer Simmons."

Dr. Walters nodded. "We're ready."

"Thank you. Let me know if you need anything at all."

"Yes, ma'am." Dr. Walters stood. He nodded to all of them, "Have a good day."

Jill Hansen looked at her second-in-command and the SBI agent. "Thoughts?"

Captain Brown deferred to Sandy Davis. "Ma'am?"

Sandy didn't hesitate. "Sounds like your plan is a good one. I have every confidence that no one in the briefing this morning will inform Detective Isaacs, but for her sake I think it's helpful for her to know this much as soon as possible."

"I appreciate your confidence in the team. I, too, trust they will not tell her. I plan to call her shortly. If there's nothing else, I'll let you get on with your work. Let me know if you need anything."

Sandy stood. "Yes, ma'am." She turned to Captain Brown. "Nice to see you again." She turned and walked out.

"Jill, I think her recommendation to talk to Elliott Nelson before calling Quinn is a good one. He's from here, he knows how local folks react, and he's got a lot more experience at officer-involved shootings than we do."

"Sound advice, Frank. I'll ask you to take a walk through the building and see how folks are holding up. We both know the loss of an officer raises tensions way above normal." She looked at her watch. "We'll inform everyone what we know at the next shift change. Please let the sergeants know to keep the incoming shift in house."

"Sure thing." Frank Brown stood and started to leave. He stopped. "Chief...Jill, thanks for coming home from Atlanta—not as exciting, but you're the leadership we needed now."

"Thanks, Frank. Maybe you'll reconsider early retirement." She smiled and opened the door for him. *Be glad you don't know how many officer-involved shootings I've worked.*

"Stranger things have happened."

"Indeed they have."

Jill sat at her desk and dialed Elliott Nelson's number at the SBI.

Heading Home

The drive up to the lake on the back side of the mountain where they had hiked took only twenty minutes and there was no one there but Quinn and Billy. He took the basket and cooler to a table, shook out the table cloth, and put it on the table.

Quinn moved around to the opposite of the table. "Why look at you, going all domestic on me."

"One of has to."

"Ouch."

"Hey, that's my line." Billy was laughing.

"Okay, okay. Guilty as charged." The words out of her mouth, she went silent. Her head down still helping him straighten the tablecloth, she looked up at him. "Does every little phrase make you think...."

"No. Not every little word or phrase, but some." He stood upright and looked at her. The sunlight glittering on the lake behind her put a halo around her head. "Oh, Quinn. Don't move." He took out his phone.

She stood absolutely still. "Is there a bee on me?"

"No. Let me take a picture and show you." He took several pictures and then looked at them. "Look at this one." He turned the camera toward her. "Your halo is visible."

She grabbed the phone from him. "What are you saying?" She looked at the picture. There was a perfect halo around her head. She broke into hysterical laughter. "Well, don't get used to it. It may be the closest you come to seeing any kind of angel in me."

He stared directly into her eyes. "I see one every time I look at you. Now I have the evidence." He smiled as he walked around the table. "This is tough stuff. Our work is tough, the tragedies of it are tougher. Just don't let it make you jaded. I promise you—you'll be a stronger cop once you're on the other side of this."

"I hope I'm never a jaded one. If you see that in me, you have to promise me you'll tell me."

"I promise."

"No matter how badly I react to you telling me—you have to tell me."

He laughed. "I promise. You promise me the same?"

"Oh, I don't think you will ever become jaded." She put her arms around his waist. She didn't pull back when she felt his weapon.

He hugged her and the stood there swaying with the breeze. He kissed her gently and turned to the table. "Come on, let's eat."

"What's in this basket of yours?"

"Well, the basket is yours...but the food is cold fried chicken, potato salad, and coleslaw. That work?"

"You bet. I love cold fried chicken." She opened the cooler and took out the quart of ice tea and poured it into the glasses he put on the table. "You set a mighty fine table, Sir."

"Here to please. Let's eat."

Quinn finished her first bite of chicken and sipped some tea. "Billy, did you talk to your parents about your work?"

He nodded. "Sorry, my mouth was full. Yes, but mostly in generalities. They were strong members of our community and always interested in how they could be good citizens of it."

"Were they?"

"Were they good citizens?"

She nodded her head.

"The best. Mom volunteered at the elementary school helping kids with reading, and Dad was a pioneer in early recycling. As you know, too many ole mountain folks think their used mattresses are okay over the side of the hill. We've pretty much eliminated that in our area. Chad and Bella are working to make sure we have good recycling easily accessible."

"They are?" Quinn's voice was incredulous. "How does Chad have time as Sheriff?"

"Priorities. And, he's doing much better about letting the team work as a team. He's not working seventy-hour weeks anymore."

"Nice. Love can do that to you."

"Think it will do it for us?"

"Already has." She smiled at him.

"What do you mean?"

"You're here in my hour of need, aren't you?"

"True that."

"Thanks for it." She looked him in the eyes. "I mean it, Billy."

"I know you do. Just makes me love you all the more." He lifted his glass and they clicked their plastic glasses.

"Just not as satisfying as hearing glass, is it?" She chuckled.

"Good point. Want more?"

"No, I'm good. Thanks. It was delicious. I'll clean up and we can walk down to the lake."

"Teamwork." He held the trash bag open; they dumped their chicken bones, paper plates, napkins, and cups.

Billy's secure phone vibrated. Grateful for the open area up here so that he got a signal he looked at the text: "Chief calling QI. GM."

"Hey, Quinn."

She turned around already half down to the lake. "What?"

"Hate to be a party pooper, but we need to head down where we can get a phone signal."

"Wasn't that your secure phone? Thought it got a signal up here."

"Text works. Need the phone." He didn't want to tell her it was her personal phone that would receive the call.

"Sure. No problem." She headed toward him and saw he already had things in the car so she started jogging.

He held the door open for her. "Should get a decent signal down below the picnic tables where we were earlier."

"Okay. Sorry to keep you from work."

Billy looked at her. He never wanted to lie to her. "Quinn, it's not for me. It's for you."

"For me? Who?"

"Your Chief is trying to call you."

"Why are they texting you?"

"I told George where we were going, although I didn't know we'd go up to the lake. Didn't want any problems for you if someone needed you."

She hung her head and looked out the side window. "So she'll call on my personal phone which wouldn't receive a signal up here?"

"Exactly." *Hang in there, Quinn.* Billy started the car and drove with care but at a speed the roads would allow. Fifteen minutes later, his phone started beeping. So did Quinn's.

Quinn took hers out of pocket. "Never thought I'd miss having a secure phone. Glad you had yours, Billy. Thanks for letting George know where we were."

"Shall we pull off here and you can make your call?"

"That works."

They stopped and Billy opened his door. "I'll be right over there." He pointed to the tree line.

Easy for you. You get the tree line and I have to cross my legs. She pushed the button on the station number.

"Round City Police. How may I direct your call. Oh, hey, Detective. Who do you need?" The dispatcher was friendly as ever.

"Chief Hansen, please."

"Yes, ma'am. Right away."

"Chief Hansen's office, good afternoon Detective. I'll put you through to the Chief."

"Thanks."

"Hansen."

"Quinn here."

"Good afternoon. Hope I'm not interrupting anything important."

"No, ma'am. Out for a picnic and a hike."

"Good choicc. May I have a minute of your time?"

"Of course."

"Quinn, if it's not too personal, is there someone with you?"

Quinn caught her breath. "Yes, ma'am. Billy Williams is with me, but he took a walk so we could talk."

"Okay, good. I'm glad you have a friend there. While there is still some work to do in the process, I am calling to let you know that we have evidence from the SBI, Dr. Walters, and our techs that the only weapon responsible for the death of Officer Simmons was found on the driver."

Quinn gasped. "Oh, Chief. Are you sure?"

"As sure as we can be. Enough so that DA O'Haire is confident it would hold up in court if it came to that."

"Will it?"

"I don't get to control how other people act, but I believe the DA. I understand the angst that comes in these situations and I wanted you to know what we know." *And that you didn't kill a fellow officer.* "We're still working the case diligently, and I'll keep you informed as I can."

"Thank you, Chief. I know you didn't have to call me—thank you."

"Quinn, just take care of yourself right now. This will be behind you soon. I will let you know when I know more."

"Thanks, again, Chief. Oh, I have another appointment tomorrow with Dr. Kingston."

"Good. Let me know if I can do anything for you."

"Yes, ma'am. I will."

"Hope you can return to your hike. Good afternoon." The call ended.

Quinn looked at the phone. Then she leaned out the open window and yelled, "Billy!"

He ran as fast as he could to her door. She almost knocked him over opening it. She jumped out and he held her. She squeezed him so tightly he thought he was in a vise. He stroked her hair. "Shh...you're okay. We're together. Shh...."

After several minutes, she leaned against the car seat. Billy stood with his foot on the door frame—their legs touching.

"Chief called to tell me what she knows at this point."

Billy waited.

"I don't know whether to cry, scream, throw-up...."

"Up to you."

She whispered, "I didn't kill Officer Simmons." She pulled him to her and held on with all her strength. "I didn't kill Officer Simmons."

Billy stroked her hair again and held her. He was trying not to let out the sigh of relief that he felt. *Thank God. Major hurdle jumped. The rest is technicalities.* "I know it helps to know."

"It does." She leaned back again. "Do you want to get in?"

"I kind of like being this close to you. That work for you?"

"More than." She told him what the Chief had said. "Is it okay that I told you? Did I break some protocol?"

"Unless you do something illegal, everything you tell me is between us. Remember?"

She kissed him. "I do."

"You know the Chief will release this to the press at some point, right?"

She nodded. "Public right to know and all that."

"That's not all bad. You have a good Chief and she's not going to say anything she shouldn't."

"Will the press leave me alone now?"

"Not likely." He watched her carefully. "As I was walking, I thought of something I'd ask you to consider."

"Sure. What?"

"I think you should call and talk to your parents. Sylvia said your name was in the Maryville paper this morning. Do you want them to find out through the news?"

"Oh, Billy. I am so self-centered. It never occurred to me that they could have news hounds at their door." She picked up her phone.

He kissed her on the cheek. "Want me in or out?"

"In, please."

He walked around the SUV as Quinn put the phone on speaker.

"Quinn, darling, how nice to hear from you. Are you okay?"

"Hey, Mother. Is Daddy there?"

"Yes, you know we're at the end of term at university. Let me get him."

"Mother...."

"Yes."

"I need both of you."

"Sure. I can put us on speaker phone. Here's your father now."

"Hello, my special daughter."

"Hey, Daddy." She choked and tears started down her face. "I'm... okay... give... me... a minute, please." She took the water bottle Billy handed her.

"First..." she sniffled and wiped her nose on her sleeve. "First, I'm sorry I underestimated your interest in my work. I've realized I was trying to protect you from the seamier side of the world I see most days."

"We know." Her mother was direct but kind.

"We love you, *nuestra hija*."

Hearing her daddy say, "Our daughter," she smiled. "That, Mother and Daddy, I have always known." She took another sip of water. "Just so you know, Billy is with me and I have you on speaker phone."

"Hello, Billy." They both said.

"Good afternoon, Drs. Isaacs."

"Billy, please, call us Elizabeth and Andres." Andres's tone was clear and specific.

"Pleasure. Here's your daughter."

"Hey." Her voice was calm and she was in control. "Can you come to dinner, and maybe stay overnight, in the next few days?"

"Whatever you want, *hija*."

"Thanks, Daddy." She took a gulp of air. "Have you seen my name in the news today?"

Her mother spoke first. "No, dear. Why?"

Then her father said, "Yes."

Billy felt Quinn's grip on his arm. "Mother and Daddy, I was involved in a traffic stop yesterday which led to the death of a fellow officer and a civilian." She said it as quickly as she could and still sound professional. "My actions, as is true for all law officers, are under review and I am on leave until that process is cleared. Chief Hansen just called to tell me that I was not responsible for the death of my colleague."

"Quinn, *espera*." Her father's voice was warm and loving.

"*Si, padre*."

"*Nosotras*…sorry, Billy. We will be there as soon as we can put some things together. You're in good hands with Billy. We'll see you in a few hours."

"We love you, Quinn."

Quinn's eyes opened wide when her mother said the word, "love." *That didn't come to you easily, Mother.*

"I love you, too, Mother and Daddy. Thanks. We'll see you at home."

"See you soon." The call was ended.

Quinn was shaking. Billy pulled her to him. They hugged across the SUV's console.

Billy finally sat back against the seat. "Let's stop and run the car through the car wash and head for home."

"You think of everything." She smiled and leaned her head against the headrest and closed her eyes.

Billy drove slowly down the mountain glancing at her from time-to-time. He touched her hand. "I love you, Detective Isaacs."

She rolled her head to the side. "Back atcha." She smiled.

Chapter 11

Someone I loved once gave me a box full of darkness.
It took me years to understand that this, too, was a gift.
Mary Oliver

Days Never End

George Marshall was at the station at six am on Wednesday morning. He hoped to get some quiet time to study the crime board. *Quinn, I hope you're going to be back here soon. I want to make sure we have* everything *ready for you to jump in on this.* He entered the code in the Detectives Workroom door and flipped on the light.

SBI Agent Reg Lawton was sitting there in the dark. "Whoa, bright lights hurt the eyes."

"Sorry, didn't know you were in here."

"Couldn't sleep last night, well, early this morning and came up to check with Chuck on his latest runs."

"Chuck is still here?"

"He let me in here to spend some time with the crime board—and my thoughts. Then I think he went home to shower and change."

George pulled out a chair facing the board. "Any new insights?"

"Not one. Do you know how many rounds per second can be shot…"

George interrupted him. "…from a Glock G-18? Yep. Twenty per second."

"That means there was no time for Simmons to react."

"There was some time."

"How?"

"Lots of target practice and quick reflexes. You're assuming the civilian started shooting as soon as he raised his gun. It could have been meant as a threat."

"Fair enough."

"Look at the pictures of the convertible. What do you see?"

"Some bullet holes, but not near as many as in the police SUV."

"Right. We don't know which of the bullets from the Glock was responsible for Officer Simmons's death. We only know one of them was. Hopefully today we'll have a preliminary report on how many bullets came from each of the police officers' weapons."

"Never ceases to amaze me how different the puzzle of each case is."

"Keeps it interesting. Now, how about you go get some coffee? Heck, breakfast downstairs in the bunkroom is pretty decent. Take your time."

"Need to shower anyway. Thanks, George. Back shortly."

Don't make it too soon. I came in for some quiet time with the evidence. He pushed the chair back and walked over to the crime board. *I'll give you this, Reg. You're young and somewhat cocky, but you're pretty good at putting together a crime board.*

Morning Begins for Quinn

"Daddy, good morning." Quinn walked around the island and gave her daddy a hug and a kiss on each cheek.

"*Buenas dias, hija.* I was hoping for some alone time with my favorite daughter."

"Daddy, I'm your only daughter."

"Correct. And my favorite."

Quinn smiled. "Thanks, Daddy. Coffee?"

"Yes. Café con leche, por favor."

"Coming right up." She went to her coffee machine and heated the milk just the way he liked it. "Thank you for coming last night."

"We're always available for you, Quinn." He said it without admonishment.

"I know it in my core, Daddy. My brain just couldn't let me unload the side of life I see almost every day."

"It is often hard to see our parents as people who live in the world. Part of our job is to try and protect our children from the seamier side of life. Perhaps we should have been more realistic with you."

"Oh, Daddy, you and Mother are both great parents. I have learned so many things from both of you—as I did from Grandmother." She set the coffee in front of him and a plate of biscotti. She pulled up her stool and sat across from him.

"We enjoyed dinner at that lovely café with you and Billy last night and the conversation was most interesting. However, I need to hear from my daughter about what weighs so heavy on her heart."

Quinn stared at him. *Why have I never trusted you to understand?* "I honestly don't know all the details since I'm on leave until I'm cleared of my involvement in the shooting."

"Will you be?"

"I think so. The powers that be have declared that all the bullets which hit Officer Simmons vehicle—and him—were from the gun presumed to belong to the civilian driver. Since I am not responsible for the death of a colleague, they will review the videos from my vehicle and Officer Simmons's body camera in an attempt to determine who fired first."

"I imagine that will take some detailed work."

"It will be checked again and again by our detectives and the SBI. Sorry, State Bureau of Investigation lab."

Andres reached across and stroked Quinn's cheek. "I have never held a gun. I can't imagine the responsibility of using one. As an ordinary citizen, I am always hopeful that law enforcement officers are well trained in the use of their weapons and take their responsibility seriously. We do, sadly, need their protection."

"Like any profession, there are rogues and renegades, I suppose. It helps to believe that we each take our oath and our training seriously." She stopped and picked up her coffee. "Maybe, Daddy, that's what I need to remember about what happened on Monday. A fellow officer was doing his job in a situation he had no idea could turn out like it did."

"Do you think of that?"

"Think of what?"

"That any situation can turn from what you expect?"

"I try. A very wise woman police sergeant told me yesterday that every morning when she puts on her badge and her weapon she knows the power she has because of them."

"Do you?"

"I do. But I will think differently about it after hearing her words about the power of the gun and the badge."

"And what were they?"

Quinn smiled. "She said, 'I never want to abuse it, and I pray I am never the officer my family has to grieve over.'"

"I pray for that for you every day."

Quinn reached over and took her father's hands. "Oh, Daddy. You do?"

"I do." He looked up at Billy standing in the door. "Come in, Billy."

"Looks like I'm interrupting a father-daughter chat. I'll come back."

"No, no. Come in. I was just telling Daddy about my talk with Sylvia. Let me get you coffee and you tell Daddy who Sylvia is."

"My pleasure. In our sheriff's department, Sylvia Whitehorse is a sergeant and second in command to Sheriff Oliver. She recently became Chief of our local native tribe when her father passed away in December. She will likely be sheriff when Sheriff Oliver decides to step down."

"I hope I have the pleasure of meeting her one day."

"Oh, Daddy. I would love that. Maybe you and Mother could come to the Pow-Wow they have…."

"A pow-wow? When?" All three turned to see Quinn's mother in the doorway. She was wearing Abercrombie and Fitch pale gray slacks, a silk pearl shell under a light gray sweater, and a pair of Gucci canvas slip on shoes.

Quinn involuntarily ran her hand down her jeans. *Oh, Mother, I must always disappoint you.* Quinn walked over and gave her mother a kiss on the cheek. "Coffee or tea, this morning?"

"A cup of tea would be lovely." Elizabeth turned to Billy. "Good morning, Billy. I see I'm the late sleeper in the group."

Billy gave her what he had learned to call an "air kiss" used by many people in Latin countries. "You are lovely as always, Elizabeth. Good morning. Here, have a seat. We'll get you started with some tea and then I'll shoo you all out and make breakfast." He smiled at her.

Quinn kept her eyes on the tea kettle. *I love you to the ends of the earth, Billy Williams.* "What's for breakfast, Billy?"

"I'm happy to take orders or I can surprise y'all—you know, gizzards, runny eggs."

Quinn turned around and saw both of her parents laughing and her mother had her arm intertwined with Billy's.

"You are a humorous man, Mr. Billy Williams. You should share that wit more often." Elizabeth lightly pulled on his arm.

"Please, don't encourage him, Mother." Quinn set the china tea cup and saucer in front of her mother and winked at Billy.

"Honey or lemon, Elizabeth?" Billy pushed back his stool.

"Honey would be lovely. Thank you." She smiled at him.

Maybe I always needed a buffer. Grandmother—she was my buffer. That's been the change in the last ten years, not that I went into law enforcement. It's that I don't have my grandmother. Well, you never know what you can learn if you step back and let things evolve. "Here, Billy." She handed him the honey jar.

Conference Room Round City Police

"Morning, folks." Sandy Davis tapped the side of her coffee cup with her pencil. "Thanks for making time to meet this morning. We need to get updated and then divide and hopefully get some answers. Anything in general for the good of the cause?"

No comments or hands were raised. "Okay, hearing none, Chief Hansen would like to speak to us. Chief."

The Chief looked around the table and saw all the badges with the black bands. *Even when we have some answers, it still haunts each of us.* "Thanks. Thanks to all of you. This case, as you already know, is going to get much more complex than a traffic stop which ended tragically. I have officially notified Detective Isaacs of the evidence regarding the death of Officer Simmons. Everyone in our station has been informed. Mr. and Mrs. Simmons are making arrangements for Officer Simmons's funeral. We expect it will be on in the next few days, but will confirm when we know. Usual protocols will be followed. Questions?"

Kevin Millwood raised his hand.

"Detective?"

"Ma'am. When will we be getting Detective Isaacs back?"

"Protocols are being followed and I will let you know as soon as we have a definitive answer. Thank you for your concern."

"We need her, ma'am." Kevin looked directly at the Chief.

"I'm pleased to hear you feel that way. Let's just do this the right way and there will be no lingering questions about her return. Anyone else?"

No one raised their hand or spoke.

Jill Hansen stood. "I appreciate your due diligence in this case, as you do in all of them. You know the importance of every clue and every piece of evidence. Follow it. Thanks for your good work." She turned to walk to the door and everyone stood.

They sat down as quietly as they had stood for the Chief.

Sandy turned to Chuck as lead forensic tech. "Any news on the remains from the Young house?"

"Yes, ma'am. The female is Sylvia Phillips Young. I'm still running records on her but so far no hits in any national databases."

"How is it you found her in the run before we had her body?" Agent Reg Lawton blurted out.

"As wife of the late Mr. Young—who spent a good deal of time in prison, she had been arrested in one of his deals gone bad. However, she was dismissed with no evidence or probable cause to hold her."

Reg nodded. "Got it."

Chuck continued. "The male body at the Young house is an offspring of Anthony Young and Sylvia Phillips Young."

"Whoa." Kevin spoke up. "I thought you only found one birth certificate."

"That's true. In Tennessee there is only one as noted earlier. A male named Phillip Anthony Young current age just shy of nineteen." Chuck shrugged. "I'm still running national databases."

George raised his hand.

Sandy saw him. "George?"

"Can Doc tell if one is older than the other and by how much?"

"Not definitively. Both faces and teeth are pretty messed up, but his estimate at this time is that the man at the house is more likely to be the younger of the two. His original estimate of the one in the convertible was 18-25, but now he's estimating closer to thirty. The forensic artist's rendering added to his information."

The table went quiet. They knew the ME used teeth as a central determinate of age. Reg held up a piece of paper on which he had drawn a line straight across connecting the two young men from the biological parents.

"Hold on, Reg." George turned to Chuck. "So you're saying these two men are full siblings?"

"Based on DNA, yes."

"Well. We've got some digging to do." George looked at Kevin.

Kevin nodded. Others murmured.

"Okay, Chuck. Anything else at the moment?" Sandy tapped the table with her fingernail.

"No ma'am."

"Thanks for your work, Chuck, and for a very late night as I understand it. We'll divide this up and you go get some sleep. We'll need you as we go forward."

"Yes, ma'am. I'm going to grab some sleep in the bunk room if you need me." Chuck stood and walked out.

"Steve, any updates from the Young house?"

"Still working the scene. We're doing shifts so I can keep my team on it. Means it's fewer people at a time but we're on it twenty-four/seven. As the evidence suggested, there was no fuel in the tank of the truck. We found multiple holes from rust, so whatever had been in there had long ago evaporated. It probably saved the crime scene. The team found the gas cap and the timing device from the make-shift bomb. The latter is in pieces, but the techs think they can reconstruct it. That's all I have at this time. We're working the house top to bottom today."

"Questions for Steve?"

All heads shook no.

"Sam, anything from DEA you want to add?"

"Chief Hansen had custody for the fentanyl signed over to DEA and our labs are working to see if it matches any known sources of manufacture and/or distribution. It will take several days—maybe longer."

"Thanks. Okay, let's take a stretch break and regroup to divide up the work to be done."

The scraping of chairs on the tile floor indicated everyone was ready to move about.

Breakfast at Quinn's

"Mother and Daddy, let's give Billy some room to do his culinary work. I'll get you settled in the great room and then get the table set. Mother, shall I get you a fresh cup of tea?"

"No, darling, I'm fine. Perhaps a glass of sparking water for the moment."

"Sure." Quinn saw Billy was already headed for the cabinet with the Waterford crystal.

"I've got it. I'll bring it in." He looked at Elizabeth. "No ice, right?"

"Aren't you observant?" Elizabeth smiled at him. "No ice."

Quinn spoke before she thought. "Mother, he's a detective." She bit her tongue.

"Of course, he is. It was just an expression." Elizabeth smiled at her daughter.

"Come, dear, let's go in the other room." Andres took Elizabeth's arm and moved his wife into the great room.

Quinn stepped over to Billy to get the glass of water. "Thanks." She kissed him lightly.

"Anytime." He pulled her into an embrace. "Relax. They don't bite. Let things settle."

She looked at him. "You're right. Thanks." She kissed him again and walked out with the glass of water.

Andres turned from the French doors. "The house looks lovely with the back garden in bloom."

"I can dry off the morning dew from the chairs and we can sit out there."

Her father started toward the kitchen. "I'll do that. You and Mother sit and visit. I can set the table and help Billy if he needs it."

Quinn felt like she'd been asked to sit with Dracula. *Stop it. Your mother loves you. Be a grown-up.* She sat in the wing back chair facing the one her mother had chosen.

"How are you today, Quinn? I know your work is way out of my realm of knowledge, but I want to help you any way I can."

Quinn felt a tear forming in the corner of her eye. *Why am I always in competition with you, Mother?* "Just having you here helps. Honestly."

"Are you sure?"

"Yes. There is nothing I can do until I am cleared to return to work. I have a meeting today at eleven with the psychologist who is responsible for assessing my fitness for work."

"Have you met him before?"

"Her. Dr. Ivy Kingston. Yes, we met the morning of the shooting." She caught her breath and looked at Elizabeth.

"Darling, I know it was a shooting. I don't have to like it. I try not to wish you had chosen a profession that didn't put you in harm's way." She gave a gentle smile. "I'm also aware that you have always been a good problem solver and had a deep sense of responsibility to others from the time you were a young child. And I know your role helping others in...the shooting in high school...and...perhaps...in some way your choice of professions made sure it was as different from mine as you could possibly choose."

"Mother...." Quinn had never heard her mother use the word "shooting."

Elizabeth held up her hand. "This talk is long overdue, Quinn. It was your choice and I have respected it. I could not be prouder of you if you were the top corporate lawyer in America. You are happy in your work, you do good for your community, and it is obvious you are respected by many. What more would a mother want for her child?"

Tears welled in Quinn's eyes—but did not drop.

"I'm your mother. I should have told you this long ago. I'm sorry it took a personal and professional tragedy for you for me to do so. Can you forgive me?"

Quinn stood and went and sat on the arm of the chair—something she would never have done at home growing up. She leaned in and kissed her mother's forehead. "Mother, I know—have always known—you love me. I did think you were disappointed in my career choice."

"Not disappointed. Scared, Quinn. I don't want to lose you."

"I know, Mother. I know." She rested her head on her mother's and was surprised her mother didn't pull away. She saw her father come in from the terrace. He smiled at her and nodded.

"You have the fearlessness of your father, too. Sometimes I forget that. So, let's make this a new beginning. I can't promise you I want to know the horrid details of your day-to-day work, but I would like to know those things that engage you and intrigue you. Is that okay?"

"More than fair. More than fair." She kissed her mother's forehead again and returned to the other chair.

Elizabeth looked at her daughter. "Shall we plan a late lunch downtown after your appointment? Billy was telling me the wife of one of your colleagues has a lovely bakery."

"Oh, that would be great. It's called Sweet Creations. You'll love it. Carrie's croissants are as authentic as you can get this side of the Atlantic."

Her mother smiled. "Then we shall do that. Now you go help that young man of yours."

Quinn stood up. "Thanks, Mother. Thanks for coming. I love you."

"I love you, too, Quinn." She looked her daughter in the eyes. "By the way, I noticed Billy has the same lovely hazel eyes you do."

"So he does. So he does." Quinn stepped into the kitchen.

"Smells good in here. What can I do to help?"

Billy leaned over and kissed her. "Your father has the table set outside. The teapot is hot and ready for fresh tea. Want to take care of that? I've got the rest."

She threw her arms around him. "I love you, Billy. Do you know that?"

"I do and I love you, too. For now, let's eat."

Fifteen minutes later, the four were engrossed in small talk about gardens as they ate biscuits, a spinach and mushroom omelet with gruyere cheese, and ham steak perfectly browned in the iron skillet. Billy had even made grits.

"Fine breakfast, Billy." Andres reached over and slapped Billy on the shoulder.

Quinn saw the wince. *Oh, Daddy, that's his bad shoulder.* She watched Billy.

"My pleasure, Andres. Glad it's edible."

Elizabeth set her napkin back in her lap after dabbing her mouth. "When do you find time to cook, Billy?"

"Well, the truth is this is all new to me. I've had a lot of take-out food from The Corral, our restaurant in the Valley, especially since my parents passed away. However, I've met this woman with whom I have fallen in love and I decided I might get to her heart if I could cook."

"You have." Quinn leaned over and kissed him on the cheek. "He made fettuccini Alfredo with shrimp night before last. Can't beat that!" She smiled at Billy.

Elizabeth smiled. "That would work with me. Of course, I'm already spoken for."

Andres took her hand. "Forever."

"More orange juice, anyone?" Quinn lifted the pitcher. She saw the heads shake. "Since no one is interested, I'll go put it in the fridge and if you'll excuse me, I need to shower and dress for my appointment."

"Go ahead, dear. By all means." Her mother smiled at her.

Quinn nodded, stood, and left.

"Billy, excuse my boldness," Elizabeth looked directly at him.

"No problem. I assume you have a question?" Billy was used to the formalities of her speech even though he still found them a little strange given his day-to-day world.

"Yes. Have you experienced what my daughter is going through?"

"Elizabeth!" Andres looked at his wife.

"Hey. No problem. Yes, I have. I've been involved in several shootings, but I have never been responsible for taking someone's life. I hope I never am." He looked directly at her. "However, I will do so in a heartbeat to save someone else's life." He was polite but somber.

"Thank you for your honesty. It gives me comfort to know you can support our daughter in a way that we have no understanding of how to do. I apologize for my directness."

"No apologies needed. My mother always said this to me: "Tell me what you need to get off your chest and know that I will listen. I'll only ask questions to know that you are okay."

"I would have liked your mother. I'm sorry you don't have her anymore."

"I'm a very fortunate man even though I've lost both of my parents. They taught me well and I carry them in my heart every day. I talk to my dad when I'm afraid I'm going to mess up and lose your daughter. He had great wisdom."

Andres perked up. "Really? What do you say to him, if I may ask."

"Most importantly, he told me when you meet the love of your life, you'll know it. Be patient and treat her right. I try."

Elizabeth reached over and touched the top of his hand. "It is obvious you do it well. We are grateful you have found each other. Thank you for being patient with Quinn. She's always been strong-willed."

"Only one of the many things I love about her." He saw Quinn at the French doors and stood. "Speaking of…." He got up and opened the door for her.

Quinn stepped out in an Alexander McQueen blazer in pale blue with dark blue slacks and her navy blue Prada heels. She had a simple but elegant gold broach on her lapel.

Billy kissed her and whispered so only she could hear. "You look stunning. That's my cop." He kept moving. "I'll get the tray and clean up."

Andres stood. "I can do it. Quinn might enjoy your company to her appointment and to get past the remaining newshounds."

Billy looked at Quinn. She looked at her watch. It was ten-fifteen. "You okay to drive me?"

"Of course. Give me fifteen minutes and I'll clean up."

"Good idea. Mother and I decided we'd go to Sweet Creations for lunch afterwards."

"Perfect. We can swing back by and pick them up."

"That will work. Here, Daddy, let me help."

"You sit with your mother. I'm perfectly capable of cleaning up from breakfast. Why don't you two move over there and I won't worry about spilling anything on you." He laughed.

Elizabeth stood, reached for Quinn's hand, and smiled. "Come, darling. Let's leave the men to the work."

Chapter 12

While trauma can be hell on earth, trauma resolved is a gift of the gods —
a heroic journey that belongs to each of us.

Peter A. Levine

Detectives Workroom

George, Kevin, and Reg left Sandy and Sam in the Conference Room and headed to the Detectives Workroom. Steve headed out to the crime scene at the Young house.

"Let's get this board updated and then get to the grunt work to try to figure out who the guy in the convertible is: Phillip Young or the other offspring?" George sat in front of a computer.

Reg moved to the crime board. He put a box for the male from the Young house and drew the line connecting them as siblings.

Kevin watched him.

George was intrigued. "Reg, do you spend time doing research on those sites where you can track your ancestors?"

Reg nodded and grinned. "My mother works for the state archives. It's in my blood."

"Got it." George nodded his head.

Kevin rolled his eyes.

"Okay, fellows, let's lay out our first line of attack and get these computers and phones working on tracking down identities, last known addresses, and life styles. One thing I'll tell you is that the black walls in the room at the Young house tells me that was a pretty unhappy man—no matter how old he turns out to be.”

“Black walls?” Reg made a note by the box for the male from the house. “Hmm...black walls.”

“Yeah, yeah. Now, let's get on with this.” George laid out the pieces he thought they should focus on and then asked for comments from the other two men.

“Looks like a plan to me.”

“Thanks, Kevin. Clear on your part?”

“Yep. Sure wish Quinn was back.” He looked at George. “No offense. You're doing great, I just know it's not your cup of tea—so to speak.”

“No offense taken. Reg, you good with running that search?”

“On it.”

“Okay, then. Let's plan to regroup at three and we'll be ready for the meeting with Sandy at four.”

Leaving Home

Billy pulled out of the garage. “Looks like all but the intrepid reporters have given up. Down to two and your patrolling officer has them under control.” He turned to watch Quinn. “And he has them facing the other direction—should be good for avoiding cameras.”

“Guess I'm old news now that the Chief has made a statement. It's a relief, honestly.”

“Once you're reinstated, I suspect the Chief will have you do a press conference and that will end this.”

“I hope you're right—on both counts.” Quinn gave a slight nod of her head.

“Both counts?”

“Yes—that I'm reinstated and this will end.”

“Hang in there. You're doing just fine. Better than most, I'd say.”

“Based on what?” She turned to look at him.

"We lose people in our profession over these situations. Some leave the profession altogether; others hit the bottle and end up drowning in it."

"Oh, Billy. I never thought of either. Does that make me weird?"

"I think it means you're well-grounded in your profession and figuring out how to cope with one of the worst things we can face."

"You're too kind. Mostly what I am is—lucky."

"Lucky?"

She reached over and put her hand on his arm. "Lucky to have you loving me, and lucky my parents are wiser than I've given them credit for."

He smiled. "Wasn't it Mark Twain who commented about how smart his father became when he was twenty something?"

She laughed. "Indeed. I realized this morning that my grandmother was my buffer to mother. My mother is a very smart and talented woman. Her standards are so high for herself that I always felt I was in competition. This morning she told me she thought perhaps I chose law enforcement so I could be different from her."

"Did you?"

"Not consciously. The shooting in high school has always been a big part of my decision. I just never said that to her...or anyone, really. She also said I was always good at problem-solving and caring for others, so she wasn't surprised at my choice."

"Did you know she felt that way before today?"

"Not all of it. They were good at encouraging me to solve problems and help others, but I don't think it was what I thought about when I chose law enforcement."

"Well, I say it's always a good day when you learn something—even when it's about yourself...or your mother." He took his hand off the steering wheel and took her hand. "Thanks for sharing that with me."

"They like you, Billy. That's not easy to achieve in their world."

"You're much too hard on your parents. Give them some slack. They're human just like the rest of us." He lifted her hand and kissed her fingers then put his hand back on the wheel. "By the way, I like them, too." He pulled into the parking lot at the psychologist's office.

Quinn sighed. "What a difference forty-eight hours can make."

"Yep. Especially when you have folks determined to get to the bottom of this case."

"Ha. I don't even know what the case is."

"Something tells me you will soon." He backed into the parking space and parked.

"I just hope you're right, Billy. I just hope you're right."

"Well, get in there and show this doctor what you're made of. I'm on your side."

She leaned over and kissed him. "And, I'm so happy you are. Love you." She opened the door and was gone.

Billy watched her golden brown hair swing across her shoulders as she walked to the door of the office building. *You're going to be fine, Quinn. Thank, God.*

Chief Hansen's Office

SBI Agent Sandy Davis entered the outer office of the Chief. "Any chance of a few minutes with the Chief this morning?"

The Chief's assistant, Ms. Leonard, smiled. "If now works, she may be available. Let me check." She stood and knocked on the Chief's door.

"Come in."

Ms. Leonard stepped inside and shut the door behind her. "Chief, Agent Davis needs a few minutes this morning. Is now a good time?"

"Better than later, right? What time is my meeting with the mayor?"

"Noon. He said it would be a 'lunch chat.'" Ms. Leonard made air quotes when she said lunch chat.

Jill looked at her watch, it was ten after eleven. *I've kept the Mayor informed. Wonder what this is about?* "Send her in." Jill stood and Ms. Leonard opened the door.

"Please come in." She waited until Sandy was through the door and shut it behind her.

"Thanks, Chief. This should only take a few minutes."

"Sit. I've got twenty minutes. If you need more, we can schedule this afternoon. What's up?"

"I just received a preliminary report from the SBI labs on the video and the convertible."

"Yes?" Jill sat up straighter, if that were possible, in her chair.

"On the video, there is no evidence of tampering with the videos from either Isaacs or Simmons. They have been time frame run, had audio analysis, and all voice orders transcribed."

Jill all but held her breath.

"Officer Simmons was clear in his direction to the driver in the initial stop which is consistent with Detective Isaacs's verbal reports. The time on Officer Simmons's video shows his return to his vehicle in a timely manner to run the license handed to him, which we now know is a stolen license—reported months ago. Officer Simmons's directions to the driver had been to keep both hands on top of the wheel. When the driver aimed the gun, Simmons gave clear directions to drop the weapon, had his weapon at the ready in less than seven seconds, and Detective Isaacs was out of her vehicle in the same time with her weapon and calling for backup. This time stamp is verified on the recording here in your station as well. The preliminary report from the stop frame on both videos is that the civilian driver fired first aiming only at Officer Simmons." She stopped and waited.

"And?"

"And, both Simmons and Isaacs fired at the driver. The ME said his final report on the driver will be available later today, but he had multiple headshots and other than the video it is not possible to determine which bullet caused death."

"Do we know how many casings were fired from each weapon belonging to one of our officers?"

"Yes, ma'am. Two from Simmons and six from Isaacs—she emptied her magazine."

Jill sat there with her hands steepled in front of her. She nodded her head. "Anything else critical at the moment?"

"No, ma'am. We should have the preliminary report from the SBI lab no later than this afternoon and maybe even the final. They have had teams working on this around the clock."

"That is evident, Sandy. I will be in touch with Director Nelson to thank him for this extraordinary support. Thank you for your continued leadership. What time is your briefing this afternoon?"

"Four pm, ma'am. Will you be able to join us?"

"I'll be there." She stood and extended her hand. "Thank you, again. I'll see you at four. If you need me before that, just check with Ms. Leonard."

"I will. Thanks for making time for me." Sandy shook Jill's hand and left.

Jill walked toward her desk. *So, Simmons was able to fire before he died.* She slowly nodded her head. *That will matter to our folks. And to know that Quinn backed him up like a good cop does—well, none of us could expect more.* She closed her eyes for a few seconds. *We'll see what the State District Attorney General says when he reviews the evidence.* She sat down and readied her notes for her meeting with the mayor.

Cleared or Not?

The door to Ivy Kingston's inner office was closed, so Quinn sat down on the sofa. She was no sooner seated than the door opened.

"Quinn, come in. Nice to see you."

"Nice to see you, too." Quinn glanced around the room. *I didn't notice the other door out of this room when I was here the other day.*

"Coffee? Water?"

Quinn realized Ivy was talking to her. "Sure, I'll get some water, thanks." She picked up a glass and poured her water.

"Me, too, this time of day."

"Here, allow me." Quinn poured water into another glass and handed it to Ivy.

"Thanks. Lovely outfit. I'm a fan of Alexander McQueen—love the jacket."

"My mother dresses me well."

"I beg your pardon."

Quinn laughed. "I enjoy wearing nice clothes, but honestly won't take the time to do anything about having them. My mother loves to shop so she keeps my closets full."

"Lucky you."

Quinn nodded. "I am—in ways I'm learning more each day."

"Care to share?"

Quinn sipped her water. "I'll assume you know I've been cleared in the death of Officer Simmons. The loss is no less tragic, but I can process it a whole lot differently than if it had been my bullet. Anyway, I called my parents and they came down from Knoxville last night. Billy helped me realize they may well have seen my name in the paper and would be worried." She stopped again.

Ivy waited.

"I've always felt I was keeping the seamier side of life from them by not sharing my work. I view my parents as very formal and I know their wealth and privilege shields them from many of the mundane things in life that average people have day-to-day—to say nothing of the tragedy." She sipped water. "Now I know I was wrong."

"Oh?"

"It had never occurred to me that anything I do could make the paper or some news media they, or friends of theirs, would see. Even my very formal mother told me this morning that our conversation about the broad view of my work was a long overdue conversation—on her part and mine."

"Did that surprise you?"

"Yes. It also made me feel ashamed that I didn't trust their world experiences to understand. We'll grow from this—already have. I have always known my parents love me and would do anything for me. I just didn't know how to share my work with them."

"Do you have a better idea now?"

Quinn smiled. "I'll learn. It actually feels good that I figured out my grandmother was a buffer between my mother's very reserved nature and my 'take on the world' nature. This morning Mother said I have the fearlessness of my father. I heard pride in her voice with that—of him and me."

"Tell me how you are feeling now?"

"Sad for the loss of a fellow officer and the grief his family will endure forever. Unsure as I still don't know any official details of what happened Monday morning or what has happened since. Cautiously optimistic that I can heal and that I might even get to keep my badge." She never took her eyes off of Ivy the whole time she was speaking.

Ivy cocked her head. "Those all sounds pretty healthy to me. Do you want to go back to work?"

"I do. I also want someone who can be objective about what has happened—and about me—to agree when the time is right."

"I don't have any answers for you at this time, but hypothetically, if I said, 'you can go back tomorrow,' what would you think?"

"I'd tell you that if it is agreeable with the Chief, I'd prefer to wait until after Officer Simmons's funeral. I think after that I'll know when I'm ready."

"There is no mandatory leave requirement. My recommendation will be part of what is considered by your Chief once she has the decision of the State District Attorney General. You know that, right?"

Quinn gave a slight smile. "This is a whole new chain of command for me after ten years in federal Immigration Service. I've read the rules and the manuals, but as in most things they are much more real when they impact your life directly."

"I can imagine."

Quinn looked at the painting of the mountains on the wall. "Is it okay for me to ask the Chief if I am allowed to attend Officer Simmons's funeral?"

"You are free to ask her whatever you like. Are you prepared for her answer?"

"In my normally logical brain there are at least three responses: 'Yes, no, and it's up to you.'" Quinn looked up at the ceiling. "Wait, there could be another, 'I can't give you an answer at this time.'"

Ivy laughed. "You do know yourself pretty well—you *are* very analytical. Maybe you could work on not making things so hard on yourself. It might be easier to first decide what you want to do, how you will deal with a response that doesn't agree with what you want, and then ask the question."

"I could only hope to mature into that level of operating day-to-day." Quinn smiled.

"Try it. You might find you like it."

"Is there anything you need me from me, Ivy?"

"Not at this time. I'll let you know if we need to schedule another meeting. If you want to meet with me, you know how to reach me."

Quinn nodded her head. "Okay. That's straight-forward enough. My early life experience with the power of guns helped me learn that you can't always control your emotions. I'm smart enough to know that grief and trauma can boomerang on you and come back when you least expect it. I may call at some point."

"I would be pleased to see you whenever you need to talk. Anything else?"

"No. Thank you for being patient with me and for the quiet competence you present. It helps."

"Thank you, Quinn. I hope to see you again, under better circumstances."

Quinn stood. "Me, too. Thanks, Ivy."

"Have a good rest of the day."

"I'm having lunch at Sweet Creations with Billy and my parents. What could be better?"

"Enjoy."

Quinn felt a weight shift on her shoulders. *Another step toward understanding and healing. It matters.* She smiled as she saw Billy get out of the SUV when she exited the building.

Mayor's Office

"Chief Hansen, good morning." The Mayor's cheery assistant smiled and stood as Jill entered.

"Good morning." Jill looked at her watch. "It is still morning?"

"For a couple more minutes. The Mayor is expecting you. This way." The assistant walked toward the conference room.

Jill was surprised. She had met with the Mayor over lunch before, but always at the table in his office. She wasn't even aware she reached up and straightened her badge until she touched the black band around it. She dropped her hand and entered.

"Chief, nice to see you this morning. Know I called you, but again, sorry for the loss of one of our officers. Didn't mean to surprise you with some other folks, but we have a call coming in. Thought it was best we all hear it together." The Mayor shook Jill's hand.

"Nice to see you, Sir." Jill continued to Peggy O'Haire, the local district attorney, "Peggy," Jill shook hands, and then the Vice-mayor, "Morning, Harriett."

"Sit everyone, sit. We're ready for the call. Then we'll have lunch."

The Mayor's assistant sat at the computer and opened the video conferencing software. The three women at the table looked at the screen and then the Mayor. Already on the screen was the State District Attorney General.

"Ladies, Mr. Mayor, thank you for making time to meet with me. Please accept my personal condolences and that of my entire staff on the loss of Officer Simmons. I have reviewed the reports currently available and asked the Mayor to set up this meeting."

Although from Round City, her prior position as a detective had been in Atlanta, so Jill had no experience with how the system in Tennessee really played out, nor the political machinations she felt might be in play here. *It is an election year.* She brought her eyes back to the screen.

"Chief Hansen, you are to be commended on your quick action in notifying my office and DA O'Haire on Monday morning. It should also be noted that Assistant Director Nelson of the SBI has spoken of the professionalism of your folks. You did the right thing in calling in the SBI right away." He picked up his coffee cup.

Is this a review of my command or a ruling on Detective Isaacs? Jill picked up the water glass in front of her and listened as he outlined the reports and information he had read.

"Now, regarding Detective Isaacs...."

* * *

Part II
Follow the Clues

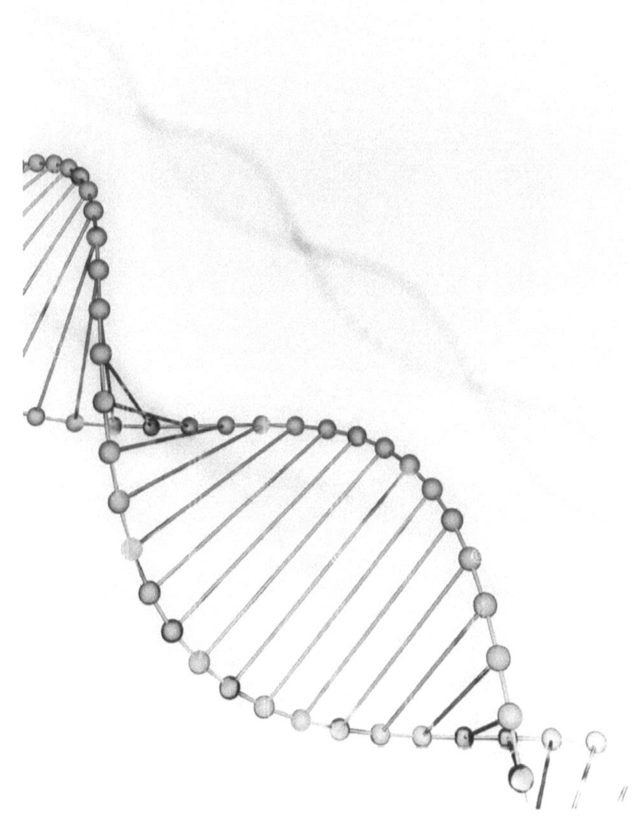

Chapter 13

The beginning of wisdom is to do away with fear.
Yohannes Gebregeorgis

Burying Our Own

The lineup, sometimes three deep, of law enforcement officers from all over the state of Tennessee filled the streets of the small town of Round City. The local officers walked behind the hearse carrying their fellow officer, Albert Simmons. They were led by Chief Hansen, Captain Brown, and Lead Detective Quinn Isaacs all in uniform—their badges covered with a black band. Quinn reached up and touched hers. *Even though I haven't been cleared for work, it was nice of the Chief to let me wear my badge.* It was a short distance from the First Baptist Church to the cemetery where Simmons would be laid to rest among his ancestors.

Billy stood with the representatives from the Valley Sheriff's Office including Sheriff Chad Oliver, Sergeant Sylvia Whitehorse, and every other deputy not needed to maintain a presence in their own community. Billy watched Quinn with both love and professional admiration. *It's not easy, Quinn, but no one would know it to look at you.*

As the Simmons's family was escorted to their seats under the tent by the grave where Albert would be buried, the officers lining the street had fallen in behind the Round City Police and walked up the hill to join them.

Dan Davis, Director of the funeral home, stepped up to Chief Hansen and spoke to her.

"By all means, I will speak to her." Jill nodded and stepped over to Quinn.

Along with all the other officers, Quinn was standing at attention. She looked at Jill.

"Detective, Mr. and Mrs. Simmons have requested that you join them at their seats."

Quinn tried to catch the breath that escaped her. She whispered, "Chief, it wouldn't be right."

"Correct. It wouldn't be right not to honor their request. Mr. Davis, standing over there, will escort you." She leaned in slightly and whispered. "It's the right thing to do. You'll be fine."

Quinn stared straight ahead. When the Chief stepped back to her place, Quinn joined the funeral director.

The empty seat was next to Mrs. Simmons. Quinn drew on every ounce of her privileged upbringing and professional training to get through this. She leaned to Mr. and Mrs. Simmons and spoke softly. "I'm deeply sorry for the loss of your son."

Mr. and Mrs. Simmons both stood and hugged Quinn. Mr. Simmons spoke as Mrs. Simmons stifled a sob. The entire gathering watched as many tried to figure out what was happening.

"Thank you for trying to protect our son and for being there with him in his last moments." Mr. Simmons shook Quinn's hand.

Quinn almost crumbled to the ground. She felt her legs stiffen and her resolve sharpen. "He was a fine young man and an excellent officer. I know you were proud of him."

Mrs. Simmons seemed to slide down into her seat while she held Quinn's hand. "Please, sit here." She patted the chair.

Quinn sat to the right of Mrs. Simmons. They both stared at the coffin in front of them holding the remains of a son and a police officer.

The pastor from the First Baptist Church read scripture and offered a prayer for the deceased followed by one for the living. The final "Amen" seemed to pass across the large crowd like a wave.

Three Round City officers stood off to the far side of the tent. The gathered crowd, all standing, felt the reverberations of the three volleys fired by three guns in a farewell salute to their fellow officer as all the law officers held their fingers against their hats in salute. Then a lone bugler standing under the flag pole in the cemetery started the slow cadence of "Taps."

Quinn felt Mrs. Simmons's grip on her hand tighten as the notes sounded the finality of her son's life. She felt Mrs. Simmons's hand loosen and her arm start to slip. Quinn steadied Albert's mother by supporting her right elbow and realized Mr. Simmons was doing the same on the other side. Quinn dropped her already awkward salute, and steadied Mrs. Simmons.

"Thank you, Detective. We will always be grateful to you." Mrs. Simmons turned and hugged Quinn.

"I hope you can find peace in the knowledge he served his community well." Quinn stepped back as relatives and friends moved-in to surround the parents. She walked off to the side and saw Billy, Chad, and Sylvia from the Valley Sheriff's Office and her detectives, George and Kevin waiting for her.

George spoke first in a quiet voice. "Carrie closed the bakery for the day, but she's there waiting with coffee." He looked around the small group. "Please come over. The back door is unlocked." He stepped away and Kevin joined him.

Quinn looked at Chad, Sylvia, and Billy. Then she saw Sam Nations talking to George and Kevin. He turned and walked away with them.

"Thank you for coming, Chad." She reached to shake hands and he pulled her into a hug. Sylvia hugged her and heard Quinn whisper. "You, too, Sylvia. You'll never know how much you helped me."

"Be at peace, Quinn." Sylvia whispered back.

Quinn turned to Billy. "Thank you for being here for me all week." Then in a whisper as she leaned in to him she said, "And I hope for the rest of my life."

Billy gave her a hug and said, "Forever. Now, let's slip away."

Sweet Creations

Billy drove slowly to give the others time to get to Sweet Creations. He was holding Quinn's hand.

"How you holding up?"

"Numb. Mostly I think I'm numb. Billy, I didn't know if I could get through the funeral. Then when the Chief told me the Simmons wanted me to sit with them, I almost collapsed."

"Well, it never showed. I have watched you like a hawk and, believe me, if I thought you were going to faint I would have swooped in and grabbed you—protocol be damned."

She squeezed his hand. "Thanks, Billy, I can see your shiny armor now."

"Or maybe my majestic wings." Billy's banter was easy as he pulled into the back parking lot of Sweet Creations. He also saw the sign on the back entry with a black border: Closed to honor Officer Simmons. *Don't focus on it, Quinn.* He pulled the door open. "After you."

"Thanks."

Quinn walked into the side room of the bakery and everyone gathered stopped their chatter, came to attention, and saluted Quinn. She saw her law enforcement friends from the Valley and Bella Anderson, Chad's wife. The SBI agents and Director Nelson, Agent Sam Nations from the DEA and her college love, her detectives, Chief Hansen, Captain Brown, and her parents were there too. *Stay under me, knees. I can't collapse now.* Not one word was said. It didn't need to be. *I tried to save him; honest I did.*

"Coffee, Quinn?" Carrie broke the tension.

"Thank you, Carrie." She gave George's wife a hug. "Thank you for giving us a space to be together."

George had walked up behind his wife. "Heck, she gave us breakfast." He pointed to a small buffet at the side of the room. "Welcome back, Quinn."

Bella was the first to hug Quinn. "You are a credit to yourself and all who love you, Quinn. I'm grateful for your friendship."

"I wish we had more time to get together, Bella."

"Let's work at making that happen."

"Agreed." Quinn turned as others came up and spoke to her. Others moved to the buffet.

"Director Nelson, thank you for coming. I'm sorry you're back with us for another loss." *I can't imagine what this like, having buried your brother, the former chief, a few months ago.*

"Quinn, as you know, this is home for me. I'll be back here one day and I'm grateful it is a community so well protected." He moved toward the buffet.

Jill Hansen stepped up. "Quinn, Ivy Kingston said to tell you she's in her office all afternoon—next to last step to having you back."

"Thanks, Chief."

"Let me know when you're ready to return. Now, get something to eat. We need you ready to go."

Sam Nations came up to her. "Hey." He hugged her. "Sorry for the loss. Let me know if I can help in any way."

"Thanks, Sam. Thanks for coming." She kissed him on the cheek. They had remained friends for the last decade.

Quinn's parents were next. She hugged each of them. "Thanks for being here. It means the world to me."

"We've left you alone too long, *mi hija*." Her daddy hugged her tight.

"Quinn, I'm touched, but must say I'm not surprised, at the obvious respect your colleagues have for you. In the worst of times, a person's true character is on display. I love you."

Quinn was not accustomed to her mother verbally expressing love and it was starting to feel comfortable. "Thanks, Mother, I love you, too. Now, let's get something at the buffet." She took her mother's hand and walked toward the table spread with croissants, biscuits, pans with eggs, bacon, ham, and grits.

The talk around the tables was quiet and subdued. Carrie sat between her husband and Billy across from Quinn, who was flanked by her parents. Quinn was sipping her coffee as she saw people finishing their food. She stood, walked to each table, and thanked everyone for their support and their work.

Agent Sandy Davis stood. "Quinn, it's been an honor to work with your team. Sorry for your loss."

"Thanks, Sandy. I appreciate all you have done. Your demeanor made it possible for me to recount my memory of events a third time without falling apart."

"Quinn, I doubt you'll fall apart. Stumble, maybe—we all do. Let me know if I can help in any way."

"Thank you for being here today." Quinn moved on.

The last people left in the room were her team and Chief Hansen. Even Billy had stepped outside with the folks from the Valley.

They turned as Chief Hansen cleared her throat. "I'm going to head out now. Thank you for your good work this week. We'll let you know when Quinn is returning. In the meantime, take some time with your families. The work to be done will wait until Monday. Have a restful weekend." She shook hands with George, Kevin, and Chuck. "Walk me to the door, will you, Quinn?"

"Of course."

The two women crossed the room and Jill Hansen faced Quinn. "We're ready when you're ready. If I can give you some advice, not as your Chief, but as a police officer who has been there. Take as much time as you need, but not too much."

Quinn nodded. "I think I understand. Thank you for your support personally and professionally. I'll see Dr. Kingston this afternoon."

"Look forward to hearing from you. Good afternoon." The Chief walked out without further comment.

Quinn walked over to her team. George, whose back was to her, was talking. "Let's get that Board cleared and ready for the rest of what's coming." Then he saw the look on Kevin's face and turned. "Oh, hey, boss."

"Sorry to interrupt."

"No interruption. Just wrapping up loose ends."

"Fair enough, George. Fair enough. Thanks for all your work and I plan to be back with you shortly."

"How shortly?" Kevin blurted.

"Kevin!" George stared at him.

Quinn smiled at them. "It's okay. I'm glad you missed me. I missed you guys, too. You want me fully fit for duty as the saying goes. I'm aiming to be that way. So, as soon as I let the Chief know, you'll be next."

Kevin frowned.

"Relax, Kevin. I'll be your worst nightmare before you know it." Quinn winked at him.

"Counting on it, boss." He extended his hand and shook hers.

"Now you guys get out of here. Thanks, George, Kevin, Chuck." She shook hands with each one.

The men turned and left the room. Quinn looked around expecting to see her parents and realized they were not here—no one was. *Ten years I spent in Immigration service here. Not once did our director bring us together around loss or a difficult case.* She walked through the side door into the front of Sweet Creations.

"Carrie?"

"Back here, Quinn." Carrie walked out of the kitchen.

Quinn gave her a hug. "Thank you for taking care of us. I am grateful."

"Just take care of yourself. My husband is the happiest he's been at work for decades and it's because of you and Chief Hansen. I can tell you from the chatter in town that folks feel so much safer because of you."

"It takes all of us, Carrie. Thanks, though." She hugged her again and headed out the back door.

Billy was leaning on her SUV talking to her parents seated in their car. Their doors opened as she approached and she saw Billy grab the door for her mother. She smiled. *As rough as I can be on him about opening my door, I know it matters to my mother.*

The three of them were together when she reached them.

"Group hug." It was so spontaneous on her part she never considered her mother might find it awkward. She relaxed when Elizabeth joined in easily.

"*Hija*, we're headed home. You're in good hands and I'd say you're pretty much back to yourself." Her daddy kissed her on the forehead.

"Thanks, Daddy. Thanks for coming and for staying for the funeral. Means a lot to me."

She turned and pulled her mother into a hug. "Thanks, Mother. I've grown up a bit this week and I'm sorry I kept you at arms-length about my work life."

Her mother kissed her on each cheek. "Perhaps we've both grown a bit, my dear. I love you. Now go spend some time with this fine young man. We'll text when we get home."

Billy and Quinn stood with their arms behind each other's backs watching her parents drive away. As they turned the corner, Quinn turned to Billy.

"I want to go see Ivy Kingston. Do you want to go or should I drop you at home?"

"I'm with you. Your chariot awaits."

They got in the SUV and Billy turned toward the office building two blocks down.

"Thanks, Billy. I have so much to talk to you about, but I want to do this and then we can go home."

"Sounds like a plan." He backed the SUV into the parking space, leaned over and kissed her.

She kissed him gently. "Let's go."

"What?"

"I want you to meet Dr. Kingston."

"I have."

"I want you to meet her as part of my life, not from your official capacity."

"Then let's do it." He turned off the car and they walked hand-in-hand toward the office.

"Thanks for staying with my parents."

"My pleasure. By the way, they invited us to Sunday dinner. I said we'd let them know."

"Nice of them. Let's see what the rest of the day brings." She opened the door to Dr. Kingston's office.

Round City Police Station

"George, you sure you have pictures of everything on this board?"

"Yes, Kevin. Checked and double checked. The only thing we need to leave up is the evidence from the trunk of the convertible."

"Do you think it would upset Quinn to see this?"

"Don't know, but don't need to find out. We've got the shooting part of this incident solved and now we have to figure out the rest of it."

"Do you want the part relating to the Youngs and their offspring?"

"What do you suggest?"

"I suggest we build a new board focused on solving their deaths, the stuff found in the convertible, and whether these people have any connection to each other."

George smiled. "That's why we work well together, Kevin. You don't need my permission to sort out the right process." He walked over and started helping Kevin remove the photos from the crime board.

Kevin stacked the photos specific to the Young residence and the convertible on the corner of the table.

George put the other photos in a folder and labeled them. Both men knew there were electronic copies of everything, but they both valued the importance of elements that led to the information around the shooting.

George started to wipe off the white board. "I'll tell you, Reg Lawton sure can lay out a crime board."

"Yeah, I thought so, too. Learned a thing or two."

George slapped him on the back. "Me, too. Not bad for two old war horses." He stepped back and all the evidence was off the board.

"Build the new crime board?"

"I think let's wait. We still have some research to do before the end of shift and it might be good to do it after a break."

Kevin nodded. *And to do it with Quinn.*

Office of Dr. Ivy Kingston

Ivy Kingston stepped out into the waiting room. "Quinn, nice to see you. Hey, Billy. Glad you came along."

"Hey, Ivy. Hope this is alright. Chief Hansen said you'd be in all afternoon." Quinn stepped forward.

"This is fine."

"Would it be alright if Billy sat in with us for a little bit?"

"Absolutely." *I'll appreciate having his perspective.*

They walked in and sat in Ivy's office. Quinn sat in the same wingback chair as in her previous visits. Billy sat on the sofa. She started to move to the sofa and Billy put his hand up.

"You look comfortable there. I'm good."

"Thanks, Billy." She turned to Ivy. "As you know, the funeral was this morning. Afterwards a number of people from the station, SBI, DEA, and Valley Sheriff's Office gathered at Sweet Creations." She took a breath and glanced at Billy. "I was asked by Mr. and Mrs. Simmons to sit with them at the gravesite."

Ivy had both Quinn and Billy in her line of sight. She saw the warmth in Billy's eyes as he looked at Quinn. She waited on Quinn since she had stopped talking.

"And?"

"And I did. I was reluctant, but now I'm glad I did. I think I was of some comfort to them."

"I'm sure you were."

"It was hard for me to process their thanks for trying to save their son and being the last person to be with him." Quinn's downturned eyes and slowed breathing wasn't missed by Billy or Ivy.

"Do you want to talk about it?"

"No, I just wanted you to know what happened." She glanced at Billy. "At Sweet Creations, the hardest part for me was when I walked into the room and everyone stopped talking, turned toward me, and saluted."

"Do you know why they saluted?"

Quinn looked at her. She nodded her head.

Ivy smiled. "Does it bother you that they did it out of respect?"

Quinn looked at the painting of the mountains on the wall. *I wonder how many officers sit here and look at our mountains. It's a good reminder of where we live.* "No. I would have done the same thing. It's just not easy to reconcile their need to show respect and my feelings of unworthiness when I couldn't save his life."

Billy sat forward and then caught himself. He leaned back.

Quinn looked at him. "Something you want to say?" She smiled at him.

Billy shook his head. "No, I'm good."

"Look. I know the difference in my intellectual understanding of what happened and my emotional acceptance. Although I have not reviewed any of the evidence, I believe I did everything I could to save his life—both lives. The reality is...I didn't."

You could hear a pin drop in the room. Quinn leaned forward and poured a glass of water and took a sip. "I learned many things that morning."

"Care to share?" Ivy cocked her head to one side.

"Training is just that—training. It matters and it will prepare you for many possible outcomes but it will never be the same as the real thing. Loss and grief are real. Even when you play and replay the events in your head, you are still left with the reality that lives ended that day. The challenge is putting it all in perspective."

"And have you?"

"Honestly, I hope I never think I have completely. It would feel to me that I had dismissed the loss and I don't ever want to do that. I will try not to let it consume me, to interfere with my ability to do my job, but I don't ever want to be jaded about my commitment to human life, my community, or my work."

Billy gave an almost imperceptible smile.

Quinn continued, "There's one more thing I want to say with Billy here and then I suspect you need to talk to me alone."

"Go ahead."

"Billy has told me he has met you before. I don't know, nor need to know the circumstances. I wanted you to meet him as part of my life. He has been with me all week and has supported me, given me space when I needed it, and helped me connect in a new way with my parents. I don't have any idea how you determine my fitness to return to duty, but I wanted you to know that I know how fortunate I am to have his love. It has me wondering why so many relationships don't work out among law enforcement officers."

Ivy smiled. "Relationships, whether among law enforcement officers, teachers, farm workers, whatever work one does are as random as the people who enter into them. Don't spend too much time trying to sort that one out."

"Fair enough." Quinn smiled. She looked at Billy. "Anything you want to say?"

"Just thanks for letting me walk beside you through this. Do you have any questions for me, Ivy?"

She shook her head. "If you'll give me a couple of minutes with Quinn, I'll send you on your way."

Billy stood. He kissed Quinn on the top of her head and shook hands with Ivy. "Take care of her for me." He walked out.

"Was I wrong to bring him?"

"Your session. You can have whomever you wish. I have the feeling you are fully aware that the more I know about you the better picture I have."

"Smart woman."

"Thank you. Now, I asked you a hypothetical the other day about returning to work. Now, I am asking you the real question. Are you ready to go back?"

"I am. I didn't expect to sit with Officer Simmons's parents at the gravesite. Now I'm glad they asked me. I think I was able to be supportive of them—and his father said it mattered to them that I tried to save their son's life and was with him at the end. Somehow I don't think many officers get to hear that. It means a lot to know I was some small comfort to them."

"Have you considered how you will handle having access to information about the incident?"

"I have. I've also thought about making sure I talk with the Chief about protocols related to the information. I also want to know if I come see you on my own dime if I need to."

"For the first, I think it's important you talk with the Chief. Sometimes knowing the facts help us heal, sometimes they are like scratching a sore and never having it heal."

Quinn nodded.

Ivy continued, "You can see me when you need to do so. We'll sort out what is within the scope of support from the department and your insurance."

"Thanks. I know the Chief wasn't sure the funeral would be today but since it was, and today is Friday, I will go with your recommendation on my return to work."

"You will be cleared for work, which I assume you have already figured out. I will notify the Chief. It is up to her when you return."

"Do you have a recommendation?"

"From an employment point of view, no. From a human point of view, I'd tell you to take some time to get out and see the world from your new lens and start the week rested and ready for whatever comes your way. There will be a mandatory review in three months, so I will see you then. I'm available when you need me."

"Thanks, Ivy. I'm sorry we met under these circumstances—I am also grateful."

"I'm glad to have met you, too. Take care, Quinn."

Quinn stood. "You, too. And, as one professional woman to another, remember to take your own good advice: get out and see the world. It's a beautiful spring we're having."

The two women shook hands and Quinn walked out.

Billy stood and took her hand.

"Billy, I have an idea."

"Only one?"

"Oh, do you think I'm ready for banter?"

"No doubt. What's your idea?"

"Let's go over to Gatlinburg tomorrow. I love some of the old shops there and it would be good to see people enjoying our mountains."

"Works for me. Want to spend the night?"

"Let's talk about it after I hear from the Chief."

Chapter 14

Don't fear failure so much that you refuse to try new things.
The saddest summary of a life contains three descriptions:
could have, might have, and should have.

Louis E. Boone

Sunday Evening

"Thanks, Mother and Daddy." Quinn gave Spanish cheek kisses to her parents and her mother pulled her into a hug.

"Thank you for spending the afternoon with us. It sounds like you had a great day in Gatlinburg and it was fun to see your face light up when you mentioned watching them make taffy at the Ole Smoky Candy Kitchen. It brought back memories of all your questions about how the wooden wheels pulled the taffy. However, I'll limit myself to one piece a day."

Quinn stepped back from her mother. "What's the fun in that? Have two." She kissed her mother's cheeks again. "We have to go, but we'll see you for Memorial Day weekend if all goes well."

"Look forward to it. Text me when you get home."

"I will." Quinn turned to see her father shaking hands will Billy. "Ready?"

"Let's go." Billy opened her door and Quinn didn't comment—out of respect for her mother. *Mother will always support equality issues but she'll never give on a man being a gentleman.*

They waved as they drove down the long drive to the front gates of her parents' home.

Quinn put her seat back and stretched her legs. "Thanks for driving, Billy. If you want me to take over, just let me know."

"It's not that far. Thanks, though. How are you feeling? Ready for tomorrow?"

"I have had the most bizarre seven days of my life; part of me waits for something else to happen—something unexpected, part of me feels guilty that I've had a wonderful weekend with you and my parents, and part of me is itching to get back to work."

"Sounds pretty healthy to me. You'll get back into the routine and things will settle. I promise."

She reached over and touched his cheek. "I love you, Billy Williams. Do you know that?"

"Part of me is absolutely confident about that, part of me is scared to death you'll find someone much more sophisticated and drop me, and part of me is grateful we can start to settle into some sort of normal."

Quinn laughed. "I suppose we'll both be surprised if our lives are ever normal."

"Yeah, let's leave that for another day. We should be back in Round City by seven or seven-thirty. Do you want me to stay over?"

"Always. Are you going back to work tomorrow?"

"Yes. I told the Sheriff I'd be at work."

"Did you use all your leave on me?"

"Ha. I have so many hours I'll never be able to take them. However, love of my life, even if I had to take leave without pay..." He glanced over at her. "I would have been with you."

"You're sweet."

"Shhh...don't let that get around."

"Okay. Our secret. I always love having you stay but I also understand that you probably have things at home to do before you go to work."

"Let's see how we feel when we get you home."

"Works for me." She turned on the audio in the car and chose an album on her phone, picked a song, and Dolly Parton started singing, "The Day I Fall in Love." Quinn closed her eyes and smiled.

Billy backed into Quinn's garage and reached over and gently shook her arm. "Hey, sleepyhead."

Quinn sat up and jerked her head toward him. "What? Where are we? Oh, my gosh. I slept all the way home?"

"And didn't snore once." He leaned over and kissed her.

"Now I'll never be able to get to sleep." She stretched.

He ran his hand down her arm. "Well, how about I stay for a while and see if I can help you get to sleep? Then I'll slip out and go the Valley."

She lifted his hand, kissed his fingers, and looked into his eyes. "How could I refuse?"

They entered her kitchen and Billy put his service weapon and badge in his safe. He wanted her to accept it as the routine they both had when she had her weapon. "Hungry?"

"No. You?" She turned to him.

"Are you kidding? That late lunch was enough to last me for four days. Send your mother a text."

"Oh my gosh. Thanks." She sent the text: "Home. Thanks again. Love you." She put the phone in her pocket and grabbed Billy's hand. "Done. Let's see how good you are at helping me get to sleep." She pretended to be running down the hall to her bedroom.

Billy pulled on her hand as if trying to stop her.

She kicked her shoes off, pulled back her covers, and sprawled on her bed.

Billy did the same and they were soon lost in the kisses, and murmurs, and promises.

Monday Morning

Quinn sat straight up and bed. Her heart was racing and she couldn't get her breath. "Billy?" She looked to the other side of the bed. It was empty. She ran her hands through her hair and looked at her clock. It was flashing five-thirty and her phone started playing "Boogie Woogie Bugle Boy." *Oh, Billy, Billy, Billy. You not only put me to sleep, you set my alarms. I am going to change that song, though.* She pushed stop on her phone and the alarm clock.

She swung her feet over her bed, sat up, and stretched as high as she could reach. She slipped on sweatpants and a top and ran down to her gym. *Twenty minutes, a shower, and I'm outta here.* As she finished her treadmill run, she saw a banner on her phone with a text. *No, two texts.*

Billy had written: "Morning, sunshine. Call if you need me."

She wrote back: "How about if I don't need you?"

Billy wrote back: "Call anyway."

She wrote back with a heart emoji.

The second text was from George: "Pick you up at six-thirty? That work?"

Quinn looked at the message again. "Why?"

"We can catch up and you don't have your detective wheels."

"Right. Thanks. C U then."

She stepped into the shower. *Two thoughtful men: one in my bed and one at work. Doesn't get much better than that.*

She was headed for the front door at six-twenty-five when she remembered she had her badge from the funeral. She opened the safe in the kitchen, put her badge on her belt, and walked back in the living room running her fingers over the black band.

Billy had opened the heavy drapes so the sheers let the morning light in. *No more patrols and no more newshounds. Thank you, Chief Hansen.* She stepped out on the porch and made sure the door locked behind her. She waved when George drove up.

"Morning, Quinn." George had leaned over and opened the door.

Quinn grabbed the handle and pulled it open. "Morning to you. Thanks for thinking of this. Otherwise I'd have had to bug you later in the day to bring home my own SUV."

"Kinda figured. How was your weekend?"

"Restorative, thanks. Yours?"

"Quiet. Chief insisted Kevin and I stay away Saturday and Sunday. Hardly knew how to act."

"Good for all of us." She smiled. "It was very sweet of Carrie to fix breakfast for us and have us at her bakery on Friday. I'll write her a note, but please tell her how much I appreciate it."

"She was glad she could contribute in some way. It was a first in my time in this department. When I talked to the Chief about it, she thought it was a great idea and...well, you can see. She was there."

"Thanks, George. You're the best."

They pulled up to the gate at the station. George gave the code word for entry for that day and the officer on duty saluted both of them after checking the vehicle. "Have a nice day, Detectives."

Quinn let out a long, slow, quiet breath. "I didn't know the code word."

"You didn't need to, I did." He turned and smiled at her. "We've got you, Quinn. Just don't be shy to say what you need. Kevin and I have both been through this. You'll settle into a routine and find that time and space help."

She turned to look at him. "George, I had no idea."

"Just as well. Part of putting it behind us and still being able to do the job."

"Got it."

George pulled into the parking space that had been added for him: "Senior Detective."

"When did this happen?" Quinn looked down the row of cars. "I mean, I'm glad. I just didn't know it had happened."

"Chief Hansen came down on Tuesday and said you had requested this several months ago but the sign had just come in." He looked at her. "Thanks, Quinn. Wasn't necessary, but I appreciate it."

"Great. Well, Detective Marshall. Let's go catch the bad guys."

"On it, boss." *Wait until you see what we have to unravel.*

Chief Hansen's Office

Quinn turned the opposite way from George after he opened the door. Then she turned back.

"George." Her voice was soft but urgent.

He turned back. "You okay?"

"Yes. But should I have come in the front door? I just realized I didn't have my ID to swipe."

"You're good. I cleared it before we came in. Relax."

"Okay, thanks. Off to see the Chief." She continued the short walk to the Chief's office. The outer door was open even though Ms. Leonard was not in yet. Quinn stepped in and saw the Chief's door was open.

"Chief Hansen."

"Come in, Detective."

Quinn entered the inner office.

"Shut the door behind you, please."

Quinn did and stood just inside it.

"Morning, Quinn. Nice to have you back. Have a seat. Coffee?"

"Morning to you, ma'am. No, I'm good at the moment." Quinn sat and faced the Chief.

On the table were Quinn's ID, car keys, and service weapon. Quinn saw the document beneath them and the four bulleted items which included her badge. There was a note beside "badge" [Delivered by Chief Hansen on...] and the date of the funeral on Friday.

"Please initial each item indicating you've received them and then sign at the bottom after you read the statement."

Quinn initialed the ID and put it on. She took her service weapon and shoulder holster and laid them in her lap. Then she took her official vehicle keys and put them in her pocket. She read the statement which indicated she was restored to full duty with all rights and responsibilities. She glanced up at the Chief—then she continued reading. The next sentence stated that she was required to submit to a three month evaluation with the psychologist of the department's choice.

Glad I already knew this. The last statement indicated she would be given a prompt when she signed into her computer to create a secure new password. *No surprise there.* She signed and dated the document. She slid it toward the Chief.

"Ms. Leonard will see that you receive a copy through secure channels." She pushed the paper to the side. "Now, how are you, Quinn?"

"First, Chief, thank you for your support of me personally and professionally during this difficult time and for supporting our detectives during what had to be a very stressful time for them." She took a breath. "I'm ready to return to work. I'm aware I may have some setback moments, but I will talk with my team and make sure they know I expect them not to ignore anything they notice about me that is out of the ordinary. I've asked Dr. Kingston if I can contact her if I need to do so." She stopped and watched the impassive face of her boss. She smiled. "Most of all, I'm grateful to be back on the team. Thank you."

"I'm glad you're back. Your team did great work and they were textbook perfect in managing the situation. It was clear from the beginning that it was important to them to get it right."

"I would imagine. They are competent folks."

"And they wanted you back." The Chief let that hang in the air.

Quinn felt the blush rising up her neck to her face. "Thank you, Chief."

"If at any time you need to step away—take time—do it. We will get by. Let's get you back to full service and this loss behind us."

"Yes, ma'am."

"You are going to be briefed by Detective Marshall and you will see that we've got a case that goes beyond the loss of Officer Simmons. I have every confidence you can lead this team in trying to solve what may be a very complex situation. Let me know if you need additional resources."

Quinn felt the energy return and her pulse quicken—not from fear but from anticipation of a crime to be solved. "Yes, ma'am. We'll leave no stone unturned."

"I'm sure of that. Unless you have anything else, I'd like you to be at roll-call at eight, please."

"Yes, ma'am." Quinn knew the words of dismissal. She stood, holding her service weapon and holster in her left hand, and extended her right hand. "Thanks again, Chief."

"Thank you for your excellent performance in a very difficult situation last Monday. See you at eight."

Quinn left the office and walked slowly down the hall toward her own office. *Excellent performance in a very difficult situation. Is she sure?* She stepped into the women's restroom to put on her gun. Then she looked at herself in the mirror. *Remember what Billy said, "You've got this."*

She entered the code in the door to the lab and her office. The lights were on so she knew Chuck was already here. "Hey, Chuck. It's just me."

He scraped the stool on the floor when he jumped up. "Quinn, hey. Welcome back." He came around the corner and almost knocked her over. He jumped back. "Welcome back."

"Yes, you said that." Quinn laughed. "Thanks, Chuck. Glad to be back. I'm sure you've got plenty to update me on, but if it can wait, the Chief wants me in roll-call at eight and then I'll meet with George to get up to speed. So, maybe we could get together around eleven?"

"Perfect. You'll know what's going on by then and it gives me more time on the run I'm doing."

"Thanks, Chuck." She turned toward her office. Sitting on the floor outside her door was a vase with flowers. She opened her door, bent down, and picked them up. Once in her office, she took the card off of the flowers. "Welcome back, boss. George, Kevin & Chuck." A tear ran down her face. She took a picture with her personal phone and sent it to Billy.

A text popped up immediately. "Go get 'em, Tiger." He put a heart emoji.

She stepped out to the counter and fixed a cup of coffee and then closed her door and started her computer. After multiple security questions and a phone call from Officer Gilbert, the head of technology, she was able to access her email and memos. A scan of her emails resulted in half of them being from others in the department thanking her for being back-up for Albert Simmons. She filed them. When she looked at the other emails, she realized she would not have been copied on anything related to the incident involving her. The rest were routine notices and policy updates. She leaned back in her chair. *Don't know what I expected. Of course, I would not be in the loop on that investigation.* The light knock on her door startled her. She jumped up.

"Yes." She pulled the door open. George and Kevin were standing there. "Time for roll-call."

A sudden dread came over Quinn. *What's going on?*

They walked down the hall to roll-call together. Quinn saw Chief Hansen at the front of the room with the duty sergeant and Captain Brown. The chatter stopped and all heads turned toward them. Her heart skipped a beat. She and the detectives and Chuck moved to the chairs on the side.

The duty sergeant gave a single command. "Ten-hut." Everyone in the room stood and came to attention. Chief Hansen stepped to the microphone.

"I've asked the Police Chaplain to start us with a word of prayer."

The Chaplain stepped forward. "Lord, we ask blessings on all the departed with special blessings on the latest among us to fall. We pray you will provide safety for all police officers and especially for those who stand with their fellow officers in times of crisis. Amen."

The "Amen" around the room was subdued but enveloped everyone.

Chief Hansen stepped back to the microphone. "Detective Isaacs, please step forward."

Quinn looked at George and Kevin who took a step back as she stepped out. She went up and stood to the side of the podium.

"On behalf of a grateful department, I hereby award you a Medal of Valor for your efforts to protect a fellow officer and to serve and protect under hostile fire." She held out a medal on a ribbon and placed it around Quinn's neck. Then she saluted Quinn.

Quinn returned the salute and then her eyes caught the movement of arms throughout the room moving to salute her. She returned the salute to all in the room, stepped back, and turned to walk back to her team.

The Chief said, "At ease. Be seated."

As soon as she said, "At ease" the room burst into applause.

Quinn felt her face redden. She stopped and stood at attention.

The Sergeant on duty stepped forward, raised his hands, and the officers quieted. "Thank you, Detective Isaacs. We will all sleep easier knowing you are among us."

Chief Hansen walked in front of Quinn and the detectives on her way out. "Let's go." They followed her.

Outside the door, the Chief stopped and shook hands with each of them. "Thank you each and all. Now let's get this case solved." She turned and walked away.

The detective team headed for the workroom.

"I need to stop here, but I'll be with you in a moment." Quinn entered the women's restroom and headed straight for a stall. She hoped she wouldn't throw up. Her head rushed with the flash of gun fire from last week and she leaned against the wall trying to get herself calmed. She took several deep breaths and let them out slowly to the count of ten. The reel in her head stopped spinning and she stepped out to wash her face. It was then that she looked in the mirror and actually saw the ribbon and medal. She touched the bronze with her fingers tracing the shield and the lettering. She flipped it over and on the back it read: "Quinn Isaacs, Detective. For valor in service to RCP." The date was in small letters underneath it. The red, white, and blue grosgrain ribbon had a bronze circle holding the medal. It felt as sturdy as the medal itself. *Oh, Albert, I wish I could have saved you. You went out of your way to make sure I was welcomed here.* Another tear fell on her cheek. She took the paper towel and wiped it off. She straightened her shoulders and ran her fingers through her hair. *I hope no one expects me to wear this all day.* She pulled the collar of her jacket over the ribbon so the medal lay below the front of her jacket. She walked out the door and was grateful no one was in the hall at the moment.

She entered the code in the Detectives Workroom door and saw that only George was there.

"Where are the others?"

"Let's get you up to speed and then we'll have a team meeting. That work?"

"Sure."

George reached out and handed her a leather box. "Chief dropped this off for you."

"Will it be disrespectful if I put this in it?" She lifted the medal.

"Wouldn't want it to get messed up as you get your hands dirty in this work." He smiled and shook his head. "It's okay."

"Thanks, George." She put the medal in the box and took the cup of coffee he offered. "Let's get to it."

Chapter 15

Learning the truth about ourselves is a lifetime's work, but it's worth the effort.
Fred Rogers

Detectives Workroom

"George, before we get started, am I allowed to see the camera footage from Monday?"

You know the answer, but not surprised you asked. "Do you want to?"

"Yes—at some point." She turned and looked out the window which overlooked the back parking lot as she pulled her hair into a knot at the base of her neck.

George smiled at the gesture. *She's getting ready to dig in.* "Makes you normal, Quinn. Hard to go through a loss and not want to know if your memories are accurate."

She turned and looked at him. "Thanks, George. *Should* I see it?"

"Here's my advice—for what it's worth. Let's get into the extension of the case. We can read the reports as background. Then you can decide if you want to see the video."

She nodded her head. *If it's not already out in the media, it will be. Freedom of Information Act will give it to anyone requesting it. No choice.*

"You're aware it will be requested by media and nosy people under FOIA."

"Mind reader?"

He smiled. "Been there."

"That makes your advice more golden. I will heed it. Let's get started."

George arranged the photos from the convertible trunk starting with when they were in the SBI bomb truck. He walked to the crime board. "You missed a mighty fine board creator in Agent Lawton. Mine won't be nearly so technical."

"You do a great board, George. I've told you that. Where's that picture taken?" She pulled her note pad in front of her.

"We had to call in a bomb team because the SBI dog handler was concerned the gun powder from the shooting might cause the dog to miss something. The SBI brought in a robot which took the box from the trunk into the bomb truck and removed these items." He labeled the pictures as he put them up:

Glock G-18 (6)

Cash- $480,000

Fentanyl laced with xylazine - +/- 2 kilos = +/- $500K-1M

"Whoa. Where exactly in the convertible was this?" Quinn stood up and studied the photos.

"In the wheel well under the mat. The Glocks were lying on top of the black box." He pointed to the box at the top of the pictures of the money and the fentanyl. "We've got pictures of it before it was removed."

Quinn ignored him. "What was the weapon of the driver?"

"Glock G-18 with a thirty-three clip." He waited to see if it upset her.

"Glock recovered?" Her question was direct.

"Yes, it bounced under the car." George had already decided he was going to play it straight with Quinn and not try to sugar coat anything. They'd deal with any effect it had on her as it came up.

"Good to know. All cartridges spent?"

"Yes."

"Retrieved?"

"Yes."

"Where are the drugs and money?"

"Chief transferred custody of the drugs to the DEA. Sam Nations from DEA has been read in and is waiting to hear from us. Money is being analyzed."

"Has Alcohol and Firearms been called in?"

"No. We're just setting up this case—it's separate from the one on Monday. The driver was not stopped in relation to these items."

"Do we know the identity of the driver?" Quinn tried to keep her voice even. She felt the slight race in her pulse.

"We're working on it. Although we have no name at this time, he was the genetic descendent…"

"He?" Quinn's brows furrowed. She looked over at George.

"Yes. He. The reason for the female clothing has not been determined."

Quinn nodded. "Go on."

George explained the driver's DNA matched a now deceased woman and a deceased criminal buried at the prison where he was last incarcerated.

"How recently is the woman deceased?"

"Monday."

"Okay, I think I need to sit down for this part."

George put up the pictures of the Young house, the exploded truck, and the bodies.

Quinn studied them. "Is the second body also a genetic match to the woman?"

"Yes. And to Mr. Young, now buried at Riverbend Maximum Security Prison graveyard."

Quinn nodded. "Looks like I have some work to do to catch up on what we know."

"I can share or you can read. What's your pleasure?"

"Let me read and then I can ask. That work?"

"Yep. The files are in the system. You going to do it here or in your office?"

"What do you need to do?"

"I'm working on some searches for the young man for whom we do have a name—we just don't have it matched to the remains. Had to get a warrant, but have it now, so should be able to get what we can from the local school and other sources."

"Work for you if we do it in this room together? I'll start reading and you can search."

"Sounds like a plan. I need fresh coffee. You?" *Whew. Thanks, Quinn. I want to keep a close watch on you for a day or two. You'll get through this with our support.*

"For sure. Let's take a walk to the break room. Then we can work until I meet with Chuck at eleven."

George opened the Detectives Workroom door and Quinn walked out ahead of him. They were just outside the break room door when Quinn looked through the glass and saw several officers inside. She stopped abruptly almost causing George to run into her.

"Sorry, Quinn." He stepped back extending his arms to his side so as not to push her.

"My fault. I don't know if I'm ready…" she nodded toward the door.

"Good day as any. I've got your back. Just smile. Say thanks, if you're up to it. Fill up your coffee cup and let's turn around and walk right out again."

"10-4." She opened the door. She was not two steps into the room when it started.

"Thanks, Detective Isaacs."

"Good work."

"Thanks for your efforts."

She gave a wan smile, nodded, and kept walking—each step hoping she wouldn't melt into the floor. She filled her cup and turned to exit.

A female officer walked up to her. "Detective?"

"Officer Evans, good morning."

"You made us proud—just needed you to know that." She walked out ahead of Quinn.

George was right beside Quinn and held the door. He spoke in a voice barely above a whisper. "Next time will be easier."

They headed down the hall and entered the workroom. Her personal phone vibrated and Quinn caught herself before she tripped and spilled her coffee. She set the cup on the table and sat down. She pulled out her phone and saw the text.

It was from Billy: "The first few hours are the hardest."

She stared at it: "Thanks. TTYS." *Bless you, sweet man.*

The Young House

Sergeant Steve Clark gathered his A-team. "Okay, folks, we're doing one last sweep here and then we'll wrap it up until we're told something else is needed."

His lead forensic officer looked at him. "Sarge, when we finished up on Saturday, the team had done a thorough search just short of breaking into walls or floors."

"True, Officer DeLoach, and we may be breaking into walls or opening floors—we'll see what the detectives decide today. Anyone notice anything we should have another set of eyes on?"

None of the team spoke.

"Okay, then you have your assignments. If I assigned you to an area you've already studied, tell me now." Steve looked from one to the other. Each gave an imperceptible shake of the head. This team had been together for a number of years and were known throughout the area for their expertise and precision.

"Then let's get to it. DeLoach, let's hit that back bedroom."

The team broke off with almost perfect military precision—three of them rewalking the perimeter and four inside.

DeLoach and Clark pulled on gloves as they approached the room where they had found the young man. The lighting in the room was dim and the black walls made even that light pretty useless. The team had set up the bright lights usually limited to outdoor night work.

"These lights help, Sarge. We looked around and under furniture but didn't move it. Any reason not to?"

"It's time. Pretty good likelihood in a teen's room with black walls that something is hidden somewhere."

"Not in places we could access. That's why I mentioned walls and floors."

"You start over there with the dresser; I'll start here in the closet. We'll work to the center and then move the bed."

Ruth walked to the far corner of the small room where a three-drawer dresser was pulled slightly away from the wall. It was on rollers and painted as black as the room. She judged by the weight it was made of cheap particle board. The clothing had already been taken in for the techs to examine. She was able to slide the dresser with no effort and moved it out from the wall. She took her flashlight and ran a beam from the corner to the bedpost. She stopped and went back a few inches.

"Hey, Sarge."

"Yeah?"

"Look at this." She pointed just in front of the baseboard. "See that small board?"

Steve bent down and put his own flashlight on the spot where she pointed. "Screws, not nails like the rest. Puttied over although not very well—looks pretty new." He looked up at her. "Let's get it open."

DeLoach pulled out a small pouch from their field kit and took out a screwdriver. She took pictures and measurements of the length of the board and it's position from the walls.

"Got my photos. Let's see if it's anything more than someone stopping a squeaky board."

He nodded. "Have at it."

She easily scraped away the putty and turned the screwdriver in the first screw. As she unscrewed the last one and dropped it into a small plastic bag, she lifted the board. She shined her light, reached in, and pulled out a gallon plastic bag which was hanging on a cup hook on the floor joist. "Clever young man to figure out a hiding place." She handed the bag to Steve.

"They look like ordinary envelopes, but this top one doesn't appear to be addressed or mailed. Looks like there's money in there, too."

"Take it out." Her voice was clipped.

He looked up at her.

"Sir." She glanced at him waiting for a reprimand for being curt.

"DeLoach, that look wasn't about the 'sir.' It was disbelief that you would consider that I wouldn't take it out."

"Sorry."

"No need. So what do we have here?" He pulled out the first envelope, opened it and pulled out a piece of paper and read it aloud: "'Phil, Monday's the day. No more notes. You in or not? Andy'"

"Is there a date on it?" DeLoach was looking over his shoulder.

"No. Just says, 'Sat.' Could be any Saturday." Steve held it up for her to see.

"Or it could be the Saturday before last Monday."

"Yeah, that too." He sat back on his haunches. "I don't want to run the risk of contaminating any of them. Put this one in an evidence bag by itself and the plastic bag in a second. Let's get these to the station ASAP. I'd prefer you take them. Use the van so you can put them in a secure drawer. I'll keep working this room."

DeLoach stood up. "On it, Sarge." She gathered the evidence and headed out to the van.

Steve spoke to the room in a soft voice. "Well, well, Mr. Young, or whoever you were, you were pretty mysterious and sneaky...or maybe just very careful."

Round City Police Station

"Hey, Quinn." George tapped the table with his fingernail.

Quinn looked up from the computer. "What's up?"

"Whichever one of these young men is Phillip Anthony Young..."

Quinn interrupted him. "IF one of them is Phillip Anthony Young." She watched his face.

"Touché! We've got two male DBs directly linked by DNA to two people who are deceased and we have one birth certificate in the state of TN. Maybe there were more kids by the Youngs."

They both turned as they heard the keypad on the door beep. Chuck walked in.

George stood up to stretch. "How's the best forensic tech doing today?"

"Best where?" Chuck bantered.

"Anywhere?" George was quick to give it back to him as a question.

"I'll take that as everywhere. Anyway, I'm good." He turned to Quinn "It's eleven and I'm just checking to see if you're ready to meet."

"Eleven, already? Sorry. Should have set an alarm." She stood and walked over to the crime board. She pointed to the pictures. "All of this did not just magically appear in the trunk of a convertible. Do we know yet who owns the convertible? I saw in the report that the dash identification number had been scratched up and the license plate stolen."

"Yep, got all that for you." Chuck's secure phone rang. "Johnston." He listened. "Got it. I'm here."

He hung up and turned to Quinn. "That was DeLoach. She's on her way in with some evidence they just found at the Young house."

George's voice was too loud for the room. "Found? Where? Why wasn't that house already covered top to bottom?" He stopped. "Sorry, didn't mean to shout."

Quinn nodded. "No, problem. We all want everything done yesterday. I, for one, am glad they're being thorough at the site of two deaths from unknown causes." She turned to Chuck. "Are the causes still unknown?"

"Quinn, it's been a week." George paced.

Quinn's voice was as calm as it had ever been. "And, we've buried an officer and have a part-time ME who has had four bodies to exam."

"Welcome back, boss." George turned and smiled at her. "We've missed you."

"What does that mean?" She put her hand on her hip and cocked her head.

"Calm, intelligent sanity is back in the house. Simple as that."

"For the moment, anyway." She smiled and looked at Chuck. "And, yes, I'm ready to meet. George, do you have time to join us?"

"Bathroom break and then I'm good."

"Good idea." Quinn headed for the door. "Back here in ten ready to go." She took her coffee mug and went across the hall to the lab and her office.

She rinsed out her mug and left it on the counter. She went into her office, closed the door, and took out her personal phone.

She sent a text to Billy: "Got a minute?"

Her phone rang. "Hey, thanks for taking a minute."

"For you, almost always." Billy's voice was light and playful.

"Thanks for your earlier text."

"Sleep well?"

"Perfectly. Thanks for setting my alarms."

"Two of them too much?"

"Normal for me."

"Fair enough, then. Fair enough."

Quinn settled in her chair and smiled at the mountain double speak she found so reassuring. "How's your day?"

"Things have been quiet on this side of the mountains. Just catching up on the usual: domestic violence, petty theft." He stopped. "How about you? Doing okay?"

"Better than I thought I'd be. Good to be back into the routine." She took a breath. "I had a rough moment after roll-call."

Billy stayed quiet.

"The Chief awarded me the Medal of Valor." She stopped to see if he would comment. "Everyone saluted me." She took another breath. "I think I held it together in the moment, but I hurried to the women's room thinking I'd throw-up or pass out."

"You okay now?"

"I am. George is being helpful in getting me into the case that is growing out of the stop that ended Officer Simmons life."

"He's one of the good guys."

"He is. They're all being helpful and seem glad to have me back."

"No doubt."

"Anyway, I need to go into a meeting. I just needed to hear your voice."

"Check in anytime. If you want to have supper together, let me know."

"I'll call you later. I love you, Billy."

"I love you, too. Take care of my detective."

She smiled. "And you take care of mine. Later."

"Later."

Quinn sat looking at her phone. *I do love you, Billy Williams. I wondered if I would ever have someone to share my life: the good, the bad, and the ugly. And this past week, uglier than I ever really imagined.* She picked up her Yeti cup and headed back across the hall.

Detectives Workroom

Quinn walked in and sat down. "Okay, gentlemen, let's get this board built and solve this crime."

"Yes, ma'am." Chuck pointed to the screen where he was projecting several screenshots. "One of the questions was about the identity of the driver of the car and the young man in the bed at the Young residence."

Quinn and George nodded.

"A national database run on DNA, now enhanced by all the folks giving no consideration to their privacy when they do an ancestor hunt, identifies four first degree relatives as descendents of Anthony Young and Sonia Phillips Young. Three of them were born in Ohio."

Quinn studied the screen. "Two females and one male born in Ohio."

"Yep. And the two females still live in Ohio."

"Addresses on them? Any record?"

"Current addresses and no criminal record on either."

"Any known address on the male born in Ohio?"

"Most recent was in South Carolina. There is currently a bench warrant for failure to appear on a domestic violence charge. I checked the last known address and he left there two months ago—owing four months' rent."

"George, want to get this on the board, please?" She looked over at the board.

George was drawing boxes and lines. "So that means there's DNA in a national database on him. Is he the driver or the one in the house?"

"No DNA." Chuck looked at George.

"I thought you said there was information in a national database and a bench warrant."

"Right. Not all DNA data is in law enforcement data bases. As for the bench warrant, it's for failure to appear. He was charged in absentia and the judge found probable cause of guilt and issued the bench warrant. Thus, no DNA."

Quinn asked, "What's his name?"

"Anthony Young, Jr."

George tapped the board with the dry erase marker. "If this guy has a bench warrant in South Carolina, he's likely got something somewhere else."

"Not that I've found—yet. If it's out there, we'll find it. Remember we have his DNA— that's how I found the parental match. The parents are in the SBI and FBI systems, but so far none of the kids."

Quinn stood and was leaning against the window frame looking at the crime board. "What's the current age of the son born in Ohio?"

"Twenty-seven." Chuck pointed to the date of birth.

"And the one in Tennessee?"

"Almost nineteen."

"How long had Mr. Young been at Riverbend?"

"Total of fifteen years. Died of a heart attack five years ago."

"Do we know how long Ms. Young has been living here?"

"The house is in her name only, paid cash, and she's been there for fourteen years." Chuck recited the information without notes.

"So..." Quinn walked to the table and leaned on the back of a chair. "One year after her husband died. Maybe she had a life insurance policy on him."

Chuck lit up like a Christmas tree. "Good thinking, Quinn. I'll check that."

"Find her address at the time she purchased the house."

"Already checked that. She was renting the same house for the previous four years."

"Okay. So, she's been there since close to the birth of the Tennessee born son. Might bode well for the body at the house being Phillip." She nodded her head. "Good work, Chuck. George, the board is looking good. Let's sit for a minute."

George wrote "Sr." next to the elder Young and a red 'X' across the box.

Quinn took a drink of water. "Since we have a positive ID on Ms. Young, we need to notify the daughters. I'm assuming the information on the daughters is current. Right, Chuck?"

"Hot off the press just before I came in here."

"Good progress. George, would you please take care of drawing up the papers and figuring out which agency has jurisdiction in their places of residence?"

"Sure, do you want me to notify the law enforcement agency?"

"Let's get everything ready and then talk before you do."

"Thinking about going to Ohio?"

"Not at the moment. Should we?"

"Well, we can't do the notification. But, we might want to think about how we can get information on the two brothers."

"That's senior detective thinking." She patted George on the back. "Chuck, you get on tracking how she paid for that house and let me know when DeLoach gets here, please. George will get the notification ready. I'm going to talk to Doc." She saw the look on George's face.

"Something I can do for you with Doc?" George watched her.

"I'll be fine, thanks. I appreciate the concern." She clapped her hands together. "Also, could we meet at four? I'll ask Sergeant Clark to be here and brief us on what they know from the house."

"On it." Chuck left the room.

"George, thanks for your concern. I promise I'll call from the morgue if I need support."

"Sure, Quinn. Just want to be here for you."

"I appreciate it more than you know." She opened the door to walk out. "There is something you could do for me."

"Sure, what? Anything."

"I didn't bring lunch. Think Carrie could whip us up sandwiches?"

"In a heartbeat. Great idea—wish I'd thought of it. Heck, might was well include boy wonder across the hall. What do you want?"

"Ham and Swiss on a croissant. Carrie knows. You fly, I'll buy."

"Not to worry. I know the owner. Back in twenty."

"Detective. Do not speed."

"Yes, ma'am." George was gone.

Quinn sent a text to Steve Clark to meet at four. She walked the hall toward the door down to the morgue. *Here I come, Doc. Don't know what my reaction will be.* She turned the handle and felt her heart skip a beat.

Chapter 16

Your willingness to wrestle with your demons will cause your angels to sing.
August Wilson

Sweet Creations

George walked in the back door of his wife's bakery grateful that Monday's lunch time was not as busy as the rest of the week.

Carrie stepped up and kissed him. "Hey. I got your text. Feeding an army are you?"

He pulled her into a hug. "If need be. Right now I just need a moment with my wife."

She hugged him and rested her head on his shoulder. "Lucky for you I'm not covered in flour."

"I wouldn't care. I need you close."

She leaned her head back. "George, are you okay?" She searched his eyes.

"Better now. I think I'm so nervous for Quinn that I'm not on my game. I snapped at Chuck. He didn't deserve it."

"Did you apologize?"

"Hoping that lunch will make amends. Okay if this meal is on the Marshalls?"

"I'd have it no other way." She kissed him and stepped back. "How is Quinn?"

"Mostly better than I could have expected. Maybe women process this stuff better than men do. Most of us put on a bravado and act like it never happened."

Her expression was direct and intense. "Just different, I think. Is it causing you to have flashbacks?"

"Not to the incident I had. Just the aftermath surfacing, I think."

"Will you promise you'll talk to me about it if you're slipping into it?"

"I will." He stepped over and kissed her. "And, I promise I'll go see Dr. Kingston if it's too much."

"That's my hubby." She kissed him. "I love you."

"I love you. I'm about to make big brownie points at work." He wiggled his eyebrows as he lifted the bag with their lunches. "Thanks, honey. See you at home." He kissed her again and left just as the bell on the front door of her bakery jingled.

"Take care of my detective." She waved as she walked to the front of the bakery.

The Morgue

Quinn called out as she started down the stairs. "Hey, Doc. It's Quinn." She stopped at the bottom of the stairs and looked around the room.

Dr. Walters stepped out of his office. "Hey, Quinn. Come in. Come in." He stepped back as she approached his small office. He quickly moved the medical journals off the chair. "Have a seat. Coffee? Water?"

Quinn smiled. "Water would be great. Thanks."

Dr. Walters reached in the small fridge outside his office door and handed her a bottle of water.

"Where's Sue?" Quinn looked around the morgue and didn't see the ME's assistant.

"Not here today. We've finished the autopsies and I'm working on final reports." He watched her face. "Doing okay, Quinn?"

"I have my moments. Just trying to be honest with myself about them and keep moving."

"That's just what this doctor would prescribe. Good for you. That said, I'm here if I can help in any way."

Quinn smiled at him. *You are the absolute right temperament for this job, Doc.* "Thanks. I did actually come for your counsel."

"Oh?"

"Yes. On the one hand, I'm relieved that Officer Simmons is no longer down here. It made it easier to come down the stairs."

He nodded. "I can understand that."

"On the other hand the remains of the other three are still here, right?"

"Yes. I'm waiting on identification on the two males and then we'll have to notify the next of kin."

"We're making progress. Not sure how long your day will be today, but we're meeting at four, if you can join us. You can go first if you have anything and then head out."

"I'd like to be there, but can't today. My wife has figured that a part-time retirement job means part-of-the-time I'm home and part-of-the-time I'm here. She needs me home this afternoon."

Quinn laughed. "That's a good one. Smart woman."

"I'll likely be a day or two more on these final reports. Your team has the basics."

"Sure, I understand. We'll generate any questions we have for you and I can check with you afterwards." She looked at the physician who had served this community as a general practitioner and now its medical examiner. "I hope we don't keep you too busy."

"Most days not—that speaks well for our community."

Quinn looked around the office. "I think your office is even smaller than mine."

He laughed. "For me, I just need the computer and people not being bothered by the clutter." He pointed to the stacks of journals and books.

You could use a bookcase. I'm going to take care of that. "No bother for me. Anyway— normally I would see the remains of the people we are investigating. I'm not sure I'm up to that at the moment." *I still don't know if I killed the driver.* "However, is there anything you found unusual or noteworthy to help us figure out what might have been going on? Do we know how the mother and son died?"

"If I can give you a bit of grandfatherly advice as well as my best medical perspective…"

She nodded. "Please do."

"…don't see them. The reports will tell you everything you need. Sometimes it does help to see the remains. Sometimes it's better to let it be."

"I value your opinion and your wisdom. That question is settled. Thanks."

"Now, as for anything unusual." He raised an eyebrow. "There is."

Quinn sat up straight and looked at the ME.

"All three of them have a brand on their right hips." He watched her carefully waiting to see her response.

"You mean like a tattoo in the form of a brand?"

"Welcome back, Quinn." He smiled and was relieved this smart young woman was doing so well. "No. I mean a brand. Burned into the flesh."

"With a hot branding iron?"

"Can be. Can also be a frozen branding iron. Either one will destroy layers of skin tissue. Tennessee considers scarification…"

"What? Scarification?"

"Yes, that's what it's called in medical terms. Anyway, Tennessee considers scarification a medical procedure and, in fact, it's been ruled as surgery."

"So, it's illegal in Tennessee?"

"Technically. However, I suppose it would require someone reporting the individual getting or giving the scarification."

"Oh, Doc, for someone who has seen as much as I have in ten years in Immigration service, this is a new one on me. Can you tell how old the young men were when they got them?"

"Not recent. Based on the distortion from expansion, I'd say soon after infancy."

"And can you distinguish the brand?"

"Got one of the techs running it, but we may never find it. If it's tied to a cult that is known, for example, there may be other examples out there. If it's a family brand, we may not find it."

"Can I see..." Quinn hesitated. She took a breath and continued, "...a picture of one?"

"Can do." The ME pulled up a picture on his screen. All that was visible was the design and surrounding flesh.

Quinn looked at it one way, then turned her head to the other side and looked at it. "It looks like a lion's paw and a lamb."

"That's right. You're seeing the one on the woman, so it must have been as a late teen or adult to have retained its shape."

"Okay, one more thing for us to check out on the sisters."

"Sisters?"

"Yes, Chuck has identified two genetically related sisters living in Ohio. George is working on notification documentation and jurisdiction. We'll let you know as soon as we have it sorted out."

The ME nodded slightly. "Two sisters." He sat silent for a moment. "Wonder if they have the brands?"

"We may need to find out. It would appear, if the data we have is accurate, that the oldest daughter was born when Ms. Young was sixteen."

"I see."

Quinn leaned back in her chair. "Doc, one of these days I may need to talk to you about the driver of the convertible. Not today. Maybe never. Just don't have it all sorted out."

"Quinn, may I speak candidly?"

"Please."

"No matter what you learn about the incident, it's not going to change one thing. You've been cleared in both deaths, as I understand it, so try to just trust the system. You have to believe you did the right thing, in the moment, and that all your training and discipline allowed you to do so."

She tilted her head and looked at him. *Cleared in both deaths—have I?* "I wonder if it's ever possible not to question yourself."

"I think it's healthy. What's not healthy is to over dwell on it. I'm not the expert here on procedures, but I should think you could recuse yourself from this extended part of the case, couldn't you?"

"Yes. We could ask the SBI to help since this is shaping up to be more than it first appeared. At this moment, I'm actually finding that attention to the detail is a good antidote for me. I can be objective and should I lose that, I have no doubt the Chief will remove me. I'm grateful if I had to have this experience that it's in this department."

"And, that young lady, is why I am still working as ME. We're in a good community and this department gets better every day. Now ole' Doc Walters' prescription for you is to get out of this morgue, go have some lunch, and solve some crimes."

Quinn stood. She extended her hand. "Thanks, Doc. I needed your medicine." She smiled.

"Take care of yourself, Quinn. Don't get too worn out too soon."

"You mean like work an eight hour day?" She winked at him.

"Or even six." He raised his left eyebrow as he looked at his watch. "I suspect you've already been here that long."

She shrugged and headed for the door. "Thanks, again, Doc—for everything."

Lunch

Quinn stopped at the women's restroom and washed her hands and face. She looked in the mirror. *Listen to Doc, and Billy, and George. They're all on your side.* She turned as she heard the door opening. She nodded at the woman from the records division and walked out the door she held open for Quinn.

"Hey, Detective."

Quinn turned. "Detective Millwood. Coming up for air?"

"Well, yes, but more importantly, coming up for lunch. George called and said he was bringing lunch for us."

"Well, I'd say that's worth taking a break. Where to?"

"Apparently he managed to get the conference room. So, let's go."

Quinn fell in step with Kevin. "Hope you were able to get some rest over the weekend."

"Hardly knew how to act with two days back-to-back—on a weekend. Actually took a ride up to Fort Loudin Lake with some family."

"That's great, Kevin. I'm glad you could get away. I've never been to Fort Loudin Lake even though it reaches almost to Knoxville." She chuckled. "My folks weren't the outdoorsy type."

"Well you couldn't have landed in a town much more outdoorsy than Round City."

"I know and I love it." She reached for the door into the conference room. "Allow me."

"Thanks." Kevin walked in and whistled. "Did Carrie send the whole bakery?"

George laughed. "She made me promise to send some home with each of you and she even sent a box of cookies for the breakroom. I told her it better be the day old ones."

"George!" Quinn shook her finger at him like a school teacher chastising a student. "Not nice. Not nice."

"Yes, ma'am." George feigned remorse. "Sit. Sit. Tea's already poured. And, Kevin, don't get used to this."

"Yes, sir!" He gave a mock salute.

Chuck was watching the exchange. *Wouldn't have seen that joking with the old lead detective.* "Hey, come on. It's hungry out."

Quinn turned and looked at Chuck. "Hey, didn't see you hiding over there."

"Not hiding. Just getting the best seat for the food."

"Then let's eat." She sat and George passed out the food.

"Lunch is on me and Carrie. She said to tell you there was one caveat."

Everyone held their sandwiches in their hands and waited.

"No shop talk for twenty minutes—aids in the digestion."

They looked at each other, shrugged, and Kevin said, "Okay, who's going to win the pennant this year?"

They all laughed and started eating.

Twenty minutes later, they were each eating a cookie and Quinn said, "Steve said he would be in at three and could meet then. Has another meeting at four-thirty. It's one…" she looked at her watch, "oh, my goodness it's twenty after two already." *How long was I with Doc Walters?* "I'll clean up the room." She heard the moans around the table. "What?"

"Think we're not capable?" Chuck shook his head like she'd told a bad joke. "My momma would tan my hide if I didn't clean up. You go do what you need to do. I'll be there at three."

"Go on, Quinn. We've got this." Kevin said.

"Okay. Thanks. Thanks for everything." She left the room and the three men. She almost ran into the Chief she was so lost in thought.

"Detective? You okay?"

"Oh, Chief! Ma'am. I'm so sorry." She shook her head. "I'm fine, thank you. I was just thinking how fortunate I am to work here." *Oh, Lord, did that sound like buttering-up?*

"No harm, Detective. Detective Marshall told me your team was having lunch together. Glad to hear it."

"And, the men are cleaning up the conference room."

"Even better." She winked. "Let me know if you need anything." The Chief turned the corner and headed toward the back of the building.

"Yes, ma'am." Quinn kept walking. Almost to herself, she repeated it, "Yes, ma'am."

Detectives Workroom

"Thanks for joining us, Steve. As you can see, we've got a start on a crime board. We have three deceased adults who are all genetically related."

Steve looked at her. "I see that. Didn't know it."

"We'd like your observations at the home of the Youngs and we'll add any new information we've collected today."

"Sure. Chuck, any luck on the contents of the plastic bag?"

Chuck nodded. "Got pictures of everything. Want them now?"

Quinn held up her hand. "Background, please. What plastic bag?"

Steve brought them up-to-date on the search of the residence and how they found the plastic bag. "Knowing the contents may give us some clues."

Quinn looked at Chuck. "Indeed. Chuck, would you share the pictures?"

One by one, Chuck put up the photos of the notes which were inside the envelopes. Chuck pointed to a picture of all the envelopes. "Only three of them were actually mailed. They came from Columbia, South Carolina, but there was no return address. You can see they were addressed to Phil Young at his mother's residence."

"So how did he get the others?" Kevin looked from one person to another.

"Question which may never be answered." Steve's voice was flat.

"A question to be researched, nonetheless." Quinn's voice was equally flat. She saw that George had drawn a line from Phillip and Anthony and written: "eight notes/letters. Timeframe?"

"Anything else, Steve?" Quinn wanted anything they had from the house on the Board as she had not been at the scene.

"There was money in the bag, too. How much was it, Chuck?"

"Just over ten thousand."

All heads turned toward him.

"Yep. I'm running it for serial numbers, prints, and anything else that might link it to the money in the convertible."

Steve jumped in. "So, other than that, we didn't discover anything else. As our techs said, 'without opening walls.'"

"Do we need to open walls? Any reason to think we should?" Quinn looked at each of the men.

All heads shook "no."

"George, something you want to say?"

"I'd just like that to be a qualified 'no.' We don't know enough yet. We may have to tear the whole house apart."

"Could be. But not today." She smiled at him.

"Chuck, what have you learned?"

"The handwriting on each of the notes appears to be a match, including with the three envelopes sent by mail from Columbia. Do you want a handwriting expert to look at them?"

"Thoughts, anyone?"

Kevin spoke first. "I don't think we know enough to decide yet. Do we have anything to compare them to?"

Steve shook his head. "Not from the house. There was nothing with writing on it in the convertible either."

"Speaking of the convertible, do we know the owner?" Quinn was looking at George.

George nodded. "SBI report isn't quite finished yet, but the last registered owner was a Robert Calhoun from Sevierville. I've called twice with no answer at a landline. It's a follow-up to be sure. No missing or stolen reports on the car. Chuck may know more."

"Let's get all our follow-ups listed which will involve other jurisdictions and then we can decide our course of action. Chuck, anything to add on the convertible?"

"No. Swanson will be back in the station tomorrow. He may have something to add. The only thing he told me was that in spite of the top being down on the convertible, it smelled like someone spilled a bottle of perfume. They were still running chemical analyses on the carpets and seats as of yesterday."

"Good to know. Thanks, Chuck."

"Kevin, any updates on the identification of Phillip Anthony Young?"

"I've talked with the principal at the high school and based on our warrant, she'll have all his records available tomorrow morning. I asked if they had a picture of him. She said they have a student ID photo on everyone. She'll see that it's included."

"Did she share anything?"

"No, ma'am. She said she would release the records with a copy of the warrant and could only speak to us on any specifics if it's cleared by the school board attorney."

"Got it. We'll save that until we know more about Phillip Young."

"Anyone else?"

"No."

"Not right now."

"Good here."

"Okay. I went down and met with Dr. Walters." All heads turned toward her. "Since we're all together now, I want to say this to each and all of you. I appreciate your support and concern for me. It's been the most challenging week of my adult life and the one thing that made it easier was knowing each of you were on the case. Thank you. I want you to promise me that if you have any concerns about my ability to be a part of this investigation you will tell the Chief and she has agreed she will remove me from the case. I think I will know if there is some reason I can't do my job, but maybe not. So, I need to know you will not hesitate." She looked from one man to the next. "If you think I need to take a break, tell me. I can handle honesty…" She slid her chair back. "I don't think I can handle pity."

All four men gasped.

"Pity?" George was first to speak. "Quinn, there is no one in this room, or in this building, that has anything but the greatest respect and admiration for you and for your textbook response and reaction. I can only speak for myself, but I will tell you when I think you need to step away whether for ten minutes or a day."

"Me, too," Kevin said.

"Absolutely," Steve was nodding.

"Yes, ma'am." Chuck smiled at Quinn.

Quinn stood and turned first to Steve and extended her hand. "Thank you. Thank you for your service and for your support."

She walked to each of the men and then back to her chair. "Thank you. Now, here's what I learned in the morgue." She put the picture the ME had sent her electronically on the screen. "Oh, and one last thing. I have not seen any of the bodies and I do not intend to do so."

There were slight sighs around the table.

"Now, look at this. This is on the right hip of Ms. Young. Both males have it on their right hips, according to the ME."

All four men turned to the screen.

Kevin stood up and moved closer to the screen. "Why that's a lion's paw and a lamb's head."

"Yes, and it is branded on all three bodies in the morgue."

George stood up and moved closer. "Branded?"

Quinn nodded. "It's called scarification in medical terms. It is apparently illegal in Tennessee to be done by anyone but a physician and is actually considered surgery. We'll follow-up on the law, but in the meantime we have something else to trace."

"Whose doc would do that to them?" George shook his head.

"Didn't say one did. We don't know when or where it was done. The ME thinks the two males got theirs very young based on the distortion that would have come with their growth. He will provide those photos. I have not seen them."

George wrote on the board beneath Young, Sr. "Scarification?"

"Yes, George. That's a follow-up to be done with the prison system. We'll also need to figure out how we can learn if the two sisters have them."

The men were nodding as they studied the brand.

"George, were you able to determine the jurisdictions for the two sisters?"

"Yes, ma'am. All the information is in a secure E-folder along with what appear to be current addresses for the two women."

"Good work everyone. Steve, I know you have another obligation in a couple of minutes. Any observations or information before you go?"

"I'll just say I'm glad you are the detectives and I'm just the crime scene investigator. Looks like you're going to have some slogging work to do."

"Yep," Kevin slapped Steve on the back. "Slogging is what we do. Why do you think they always picture detectives wearing a trench coat?"

Everyone laughed.

"Okay, thanks, Steve and Chuck. Unless you have anything else, we'll let you get back to your work. Kevin, George, and I will divide up this slogging work."

"Later, folks." Steve gave a cursory wave as he walked out the door.

"Let me know if you need anything specific. I'll be in the lab." Chuck imitated Steve's wave.

The three detectives went through their list and divided up the things that needed immediate attention.

Quinn wrote a note on her pad then looked at the men. "Okay, thanks for this. I'm going to try and see the Chief before I head home. We'll need her approval to contact the out-of-state agencies. Wrap up anything you think you need to do today and then get out of here. Tomorrow's a new day."

Kevin stood up and headed for the door. "Thanks, Quinn. It's really good to have you back."

"Glad to be back, Kevin. Have a nice evening."

"George, you get out of here. Are you sure I can't buy lunch? I asked you to do it."

"Quinn, it's settled. Compliments of the Marshalls—Carrie insisted."

"Thanks. That was very nice of both of you. Thanks also for picking me up this morning. I'll see you tomorrow."

"That you will. Hang in there, Quinn. You're doing great. I second Kevin's comment. I'm glad you're back."

"Me, too. Thanks for everything. Now let's get whatever crimes we may have on our hands solved."

As the door closed behind George, Quinn leaned back in her chair, undid the knot in her hair and shook her head gently from side-to-side. She let out a sigh, stood, and headed for her office.

Chapter 17

This stepping out into what is unknown, uncharted, and shaky—
that's called liberation.
Pema Chödrön

Chief Hansen

"Chief Hansen's office, how may I help you, Detective Isaacs?"

"Good afternoon, Ms. Leonard. Does the Chief have fifteen minutes before she leaves for the day?"

"One moment, Detective."

Quinn tapped her fingernail on the top of her desk. *What's going on with this case? Connections?* "Oh, sorry, Ms. Leonard. Would you repeat that?"

"No problem. The Chief can see you at five. Will that work for you?"

"That's perfect. Thank you so much." Quinn hung up the desk phone and looked at her computer. *Time to get through some emails.* She set her phone timer for twenty-two minutes so she wouldn't be late.

She jumped when the "Boogie Woogie Bugle Boy" started playing. *I am changing that right now.* She opened the settings on her phone and chose "The Irish Washerwoman." *That's got a nice lilt and won't stop my heart and shouldn't lull me back to sleep in the mornings. Okay, that's done.* She walked out into the lab.

"Chuck?"

"Yes, ma'am. I'm around here. Got a timer about to go off."

"Just wanted to tell you to head out. Don't stay here all night."

"You leaving?"

"Seeing the Chief and then I'll head out."

"10-4. See you tomorrow."

"Okay. Night, Chuck."

She left the lab and headed toward the Chief's office. She glanced at her watch and decided she didn't have time to stop in the women's restroom and be on time. She kept going. She stopped. *Come on. Just keep moving.*

"Detective, good afternoon. Go right on in. The Chief's expecting you."

"Thanks. Have a good night."

"Well, I may be here when you finish, but if not, you have a good evening, too."

Quinn stopped in the doorway. *Ms. Leonard has calmed a lot with the new Chief.*

"Come in, Quinn. Have a seat."

"Thanks, Chief. I wanted to update you on the Young investigation."

"Haven't had time this afternoon to read any updates. Fill me in."

Quinn gave her the overview of the current findings and meetings. She didn't over emphasize any aspect of it and didn't share the part of her conversation with the ME about her own concerns.

"You saw the brand?" Chief Hansen looked at Quinn.

"Just the picture." *No reason not to tell her my decision.* "I talked with Dr. Walters and I don't wish to see the remains. He encouraged me to stay with that position—said everything I need will be in his final report."

"Any indication when he will have that?"

"Tomorrow or Wednesday at the latest."

"Good." She took a sip of coffee. "I have not had an opportunity today to tell you the preliminary report and video reviews by the SBI support that both officers acted in a timely manner, discharged their firearms appropriately, and that Officer Simmons's shot ended the driver's life." She paused to watch Quinn's reaction. "The Assistant State Attorney General's ruling supports that conclusion."

Quinn sat stone-faced. *Is that good or bad? I didn't help him at all. I...*

"Detective." The Chief's tone was firm and free of emotion.

"Yes, ma'am?"

"Questions you have?"

"Is it possible not to have questions?"

"Not in my opinion. Not if you're good at what you do."

"I prefer to stay focused on the case at hand. I understand the traffic stop was not on suspicion, but it did result in the death of two people."

The Chief let her talk.

"I think if we work the case at hand and solve it, then it will be clearer to me if I need to go back and revisit my part in the precipitating event." She reached for the bottle of water on the table. "May I?"

"Of course."

Quinn opened the water and took a long drink. She leaned her forearms on the edge of the table. "I know we have protocols and I will always do my best to follow them—but may I ask you something as a fellow police officer, not my boss?"

"Anytime. I think you know by now I won't answer if I can't, and I'll tell you why I can't answer when I can."

"Thanks." She took another sip of water. "Do most officers in an officer-involved shooting want to see the video?"

"Some do. Some don't."

"Do you think it's a good idea or a bad one?"

"I think it's very individual. Timing is part of the equation. Often the videos are under seal pending any charges. The State District Attorney General has cleared you. Of course, an attorney for the family could still name you, Officer Simmons, me, the duty sergeant, anyone he or she could think of—if they bring a suit against us. I can ask our DA if she plans to ask a judge to have the videos sealed until we know more. Would that give you some relief?"

Quinn sat looking around the wall in front of her where there were lots of awards and citations the Chief had received in her position in Atlanta. Her eyes stopped on a framed medal. Without thinking, Quinn stood and walked to the medal: *Medal of Valor*. Quinn looked at the Chief and immediately returned to her seat.

"I apologize, Chief."

"No apology necessary." She sat back in her chair. "Quinn, you will survive this—and better than surviving it you will come out of it a better police officer. Many officers never have to learn the hard lessons of all the training and the practice to defend life and liberty. You've just had a lesson. It will take time. Give yourself that time."

"I don't need to know if the DA is seeking to get the videos sealed." She took a sip of water. "Thank you for your counsel and for your professionalism. I'm a better law officer for working for you." She gave a slight smile. "Any questions on where we are at this time?"

"I think I'm duly briefed. Go home and get some rest. Don't make me order you to limit your working hours." She smiled at Quinn.

"No, ma'am. I know I need time to decompress. Can't always stop my brain, but I'll try to distract it."

"Good for you. Have a good night, Detective."

Quinn stood and extended her hand. "You, too, Chief. Thanks, again."

End of the Day

Quinn had her personal phone in her hand as she reached her official SUV—she stopped and looked at it. She had read the email from the head of maintenance explaining the SUV had been serviced and washed after the forensic techs had finished. *Nothing happened to it, so nothing to know.* She shrugged, opened the driver's door, and sat down. She reached to close the door and her heart started to race. She sat there with the door ajar.

"Sort of like falling off a horse, Detective."

Quinn looked up to see the Chief standing there.

"Just a bit of flashback playing in my head."

"Normal. First day's the hardest. How about I follow you home?"

"It's not necessary. Really."

"Probably not, but humor me. I'll feel better."

"Yes, ma'am." Quinn shut the door, started the car, and rolled down the window. "Ready when you are."

"You pull out first. I'll be right behind you."

Quinn backed out of the parking space and headed for the exit gate. The Chief was right behind her. *The car is fine. I'm fine.* She turned onto her street and decided to pull into her driveway instead of backing in since the Chief was behind her. Quinn saw the Chief stop in the street. She got out and walked down to thank her.

Chief Hansen had the passenger window down. "Seems a nice night to sit on that porch and have a long drink of iced tea."

Quinn leaned on the frame of the open window. "Yes, ma'am, it does. Thank you for your concern. I'm okay now. Just a moment of remembering."

"It will fade. You know how to reach me—or Dr. Kingston. Have a nice evening, Quinn."

"Thanks, Chief. You, too." She stood and watched the Chief drive away. She pulled out her phone and walked to the SUV. She sent a text to Billy: "Call me in 5 if u hv time." She got in, turned the SUV around in her large driveway and backed it into the garage. She had her shoes off by the door and her weapon and badge in her gun safe when her phone rang.

"Ready for supper?" Billy's voice was cheerful and lively.

"Too tired to think of it. What's on your mind?"

"Mostly you. Where are you?"

"Home."

"Good. I'm about fifteen minutes out and I'm bringing supper from The Corral."

"Really? Oh, Billy. I get to see you and have supper from The Corral? Can't wait."

"Good. Anything you need on my way into town?"

"No. Thanks, though. I'm going to go change and I'll get tea poured so we're ready."

"See you soon. Love you."

"Love you, too." She rushed to her bedroom and got out of her suit. She washed her face and put on a pair of pale green shorts and a mint green silk shell. She was standing in the kitchen when she heard the garage door open. She stepped over to open the kitchen door.

Billy backed into the garage and walked in front of the other two vehicles. He slipped out of his boots and reached for the door handle just as Quinn opened it.

"Hello, handsome."

He looked up at her and whistled. "Hello, yourself. Don't you look like spring?" He stepped up and kissed her, setting the food on the counter. Then he pulled her into a hug. "How's my favorite detective?"

"Off work."

"Good." He took off his service weapon and his badge and put them in his gun safe.

"Tea or beer?" She held up a glass and a bottle of beer.

"Tea, thanks. I have some computer work to do tonight."

She set down the glass and bottle of beer. "Billy, I'm very happy to see you, but you didn't need to drive all the way over here tonight."

"I did." He wiggled his eyebrows. "I needed to see how your day went and that meant laying eyes on you."

"Ha. You could have done that with Facetime."

He snapped his fingers. "I knew there was something I forgot." He started laughing. "Come on. Let's not waste time on trivial details. Carla said to tell you, 'Hey!' James had to go to Knoxville so she was helping out in the restaurant."

"Isn't their baby due soon?"

"Two months or so, I think. She said she's doing great but Joshua and James are always fussing at her." He laughed. "I think her exact words, 'they're like two old maid aunties—trouble shared is trouble doubled. My trouble is doubled for sure—married to one, sister to the other.'"

"I love it. Only Carla could make up a new southern saying from an old one." She poured two glasses of tea.

Billy unwrapped the foil from around the hot food and they filled their plates with pulled pork barbecue, coleslaw, corn on the cob, and cornbread. Billy held up his plate like an offering to the gods of southern cooking — "Best there is."

"Let's sit out on the front porch. It's cool out."

"Lead the way." He picked up their plates and she took the tray with their drinks, napkins, and cutlery.

She turned the corner to the right side of the porch and set the tray on a chair. She took a tablecloth off the tray and put it on the table.

"Fancy."

Quinn laughed. "Easier than wiping down the table."

The clinked their glasses of tea together.

"How are you?" Billy took a bite of cornbread.

"Better than I might have hoped. I told you earlier I had a bit of a melt-down."

He reached over and stroked her cheek.

"I couldn't have asked for better support, though. Everyone has been kind, some have offered advice when I asked, and...well, and I cut myself some slack."

"Now that's what I like to hear."

She cocked her head as she picked up the ear of corn. "What do you mean?"

"How many times have you told me you are your own harshest critic? You are."

"Okay. Fair enough. Enough about my day. How was yours?"

"If I didn't know better, I'd swear that the criminals heard I was back at work. We had a fire at cabin which the firefighters were able to get out. It was unoccupied at the time."

"Oh, I'm glad no one was hurt. Was it arson? Is that what...sorry, none of my business."

"It might be. We found a fairly large stash of fentanyl and called in Sam Nations. He didn't mention the jurisdiction, but said they just recovered some from a convertible in the area." He watched her face.

"And?"

"And, Sam took our haul to Knoxville and they'll see if they appear to be from the same source."

"How will they know that?"

"Chemical properties, packaging, could even luck out and find some fingerprints on the packaging. Some of these distributors are not too smart when it comes to handling their product."

Quinn was silent. She chewed across the ear of corn, turned it, chewed across another row and then set it down. "I think I need to talk about those trees across the road in the park."

Billy switched without a blink. "They are lovely. Which is your favorite?"

"The dogwoods. I like the pink and the white."

"Yes. They are a magnificent flower. I like the mountain laurel."

She smiled. "There are some right over there." She pointed across the table toward the side of the park.

Billy reached out and took her hand. "Thank you."

"For pointing out flowers?"

"That, too." He kissed her hand. "For stopping me. I'm sorry." He looked into her eyes.

"No apology." She leaned over and kissed him. She sat back and started laughing.

"What's funny?"

She reached over with her napkin. "I left you some corn kernels."

"Well don't wipe them off. I can save them for later."

She slapped his hand playfully when he tried to push her napkin away. "What would your mother say?"

"Okay. Okay. I surrender." He let her wipe his mouth and then smiled at her. "Quinn Isaacs, I love you."

"I love you, too. Now let's eat before it gets cold."

Sweet Creations Bakery

The tall, thin man walked up to Sweet Creations just as Carrie was locking the front door.

"Sorry, sir. We close at five-thirty. Closed out the cash drawer, so I can't even sell you a loaf of bread. Do come see us tomorrow."

"Somewhere you can recommend to stay in town?"

"There's a bed and breakfast at the end of the block." Carrie pointed to her left. "Other than that the hotels and motels are all out at the highway."

"Okay, thanks." The man turned to walk away and turned back. "Any chance you know Sonia Young?"

Carrie looked at him. She'd heard George use that name on the phone with Kevin Millwood. She hoped her face didn't betray it. "No." She shook her head, looked up to the ceiling, and pretended she was thinking. "No, I don't believe I do. Does she live around here?"

"Yeah. She's my cousin and I've been trying to reach her. Don't have her current address though. Wanted to surprise her. Just thought if you knew her you'd know if she was out of town." *Well, that's one person who hasn't heard anything.*

Carrie shook her head. "Sorry. Can't help. Come visit us tomorrow if you stay overnight. Our donuts are a hit. Have a good night and thanks for stopping by." She closed the door, locked it, and pulled down the shade with a sign which listed the hours she was open and read: "Closed—Ya'll come back!" in the center of a donut. She flipped off the light switch and walked back toward the counter and turned around to look through the plate glass window.

The man stood with his back to the bakery and looked up and down the street. *Guess the word isn't out that there are two people died out on that crummy country road.*

Carrie took out her cell phone and sent a text to George. "Call me ASAP." She jumped when her phone rang. "Hey."

"Hey, yourself. What's up? Want me to take you out to supper?"

"George. Stop. Listen to me." She told him about the man. "I know I've been a detective's wife for a long time, so I'm naturally suspicious, and you know I don't say anything about stuff I overhear you talking about, but isn't Sonia Young a name I've heard you use lately?"

George went very quiet. "Carrie, is the bakery locked up?"

"Yes. Front and back. I'm ready to walk out the back door."

"You stay right where you are. I'll meet you in the back parking lot, but don't you come out until I call you."

"Okay."

"Promise me?"

"I do. Thanks, honey. See you soon."

"In less than five minutes. Love you."

"Love you, too."

George ended the call with her and dialed Quinn's secure phone.

1211 Sunrise

The leftover food was in the fridge and the dishes in the dishwasher. Quinn dried her hands on the dish towel. "Thanks for supper—the food and the company." She kissed Billy lightly on the lips.

He pulled her to him and gave her a long lingering kiss. He whispered in her ear and took her hand and started walking toward the great room sofa.

Her secure phone rang and vibrated on the kitchen counter. She shrugged as she picked it up. "Isaacs."

"George here. Sorry to bother you." He told her what had happened.

"Where are you?"

"Headed to the bakery."

"Billy's here. We'll go take a walk in the park downtown. We can be there in five."

"I'm going to follow Carrie home and then I'll be back."

"We won't engage unless approached."

"I'll come in from the end of the park away from your part of town."

"Got it. See you in the park." Quinn ended the call and told Billy what was going on. They put on their service weapons and badges and headed into the garage.

"Let's take my car. Looks more like we're on a date." Billy grinned.

"Do you always wear a badge and a gun on a date?" Quinn opened his passenger door. "Besides, neither of my vehicles has any markings."

"Oh? No special license plate on your work SUV?"

"Oh. Yeah. There is that." She shut the door and they were headed to the park in downtown. "Carrie said the man was white, tall, and thin, wearing khaki pants and a blue open collared polo shirt.

"Up for this?"

She stayed quiet for several seconds. "Never been more ready. Let's see where this may lead."

Chapter 18

One has to shut off that nagging part of the mind and go on without it with bravo and philosophy.

Sylvia Plath

Downtown Round City

Billy drove toward the bakery and was about to do a U-turn to the parking places opposite the bakery.

"Billy, pull in front of Sweet Creations." Quinn hopped out. She called over her shoulder. "Come on, honey. She closes soon."

Billy stepped out of his SUV and spoke loud enough for her and the man walking toward them to hear. "Look, sweetie. The sign says they're already closed."

Quinn stopped and made a production of putting her hands on her hips and pouting. "You're right, again. I swore they closed at six-thirty."

Billy put a look of gloating on his face and smiled. "Sorry, babe. What'd you say we just go for a walk in the park instead."

"Let's just go sit on a bench and enjoy the cool air."

"Good idea." Billy managed to turn in time to just miss hitting the man as he walked by. "Oops. Sorry." He reached for Quinn's hand. "Come on. The bench awaits."

They looked both ways and jogged across the street and plopped on the bench. Quinn turned sideways so she was facing Billy. She could see the man on the street and Billy was looking into the center of the park. He saw George Marshall headed their way at a leisurely pace.

Billy leaned and kissed her and barely whispered. "George at three o'clock."

Quinn did not turn. "Subject looking up and down street and about to cross over." She leaned in and kissed Billy on the cheek and whispered. "Let's let George take the lead on this."

Billy just nodded, turned, and kissed her.

George watched the man cross the street and pulled his phone out. He pretended to be talking on the phone but was taking a picture. *Sure hope I can get his face.* After several snaps he dialed Quinn's phone.

"Hey." She held the phone close to her ear.

"Try to get a picture. I've done the best I can from here." His voice was low, but she heard him.

"Sure. We'll be glad to stop by. We're in the park right now, but we'll be there in thirty minutes or so. Thanks for reminding me."

Billy shook his head and made sure his voice was loud enough to be heard. "Honey, where are we going now? I told you I have an early day tomorrow."

She ran her fingers through his hair. "I know, sweetheart, but Millie wants me to pick up the cups for tomorrow's luncheon."

He sighed. "Okay."

"Hey, let's do a selfie. My folks would be so happy to see us out enjoying the park." Quinn turned and had her camera ready just as the man walked behind them. *Well, that was mighty accommodating of you.* "Smile, honey."

George managed to catch up to the man from out of town about fifty feet past Quinn and Billy. He feigned tripping and bumped the man. "Sorry, fella. Tripped over my own two feet."

"No problem. You okay?" The man was polite but stepped to the side.

"Yeah, yeah. Just trying to get a walk in before I head for another night of lousy sleep. Distracted, I guess. Sorry, again." George kept walking.

The man raised his voice to make sure he was heard. "You from around here?"

George stopped. "Been in these hills all my life. You?"

"Nope, just passing through. Trying to find my long, lost cousin. Ain't easy with no more phone books. Not real sure where she lives either—not having much luck."

"Well, maybe I can help you. Who's your cousin?"

"Sonia Young."

"Don't know her. No idea where she lives? I mean we pretty much know folks by family names if they've been here for generations, but ...well, anyway, no idea where she lives?"

"My uncle just said she was on the outskirts of town, but still in Round City."

George shook his head. He saw Quinn and Billy get up from the bench. *What's your plan, Quinn? I don't do mental telepathy.*

"When did you last talk to her?" George was winging it.

"Not in a blue moon."

"Your uncle live near here?" George tried to make his interest seem genuine.

"Over in Sevierville—when he's in the mountains."

George clapped his hands together. "Hey, then he knows the area. Call him up. He can tell me the general location then maybe I can help."

The man hesitated. "Thanks all the same. He'd be mad at me for not remembering to get her address."

George saw Quinn and Billy walking toward them. "Well, buddy, sorry I couldn't be more help."

"No problem. Appreciate it." The man turned away from George and almost ran into Quinn. "Oh, sorry."

"No harm, no foul. I should have been looking where I was going." Quinn stepped around him.

George acted like he was walking away and stopped. "Hey, maybe these folks know your cousin."

Quinn and Billy stopped. "Trying to find someone?" Quinn smiled showing straight white teeth.

"He's looking for his cousin. What was that family name again? Old?"

The man looked at George. "Young. Sonia Young."

George laughed. "Old. Young. I knew it was one of those age names." He shrugged.

Quinn's eyes got big and she let her mouth gape open. "Sonia? Of course, I know Sonia. Well, 'know' is a little strong. I met her in a doctor's office and we've run into each other several times. Chatted. You know." She grinned and shrugged. "Lives out on the edge of town, right?"

The man's face brightened. "Know where?"

"Oh, you don't have her address?"

"Nah. Haven't seen her in years. Just knew she was near here and then my uncle said to look her up."

"I know the general area from what she told me. Most folks have their names on their mailboxes out that way." She turned to Billy. "Hey, we don't have anything pressing and it's still light out. How about we lead him out there?"

The man's face paled. "Well, actually, I'd just like her phone number. She hasn't answered my calls so I'm thinking I must have written a number wrong. Wouldn't want to just drop in and all. Besides, I'm headed toward Maryville now. Just took a chance."

"Sure. I understand." Quinn tried to look sympathetic.

"Well, I'm going to leave it to you folks. Headed out to the highway myself. My motel is out there." George turned.

The man called out to him. "Know a good motel—not one of these chains that robs you?"

George turned back. "Any number of them. I'm at a small local place called The Dew Drop Inn. Can't miss it. Mile or two from here before you get on the highway—on the right."

"Thanks, again." The man turned back to Quinn. "Well, guess you can't help me with trying to see my cousin either."

"Got a card? If I run into her again, I could give it to her."

"Nah. Nothing so fancy as that. I'll just have to disappoint my Uncle Bob."

"Your Uncle Bob?" Quinn cocked her head slightly. "Bob Calhoun?"

The man stepped back. He tried to retrieve the look of shock he knew was on his face. "That's funny. How did you know…" He hesitated and took a breath. "…that name?"

"Last time I saw Sonia—actually right over there at the bakery, we walked out to her car. It was a nice Saab convertible and I commented on it. She mentioned her uncle from Sevierville loaned it to her." She turned to Billy. "Nice ride." She turned back to the man. "Sorry, I'm being rude, I'm Quinn, this is Billy. What was your name?"

"Roger. Roger…Calhoun." His stumble on the last name wasn't missed by Quinn or Billy.

"Well, see that's what's so funny. I said, 'Nice uncle,' and Sonia said, 'Yeah, Uncle Bob is a great guy. I told her…"

Billy interrupted. "Honey, Mr. Calhoun doesn't want to hear your story." He shook his head and rolled his eyes toward Roger. "Mountain folks, always have to make a story out of the least little detail." He winked at Quinn. "Some reason the name's important, honey?"

Quinn put her hands on her hips and then dropped them. She grinned at Mr. Calhoun. "He's right. I can walk you around the block to take you just across the street." She chuckled. "Well, long story short, I have an Uncle Bob and we joked about how it would be too funny if we had the same Uncle Bob—that's when she said hers was named Calhoun. No big deal." She shrugged. "I apologize. We do love our stories in these hills."

"So I've heard. I'm from Ohio. We tend to be short, brief, and to the point."

Quinn grabbed Billy's arm. "Billy, we either have to buy Mr. Calhoun a drink and give him a right proper mountain welcome or send him on his way."

Roger stepped to the side. "I'll be going. Thanks for your help." He started to walk. "One more thing. When was the last time you saw Sonia?"

Quinn shook her head and looked around like she was thinking. "Couple of weeks. Yeah, at least a couple of weeks. Well, good luck."

Roger walked toward a Mercedes SUV in the middle of the block.

Quinn had seen George pull around the end of the building. She knew he would follow and probably already had the license plate and photo being run. She called out. "Take care." Then she grabbed Billy's arm and they jogged to his SUV.

In Pursuit

"Dispatch. Evening Detective. How may I help you?"

"Sergeant on duty, please."

"Fishburn." His voice sounded drowsy with sleep.

"Isaacs, here. I need a patrol…." She gave him explicit directions to have an officer out near the highway and one near The Dew Drop Inn. "That's right. Thanks, Sergeant. Would you please transfer me to the forensic tech on duty?"

"Yes, ma'am. Lead will be Officer Jamison. You coming in?"

"At some point." *I have no idea what this night will bring.* "Call if you need me."

She heard a click. "Johnston."

"Chuck. I thought you were going home."

"Was headed…."

Quinn interrupted him. "Never mind. Glad you're still there. Did you get a photo from George?"

"Yep. License plate on a Mercedes SUV, too."

"Owner of car?"

"Robert Calhoun. Sevierville. Sound familiar?"

"Indeed. How about the photograph?"

"Not the best resolution. Running it anyway."

"I'm sending you a picture I took. May or may not be better. Call me when you have something."

"On it. Sounds like a hot lead, Quinn."

"Might be. Might not. Thanks, Chuck."

"10-4."

Quinn's eyes were on the road the whole time. She was aware of Billy's turns in an evasive maneuver not to appear to be tailing the man.

Billy hit his palm on the steering wheel. "Why didn't I think to say we needed to head back to the Valley?"

"Because you weren't planning to go home tonight?" She squeezed his arm.

He chuckled. "Could be. Anything you can share with me from Chuck?"

She told him what she knew.

"Well, well. Mr. Calhoun is a generous uncle, isn't he?"

Quinn smirked. "Yeah. Believe that one and I've got a bridge for sale."

"Which one?"

She gently slapped his arm. "Stop it, Billy Williams." Then she laughed. "Look there's George." Then she realized Billy was signaling to pull over. "What are you doing?"

"Flashing lights coming from behind."

"Great." The sarcasm in her voice was evident. "Sergeant Fishburn must have made his own decisions about this." She watched as cars ahead of them pulled to the side.

"Hey, the good news is the officer is smart enough not to use his siren." Billy pulled out as soon as the patrol car passed and pulled ahead of the Mercedes toward the entrance to the highway. Billy sped up so he could pass George.

Quinn's phone rang. "Isaacs."

"Marshall. What's going on? Did you order that car?"

"Not in that way. Sergeant Fishburn must have decided it was more urgent than I indicated."

"No surprise. Is that Billy pulling around me?"

"Yep. You pull into the Dew Drop Inn. We'll have him if he decides to get on the highway."

"You can't stop him since you're in Billy's car."

"True, but I've got you and two patrol cars out here ready to go."

"Good job, Quinn. Later." George ended the call as Billy passed him.

"Billy, watch out." Quinn's voice was calm. "Looks like Roger missed the first entrance into the Dew Drop Inn but has decided to turn into the second one."

"George is there now, too. What's he going to do? Hope he's got a room lined up."

"We know the owner. All it takes is a call and George could pick up a key like he'd been staying there for weeks. You know, 'Hey, George. Good day?' Yep, whoever's on the desk knows the routine."

"Yeah, that comes with local motels that can't compete with the newer ones in amenities. They need us, too, given the clientele they likely get."

"Look how smart you are, Billy Williams."

"Detective, remember?"

"That I do."

"Good news, my dear. I actually do need gas." He pulled into the service station next to the motel and got out to pump gas.

Quinn turned around and watched Roger, or whoever he was, walk into the office of the Dew Drop Inn just after George.

Dew Drop Inn

"Hey, George. How's it going?"

"Hey, Frank. Tired mostly. How about you?" George waited to see if Roger would come in. "How's the family?"

"Okay, except Aunt Margaret…Hang on a minute, can you?" Frank looked around George when the door opened. "Help you, sir?"

"Go ahead, I can wait." George said it loud enough to be heard by the man entering.

"Come on up. George here will move. Need to tell him about my aunt. Driver's license and credit card, please. How many folks you need room for?"

"Just me." Roger stepped around George who turned to see who had come in.

George smiled. "Oh, hey. See you found it okay. Brought you some business, Frank. Look, I need to go to the room for a minute. I'll stop by to hear what Margaret's up to these days." George walked to Room One just to the left of the desk, put the key in, and entered. He knew there was a door to open where he could hear every word said at the small desk area.

"Now, sir. Driver's license and credit card." Frank held his hand out.

"Maybe you could help me first. I'm trying to find my cousin—Sonia Young. You know her?"

"Small town, but can't say as I do. Family been here long?"

"What's long?"

"Four generations minimum." Frank laughed. "We've got deep roots in these mountains."

"Hmmm...so it seems. No, she moved here about fifteen-eighteen years ago or so."

Frank shook his head. "Can't rightly say I know anybody by the name of Young. Sorry. Now let me get you checked in and then maybe you could go check with our police station. Nice folks there and they'll help you if they can."

Roger turned. "Well, thanks all the same. I think I'll just head on to Maryville. Catch you next time."

"Whatever you like, Mr. We're here twenty-four hours. Happy to be of service."

"Yeah, thanks." Roger turned and headed for the door.

George opened the door to Room One and raised his voice. "Now, Frank, about Margaret... ." He saw Roger step out the door and double-step to his SUV. George had already alerted Quinn.

The Stop

Quinn used her secure phone to call Jamison in the marked vehicle sitting across the street.

"Officer, Quinn Isaacs here."

"Yes, ma'am."

"There's a man about six feet two inches tall, brown hair, thin, about to walk out of the Dew Drop Inn. Claims his name is Roger Calhoun. If he gets in the Mercedes SUV in front of the motel, follow him as if you're on normal patrol. Don't lose him. If he heads for the highway, I'll pick up the tail. Otherwise, stay as close as you can without raising suspicion."

"Yes, ma'am. Anything else I need to know."

"Yes. Be careful."

"10-4."

Billy had filled his gas tank and they were sitting on the far side of the gas station next to the Dew Drop Inn facing it. "He's in the SUV."

"Let Jamison take the tail. Roger may have just decided he wanted a better place to sleep."

"Fair enough." Billy pulled out three car lengths after Jamison pulled onto the road from across the street.

Quinn kept her eyes on the Mercedes. "Losing light. It's going to be harder to tail him."

"Maybe not." Billy pulled back into the right lane.

"Why?"

"I just noticed his left tail light's broken. There's no red on the outer part and the light appeared to be out."

"Really? That's a violation. Jamison can pull him over and ask for ID..." Quinn stopped talking and gasped. *Stop it. There will be a million automobile stops today. They won't turn out like Officer Simmons.* She was about to call Jamison when she saw his flashing lights.

"Is Roger pulling over?"

"Appears to be."

"Thank, God." Quinn whispered. She kept her eyes on the two vehicles.

Billy slowed down and turned right into a strip mall just before the entry to the highway. He drove slowly around the cars in the parking lot and parked at the far end next to the exit and so he was behind a tree from Roger.

They watched the officer approach the Mercedes SUV.

"Look, Billy, the other officer on patrol pulled up behind Jamison." She let out a long sigh. "That's good." *I hope.*

Round City Police Station

"Detective Isaacs, Matron here. He's booked and in holding whenever you're ready. Report is in the system."

"We'll be down shortly. Thanks." Quinn turned to George. "Let's figure out what we've got here." She opened the secure electronic file from the matron.

"Where's Billy?"

"He headed back to the Valley. He's got some stuff going on, too." She looked at the file.

George looked up at the screen where the information was projected. "With that rap sheet, we could be with him all night. The outstanding warrant is, interestingly, in South Carolina."

Quinn read the report from the arresting officer and the jailer. "So, Roger is Roger. Smart to use his real first name." Quinn was writing on her notepad.

"That's the thing with criminals. They figure out how to let just enough be known not to get caught in providing false information."

Quinn stared at him. "You're joking right?"

"Of course. They lie all the time. The funny thing is that his middle name is actually Calhoun."

"It's his last name, at least according to this record—that intrigues me."

"Yeah, let's see what he has to say about that." George turned from the crime board.

Quinn stopped reading the report, stood, and started pacing. She pulled her hair into a knot.

George watched her carefully. "Quinn, you don't have to do this interview. Let's talk about it."

"I'm fine. I can do the interview. However, I won't and neither will you."

"What? Why not?"

"I don't want any chance of Roger yelling 'entrapment.'"

"Because we happened to all be in a park at the same time?"

"George, are you willing to tell a judge that?" She frowned and shook her head.

"Nah. Just hate not being able to…" He turned as the door opened.

"Quinn. George." Kevin Millwood nodded.

"Evening, Kevin." George looked at Quinn. *You called him, didn't you. Way to go.* "Smart move, Quinn." He nodded.

"What's up?" Kevin pulled out a chair and sat down.

Quinn asked George to fill Kevin in starting with the call from Carrie.

George gave him the rundown of the last hour-and-a-half including the arrest. "Now he's downstairs in our fine accommodations."

"What's the warrant for in South Carolina?" Kevin looked at the crime board.

"Possession of a controlled substance and fleeing a police officer."

"Did we do a body search here?" Kevin was writing on his notepad.

Quinn held her finger in the air. "I need a minute, Kevin." She finished reading the report. She looked up and Kevin and George were still reading the screen. She took her secure phone and dialed District Attorney O'Haire.

"O'Haire."

"Quinn Isaacs here. Sorry to interrupt your evening."

"Hey, Quinn. Welcome back. Kinda late isn't it?"

"Ah, you know crime never sleeps."

"Actually most of the worst crimes happen in the dark."

"Or at least the privacy of someplace," Quinn said.

"Right. Well, you didn't call to talk crime statistics. What's up?"

Quinn filled her in on Roger and included the outstanding warrant in South Carolina.

"Got it. Well, first of all, we can hold him thirty days so no need to rush on our end. Not going to raise anyone in South Carolina at this hour who can do anything. Send me the particulars and I'll get on it tomorrow."

"Okay."

"And, Quinn… ."

"Yes."

"I suggest you do the same. Let him sit in our fine accommodations overnight. Might do him good to think we're country bumpkins."

"Thanks, Peggy. I'll send you the report."

George and Kevin were sitting across the table looking at her.

"DA says to let him cool his heels. Thoughts?"

George spoke first. "Sounds like a plan to me. Let's call it a day."

"Kevin, you good with that?" Quinn waited.

"Sure. Gives me more time to strategize."

"Tomorrow it is, then. Go home, gentlemen. Thanks for your extra-long day."

"No problem. I'll let the matron know. Night, Quinn." Kevin walked out whistling.

"I know it's been a long day, Quinn."

"No longer than many. Thanks for your work."

"Thank you. Glad you're back." George stood up, gave her a mock salute, and left.

Quinn took out her personal phone.

End of a Very Long Day

"Hey, love of my life." Billy's voice was cheerful and caring.

"Hey! Busy?"

"At the station, but about to call it day. Just needed to follow up on a case."

"Sorry to take you away from them."

"I'll always make time for you—unless lives hang in the balance."

"You're sweet. Just wanted to tell you I'm headed home now. We're going to let our guest, Roger, rest in what I hope will be fitful slumber in our fine accommodations." She chuckled.

Billy smiled to hear her laugh. "He should be happy—no motel bill."

"Ha ha!" She grinned.

"Anyway, he deserves a rough night in jail. You doing okay?"

"I am. Thanks. Lots of activity today and it was good to get into the swing of things."

"Glad to hear it."

"I'll text you when I get home."

"Call, if you want. I'll be home by then, too."

"Okay. One way or the other you'll hear from me."

"Drive safely. Love you."

"Love you, too." She ended the call. *Is this how other couples in love get to live—knowing their love is at the other end of a phone—anytime?*

She backed into her garage, left her work shoes at the door, and put her service weapon in the safe. Her hand pulled away when she touched her badge and felt the black band around it. She removed her badge and set it in the safe. *Rest in peace, Albert Simmons. Rest in peace.* She sent Billy a text: "Headed for shower and bed. Love U."

Billy replied immediately: "Sleep well. Miss U. Love U."

Showered and in bed, Quinn put her phone on the charger by her bed and then picked it up again. She called Billy.

"I was hoping you'd call. Everything okay?"

"Just wanted to go to sleep with your voice in my head."

"Want me to sing you a lullaby?"

"Not tonight." She smiled at the thought of it.

"Truth is, you don't ever want me to sing." He laughed. "Hey, I could whistle, though."

"Just your slow, southern drawl is all I needed. Love you, Billy. Thanks for loving me."

"More than you can ever know."

"Night." She ended the call, put the phone on the charger, and fell fast asleep.

Chapter 19

Very often, "what happened" takes years to reveal itself. It takes courage to confront our actions, peel back the layers of trauma in our lives, and expose the raw truth of our past. But this is where healing begins.

Oprah Winfrey

Tuesday Morning

Quinn scanned her ID in the back door of the station at six-seventeen Tuesday morning. It was dark. Cloud cover blocked the stars she loved seeing this hour of the morning. She pushed the door and stopped when she heard her name. She turned and saw George jogging toward her.

"Hey, I didn't see you drive in behind me."

"I didn't. I was distracted and headed for the back lot completely forgetting about my parking space." He laughed. "Lots of years of practice."

"Well, I'm glad you finally got a space behind the building." She acted like she was closing the door.

"Hey. Hold on."

"No ID scan. No entry." She grinned at him.

"Well aren't we cheery at this hour?" George scanned his card. "Can't believe it's so dark out. By now we usually have a hint of light over the mountains."

"Clouds are supposed to clear out fairly quickly this morning."

"Good. Still won't be full sun til nine or ten."

"Maybe nine-thirty this time of year."

"That's right. Split the difference." He stepped up beside her as they walked down the hall. "I'm going to grab some coffee. Meet you in the workroom?"

"I'll be there. Just need to check something in my office. See you in a few."

"Sounds good."

Ten minutes later Quinn opened the door from her office to see Kevin standing there and George putting the code in the Detectives Workroom across the hall. "Morning, Kevin. Get a good night's sleep?"

"I did. Thanks. Hope you did."

"Like a rock." Quinn smiled and held the door. She put her mug down on the table. "Okay, let's finalize our plan for interviewing our overnight guest."

Kevin smirked. "Guest, ha. He deserves to be in prison."

George put his hand up. "Now, Detective. Let's not be judge and jury."

Kevin slapped at George's hand. "Too early in the morning for that."

Quinn sipped her coffee. "What's your plan, Kevin?"

Young House

"Dispatch."

"Need backup at the Young's house. Surveillance shows an unmanned aerial vehicle overhead."

"How many officers on the scene?"

"One."

"Back up headed your way."

The dispatcher notified the duty sergeant and dispatched two vehicles. One was seven minutes away the other was ten.

Quinn picked up her secure phone from the table in the Detectives Workroom. "Isaacs."

"Dispatch, Detective." The dispatcher told Quinn the nature of the call from the Young residence.

"Thanks. On it."

George and Kevin looked at her. "A UAV flying over the Young's house." She stood. "Let's go, George."

"Need me?" Kevin looked up from the folder he had in front of him.

"This will give you a chance to see if there's any new information on this case. Decide on an officer to be with you. We'll call you as soon as we're headed back."

George called dispatch as they headed for Quinn's SUV.

"Dispatch."

"Isaacs and Marshall headed for Young's house."

"Noted, Detective. 10-4."

"10-4."

Quinn put her emergency light on but not her siren. "Dispatch didn't get any more information from the officer."

"I'm going to get dispatch to connect me with the officer. Make sure they're getting any photos and video they can." George was punching in numbers as he spoke.

"Marshall here. Try to get whatever pictures you can." He listened. "Got it. 10-4."

"It's still dark. May not be possible."

George ended the call. "Officer said she got some photos of the lights that made her think it's a UAV. Daylight will be creeping in soon, hopefully."

"Yeah, that's a challenge in these mountains. Friend of mine used to say, 'Clock says daytime, sky says not yet.'" Quinn approached the turn-off to the Young's house and slowed.

She saw a panel van parked alongside the highway and pulled in two car lengths behind it. "This could be the launch site." She pointed to a small dish antenna on the roof of the van.

George ran the license plate. "Well, well. Mr. Calhoun of Sevierville must own a fleet of vehicles."

"Just went up another notch on the 'who is he?' list." She and George exited at the same time. He went toward the passenger's side and she toward the driver's side. Each had their hand on their side arms.

The back door of the van opened just as they reached the front of Quinn's SUV. Both officers pulled their weapons.

"Something wrong, officer...officers?" The young man jumped out of the van with his hands in the air.

George moved toward him looking inside the van as he spoke. "You're doing just fine. Keep your hands over your head."

George patted him down. He turned to Quinn and shook his head.

Quinn let out a sigh. *No weapons.*

"Hey. What'd I do?"

"Nothing, if you're smart." George sounded like a drill sergeant.

Quinn stepped up and looked inside the van. Along the sides were benches and computers and several drones in clear plastic cases.

"What's your name?" George put away his weapon and held a pad and pen.

"Christopher."

"All of it."

"Christopher Cox."

"License?"

"On the visor."

Quinn walked toward the front of the van. She opened the driver's door and saw a license on the visor. She also saw there were personal belongings on the passenger seat, one of which was a woman's shoulder bag. There were drinks in both cup holders. She walked to the back.

"Who's with you?" Quinn looked right at him.

"My girlfriend, Marcia."

"Where is she?"

"Down that road." He pointed toward the road leading to the Young house.

George looked at him. "You mean the road with the barriers and signs saying 'no trespassing'? That road?"

Christopher's shoulders slumped. "Yes, sir."

"Hands behind your back. You're under arrest for aiding in illegal trespass and crossing a police barrier. And that's just for starters."

"Hey, we're just doing our job."

"Save it for the interview." George walked him to the back of the SUV and put him the back seat. "If you know what's good for you, you'll sit there and behave like a choir boy." George buckled the seat belt and walked back to Quinn.

"Look at this setup." She pointed to the inside of the van.

"Doesn't look like a news crew to me. Does it to you?"

"Nope." She turned as she heard a voice call out.

"Hey. What's wrong? Where's Christopher?" The young woman was holding a UAV. She didn't even look as she crossed the county road.

"Stop."

She did. She was in the middle of the road.

"Now walk real slow toward me." George clipped each word.

The young woman took one step and stopped like she was playing the children's game: "Mother, May I?"

"Keep walking." George shook his head in disbelief.

"Where's Christopher?"

"Who are you?"

"Who are you?" She snapped at him.

"I'm Detective Marshall and I get to ask the questions. That clear?"

"Yeah." She stepped off the road. "Okay if I set this down?" She lifted the UAV.

Quinn stepped up. "Put it right there on the floor." She pointed to the back of the van.

George stood beside the young woman. "Now, who are you?"

"Marcia. Marcia Fisher."

"Got any identification on you to prove that?"

She shook her head. "In my bag on the front seat."

He nodded to the side of the van. "Let's go and keep your hands where I can see them."

One of the police officers dispatched as backup pulled up and Quinn walked along the driver's side of the van and stood in front of it so she could see George and the young woman.

The officer was out of her vehicle and standing beside Quinn.

Marcia held her hands out to her side and walked to the front of the van. "Should I open the door?"

"Might be the best way to get your bag."

She opened the door. "Okay if I take it off the seat?"

George saw the purse was like a saddle bag. It had a flap over the top and a piece of leather as a clasp through a leather loop. "Hold the bottom with your left hand. Open the top with the right and keep your hand on the flap once it's open."

She did as he directed.

"Now empty it on the seat."

"Are you kidding me?"

"I don't kid." George glared into her eyes.

"Got it." Marcia emptied her purse on the seat. "Satisfied?"

George saw there was nothing she could use as a weapon. "Get your license."

She picked up a small cloth wallet and took out her license.

"Now, turn around and put your hands behind your back."

She put her hands on her hips. "Why?"

"You're under arrest for crossing a police barrier, trespassing, and flying a UAV in the dark."

"We have permits from the FAA." The sarcasm dripped from her lips.

George cuffed her and turned her toward the officer in front of the van. "Take her to the station and book her on crossing a police line, trespassing, and flying a UAV in the dark."

"I told you we have permits." Marcia glared at him.

Quinn jumped in as good cop. "You'll have a chance to produce them. Just go with the officer." She smiled.

"Ha! Like *that one* cares what you have to say...lady?" Marcia strung out lady with a sneer on her face.

Quinn stepped in front of her. Her tone was flat and blunt. "Let's be very clear, *young* lady. I am the lead detective here and I don't kid either."

"Got it." Marcia moved as the police officer opened her back door and slid to the other side.

George put Marcia in the seat and the female officer reached across and buckled the seatbelt. She and George slammed the doors at the same time.

"Thank you, Officer. Detective." Quinn nodded. "You can let her sit there until the backup with two officers arrive. Then one can go with you and you can take her in."

"Yes, ma'am."

The officer stood beside the driver's door of the vehicle. She saw the lights of an approaching police vehicle.

Quinn moved toward the van. "Let's have a look, George."

"Okay. Let me check on the boy genius in your SUV." He walked toward the door.

The second backup vehicle arrived and Quinn spoke to the officers.

"Both of you please go check on the officer at the house. It's at the end of that lane."

"Yes, ma'am."

"Then report back here. One of you can go ride in with one of our suspects." She nodded to the other officer standing by the vehicle with Marcia. "Then I'd like the other one to stay with the van until a tow truck gets here."

"Yes, ma'am. On it." One of the officers ran across the road, moved one of the barriers, hopped in with his partner and they drove toward the Young residence.

George met Quinn at the back of the van. "This isn't two kids playing with drones."

"UAVs."

"Yeah, whatever. Most folks call them drones."

"And so can you—just not on duty." She smiled at him.

"Yes, ma'am." George laughed. "Does everything have to be so complicated?

"No. Not everything. Just humans."

"Now, that's the truth if I ever heard it."

"I'll notify Steve Clark about the van and see if he wants someone to check it out before we move it or wait 'til it's at the station."

"Good plan." George nodded. Neither of them entered the van, but they both took pictures with their official phones.

"By the way, Quinn.... ."

She turned her head to look at him. "Yes?"

"Loved how you set her straight that you're lead detective." He smiled.

She chuckled. "You know, it felt pretty good."

"Welcome back, Quinn."

Yeah. I hope so.

Round City Police Station

Quinn gave the daily password to enter the gate at the station. The tow truck with the van was right behind them.

Quinn looked over at George. "Those kids should be in holding. I want us to meet with Kevin before we start interviewing any of them."

"Good idea. Let them stew."

"I asked matron to be sure they couldn't talk to each other or Roger. Not sure how all this is connected."

"No telling. What we know for sure is we have three vehicles connected to a Robert Calhoun in Sevierville."

"Yeah." Quinn pulled into her parking space. She looked at the clock on her dashboard. "It's seven forty-five. Have you eaten?"

"Let's check with Kevin and see if Chuck is here. We'll order in and make a decision about interviewing these folks."

"Got it." He swiped his ID card on the back door after Quinn. "As soon as I stop down the hall."

"Good plan. See you in the workroom." She headed for the women's room.

She was washing her hands when her personal phone buzzed. "Hey, Billy."

"Good morning. Busy?"

"At the station. Got some stuff going on related to a case." She assumed Billy was on his personal phone, too.

"Yeah. Me, too. Just wanted to see how you were doing this morning and let you know I'll be tied up over here most of the day. If I don't answer, call Sylvia."

"Thanks for the backup. I'll be fine, though. Slept well."

"Glad to hear it. I was restless all night." The suggestion in Billy's voice was evident.

"Patience, my love."

"Yeah. That." Billy laughed.

"I hope you have a productive day."

"You, too. Good luck with your case. Love you, Quinn."

"Love you, too. Later." She ended the call, looked in the mirror, and smiled at herself. *I am one lucky woman. I don't ever want to forget what happened last week and how it felt. I do hope I can stay focused on my work.* She ran her fingers through her hair, started to pull it into a knot, and stopped herself. *Do I really pull my hair back when I'm working a case?* She shook her hair from side to side, turned, and walked out the door.

Quinn put the code in the Detectives Workroom door and heard the three men talking.

"Hey, Kevin. Chuck. Hungry?"

Kevin shook his head. "My third cup of coffee has about run out."

"I could eat. What's the plan?" Chuck looked at Quinn.

Quinn took money out of her pocket and put it on the table. "Breakfast is on me as long as it's from Sweet Creations. Anywhere else—everyone pays their way."

"Yeah."

"Sure."

"Okay, okay. Twist my arm." George pulled out his phone. "The usual?" Heads nodded.

George ended the call. "It'll be here in thirty."

Quinn sat down. "Good. That will give us time to catch up and decide how to manage this. What's your thinking, Kevin?"

"I'm up-to-date on the information on the Youngs. I think I can handle the interview. We can talk about strategy."

"Good." Quinn nodded. "Need anything more from Chuck?"

"Not at the moment."

"Chuck, anything you want to add?"

"Yeah, don't forget to call me for breakfast." He laughed as he walked to the door.

Quinn shook her head and laughed. "No problem, Chuck." She rolled her eyes at him. "Kevin, did you think about an officer who could partner with you?"

"Yeah. You have any thoughts?" Kevin waited to see if Quinn or George would answer.

"We can brainstorm if you want." Quinn looked at George.

George leaned his head in Kevin's direction.

"Kevin?"

"I was thinking about Officer Evans. What do you think, George?"

"Haven't done an interview with her myself, but seen her handle herself pretty well in the field." George was nodding.

"Anyone know if she's in the station?" Quinn looked at the men.

Kevin answered. "Saw her in the break room at shift change, don't know if she was coming on or going off."

Quinn looked across at George. "She was in the break room yesterday morning when we were there. Must mean she's on morning shift. I'll check with her sergeant." Quinn picked up her secure phone.

"Dispatch."

"Duty Sergeant, please."

"Yes, ma'am."

"Vincent here."

"Sergeant, Quinn Isaacs here. Do you have a minute?"

"Yes, ma'am."

"Any chance Officer Evans is in the station this morning?"

"Yes, ma'am. She's backup this week on desk duty."

"Any concerns you'd have about her helping us with an interview in about an hour?"

There was silence. "Concerns about her not being available for backup or doing an interview?"

"Both."

"No, ma'am. Not at all. Could be good experience for her."

"Would you like me to clear it with the Chief?"

Silence again. "Not necessary. I can get the desk covered. Shall I speak to Officer Evans?"

"Yes, please. When she's available, please have her join us in the Detectives Workroom."

"Yes, ma'am."

"Thank you, Sergeant. I appreciate the assistance."

"Anytime, Detective." The call ended.

Quinn turned to the others at the table. "Okay, Evans is available. She'll be here in a little bit." Quinn walked over to look at the crime board. "Lots of pieces here." She tapped on the white board with her nail. "Thanks for adding the morning arrests, George."

"I brought Kevin up to speed on what we found out there."

"Thanks. Which first? Roger, Christopher, or Marcia?"

George raised his hand and then lowered it. He shrugged. "I really do prefer the informality—just hard to break old habits."

"No problem. What's your thinking?"

"I think Christopher—then Marcia—then Roger."

"Reasoning?" She turned her head at the knock on the door.

Kevin stood up and opened the door. "Officer Evans. Come in."

"Morning, Detectives. Sarge said you needed me." She looked at Quinn.

"Kevin." Quinn raised her palm toward Kevin.

"I'd like you to do an interview with me. Interested?"

"Yes, sir!" Officer Evans' eyes opened wide. "Sure. Just tell me what to do."

Quinn pointed to the table. "Pull up a chair. We're just starting to strategize and what we don't cover in that discussion, you can read in reports."

They spent the next twenty minutes discussing pros and cons of the interview order and the strategies. George picked up his phone. "I'll be right out." He ended the call. "Hate to interrupt the flow, but breakfast is here."

Quinn nodded and George got up. "Coffee, Officer Evans?"

"Ma'am. Is it okay to just call me Evans? Or DeAnn?"

"Sure." Quinn laughed. "I should have asked. We generally use first names when we're problem solving in here. Thanks for reminding me."

"So, DeAnn, coffee?"

"Yes, please."

"Come with me." Quinn picked up her cup and they headed to the break room. Quinn washed out her cup and put money in the box for coffee for both of them. "DeAnn, if you have..." Quinn opened the door into the hallway, "any concerns at all, raise them. We only get better when we consider all ideas."

"Sure. I'm just trying to take it all in. I've questioned folks in suspicious circumstances on the street, so not totally foreign to me. This, though, I know has a lot more nuances to it."

"Right. Just follow Kevin's lead. You two will have a few minutes to talk about signals you might use to cue the other. I'm pretty sure you'll be the 'good cop' in this one."

"Thanks for the opportunity." DeAnn stood to the side as Quinn put the code in the door and opened it.

"Smells heavenly." Quinn looked at George and Kevin. "Don't eat it all. I'll get Chuck."

George handed DeAnn a plate. "Dig in." He took the tops off the foil trays with eggs, sausage, grits, and croissants.

Kevin opened the paper bag. "And that sainted Carrie sent us blackberry preserves." He put it on the table.

The door opened and Quinn walked back in. "Save me any?"

"Probably not." Chuck handed her a plate and took one for himself. "Thanks, Quinn."

"My pleasure. Enjoy, folks."

They were enjoying a few minutes of eating and friendly conversation about life and the weather when Quinn heard the chirp of the code in the lock. There was a knock on the door and then it opened. Quinn knew it could only be one person. She stood.

"Morning, Chief."

The others stood immediately.

"At ease, go on with your breakfast."

"Have some?" Quinn offered Chief Hansen a plate.

"Didn't come for this, but who could resist." She took a croissant, preserves, and butter. "No one will mind if I take it with me?"

"No, ma'am. Need me?" Quinn looked at the Chief.

"I've read the reports on the events of the night and the morning. I assume you're getting ready to do interviews?"

"Yes, ma'am. Detective Millwood and Officer Evans will observe Detective Marshall and myself when we interview the two we picked up this morning. We hope they will give us something that will help with the man we arrested last night. As you know, that gentleman has outstanding warrants in South Carolina."

"Yes, I saw that. Is the DA on it?"

"Yes, ma'am. She said she'd talk to folks in South Carolina first thing this morning."

"Good. Anything you need just let me know."

"Yes, ma'am."

The Chief turned and headed for the door. They all stood again. "Have a good day."

Kevin and George were finished eating. They put their food in the plastic trash bag Carrie had sent. "I'll clean up the leftovers." George started putting lids on the food. "Okay if I call down and see if the ME and Sue want some?"

"By all means. Should have invited them up. Thanks for thinking of it, George." Quinn put her empty plate in the trash bag. "Let's regroup in ten minutes and get this done."

Kevin and DeAnn talked while George and Chuck took the food downstairs to the ME.

Chuck pushed the elevator button with his elbow. "George, did you ever think about how weird it would be to eat in a morgue?"

"No. And I don't want to consider it now." He rolled his eyes. "Then again, *you* eat with all kinds of chemicals, matter, materials, right? What's the difference." He stopped and looked at Chuck as they waited for the elevator. "Never mind. Don't go there."

When they came back, Chuck headed to the lab and George entered the Detectives Workroom. Quinn and Kevin were role playing an interview. George noticed DeAnn was watching intently.

Quinn stopped. "Welcome back. ME happy?"

"As a clam."

"Good. Let's set up our plan and get started."

They talked for another fifteen minutes.

"Kevin and DeAnn will be in observation. George and I will take Christopher first, then Marcia. We'll take a short break in the Matron's office and then George and I will go in the observation room and you two will interview Roger. Ready?"

"Yes."

"Yes, ma'am." DeAnn nodded.

"Let's do it." George stood.

"George, will you let holding know we're headed down?"

"Yes, ma'am."

Chapter 20

Inaction breeds doubt and fear. Action breeds confidence and courage.
Dale Carnegie

Tell me the Truth

Quinn followed George who was escorting Christopher Cox to interview Room One.

"Sit." George pointed to the chair facing the one way mirror. *I'll be glad when we can do away with those mirrors. All the technology—don't need them anymore.*

Quinn set the recorder on the table. *Guess this still could be backup. The microphones and the video are recording. Oh, well. Technology issues for another day.* "This is Detective Quinn Isaacs." She played it back. The recording worked. She erased it and set it down again.

Quinn totally ignored the one-way mirror behind which Kevin and DeAnn were observing the interview. "This interview is being recorded." She gave the date and time. "I am Detective Isaacs of the Round City Police, and this is..."

"Detective Marshall of thc Round City Police."

She looked at Christopher. "Please state your name, address, and date of birth."

"Christopher Cox. 453 Chapin Road, Columbia, South Carolina." He gave his date of birth.

Quinn looked at him with a slight smile on her face. *Hmmm...makes him thirty. Doesn't look it.*

"Christopher Cox, you have the right to…" She watched his impassive face as she recited the Miranda warning. "Do you understand your rights and responsibilities?"

"Yes, ma'am."

"Do you wish to have an attorney present?"

"No, ma'am."

"Please state your wishes specific to having an attorney present."

"I don't want an attorney."

"Thank you for your clarification. What is your occupation, Mr. Cox?"

"I'm a videographer."

"Who do you work for?"

"It's my company. People buy my services."

"Do you have a place of work?"

"My house."

"Is the equipment in the van all yours?"

"Yes, ma'am." He stopped—looked around the room. "Well, I mean the computers and UAVs are mine…and the printer."

"Whose van is it?"

"Mr. Calhoun."

"How do you know Mr. Calhoun?"

"He's Marcia's uncle."

Quinn studied the face of this seemingly earnest young man. *Well, Christopher, Mr. Calhoun seems to be everyone's uncle.* "Do you personally know Mr. Calhoun?"

"No, ma'am. He lets me use his van when I'm doing UAV work for him."

"Have you ever met him?"

"No, ma'am. He tells Marcia what he wants us to do."

"Like you were doing this morning?"

"Yes, ma'am."

"How long have you known Marcia?"

"We went to technical college together in South Carolina, but she's from Ohio originally."

George was glad he was looking at his notepad when a smirk spread across his face. *Ohio? South Carolina? Guess it's time to find out the connections.*

"Do you have written contracts for your services?"

"Yes, ma'am. They're in my case in the van." He took a deep breath. "Is the van somewhere safe?"

Quinn nodded. "Absolutely. It is in our back lot."

"Oh, gee. Thanks. I'd be in a big hurt if I had to replace it."

"How often do you use it?"

"This is the fourth...no, fifth time."

"Where did you drive it before this?"

"All of them have been here in Tennessee. Mr. Calhoun has us map properties he's interested in purchasing."

"Really? Even when it means trespassing?"

The color faded from Christopher's face. "I'm really sorry, Detective. When I saw the police tape, I told Marcia we shouldn't do this one, but she said her uncle would be really mad if we came back without the video he wanted."

George looked at Christopher and smiled. "Ah. Love makes most men crazy."

"*Excuse* me, Detective." Quinn had to make an effort to sound stern.

"Sorry, Detective." George winked at Christopher and nodded toward Quinn and shrugged. Then he lowered his eyes to the floor and pulled his lips in to be sure he didn't smile.

"Now, back to the matter at hand, Mr. Cox. What was so important about your videotaping of the property this morning?"

"Mr. Calhoun said he'd heard that the property might come up for sale and he wanted to beat the market on it."

"Do you do mostly real estate?"

He nodded. Quinn noticed he seemed to be biting the inside of this lip. "Yes. For the most part. Some of it is residential, some commercial. I can't remember the last time I did something that wasn't real estate."

"Who else have you done UAV work for?"

"Oh, ma'am. I can give you a whole list of realtors, mostly in South Carolina. They put the property on their websites, brochures—stuff like that. Seems like folks today want a bird's eye view of land they want to buy."

Quinn tilted her head. "Even when it's in a subdivision?"

"Oh, yes. They want to see how people keep their back yards. You know, that kind of thing."

"Marcia said you have a permit to fly the UAV at night."

"In the van. It's a Part 107 from the FAA. Yes, ma'am, wouldn't leave home without it."

"How long has Marcia been your girlfriend?"

"Well, like I said, we met in technical college, but we've only be together for six or seven months."

"When did you start doing videography for Mr. Calhoun."

Christopher looked at her. "Ha. That's funny. I never put it together before. I ran into Marcia in a bar in downtown Columbia one night—really cool area called Five Points—and the next day she asked me if I'd like to do some work for her uncle." He stopped and looked at Quinn. "Ma'am, I know we broke the law trespassing, but I didn't mean any harm. Can I ask you a question?"

"You can ask. I may or may not be able to answer it."

"Are you suggesting Marcia set me up? Is everything I've done for her uncle illegal?"

Quinn studied the young man's face. "That's a question for which I plan to find the answer."

"Detective." George leaned in toward Quinn. "This seems like an honest young man. Can't we cut him a break?"

"Detective Marshall." Quinn did not turn to look at him. She kept her eyes on Christopher. "We, you and I, do not make deals—as you well know. Our job is to get the facts. Our District Attorney, Ms. O'Haire, is the only one in law enforcement who can decide if a suspect is..."

"Suspect? Suspect in what?" Christopher's voice shook. "Honest. All I've done is not stop Marcia from going past that barrier. We were taking video of vacant land and that's legal as long as it's not for surveillance."

Quinn lowered her forearms onto the table and leaned toward Christopher. "If you continue to cooperate, assuming everything you've said so far holds up as being cooperative, I will speak with the District Attorney and urge her to give you some leeway as a cooperative witness." She smiled.

"It is. I promise. It is." Christopher's shoulders shook slightly. "Ma'am, could I have a drink of water?"

Quinn turned to George. "Detective, I think we'll let Mr. Cox have a break for now until I can talk with the DA. Please return him to holding and see that he gets some water." She turned back to Christopher. "I hope, for your sake, Mr. Cox, that you are telling me the whole truth. I want to believe you." She stood. "This ends this interview."

"Detective Marshall returning Mr. Cox to holding." George said as he walked over to help Christopher stand.

"Detective Isaacs ending interview." She turned off the recorder. "Thank you, Mr. Cox."

Christopher just nodded as he shuffled out the door ahead of George.

Quinn went out in the hall and watched them go. Then she went into the observation room. "Questions, Officer Evans?"

Getting to the Truth—Maybe

The matron took Marcia into Room One for the interview. She stood at the door as Quinn and George came down the hall.

"You sure you're okay with this strategy, Quinn?"

"As sure as I can be. I think you had a great idea." She looked at George and nodded. "Ready?"

"Can't wait." He grinned.

George opened the door and let Quinn go in first. She headed for the chair against the wall and George looked at her and then the table. "But, Detective Isaacs, shouldn't you conduct this interview?"

"Detective Marshall, I make the decisions here. Let's see if you can conduct an interview correctly—*this time.*" Quinn's stare could bore a hole in a steel plate.

"Yes, ma'am." George sat opposite Marcia. "Morning, Ms. Fisher. Just give me a minute to get this recorder started." He fumbled with the recorder, turned it on, and muttered, "This is a test." He stopped it, replayed the recording, and then erased it.

He nodded at Marcia Fisher. "Okay, let's get started." He started the recording again. "This is Detective Marshall of the Round City Police, and…"

"*Lead* Detective Isaacs of the Round City Police."

"…in Interview Room One with…please state your name, current address, and date of birth, please." He smiled at Marcia.

Marcia sat there stone-faced and silent.

"Excuse me, please state your name…" George looked at her.

Marcia interrupted him. "I heard you the first time. What if I don't want to tell you?"

George looked over at Quinn then back at Marcia. "I'll have to add obstructing an investigation to the charges against you."

"Can't make a decision without your boss?" Marcia's smile was a full-blown sneer.

George sat up straighter. "Ms. Fisher…"

"See you know my name." She laughed.

"State your name, address, and date of birth for the record."

She sighed, slumped in her seat, and stared at George. "Marcia Cox, 654 Lucky Lane, Irmo, SC." She gave her date of birth.

Quinn scribbled "Age - 28" on her pad. *Pretty big chip on her shoulder. Wonder why?* The date of birth matched the driver's license Marcia had given George earlier.

"You have the right to remain silent. Anything you say can and will be…" George read the Miranda warning off of a card. It was part of his strategy. He looked up at Marcia. "Do you understand these rights?"

"Yeah."

"Do you wish to have an attorney present?"

"Don't need one."

"I need you to tell me if you want an attorney or not." *Come on, Marcia.*

"I—do—not—want—an—attorney. Got it?"

"Thank you for being clear. Now, why were you flying a drone over private property?"

"It was over vacant land which is legal."

George jumped in quickly. "You crossed a police barrier which was clearly marked. Did you have permission to do that?"

Marcia stared at him.

"Detective, enough of this molly-coddling. Stand up and let me show you how to conduct an interview." Quinn was standing beside George.

George made a show of almost tipping over his chair. "Yes, ma'am. Sorry, ma'am." He pushed the chair further back and got up. He pushed the chair back toward the table and lowered his voice. "I'm really sorry, ma'am."

"'Sorry don't get the job done.' Ever heard that before, Detective?" Quinn sat and totally ignored George. She placed a folder on the table and looked directly at Marcia.

"Ms. Fisher, we have limited time to conduct this interview. I promise you in no uncertain terms that our District Attorney just loves to throw the book at someone who obstructs justice. So, you get one chance with me on this interview. Any questions about that?"

Marcia stared at her.

"When did you arrive in Tennessee?"

"Sunday, if it matters."

"What was the purpose of coming to Round City?"

"Aerial videography of property." Marcia stared at George.

"Did you see the crime scene tape and police barrier at the end of Sunset Lane and the County Highway?"

"Maybe. So?"

Quinn put a photo on the table and slowly turned it for Marcia to see herself on the road blocked by the barrier and crime scene tape. "Is this you?"

"Could be."

Quinn slapped the photo, leaned in on her forearms and said, "Last chance. You either answer these questions truthfully and fully or I'll end this interview and you'll take your chances with the District Attorney who has the information from Mr. Cox." She waited a three-second count. "And, the charges will include interfering in a murder investigation."

Marcia jumped in her chair and the chains on her wrists and ankles clanked together. "No way in hell. What are you talking about? I didn't murder anyone. Who?"

Quinn continued to stare at her.

George leaned forward but didn't move his chair. "Miss Fisher, just cooperate."

"You, shut up. What kind of man are you? Letting a woman tell you what to do." She pursed her lips as if to spit.

Quinn lowered her voice and let every syllable drag out. "Don't even think about it." She stared into Marcia's eyes. "If you spit at Detective Marshall or me, or attempt any other form of assault, I will end this interview, add assaulting a police officer—and ask the DA for the maximum sentence."

Marcia swallowed. "Yeah, how long can that be?"

Quinn looked at George. "What do you think Detective?" She smiled at him.

George was nodding his head. "Well, trespassing, passing a crime scene tape, assaulting a police officer – all told those are about five to six years. Add murder—life." He sat back, put his right ankle on his left knee, crossed his arms and smiled.

"Whoa, whoa, whoa. You're trying to blame me for something I didn't do." A tear formed in Marcia's eye.

Quinn leaned in on the table and spoke in a soft voice only loud enough to make sure it would record. "Then listen very carefully. Starting now, no bull thrown in, tell me everything you've done since you entered the state of Tennessee. Make no mistake if you get off-track, make excuses, or I find you've left anything out, I will throw the book at you—and press the District Attorney to go for the maximum sentence on every charge." She stared into Marcia's eyes again. "Any part of that you don't understand?"

The façade dropped; Marcia whimpered. "I understand, Detective."

"Good. Now let's have it."

"We drove from South Carolina on I-26 through Asheville, to where I-81 meets I-40 in Tennessee. We got to this hick...uh, Round City, on Sunday night... ." She gave details of the hotel where they stayed, a little too much detail about how she and Christopher spent their evening in the hotel room, and how they spent Monday test flying the drone in a park so they could be sure they knew heights and how well their topographical maps matched the actual land in the area. "Uncle Bob was very specific about the property he was interested in and we were to get as much of the house at the end of the road without trespassing onto it."

Quinn sat with her arms crossed, her head slightly tilted, and watched every movement of Marcia's eyes, mouth, and upper body.

"We had pretty much finished when I came out and you were standing there. I had lost communication with Christopher so I didn't know what was going on."

"Did Uncle Bob give you that tattoo on your hip?"

Marcia tried to move her hands which were still chained to her waist toward her hip. The irritation in her voice leapt from her lips. "How the hell do you know... ."

Quinn was shaking her head. She pushed back her chair and acted like she was going to stand up.

"Wait. Wait. I have a temper. Okay? I forgot the rules."

Quinn slid her chair back toward the table. "Well?"

"We all have them. Everyone in the family."

"What do they mean?"

"They mean you are part of the family."

"And what obligation does that carry?"

Marcia bit her lip. "You won't have to worry about me serving a prison sentence. If I tell you about the family, they'll find me and take care of me."

"They can't take care of you in prison."

"Ha. That's the one place they can probably most easily take care of me. You know—kill me."

Quinn turned to George, "Detective, will you please get Ms. Fisher a bottle of water?"

"Detective Marshall exiting interview Room One."

"Take a breather, Marcia. I think we have a lot to talk about." Quinn stood up and stretched.

Marcia lowered her head and started clicking her tongue against the top of her mouth.

Quinn glanced at Marcia's face in the mirror. *What secrets do you hold, Marcia?*

Observation Room

Officer Evans turned to Detective Millwood. "Wow! Did Detective Isaacs know she would get that from this woman?"

"We have some suspicion this is a cult. Look at the tattoo again on the crime board when we go upstairs. Sonia Young and both her sons have it. We have learned from the records from Riverbend on Mr. Young that he did not have a tattoo. He was a pretty bad guy in his own right, but we don't know why they came to Tennessee when the others seem to have an Ohio and South Carolina connection."

DeAnn Evans nodded her head. She sipped her Yeti of water and watched Quinn pace. "Detective, do you think most law officers can play off each other the way they do." She pointed toward the window.

"Ha. They've both had lots of practice and both of them have some natural instincts which make getting to the truth just seem to work. Here's a question for you. If you were called into court as someone who witnessed the interview, do you think at any time the suspect was coerced into saying something incriminating?"

DeAnn sat there for several seconds. "That's what's so fascinating to me... is it okay if I use their first names in here?"

Kevin laughed. "No problem."

"George played the bumbling detective almost afraid of his boss, but it was believable. I've seen him at crime scenes and he is top notch. Part of me wondered if it was his twin in there."

"Good observation. And, Quinn?"

"Whew. I can't see how she could ever be accused of coercing a suspect. She was clear in her expectations, delivered them in a no-nonsense tone of voice, but not threatening, and I think I actually saw the suspect's expression change when she realized she couldn't bluff her way by being a spoiled brat."

Kevin raised his hand in a high-five. "Good attention to detail. You'll need that when we do this Roger fellow."

"Hope I'm up to it."

"Wouldn't be here if I didn't think you were. Given what's happening in there, I suspect we will regroup before we interview him."

She gave a soft chuckle. "Yeah, guess he's not going anywhere."

"Right."

Interview Room One

George knocked on the door, opened it, and stepped in. He turned back to the matron who handed him two bottles of water. He gave one to Quinn and set one on the table. He went back to the door and took the third one.

Quinn turned on the recorder. *We need to talk about no longer doing this. Every second is recorded on video and audio already.* "Detective Isaacs of Round City Police restarting interview."

"Detective Marshall reentering interview room."

"Ms. Fisher, to verify your presence, please state your name."

Marcia rolled her eyes, stopped, and lowered her head again. "Marcia Fisher."

"Detective, will you please release Ms. Fisher's cuffs from her waist so she can drink her water?"

George walked to the table. "Please push your chair back." Marcia did. He unlocked the cuffs from the chain around her waist. "Cuffs, too, ma'am?"

"Maybe later." Quinn turned the lid on the bottled water but did not remove it. She sat it on the table in front of Marcia.

Marcia picked up the bottle, managed to get the lid off, and took a drink. "Thanks."

"Now, Marcia. I need to know exactly why your Uncle Bob sent you here to do aerial photography."

Marcia drank slowly. Her eyes darted around the room. "Isn't there some kind of program that will protect me? I don't know what you call it." She put her water bottle on the table and lowered her hands and was wringing her hands as she stared at them. "If I tell you anything, they'll find out—and I'll be dead." She lowered her voice to barely a whisper. "Just like Sonia and Phillip."

George looked at Quinn and raised his eyebrows.

Quinn's secure phone buzzed.

Chapter 21

It does not require many words to speak the truth.
Chief Joseph

Quinn's Office

Quinn read the text from the district attorney, ended the interview, and told the team they would meet in the Detectives Workroom in thirty minutes. She gave George a specific assignment and headed for her office. She sat down and picked up her desk phone and dialed the DA's number. "Hey, Peggy. It's Quinn. Got your text."

"Thanks for calling so quickly. I wanted you to stop the interview because I think we need to have you folks do some serious background work before we go on. I assume Marcia Fisher is in a secure place?"

"She is. We have eyes on her and she seems calm at the moment."

"Don't want to tell you how to do your job, but we're going to need to hold these two and we can't do it more than twenty-four hours on trespassing. If either of them change their minds and ask for an attorney, it could derail everything."

"I know. George is checking with the SBI, FBI, and DEA to see if there's more to this 'family' than we've found so far. Peggy, I don't think this young woman was bluffing. She had a lot of bravado at the beginning…"

Peggy interrupted her. "Yeah, I was watching the whole time—by the way, good to have you back, Quinn."

"Thanks. Good to be back. Anyway, my sense is she has built up a defense to cope in whatever this 'family' is and her role in it. When I took a hard line with her, it's clear she has been well-conditioned to authority. Maybe not police authority, but someone being in charge."

"I agree."

"I have some questions about how we manage the interview with Roger Calhoun Young. I've been curious about the last name since we found it. Now, I need to figure out how to handle this interview. According to our jail staff, he doesn't have the tattoo. Can't figure that one if he's in the 'family.'"

"So, what's your concern?"

"You've read the report on our observations and tail, right?"

"Yes."

"Any problems?"

"You have four bodies in one day and any reasonable person would accept that surveillance of someone looking for at least one of them as a 'long-lost cousin' was justified. What's your concern?"

"George and I talked about having Kevin and a female officer do the interview so we don't get tangled up in possible cries of entrapment."

"He was stopped by a police officer for a violation of code on a broken taillight and a run of his license brought up his arrest warrant. I'm not worried about it."

"Okay." Quinn was running scenarios through her head. "I want to give Kevin and DeAnn a chance on this one. We'll talk it through and maybe use me or George if we need to unsettle this guy."

"That's your bailiwick. On my end, I'm not worried about you or George being involved in an interview with Roger Calhoun Young."

"Okay, thanks, Peggy. Where are we on the South Carolina warrant on him?"

"These things take time. Things are in motion down there. They'll want to make sure the warrant is still valid, decide if it's worth extraditing him, and so forth. So, we've got a day or two, at least, to see what he was really doing here. We can hold him for thirty."

"Okay, thanks. We're on it."

Detectives Workroom

Quinn looked around the room. "Everyone ready?"

George, Kevin, and DeAnn nodded their heads.

She heard the chirp of the lock on the door. She stood as did the others.

Chief Hansen entered and stood just inside the door. She put out her hand for them to stay seated.

"Good afternoon, Chief."

"Please continue."

Quinn looked at her watch. It was twelve-ten. *Wow. Afternoon already.*

"Updates?"

George jumped in. "No records specific to the tattoo or family name showing up in Tennessee. My initial search through the FBI has me in a search loop which is still running, but my search with the DEA got me an immediate call from our friend, Agent Sam."

Quinn waited to see what Sam Nations had said to George.

"He's on his way here."

Quinn was not surprised. "Did he give us anything to go on?"

"Nope. Said he would be here by one."

"Anything else pop-up?"

"Not yet."

"Anyone have something they want to discuss about this morning's interviews?"

"No." DeAnn spoke first.

"Not right now." Kevin wrote a note on his pad.

"Nope." George shook his head.

"Then let's break and have lunch. I'll let you know when Agent Nations arrives." She turned to the Chief. "Anything to add, Chief Hansen?"

"We have two out of four deaths last week that we have no idea who the responsible party is. We need all your good thinking focused on any possible leads. Let me know if you need anything." She opened the door and left.

"Get some lunch. I'll let you know when Sam arrives and we're ready to meet." Quinn leaned back in her chair.

The two detectives and police officer stood and exited the room without a word.

Quinn stood up and walked over to the window overlooking the back lot. *What's the linchpin to all this? A cult? Drugs? How did Sonia Young buy that house? Money laundering?* She leaned against the window frame. *And who is Robert Calhoun?* She stood straight up and headed to her office.

Quinn's Office

She stepped into the lab and turned for her office door when she heard Chuck call her name.

"You need me, Chuck?"

"Hey. Had lunch?"

"No. About to get a protein bar. How about you?" She walked to the corner and saw him sitting at his desk.

"I just got a sub that's big enough for six people. Want some?"

"You sure?"

"Look at this!"

"Didn't you know what you were ordering?"

"I said a large whole-wheat sub with ham, extra pickles, Swiss cheese, lettuce, tomato, mayo, and mustard."

"Something unusual about that?"

"Not really. When the kid delivered it he said, 'Gilda made it special for you.'"

"Who is Gilda?"

Chuck blushed.

"Never mind." She walked over and looked at the sandwich. "Looks to me like she cut the ends off of two large subs and put them together."

"Exactly." He was still light pink.

"Well, Chuck, always good to have friends." She smiled at him. "I'll take a third of one of those pieces."

"Take the whole half."

"Oh, no thanks. A third is more than enough for me. Need a drink?"

"I was just headed down to the break room to get something."

"You sit tight. I need to go down the hall and I'll get us both an iced tea. That work?"

"Perfect." Chuck walked to the far table where they sometimes ate. "I'll scrub it down."

"Back in a few minutes." Quinn walked toward the door and headed to the women's restroom. She washed her hands and then looked in the mirror. *This could be big. I can't blow it.* She ran her fingers through her hair, took the paper towel and opened the door before she threw it away.

Two bottles of iced tea from the vending machine in her hands she pushed the code on the door with her finger and shifted one of the drinks so she could turn the knob. One of the bottles started to slip and she managed to grab it and push the door with her hip.

"Quinn, you okay?" Chuck was headed toward the door.

"Did I make that much noise?"

"Uh, no. I think it was the expletive that told me you were in trouble."

They both started laughing. She handed him a bottle. "Don't you dare remember that!"

"Yes, ma'am." They both laughed again.

They sat at one of the stainless steel tables which Chuck had cleaned with antiseptic.

"I can't believe I'm not squeamish anymore about eating in here."

"I don't ever put anything on this particular table but boxes and cartons. No lab work is done here—nothing to worry about."

"Do I want to know what's in those boxes and cartons?" She tilted her head and looked at him.

"Uh, probably not. Anyway, nice to have lunch together. Glad you're back, Quinn."

"Me, too. Now, any word on how Sonia Young paid for her house?"

"It was a cashier's check drawn on The First Bank of Calhoun."

"Of course it was."

"Seriously, Quinn. That's the name of the bank."

"And let me guess, it's in Calhoun, Ohio. Right?"

"Close. No such town, but lots of Calhouns in central Ohio."

"I'm sure some of them are fine upstanding citizens. Just need to figure the connections to the Calhoun name that keeps popping up here—if there is one."

"You'll need a warrant to get the bank records."

"We're doing a strategy meeting when Sam Nations gets here."

Chuck wadded up the paper from his sandwich and threw it like a basketball at the trash can. "Woohoo. Three pointer."

Quinn clapped. "Thanks, Chuck. I owe you."

"Nope. This one's on me. Just glad you're back." He stood. "Okay, back to work."

"Do you have final reports on the COD on the bodies from the Young house?"

"Yes. There was a 9-millimeter to the head on the male with a pillow held over his face."

"G-18 Glock?"

"Don't know. Could be a number of different guns. You know the Glock G-18 is illegal in the U.S., right?" He looked at her.

"Yes. We have that noted in our earlier reports. Doesn't seem to keep them from being here, though, does it?"

"No, ma'am."

"Do we know how Sonia Young died?"

"It appears to be a self-inflicted gunshot from a 9-millimeter, but the ME is not willing to make that definitive. We have no weapon. It's possible to stage a murder to look like a suicide."

Quinn stared at the wall. *So who was in that house? The Young who was driving the convertible or was Roger Calhoun Young in that house? Or both?* "Chuck, please send me the reports on all the prints lifted at the Young house as soon as possible." She walked toward her office.

"On it."

"Thanks, again, for lunch." It carried the tone of a well-practiced afterthought.

"Anytime."

Her secure phone was buzzing as she walked in her office.

"Isaacs."

"Detective, Agent Nations of the DEA is at the front desk."

"I'll be right up. Thanks."

She set her bottle of tea on her desk, turned to walk out the door, and found herself glancing in the small mirror she had placed to the right of her door. *Ohhh, old habits die hard. Sam Nations, I will always love you, but you are no Billy Williams.* She straightened her shoulders and headed for the front.

Detectives Workroom

The desk officer released the lock on the door as Quinn approached. She extended her hand, "Hey, Sam. Thanks for coming."

"Hey, Quinn. Good to see you. You look lovely as always."

"Flattery will get you nowhere, Sam."

"Yeah, yeah. I know. My own fault—more than a decade ago."

"Water under the bridge. So, how's my favorite DEA agent?"

"Doing fine. How's my favorite detective?"

"Oh, this mutual admiration society could get sappy if we're not careful." She punched the code in the Detectives Workroom door, pushed it open, and let Sam pass.

"Yeah, who would want that?" He chuckled. When the door closed behind Quinn, he said, "Seriously, Quinn. How are you?"

"Doing well, thanks. Rough week behind me but I'm back in the game."

"No surprise to me. May I ask a favor, as an old friend?"

"Anytime."

"Please take care of yourself. What you went through can come back to bite you when you least expect it."

"I am, Sam, and I will. I've got lots of good folks around me and a Chief who is the boss of your dreams."

"And, don't forget Billy." It was a statement, not a question.

"And, Billy. Yes, Sam. I have Billy." She felt a tingle go through her body. *I have Billy.*

"I'm happy for both of you."

"Thanks. Have a seat." She realized he had moved over to the crime board. "Or better yet study the board while I call our folks."

"I saw the early part of it. I'll take a few minutes. Thanks."

Quinn punched in George's number. "Hey. Sam is here. Would you let the others know and may I ask you to bring some waters with you?"

"They're already there. I brought in a fridge last week. Decided we needed one."

Quinn looked around the room. She saw it in the corner. "George, you should..." she stopped herself "be awarded the good Samaritan medal. Thanks." *I have to do better about accepting others wanting to do things for the good of the team.* She walked over next to Sam.

"What's this?" He pointed to the photograph of the brand on Sonia Young's hip.

"Scarification." She looked at him and smiled. "New word for me. I was a bit crasser and called it a brand."

"Same difference, right?"

"True. I'll leave it to the DA to parse words if it comes to that. Our reports have the medical term."

"Scarification, it is."

The door opened and George, Kevin, and DeAnn entered.

"Sam, you know George and Kevin. Have you met Officer DeAnn Evans?"

Sam extended his hand. "Don't think I've had the pleasure. Sam Nations."

"Nice to meet you." She smiled at him.

"Sam is with the DEA." Quinn could swear she felt some electricity off the handshake between them. "Shall we?" She pointed to the chairs around the table.

Everyone pulled out a chair and sat.

Quinn opened a document on the computer and a blank sheet appeared on the screen.

"We've been moving fast and new things today appear to have a link to them—all of which has us jumping. We're going to step back and make sure we know everything we have to address."

Heads nodded.

"Sam, we'll bring you up to speed on the two interviews we did this morning and that will get us started on a list of things we need to track down. DeAnn would you give us a recap as an observer?"

DeAnn identified the highlights of the interview and what she believed were the take-aways. She looked at Quinn.

"Nice job. Questions, Sam?"

"Nope. Think I've got it."

"Alright then. Now I want to make sure we have noted anything you have questions on so they don't slip through the cracks. I'll start:

1. Notification documentation to the two daughters of Sonia Young.

2. Do the daughters have scarification?

3. Was the oldest son of Sonia in the Young house?

4. How did the oldest son end up with the convertible?

5. Source of funds in First Bank of Calhoun for Sonia Young to buy a house? Were the contents in the trunk or did the son have them?

6. Did Roger Calhoun Young have a part in the deaths of Sonia and son, presumed to be Phillip? Fingerprints?"

Quinn stopped typing.

"What else?" She heard George laughing. "George?"

"Well, I do have something to add to the list, but seriously, The First Bank of Calhoun?"

"Yes, Detective. Problem with that?"

"No, ma'am." He stopped laughing.

Quinn chuckled. "Relax, George, I had the same reaction. Now what do you have to add to the list?"

"What is the evidence for the warrant on Roger from South Carolina?" Quinn typed it onto the list.

De Ann raised her hand. "Is there any record of mental health issues on Marcia Fisher?"

Quinn nodded and typed it on the list.

They continued for several minutes and entered all the pieces they felt were threads at this point. Quinn typed the last word from Kevin and turned to Sam.

"Sam?"

"It turns out we've intercepted fentanyl from four different sources in this region in the last week. Our initial runs at DEA indicate three of them have the same chemical makeup and none of them have xylazine except the batch from the trunk of the convertible."

Quinn had her eyes focused on Sam. *So it would appear Billy's case doesn't intersect with ours.* "What are the implications of that for what was found in the convertible?"

"Just to make sure we're all on the same page, the batch confiscated here is far more lethal than the other three—though the others are bad enough." He looked around the table. "Further analyses are being run to see if there's a connection in the base powder used, but even if there is it may simply mean the original chemical came from the same place. The major supplier is China but most fentanyl comes in through Mexico where it is made into tablets—all of this was powder. Anyway, we're continuing to work on it in the lab and folks are looking for possible connections to known sources of both forms."

"Thanks, Sam. Questions for Sam?"

There were none.

"Let's make a plan."

George walked over to the mini-fridge. He held up bottled water and tea. "Anyone?" He passed them around and discussion began.

"Anyone think we need to reinterview Christopher Cox at this time?" She looked around the table. "Yes, Kevin?"

"We can't find any record on him except his business license in South Carolina. The downstairs techs are still working on the van, but all his equipment inside it seems to be straightforward and we're working on the paperwork that was in the van. There is an FAA 107 permit for night flying just like he said. There is paperwork on a contract with Robert Calhoun of Sevierville. I think you nailed it when you helped him realize Marcia was using him."

Quinn nodded. "Anyone else?"

"He seemed a pretty straight arrow to me." George looked at Quinn. "I think our time and resources are better spent on Marcia and Roger."

DeAnn raised her hand.

Quinn smiled at her. "DeAnn, just jump in. We do a pretty good job of handling interruptions and 'next in line' stuff. So feel free to say what you need to say."

"Thanks. I'm about the same age as Marcia. I know you have her in isolation at the moment…" She looked around the table. "I have an idea."

All heads turned toward her.

"What if you put me in a cell with her wearing a wire? I could go in on something like shoplifting which she wouldn't see as threatening and see if she'll talk to me."

Quinn looked around the table. "Risks?"

They discussed pros and cons. "Before or after we talk to Roger?" Quinn looked around the table.

DeAnn started to raise her hand then dropped it. "I've read the reports on intercepting him and following him. I could make some comment about running into him and him offering to help me."

They kicked around ideas for several minutes. Finally, George spoke up. "I think DeAnn could be a back-up plan, but first I think we need to make one more run at Marcia and see if we can get anything that we can use with Roger before we interview him."

"I agree. Let's take a break and regroup and decide if this is going to happen today." Quinn stood. "Sam, may I see you in my office?"

Quinn's Office

Sam followed her into her office. She shut the door. He sat in one of the two chairs and leaned back.

"You know me as well as anyone—and better than most." She took a deep breath. "I honestly don't see any personal risk to DeAnn Evans in this plan. That said, I need a calm, rational perspective."

"Without being presumptuous about how you're handling last week, I see the Quinn I've always known—the one who used to beat my ass in every case we analyzed in graduate school. If anyone...the psychologist, your Chief, anyone—and no one has just so you know—had asked me if you were fit to return to work, I would have told them you are the last person they needed to worry about. So trust your gut."

"Thanks, Sam. Just for the record, is there something you *do* worry about related to me?"

He gave her a gentle smile. "There is. I worry that you won't cut yourself any slack and be human like the rest of us when crisis hits."

She rolled her desk chair forward and was almost knee to knee with him. "Thanks, Sam. We're done expressing regrets that we were never to be a couple for life, but I am always grateful you are my friend."

"For life."

"Thanks. I count on your honesty." She smiled. "You might be pleased to know that I've actually cut my parents some slack and trusted that they were mature enough and smart enough to know something about my work."

Sam sat up straight and clapped his hands. "Well, I'll be a son-of-a-gun. When did this happen?"

"Last week. They came and stayed a couple of nights and I've quit trying to hide the ugly side of what I do."

"How did your mother handle that?"

Quinn laughed. "She told me she couldn't promise she'd want to hear the horrid parts of what I have to deal with—but we have a new beginning."

"Good for you, Quinn. Good for you." His grin spread across his face.

Quinn settled back and let herself relax in the comfort of the mountain double speak.

Chapter 22

You gain strength, courage, and confidence by every experience in which you really stop to look fear in the face. You are able to say to yourself, 'I have lived through this horror. I can take the next thing that comes along.'
Eleanor Roosevelt

Detectives Workroom

"Ready?"

George, Kevin, DeAnn, and Sam quit talking and turned toward Quinn who was standing at the crime board.

"We agree that the connecting figure among the Young family, Roger, and Marcia—and by extension Christopher Cox—is Robert Calhoun. George, before the break you felt pretty strongly about another round with Marcia Fisher before we talk to Roger. Further thoughts?"

"Based on the registration of the vehicles, we're running Robert Calhoun. So far, nothing has popped on him. No question he's the linchpin."

Kevin snorted. "Kingpin is more like it." Heads nodded.

"Anyway," George picked up again. "Marcia appears to be the least seasoned of the two clear connections we have to Calhoun. So I think we try to find out what we can about him from Marcia."

On a clear part of the whiteboard, Quinn had drawn a Venn diagram of the connections. She tapped it with her dry erase marker. "George, any concerns about trying DeAnn's plan?"

"I think it's worth a shot."

"Kevin?"

"Seems to me she'll be off-guard—you know, not a formal interview, that kind of thing."

"Sam?" Quinn looked at him.

"No evidence she's involved in the drug side of this, so it's out of my playing field. As I listened to your strategy discussion, it seems solid."

"DeAnn, this is your idea. Any additional thoughts?"

"I'd love to try, ma'am. I verified what I would have to have stolen to constitute a Class E Felony, so I'm good."

Quinn raised an eyebrow. "Really? And what have you stolen?"

"An Apple Watch Ultra—$750.00 worth." She smiled.

Kevin tapped the table. "Aren't those under lock and key in most stores?"

DeAnn grinned. "Yes. However, our local jewelry store has three on display in individual plastic cases on the back counter. You'd be amazed at how fast I could grab one and run out the door."

Everyone laughed and the tension in the room broke. Quinn drew an arrow to Marcia and walked to the table. "Then show us what you've got Officer Evans."

DeAnn spent the next ten minutes going through her plan step-by-step. "Comments? Questions?"

"Sounds solid."

"Can't find any holes."

Sam nodded. "Not my show, but I think it will work."

Quinn said, "I think you'll be credible and relatable. I suggest this time-frame." She looked at her watch. "It's five after four. I agree with DeAnn that it's most likely to try such a crime just before closing—which for our local store is six p.m. That would have Matron putting DeAnn in a cell about seven. Kevin, you take seven to eleven; George, eleven to three; and I'll take three to seven. That work?"

Heads nodded.

"I suggest everyone head home, get some rest, and let's see if we can bait this hook. DeAnn please stay for just a minute."

Sam stood first. "Sounds like a plan, folks. I'm going to head out. Hopefully by morning we'll know if there is a connection to the drugs they took from Roger in South Carolina and what was in the convertible. Happy hunting...or fishing." He walked out the door.

Kevin and George wished DeAnn good luck and left.

"DeAnn, I am impressed with your plan. I talked with your sergeant and you are assigned to us for the time needed in this investigation."

"Thank you, ma'am. I don't mind being backup for the desk, but I love that I'm getting learn from you."

Quinn gave a slight nod of her head. "Glad to have you on our team. Now what do you need from me to get started?"

"I'm going home and get into clothes that make me believable, I hope, and get back here to get wired up."

"I spoke with Officer Gilbert in the tech unit and he's going to take care of it himself. So plan to meet with him at six. Then Matron will be expecting you."

"Yes, ma'am. Thanks, again, for the opportunity."

"Let's go catch a fish." Quinn rolled her eyes. *Not the best metaphor I could have chosen.*

1211 Sunrise

Quinn backed into her garage and was thinking about what she could eat for supper. She put her badge and service weapon in the safe by the kitchen door and walked toward the fridge. She took out her phone and sent a text: "Time to talk?"

Her phone buzzed before she could set it on the counter. She answered.

"I thought you'd never ask."

"Ha! Ha! Aren't you the funny one, Billy Williams."

"Been accused of it more than once. How's your day?"

"Getting longer by the minute."

"Oh." The disappointment came through in his voice. "I was hoping we could have supper together."

She opened the door to the fridge. "It's possible."

"Really?!" His tone shifted to excitement. "What time? What do you want? I'll pick it up?"

"I'll order from Asian Deli. What time can you pick it up?"

"What time can you be home?"

"I am home."

Billy was silent. "Quinn…is everything okay?"

She laughed. "It is. I should have told you. Sorry. I'm home because I have to be back in the station at three am."

"Well that will shoot a night's sleep all to…smithereens."

"I know the other word, Billy. In fact, I apparently used it when I almost dropped two bottles of tea opening the door to the lab—and Chuck heard me."

Billy laughed. "That's my detective. Okay, Asian Deli it is. Order it for five-thirty pickup."

Quinn looked at her watch. It was four forty-five. "You sure?"

"I'm walking out the door now."

"Okay. See you soon. Love you."

He stopped walking and smiled. *See how easy that was, Quinn.* "I love you, too. See you soon."

Quinn decided this would be a two shower night. *For sure I'll need one when I get up at two-thirty just to wake myself up.* She turned on the steam feature on her shower, undressed, walked in, and sat on her teak bench. She leaned against the wall and let the steam surround her.

She was reading a magazine in the great room when she heard the garage door open. She jumped up and ran to open the back door. She and Billy had their hands on the knob at the same time. When he tried to push it open, she pushed it closed.

"My, my. Someone's feeling feisty tonight." Billy used his shoulder and pushed the door.

She stepped back but held the door so he wouldn't fall through it. As he took the single step up from the garage, his shoulder still against the door, she kissed the top of his head.

Billy stopped, put the food on the counter, and pulled her into a hug. "If there were enough space here, I'd twirl you around the room." He gave her a long, slow kiss.

She hugged him tightly and returned the kiss. As she turned her head, her wet pony-tail hit the side of his neck. "Oh, Billy. I'm so sorry. I knew I should have dried my hair."

"I'll live." He winked at her. "Let's eat. I have strict orders from your favorite chef not to let the shrimp sit."

Quinn grabbed the food and started putting it on the plates she had set out.

Billy put his badge and gun in his safe and walked to the sink to wash his hands. "Okay if I have a beer?"

"Whatever you want. Iced tea for me, please." She took the plates into the great room and put them on the table.

Billy was right behind her. "One iced tea." He lifted his beer. "Cheers."

She clinked her glass to his beer mug. "Cheers." They sat down next to each other looking out the French doors to her back yard.

"How was your day?" They said it in unison.

Quinn started laughing. "Is this what happens to couples when they get to know each other well?"

"Perhaps. I wouldn't really know." He leaned over and kissed her cheek. "I promise we'll keep the spice in our lives."

She lifted her glass. "Deal. Now, how was your day?"

"Busy, but fruitful. Sam Nations was in the station today. Apparently there's not likely a link between our recent fentanyl haul and yours."

"I know. He must have come here from the Valley. Worrisome that there have been four different confiscations in the last week in our area."

"Seems ours was the biggest, but that doesn't make the smaller ones any less lethal."

Quinn took a bit of the shrimp korma. "Are Chad and Bella making any progress on their youth activity center?"

"They are. There's a large complex of sports fields and an activity building being designed. Seems Joshua, Carla, and James are spearheading the fundraising for it."

"Wow! That's great news. Amazing what the prospects of a child in the family will do for folks wanting their families to have safe places to engage in the world. Where is it?"

"That vacant land below the Tribal Center behind the library. The county owns it so the County Commission has approved the land use."

"That's great." Quinn took a bite of shrimp.

"What made you think of it?"

"Just that we spend our time trying to catch the people trying to poison our kids with drugs and Chad spoke many times of wanting to do preventive work."

"As Sheriff, he always felt his time had to focus on crime-fighting too. I think Bella helped him see that prevention is also fighting crime."

"Need to look more closely at Round City. Pretty sad I've lived here ten years and don't know any place other than the park across the street, the one downtown, and the one off of Maple..." she halted "Street."

Billy took her hand. "Good recovery. You, okay?" *Yes, love, that was where it happened. It will get easier.*

She squeezed his hand. "I'm good. Thanks. Now don't let this shrimp get cold." She took a bite. "You know I'm glad that my Asian Deli has now added some Indian curry dishes."

Billy lifted the shrimp on his fork. "Me, too." He bit into the shrimp.

They ate and chatted about the flowers blooming in the back yard, Billy's latest woodworking project, and the weather.

All nice safe subjects, Quinn. "Here let me clean up the dishes." He pointed to the magazine on the floor. "If I didn't know better, I'd say you were reading a magazine before a handsome prince entered your garage."

"Puh-leeze, spare me." She gave him her slowest, mountain, southern drawl. "Let's do the dishes together. I'd rather be with you."

"Many hands make light work."

"Arghhh, you are full of platitudes tonight."

"The better to charm you, my dear."

She swiped at his arm with the cloth napkin. "Stop it." She was laughing so hard she almost tripped as she turned toward the sink. She laughed even harder as she set down their glasses. She threw her arms around him and drew him into a long passionate kiss.

"You keep that up and the dishes can wait."

"They can." She took his hand and headed for her bedroom. She started skipping.

"Hey, stop. I never could skip." He was laughing now.

They entered her bedroom and fell on the bed. Billy reached across her for her alarm clock. "What time?"

"Two-twenty."

"In the morning?" He feigned disgust on his distorted face.

"Yes, love. In the morning. You are welcome to sleep in. Thanks for setting the clock." She set her phone, put it on the night stand, and turned her face to him.

He kissed her gently as he undid the buttons on her blouse. "I love you, Quinn Isaacs. I hope you know that."

She stretched her arms around him. "I do, Billy Williams. Now stop talking."

Round City Jail

DeAnn had been in the cell with Marcia for almost two hours. She made a show with the Matron about not belonging in jail.

"Leave it to the jury."

"Jury? I won't be in front of jury. You're nuts." DeAnn had pulled her arms away when the matron undid her cuffs.

"Little piece of advice, young lady. Cooperation goes a long way in here. You might start now."

"Yeah, yeah. Okay." DeAnn had rubbed her wrists and sat on the cot.

The matron left and muttered, "Class E Felony and she's whimpering about *my* jail."

DeAnn spent those first two hours lying on the cot, rolling over, getting up and walking the length of the cell. Then she pulled out the metal chair chained to the metal table. "Not even anything here to read or do."

Marcia stayed on the cot facing the wall.

"Hey, whatever your name is. Do they feed us?"

"At five. You missed it." Marcia never turned to look at DeAnn.

"What? I have to wait until breakfast?"

Marcia didn't answer.

Well this is going well. Hope Detective Millwood brought something interesting to read while he listens to the white noise.

DeAnn sat on the edge of the bed and started humming and tapping her hands on her legs. She sang to herself.

"Hey, what's that song?"

DeAnn ignored her. *Two can play your game, Marcia.* She continued to hum, "When I'm Gone." She had the rhythm of her taps down perfectly to match the popular version of the song where people use cups.

"Hey, my name's Marcia."

DeAnn continued singing softly and shifted the tapping to the side of the metal bunk.

"Okay, okay. I'm sorry I was rude. My name's Marcia."

"Yeah, so you said." DeAnn went back to singing.

Marcia tried to imitate the tapping but her beat was off.

DeAnn stopped, looked across at Marcia, and held up her hands. "If you want to do it, it's like this. Clap, clap, slap, slap, slap, clap."

Marcia did three claps before she did a slap on the side of the metal bunk.

DeAnn slid over on her bunk so she was directly opposite Marcia. "Look. Let's do it slow. Clap...clap...slap...slap...slap, clap." She moved her hands and watched Marcia who was staring at her hands. "Good, you got that part. If we were in the real world, and not this dump, we'd have a cup."

"That's it. I knew I'd heard it. It's the 'Cup song.' Right?" Marcia smiled.

"Unless you're from the mountains."

"What do you mean? It was in a movie."

"Yeah, the clapping part was, but the song is an oldie from these mountains. Ever hear of the Carter family?"

"Are you kidding? I'm a huge Johnny Cash fan—I'm into melancholy."

"Well two points for you. But Johnny Cash married June Carter who is from the Carter family—anyway, we were singing this song long before the movie. Now you want to learn this or not?"

The two young women spent the next few minutes perfecting the clap sequence until DeAnn held her hand up. "Okay, I think you've got it. Do you know the words?"

"Most of them. You start."

DeAnn started clapping and tapping. Marcia joined in. They both started singing the song.

About half-way through, Marcia stopped. DeAnn sang a few more lines and stopped. "What's the matter? Forget the words?"

"No. I forgot where I was."

"Isn't that the point?" DeAnn rolled her eyes. She leaned toward Marcia, "My boyfriend will have hightailed it out of here. I got caught shoplifting a stupid Apple Watch Ultra which he just had to have. SOOO...the words of this song are going to become my calling card."

"Well, maybe we'll go sing it together on stage in some hick bar. I'm pretty sure my boyfriend is smart enough to figure out I used him."

"Really?" DeAnn leaned further and almost fell off the bed. *Couldn't have planned that one and it was perfect.* She tried not to smile. "What'd you do?"

"Not important. Look, let's try this one more time. Then I can go to sleep with it in my head."

Maybe you'll open up... DeAnn started the clapping and tapping again.

They finished the song and Marcia rolled over on the bed, faced the wall, and kicked it.

"Get some sleep, Marcia. Tomorrow's a new day." DeAnn rolled over on her back, bent her knees, and put her hands behind her head. *Hope you change your mind so the matron doesn't have to wake up the whole place with an alarm. I hope I can stay awake.*

Round City Jail – 2:45 a.m.

George turned as Quinn entered the small room off the matron's office where they had a listening station for the wire on DeAnn.

"Morning."

"Morning, Quinn. Get some sleep?"

"I did. Did you?"

"Could have slept here it's been so quiet. Hopeful… ." he held up his finger.

"Well, go on. Get some sleep. See you a little later in the morning."

"Wait. Hear that?"

"Sounds like tapping?"

"Yeah." He grinned. In barely a whisper, so as not to miss what was happening, he said, "DeAnn connected with her about nine o'clock over a song. Then Marcia stopped talking."

"So, what's the tapping?"

"The good news is if this is as accurate as our tech guru says, it's coming from Marcia's bunk." He held up his finger again. "Hear it? Now it's coming from both bunks. Go, DeAnn."

I can't wait to hear what this is all about. Quinn sat down and moved closer to the table. She focused on the tapping. *I've read about prisoners using codes. Is that what this is?* She listened for a pattern.

On a pad of paper on the table she wrote: "Cup Song?"

George nodded. He wrote: "I'm staying."

Quinn drew a smiley face on the pad of paper.

Marcia started singing.

DeAnn sat up on the side of the bed. She sang softly and continued the tapping and clapping to the song.

Marcia stopped at the end of a verse. "So, what do you say? Shall we leave?"

"What?" DeAnn acted surprised. "If that cop who interviewed me is right, I could be looking at one to six years in prison." She leaned forward.

"My stupid boyfriend said it was a misdemeanor—slap on the wrist if you return the item."

"Did you?"

"Did I, what?"

"Return the item?"

"Yeah. The cop has it."

"Then they'll let you go unless you have a record."

"How do you know?"

"Family history."

"Ha. First I'd have to have a family—to have any history, that is."

"Where's your family, DeAnn?"

"Damned if I know. I was in and out of foster homes until the state had to set me free at eighteen. I managed to get into Tennessee Tech."

"Did you graduate?"

"Yes. In music. Wanted to work in Nashville."

"Ah, now I get the singing part."

"I wasn't a voice major." DeAnn stopped. "What about you? Did music bring you to Tennessee? You have a good voice."

"If only. I got my boyfriend to bring me up here to run a drone over some property for my uncle."

"Wow! Really? How cool is that? You can really fly a drone?"

"Yeah. Not difficult. It's fun though and I can get pretty wrapped up in it."

"Then how'd you get in here. Sounds pretty normal to me. What kind of property? I mean you weren't trying to get national secrets or anything, right?" DeAnn laughed.

"Hardly. I crossed a 'no trespassing' sign."

"Seriously? What's the big deal about that?" DeAnn waited a few seconds. "I mean did the property owner call the cops?"

"Nope. The cops were already there—crime scene."

DeAnn widened her eyes. "Did you know it was a crime scene?"

"Kinda. Hard to miss the yellow tape."

"Then why did you cross it?"

"If you knew my Uncle Bob, you'd know why."

"Oh, crap. One of those." DeAnn pulled her pillow in front of her and hugged it.

Marcia sat with her elbows on her knees and her chin in her hands. "Yeah."

DeAnn clapped her hands together. "Hey, my boyfriend—ha, ex-boyfriend—spent hours and hours watching all those cop shows. I did, too, just to be with him when I wasn't working. Can't you tell the cops your uncle made you do it?"

Marcia looked across at DeAnn. "You are naïve. How old are you?"

"Twenty-six. You?"

"Twenty-eight. You don't look twenty-six."

"My last foster mom would say I don't act it either. Guess I wouldn't be here if I did. I was so stupid. I tried to tell him I was saving to buy him the damn watch. Apparently while I was waitressing to make enough to pay for the lousy motel room we lived in, he was out scouting stores."

"Men. Can't live with them—can't live without them."

"Ha. I'm ready to try." DeAnn made a show of hugging her pillow tighter. The light from the hall outside their cell cast shadows on the wall making her look like a troll. "So, about your uncle. What're you gonna do?"

"I think I'm going to see if the lady detective will help me get away from him."

Quinn had been leaning on her forearms. "Let's go. The recording will continue. Let's strike while the iron's hot."

Quinn stepped out of the small office. "Matron, I want George to go with you to get Marcia Fisher. Now."

"Yes, ma'am."

Quinn grabbed a bottle of water and went to interview Room One while George and the matron went down the short hallway to a locked door. The two women were in the first cell which was isolated from the others.

George stepped in. "Let's go Ms. Fisher. My boss wants to see you now."

DeAnn pulled her legs up onto the bed and slid into the corner away from the commotion.

George looked over at her. "You. Don't move."

"No, sir. I won't." DeAnn tried to make herself small.

The matron had the cuffs and was about to put on the ankle chains.

"Leave them off. Orders from Detective Isaacs."

The matron shrugged and stepped back. "She's all yours."

George pointed toward the door. "Let's go. And don't try anything with those feet." He shut the door behind them and walked toward Room One. "Don't know why you're so special you get to have your feet free."

Marcia walked along the short hall.

George opened the door to Room One.

Chapter 23

Success is a collection of problems solved.

I.M. Pei

Interview Room One

"Sorry to wake you, Marcia." Quinn smiled at the young woman and turned the lid on the water. "Detective, please uncuff, Ms. Fisher."

"But, Detective Isaacs... . "

"Detective." She let it hang in the air.

"Yes, ma'am." He leaned down and uncuffed Marcia's cuffs from her waist chain and stepped back.

"The cuffs, Detective—now." *Sorry, George. That was a bit sharper than I meant it to be.*

George unlocked the cuffs and whispered to Marcia. "Don't you dare try anything."

"Detective. Have a seat." Quinn glowered and nodded toward the chair.

George made a point of scraping the chair against the concrete floor when he moved it.

Quinn ignored him. "As I said, Marcia. Sorry to wake you, but I was awakened a little while ago by our district attorney. I just need to get this on the record."

"This is Detective Isaacs of the Round City Police..." she pointed to George.

"Detective Marshall of the Round City Police."

She pointed to Marcia.

"Marcia Fisher." Without prompting she gave her address and date of birth. Then she looked at Quinn. "And I don't want an attorney."

"Thank you for cooperating, Marcia. Anyway, I got here as quickly as I could. Detective Marshall was on duty, but I wanted to be the one to tell you this." She glanced over at George.

"Why is a district attorney calling you in the middle of the night?" Marcia squinted her eyes.

"Because everyone has a boss and hers called her at that hour."

"So the district attorney is your boss?"

"No. But that really doesn't matter. She's the one who controls what charges are finally filed against you."

"Oh."

"It seems another one of your uncle's...uh...relatives has been arrested in our mountains." Quinn was very careful in how she said the next part. "There has been a significant amount of cash and very lethal fentanyl confiscated." She stopped.

"Whoa. I don't know anything about that!"

"Really? Apparently he told the SBI—sorry, State Bureau of Investigation agent—that you were up here working for his uncle, too."

Marcia squeezed the bottle of water causing some of it to spill on the table. She took her hand and wiped it onto the floor.

Quinn ignored the water.

Marcia leaned forward. "I was wrong to cross that property line. I know that. But, I have nothing to do with any murder—or drugs—or cash—or whatever else." She took a deep breath. "If you don't help me get a new name and a new place to live, Uncle Bob will have me killed." A tear fell on the table. "I mean it."

"Because you got arrested for breaking the law?"

"No matter what I say, he'll believe I squealed on the family. There's no way on earth you live if you do that."

"Where is your Uncle Bob?"

"Probably in South Carolina. He mostly handles things by burner phones."

Quinn knew George was watching and listening with an intensity that he would be able to quote Marcia verbatim.

"Then why did he send you to Tennessee?"

"I told you the truth. To videotape the property."

"Is that all the truth?"

Marcia lowered her head. "Yes, but not all the information."

Quinn waited.

"Part of his control over the family comes with making sure you know something really bad happened to someone in the family who didn't follow his orders..." She gulped water from the bottle, "and if you don't do what he says, that's what will happen to you—only worse."

Quinn leaned in and spoke in a quiet and caring way. "Marcia, what happened that has you so scared?"

Marcia glanced at George who was looking at the floor. "I don't know who lived in that house, but they were family members." She took another drink. "That's why I knew I had to cross the crime scene tape." She set the water bottle on the table and rubbed her eyes with her sleeve. "Please, you have to help me."

"I can't make any deals with you, Marcia. That's the job of the District Attorney—that's why she called me. If you tell me everything you know about the family's operations and how your uncle runs things, she is willing to talk about a deal and work with the FBI to get you into witness protection."

"No, no, no. Don't you get it? Everyone in the family knows he has people everywhere who can get information if one of us is arrested. Just going to jail can get you seriously hurt—if he thinks you're still useful to the family—if not, then you get dead."

Why aren't we finding anything on this Robert Calhoun besides property records and automobiles? What's his...

"Marcia. What is Uncle Bob's last name?"

"Calhoun."

"No, I mean his real last name. Calhoun is the name used for the family." She said it with as much conviction as stating her own name.

Marcia looked up at her. The pulse in her carotid arteries was beating so hard it was visible. She whispered, "Do you know?"

"What is his real name, Marcia? This is really important to help you get a deal." Quinn kept her gaze on the young woman.

"No one in the family is really a Calhoun—like my parents are Fishers. Uncle Bob is a Carter. Robert is his real first name, but none of the older folks use anything but Calhoun when doing the family business." She gave a nervous laugh. "Heck, we're not even family biologically as far as I know."

"Does Uncle Bob have a middle name?" Quinn kept her voice calm and steady.

"Oh, yeah. He makes sure every member of the family knows who he is: Robert Kemp Carter. And we know the penalty for giving that name to anyone." She slumped in her chair and drew her finger across her throat.

Quinn saw the gesture. "One more question."

"How old is he?"

"Around fifty. My mother remembers when he took over the family."

Quinn wanted to explore that bit of information, but for now she knew they had much more important things to find out.

"Marcia, I'm going to let you go back to bed while I talk with the District Attorney. The Matron will get you up and make sure you have breakfast before we meet with her to talk about your plea deal—and your protection."

"Sure. Whatever." Her voice was barely audible.

"I'll ask the matron to move the young woman who is in with you. I want you to feel safe."

"No. Please don't. She's nice." Then she glanced at George and then Quinn. "Do you think I'm in danger from her?"

Quinn tapped the table with her nail to get Marcia to look at her. "Marcia, look at me. She's a local girl who made a bad decision. She's a waitress and she sings at one of the local bars. Has Nashville ambitions, I think." She turned toward George. "Is that right?"

"Yes, ma'am. Pretty good voice on her. She might get there."

"Okay. I have to trust you at this point. I'll take your word for it." She stared into Quinn's eyes. "Please tell me you'll help me."

"I promise you I will do everything I can to help you. Go get some sleep." She turned to George. "Detective." *Marcia, you have no idea how safe you are with your cell mate.*

George stood and walked toward the table. "Have to cuff you. It's protocol."

Marcia held her hands out.

"Detective Isaacs ending interview."

"Detective Marshall leaving interview with..."

"Marcia Fisher." Marcia jumped in before he could say her name.

Quinn followed them out and headed straight for the Detectives Workroom.

Detectives Workroom

Quinn was at the computer when George walked in. "Find anything?"

"Just got logged in." She typed: "Robert Kemp Carter"

"Were you surprised she gave it up so easily?"

"Hard to know. I think DeAnn Evans made a significant difference in it happening."

"How's that? I mean—granted she managed it well, but is there something in particular?"

"Maybe DeAnn came across as just normal enough for Marcia to think she could have a life outside the family."

"Hmmm...good point."

"Let me watch this screen. Want to get us coffee? You fly, I'll buy."

"I think I can handle the break room coffee price since you guys are out of coffee pods on that fancy new machine in the lab. Back in a few." He stepped out of the workroom and headed down the hall.

Quinn sent herself a note to buy coffee pods. *Please let the name be right.* She got her first hit. George opened the door.

"Come on, George. We've got something."

He passed her coffee across the table and sat down.

Quinn put the image up on the screen and started to scroll.

"Slow down. I flunked speed reading in high school." George laughed.

"Sorry. I want to get to something that…Bingo. Look." She used her cursor to point to an entry. She started making notes.

So did George.

"I need a break." Quinn stood up and looked at the wall clock. It was five-thirty in the morning. "George, you should go downstairs and get some sleep. I'd tell you to go home, but once I talk to Peggy O'Haire, we may be moving fast."

George was standing by the window drinking the last cold sip of coffee.

They both turned when they heard the chirp of the lock on the door. Then the tap as it opened.

"Good morning, Chief." Quinn nodded to Jill Hansen.

"Good morning, Detectives. Looks like a long night."

"We both had some down time. Want an update?"

They ran through the use of DeAnn Evans in the cell, what happened in the interview with Marcia, and the search they were still trying to process.

The Chief nodded. "Well, he may not be on the Ten Most Wanted List by the FBI, but sounds like you may have located someone the FBI is going to be very interested in finding."

"So am I." Quinn glanced at George. "We were about to take a break and then strategize next best steps."

"Have preliminary thoughts?"

"Yes, ma'am." She outlined them for the Chief.

"Let me know if you need help with the FBI. You've built your contacts at SBI, so that shouldn't be a problem."

"Ma'am, I've worked with Agent Bill Michaels, a regional FBI agent. Okay to start with him?"

"Good choice. Need anything else. Let me know. Now both of you go home for an hour or two, no less. That's an order." She left the room.

"Well, Detective Marshall, we've been given a direct order. I'm headed home to stand in a very hot shower, stop at my favorite bakery and buy breakfast, and I'll be here by seven."

"Well, Detective Isaacs, I can follow orders and I'm going home to take a hot shower, call my wife who owns that very fine bakery, and ask her to have our breakfast ready. I'll stop and have five minutes with her, pick up our breakfast, and be here by seven."

They walked out the back door together.

Quinn's House

Quinn backed into the driveway but didn't put her SUV in the garage. She ran up to the porch and put the code in the front door. She opened the door and was about to close it when she heard Billy.

"Halt. Who goes there?" He was coming out of the kitchen dressed for work.

"What? No weapon?"

"Was about to get it when I heard the door lock. I saw your SUV out the side window so wasn't too worried about it. Good morning, lovely lady."

She kissed him and took his hand. "Good morning. I'm headed to the shower. Do you have to leave right this minute?"

"No, if I'm out of here by six-thirty or so, I'm good."

"Perfect. I'm going to run shower and change. Any chance of having a cup of coffee together after?"

"I'll make you breakfast." Billy squeezed her hand.

"Thanks, but George is bringing breakfast to the office."

"Oh, sure. You'd rather breakfast from Sweet Creations than Billy Williams' fine cooking." He laughed. "Me, too."

She put her badge and service weapon in her safe and turned for her bedroom.

He kissed her and then patted her on her bottom. "Go. Shower. I'll make real coffee for you."

She was taking her clothes off as she went.

He stood watching her. *Not fair, Quinn. Not fair.* He watched anyway.

Fifteen minutes later she walked in the kitchen and Billy whistled. "Wow! You seeing another guy?"

She put her hands on her hips. "What is *that* supposed to mean?" She tried to look angry.

"Bad compliment. I apologize. Let me try again. You look stunning, love of my life." *You would look good in sack cloth as my grandmother used to say. But...those expensive suits you wear the way I wear jeans make you a knock out.*

She kissed him on the cheek. "Redeemed." She sniffed. "And the coffee helps."

They sat at the counter and she gave him the overview of the night and the morning search.

"Sounds like you're on a roll. I know Sam said it's unlikely these fentanyl packets are connected to the same source. If something turns up, I can be back over here in thirty minutes—or less with my lights."

"Don't know enough at the moment. You know I will call you if there is." She ran her finger down his cheek. "Or I might just call you for no reason." She smiled.

He leaned over and kissed her. "You can call me anytime."

"Same to you. I hate to drink and run, but duty calls."

They both stood.

She put her arms around his neck. "Thanks for loving me. I was so caught up in the information we found that it never occurred to me you would still be here." She kissed him softly. "I'm glad you were."

"I'm glad I were, too." He winked.

She gently slapped his hand. "Lucky for you I'm not an English teacher." She headed for her safe and put on her badge and service weapon. "Come on, I'm not superstitious. I'll go out a different door than the one I entered."

They walked into the garage together and she kissed him. "Be safe and take care of my detective."

"Quinn, thanks for loving me. You take care of *my* detective."

"I'll do my best. Later." She walked to her SUV, got in, and drove down the driveway.

Billy followed her and realized she had hit the garage door button. *Oh, Quinn, if you had more time I'd drive you nuts by opening the door again.* He chuckled and turned the opposite direction and headed for the Valley.

Detectives Workroom

Quinn walked through the back door of the station at six fifty-one. She went straight to the workroom and took out her secure phone.

"Jackson."

"Good morning, Agent."

"Good morning to you, Quinn. Trust this is a social call."

"I wish." She filled him in on what was happening.

"Agent Davis is back in the office. I'll send her your way and she can muster anyone else you need. Safe to assume you're calling in the FBI, too?"

"Yes, sir. I'll try to reach Agent Michaels as soon as we hang up."

"I'll let you know when to expect Davis."

"Thanks. Appreciate the help. Don't forget to come visit."

"I was just there…" He hesitated. "Take care of yourself Quinn."

"Hopefully it can be a time when you're here to enjoy our fine little town." *I know you were going to say I was just there on Friday—for a funeral.*

"Sure thing, Quinn. Talk to you soon."

He knew—and I knew—what he was thinking. Hope my voice sounded normal. She forgot she had dialed Agent Michaels at the FBI.

"Michaels."

"Sir, this is Quinn Isaacs with the Round City Police."

"Hey, Quinn. I heard you had left Immigration. Lead detective is the rumor. That right?"

"Yes, sir."

"Congratulations. Hope you aren't getting a baptism by fire in your first year."

"Sir, I had it in my first week." *To say nothing of the last week and a half.*

"Well, then you're seasoned. What can I do for you?"

"Do you have a few minutes so I can tell you what we're dealing with here?"

"Hold on. Let me grab fresh coffee and sit down. You liking the work?"

"It's challenging, which I love. Good folks here. I'm learning so many things I'd never have learned in Immigration. More than that, it lets me live here in a place that's been home for ten years."

"Then you can't beat that. I like living in Knoxville which is my hometown. No desire to head to D.C. Don't see the appeal. Okay, got my coffee and I'm at my desk. What's up?"

Quinn was in the middle of giving him the run down when George and Kevin walked in. She salivated at the teal box which she knew would hold some delicious pastry from Carrie.

Agent Michaels cleared his throat. "I've got the record up on my screen. What's your plan?"

"We need to make one. Do you have someone who can join us? I just heard from Agent Jackson at SBI and he's sending Agent Davis. She's in Maryville and will be here in forty minutes."

"I can be there in an hour."

"Sir, I wasn't expecting you to…I mean, I'm honored, but…"

"Quinn, relax. I can deploy whoever we need—to do whatever needs to be done. See you in an hour."

"Thank you, sir."

"It's Bill, Quinn. Bill is fine."

"Thanks, Bill." The call ended.

George put a plate in front of her. "Breakfast is served. Sounds like we have some big wigs coming."

"From the FBI, yes. And the good news from the SBI is that Sandy Davis can join us. Good morning, Kevin."

"Morning." He lifted his coffee mug.

"Let's eat, get our ducks in a row, and be ready for the SBI and FBI within the hour."

Round City Jail

DeAnn was sitting on the edge of her bunk when they brought breakfast. *I'm starved. Hope I can get through this meal. Glad they're not putting her in with the general population.* The tray slid through the opening in the bars.

"You." The woman pointed at DeAnn. "Matron said to tell you to be ready for interview this morning."

"Yeah, sure." DeAnn didn't look up.

Marcia stood up and took her tray. "Looks better than lunch yesterday."

The jailer moved on into the next area banging the outside door behind her.

DeAnn picked up the egg biscuit. "It's hot. I thought we'd get cardboard for biscuits."

"Better enjoy it while we can."

"How'd you sleep?"

"Fitfully. Don't you remember? They took me out of here at some ungodly hour."

DeAnn stretched. "Oh, yeah. Guess I fell sound asleep when you left."

"Lucky you."

"I've never been interviewed. Is it bad?"

"Just cooperate. I didn't. It'll make it worse if you don't."

"Is that why they came and got you in the middle of the night?" DeAnn's eyes were wide.

"Maybe." She took a bite of the egg sandwich and chewed.

DeAnn lowered her voice. "I was afraid we'd have to go eat with a bunch of really bad criminals. I'm glad we're in here."

"Yeah. Me, too." Marcia took another bite.

DeAnn took a bite of her biscuit and ate without saying another word.

Chapter 24

We have all known the long loneliness and we have learned that the only solution is love and that love comes with community.

Dorothy Day

Round City Police Station

Quinn went straight to her office and picked up the phone and dialed the DA.

"O'Haire."

"Hey, Peggy."

"What's up at this hour, Quinn?"

"You mean you slept while I used your name in vain at four a.m.?"

"Ohhh...what now?"

Quinn filled her in.

"You can use my name in vain anytime to get those results. What do you need from me?"

"Not sure at the moment, but wanted you to know in case we need warrants for anything."

"I have a hearing at ten, but it should be short. Just text me and I'll call as soon as I can."

"Thanks, Peggy."

"Quinn," she took a breath "you're amazing and I'm really glad you're back on the job. Just please don't push yourself. Sounds like even the FBI has been looking for this guy for a long time."

"Thanks for the support, Peggy. I do need reminders—especially right now—but my head's in a good place. I feel like I can say this to you—I'm sorry I couldn't save Officer Simmons—truly, I am. I also know that one way I can honor him is to pursue what he unwittingly unleashed in a simple traffic stop."

"Good girl. Just take time for a breather every once in a while."

"I will. I promise. Thanks, Peggy. Means a lot."

"We women in law enforcement have to help each other."

"I know. I'm lucky. There are some pretty good men in law enforcement helping me, too."

"True that. Now go. Talk to you soon."

"You, too." She ended the call. *I do have some good men and women helping me on reentry. Wonder if astronauts need help readjusting to earth when they return?*

There was a knock on her office door. She stood and opened it. "Come in."

"Hey, Quinn. Just wanted to tell you I'm here. Anything I need to be doing besides what I'm already doing?"

"Morning, Chuck. I think we're moving ahead. Anything left on the Simmons's case or Young residence?"

"Nope. You have all the reports from our team and the SBI."

"Including the one on the truck that was blown up?"

He nodded.

"Sam Nations told us late yesterday there are three other cases involving fentanyl in the area, but none of them have the xylazine. So, they are not being considered linked to ours—at least at the moment."

"Good to know."

"We've had what may be a break in the Young murders and the drugs and cash."

"Yeah?" Chuck's eyes lit up. "Can you tell me?"

"Chuck, you can know anything in a case unless we've locked it down for some reason. Bottom line is we have the SBI and FBI coming any minute now. We may have a lead on the head of this 'family.'"

"You mean that Calhoun guy?"

Quinn nodded. "Now we have a legitimate name."

Chuck whistled. "Good work, Quinn."

"Team work. You study the physical evidence, we detectives slog through the evidence and data we can find, and together—if we play our hand right—we might solve a case."

"Sounds to me like you might solve cases for lots of folks."

"Not willing to bet on that hand yet. Anyway, I have to get the conference room set up. I'll call if we need you."

"Thanks, Quinn. Glad you're back."

She smiled at Chuck and walked out the door. "Thanks, Chuck. Me, too." *That's the second 'glad you're back' in ten minutes. I'm so happy to be in a place where people care about the work and each other.*

Getting Ready

She opened the door to the conference room just as her secure phone buzzed. Her eyes widened as she saw that the room was set up, pastries were on a tray, and fresh coffee was brewing. *Yeah, I'm really glad to be in a place where people care about the work and each other.*

"Isaacs."

"Ma'am. You have two visitors at the front desk: Agent Michaels and Agent Davis."

"I'll be right up." She turned and almost ran into George and Kevin coming in the door.

"Thanks for setting things up. I'm glad we're on the same team."

"Us, too. We were just talking about that. Right, Kevin?"

"Yep. Feels good to be productive and respected."

Quinn blushed. She knew the reputation of the former lead detective was as a control freak. *Like my boss at Immigration. Well...sorta.* "Well, our guests are here. I'm headed to get them."

She walked to the door that opened into the reception area. The officer on duty pushed the button to release the lock.

"Agent Michaels. Agent Davis. Thanks for coming." She extended her hand to shake.

"Excited to learn what's been going on since I left." Sandy Davis shook her hand.

"Thanks for inviting me. Sorry for your loss." Agent Michaels extended his hand.

"Thank you for coming. We're in the conference room." Quinn's hand moved to touch her badge with the black band. She stopped herself and shook his hand. "This way."

"Detective Isaacs." The voice came from the front desk.

Quinn turned toward the duty officer. "Agent Nations is here."

"Sandy, would you mind showing Agent Michaels where the Conference Room is?"

"No problem. We probably both need to stop in the hall first." She smiled at Quinn.

"I'm so sorry. Of course. I'll be right with you." She turned as the door opened for Sam.

"Got your text. What's up?" Sam looked ahead and saw the two agents headed toward the restrooms.

"Big guns."

"Yeah. Including you." She smiled at him. "Thanks for coming. Stop off in the hall if you'd like and then join us in the conference room."

"Thanks. I'll do just that."

Quinn took her phone and sent a text: "Ready for you in five minutes."

"10-4." The reply was immediate.

Conference Room

Just as everyone had their coffee and pastry, were seated, and introductions made, the door opened. Everyone stood up.

"Sit, please. Thank you for coming." Chief Hansen shook hands with the agents from the State Bureau of Investigation, the Federal Bureau of Investigation, and Drug Enforcement Agency. "I won't delay your meeting. I want you to know we appreciate your support and I have no doubt with this team we can solve our local cases—and it would appear we may contribute to cases impacting your work. The full resources of my office are at your disposal." She turned and left the room.

"I want to add to the Chief's comments. Thank you for coming and I apologize for the early hour. George will get you up to speed."

George gave a thumbnail sketch starting with the traffic stop. He ended with the name they received from Marcia Fisher: Robert Kemp Carter.

"Questions or comments?" Quinn looked at each person around the table.

Sandy Davis spoke first. "Is the officer still in the cell with Marcia?"

"She is."

She nodded.

Bill Michaels lifted a finger in the air. "Am I correct you haven't interviewed Roger Calhoun Young?"

Quinn nodded. "That's correct. As you know, we can hold him for thirty days on the warrant from South Carolina and we made a decision as a team to see what more we could get from Marcia."

Sam jumped in. "How much longer are you holding Christopher Cox?"

"I'll take that one." Eyes turned to Kevin. "We have seventy-two without charging him. He's only been arrested on facilitating a misdemeanor. In two hours, he'll have been here forty-eight of those. So I assume we'll decide based on our work here."

Quinn nodded and smiled at Kevin.

Questions and answers, mostly to clarify points George had made, went around the table.

Quinn looked around the table. "Anything else? Feel free to jump in at any time, but we need to finalize these details. George will take any of you who want to see the crime board to the workroom when we finish. Kevin, will you please put the list we're going to generate on the screen so we can all see it?"

"Yes, ma'am." He had a document open on the computer and projected it on the screen.

"I'll start and then each of you can add or edit as needed. Here are the takeaways:

1. Bill will be given the paperwork on notification of Sonia Young's daughters in Ohio and the registered letter we have ready. He will send agents who will also interview the daughters.

2. Sandy will check with the SBI folks who have been working with our ME to see if they have verified the age of the two male bodies in the morgue so we know who is who.

3. Sandy will set up a liaison with South Carolina on their outstanding warrant on Roger Calhoun Young.

4. Sandy will coordinate a joint team with Bill who will go to Sevierville to see if we can find Robert Calhoun AKA Robert Kemp Carter.

5. George will coordinate a joint team with our DA and an FBI agent, to be named by Bill, for her interview and deal offer with Marcia Fisher.

6. Sam will work with Bill on the FBI history on Robert Kemp Carter and his record of drug dealing."

Quinn stopped and looked at the wording on the document Kevin had typed as she spoke. *Almost verbatim. Good job, Kevin.*

"Additions? Edits?"

All eyes were on the screen.

Quinn took a drink of water and studied the faces. *Oh how I'd love to know what you are thinking.* "Yes, Sandy?"

"When are you planning to interview Roger Young?"

"Although the DA reached out to authorities in South Carolina, they have not gotten back with us. I really want to go into that interview with as much information as we can gather. As you know, we can hold him up to thirty days just on the warrant. So, let's see what today yields and go from there."

"Sounds reasonable. Maybe we just put him on the list to be interviewed so we all have that in mind."

"Done. Thanks." Quinn pointed at the screen. "Kevin?"

"Uh, Quinn. Are you going to be in the interview with the DA and Marcia?"

"That's up to the team. I think George has a good handle on how Marcia responds and we'll finalize that interview when the DA and Bill are ready."

Finally, Bill Michaels spoke. "This may sound extraneous, but leadership matters. I worked with Quinn on a case over in the Valley and I was impressed then. The attention to detail here is commendable. You should all be proud." He was nodding his head and smiling. "I'll get our folks on notification and interview of the sisters in Ohio and start the wheels rolling to see what we can offer Ms. Fisher." He stopped. "It will, of course, depend on how useful what she has to say is to any case the FBI has. You know that, right?"

Heads nodded.

Quinn wanted it on the record that they all knew why. "As you know, Tennessee does not have a state witness protection program. Given the search for Robert Kemp Carter from the FBI level, there may be a way." She looked at Bill. "We will appreciate anything you can do to facilitate it. If my hunch is right about the deaths of Sonia and the male Young in the house, she is justified in being afraid."

Sandy jumped in. "Do you think Roger Young is responsible for their deaths?"

"I think someone in the 'family' is." She put air quotes around the word family. *And it just may be the elusive Robert Kemp Carter.*

"Anything else?"

"No."

"Not here."

"Let's get this rolling."

Quinn held up her hand with her palm out. "Thanks. Everyone knows what to do. Kevin and I will be available to any team. Just ask. We'll meet here for an update at two p.m. That work for everyone?"

Everyone nodded.

"Then let's get to it." Quinn pushed back her chair and reached out her hand to Bill Michaels. "Thank you. You're welcome to use this room to work."

"Good deal. I'll go down and see the crime board and be back."

"Sandy, thanks. You good to work in the Detectives Workroom?"

"Sure. I'll connect with George." The women shook hands.

"Sam, what do you need?"

"Some time with Bill. We'll handle it. Thanks, Quinn." He leaned in to shake her hand and spoke softly. "Good job. Always knew you were best in the class."

Quinn felt the red rising in her face. "Thanks, Sam. Thanks." She shook his hand.

Kevin stopped as he and Quinn were the last in the room. "Thanks, Quinn. I always hoped I could work in a department of top-notch folks who could respect each other and get the job done. Of course I never imagined we'd have cases that were more than our local petty crime and domestic abuse, but I guess times are changing everywhere."

"Thank you, Kevin. It's a pleasure to be part of a great team. Thanks for all you've done on this very complicated and convoluted set of cases." She shook his hand. "Now, I'd appreciate it if you'd make sure our guests know how to reach you. Call me if you need me."

Kevin walked out of the room and Quinn sighed. She walked over to the counter and smiled at seeing there were still pastries in the teal box. She picked up the box and walked down the hall to the Chief's office.

"Morning, Ms. Leonard. Thought you and the Chief might enjoy a pastry from Sweet Creations."

Ms. Leonard looked up from her desk. "Thank you, Detective. I'll see that the Chief gets them."

"You, too." Quinn winked at her and walked out.

Quinn's Office

Quinn entered the lab and saw Chuck bent over a microscope with his earbuds in. She went in her office and shut the door.

She looked at the time on her computer and saw it was ten after nine. She took out her personal phone and opened her contacts. She chose the number and it rang.

"*Hola, hija. ¿Cómo estás?*"

"Hey, Daddy. I'm well. How are you and Mother?"

"We're well and enjoying the break from teaching."

"I just wanted to let you know I'm doing fine. I can't believe it's Wednesday already and I haven't called."

"Billy called to check on us yesterday. He said you were doing well."

Quinn felt her heart race. *Billy called to check on you? Oh, you are a jewel, Billy Williams.*

"That was nice of him."

"Yes, your mother and I like him very much. He and your mother chatted for some time."

"Good. Is she there?"

"No, she's at the hairdresser. I'll tell her you called. She'll be disappointed she missed you."

"I'll try to call her later today. Big case right now and there are lots of irons in the fire."

"You just do what you need to do, *hija*. Take care of yourself, too. If you have another minute, I'd like to ask you something."

"Sure, Daddy. What's up?" *Why is always so much easier to talk to him than Mother?*

"You know we go to Spain after the spring semester at the university. We have our tickets to go next week, but I don't want to…"

"Oh, Daddy, go. Please. I'm doing fine and I'm glad to be back in a routine. Your annual trip will just make that routine seem more real."

"If you're sure."

"I am."

"You know we can be home in hours if you need us."

Quinn felt the warmth of the smile in his voice. "I always need you, Daddy—and, Mother. I just haven't always let you in—or let you know it. I'm trying to do better."

"That's my girl. We love you. Now go stop crime. I love you."

"I love you, too. Give Mother a kiss for me and tell her I love her. I'll talk to you before you leave."

"That's great. *Ciao.*"

She loved that he used the Italian good-bye. *I suppose it's become universal these days. Ciao.* She smiled and turned to her computer and entered her password to work through her emails.

Robert Kemp Carter who are you? Where are you?

An hour later she stretched, rubbed her eyes, and drank from her Yeti cup. *Administrative emails finished. Wonder if folks are being kind to me this week. Didn't seem like as many as usual.* She walked into the lab with her mug.

"Hey, Quinn. Didn't know you were in here. Got a minute?"

"Sure. I was just going to make a cup of coffee."

"Go ahead. I'll pull this up."

Quinn made her coffee. "Want some?"

"I'm good."

"Thanks for the new coffee pods. I have it on my phone to get some." She gave him a sheepish look. *And a bookcase for Doc.*

"No problem. Don't worry about it."

"Not worried. Just want to contribute my fair share."

He shrugged. "Okay. You asked me to review all the prints at the Young residence. Sorry it's taking so long but I ran into something strange and I've been digging into it."

Quinn pulled up a stool. "What?"

"On the prints, generally the forensic techs will dust the obvious places at a crime scene but they can't dust the whole house top to bottom. If there's something unusual, they'll do more than the usual doors, sills, knobs, countertops, that kind of thing."

Quinn nodded. "Yes. So?"

"Anyway, there was no evidence of anyone else in that house. The techs downstairs ran the prints and I double checked them."

"Okay. We both know in today's world people wear gloves."

"Yeah. Well, I didn't go any further because the prints were either in the system with a record—like Roger Calhoun Young—or there was nothing on them, like the two Young brothers."

"Got it. What did you find?" Quinn tried not to sound impatient.

"Well, it wasn't about the fingerprints as much as it's about the record. Look what I found on Roger Calhoun Young."

Quinn stared. "How did we miss that?"

Chuck shook his head. "Apparently we're not the only ones who did. It's not in the FBI record. I found it through a newspaper search." He grinned. "And for what it's worth, we've only been on this for a few days. Other folks have had years."

Quinn nodded. "Oh, yes, they have." She stood up, patted Chuck on the back, and said, "Way to go, Chuck. Way to go."

"I'll send this to your secure folder."

"Good work. I'm on it."

Quinn went back in her office, shut her door, and logged back on to her computer.

The Valley Sheriff's Office

Billy looked up from his desk in the detective room.

"Surprised to see you down here, Billy."

"Hey, Sylvia. Do my best work up in the lab—closer to work with our wonder tech, Elizabeth, but also gives more room in here for the other two. Anyway, my office habits aren't likely the reason for this unexpected visit."

Sylvia laughed. "No. No, they're not. Saw you in here. How's Quinn doing?"

Billy leaned back in his chair. "Better than most who have to live with it, I'd say. Her talk with you seemed to help her turn a corner."

"Good to hear. Anything I can do?"

"Don't think so. She's got a big case coming off the stop of that convertible. Thought it might intersect with our recent fentanyl haul, but so far it doesn't."

"The problems in these mountains used to be about stealing each other's moonshine, bar fights, and domestic violence."

"Still got those."

"Not as bad, I think. The influx of folks who don't have roots here make it hard to maintain community."

"That's why the work the Sheriff and Bella are doing to design and build a community center is so important."

"I agree. The Corral gives us a great place for music, but we need more. Well, anyway, sorry to interrupt. Just wanted to check on Quinn."

"Thanks, again, Sylvia. She'll be pleased you asked."

Sylvia pulled the door closed behind her.

Billy took out his personal phone and sent Quinn a text: "Hey!"

"Hey!"

"Busy?"

"Swamped. Call u later?"

"10-4. Sylvia said 'hey.'"

"Hey, back." She ended with a heart emoji.

He sent an intertwined heart back. *I hope you can hang in there.*

Chapter 25

*Don't try to figure out what other people want to hear from you;
figure out what you have to say.*
Barbara Kingsolver

Quinn's Office

Quinn looked up from her computer at the knock on her open door. "Hey, George. What's up?"

"I've checked on everyone and just took lunch orders. Folks want to stay at their tasks, so I'll just get lunches and deliver them. We're ordering sandwiches and salads from the deli next door. Want something?"

"Thanks for taking care of our guests. I lost track of time." She looked at her watch. "Oh, my gosh. It's twelve-thirty. Are they starving?"

"Relax. Everyone could take care of themselves if needed. I'm just trying to be a good host."

"You are. Thanks. Anyway, I'll have a tuna salad sandwich on whole wheat, please."

"Got it. I'll drop it off when it gets here."

"Thanks, George." She hesitated. "George, I think we have something much bigger here than the tragic loss of four lives." She reached for her wallet.

"Oh?" He leaned against the door frame. "Ready to share?"

"No. But I will be by three." She smiled. She handed him the money she'd taken out.

He put his hand up. "No need. Ms. Leonard said the Chief wants it billed to the station."

Quinn knitted her brow. "One of these days we have to figure out how to keep all this fair. We should feed our guests, but we have to eat anyway. Seems the station shouldn't pay for ours."

"Yeah, and the Chief has a discretionary budget and the agents probably get an allowance for temporary duty elsewhere. So, it all comes out in the wash. Just tell the Chief thanks."

She laughed. "I will, George. I will." She gave a slight wave as he turned to leave.

"Back shortly with sustenance."

"10-4." She turned back to the screen.

Conference Room

At two forty-five, Quinn went to the conference room to check with Agent Michaels of the FBI and get ready for their team meeting.

She tapped on the slightly open door.

Bill Michaels looked up from his computer. "Hey, Quinn. Is it that time already?"

"Close. If you have time, I need a minute with you on some evidence that hasn't been addressed yet."

"Sure. What's up?"

She pulled up the picture of the boxes with safety deposit keys. "These were in the convertible and we just haven't gotten to them, yet. I suspect they will be in your court before this is said and done. Just wanted to make sure I apprised you of them."

Bill whistled. "Wow! How many are there?"

"Fifty-two."

"Thanks for the heads-up. Depending on how this goes, we may need you to transfer custody."

She nodded. "Let's get through what we have at the moment and then decide."

Bill stood. "Unless you need something, I'll head down the hall. Back shortly."

"Sure." She pulled up the document their list of tasks.

Folks entered the room and everyone was seated ready to go by two fifty-five.

"No need to delay. Let's get started. Who wants to start?" Quinn looked around the table.

Bill Michaels went first. "Mine might be quickest. We already have agents out on notification to the Young sisters. Might be tricky to find out if they have scarification, but we'll know more when they make contact. An agent from Washington has made contact with DA O'Haire and initial conversations are in play on new identity for Ms. Fisher. It's no guarantee, but has some possibility. If you release her, they will keep her in protective custody while they see if we can find Carter. Last, but not least, we're working on a subpoena to get the bank records on Sonia Young regarding the money she used to buy the house."

"Thanks, Bill. Sandy?"

Sandy cleared her throat. "We are still waiting on the report from the forensic pathologist on the age of the two men. Preliminary reports suggest that the younger son is most likely the one in the bed at the home with Ms. Young. That would put Anthony Young, Jr. in the convertible."

Kevin interrupted. "We still don't know why?"

Quinn looked at him. "We may never know." She let that hang in the air. "We have no video at the home of Sonia and Phillip Young. The only fingerprints we've found are Sonia's and Phillip's. If Anthony was there, we don't know it. They were clearly deceased when the bomb went off in the truck, so someone was in the area at or about the time they died. Who? We don't even know where the convertible was."

Kevin squinted. "I thought we did. Didn't someone see Sonia in it?"

Quinn shook her head. "No, Kevin. I was trying to get Roger to talk when I said I had met her and seen the convertible."

Kevin turned deep red. "Sorry, Quinn. I shouldn't have made that mistake."

"No problem. Lots of information to keep in our heads." She turned to George. "Please make sure the crime board reflects that we have registration on the convertible, but not last known whereabouts." *George knows it's accurate. Hope this cuts Kevin some slack.*

George nodded.

"Quinn, I have one more thing."

"Sorry, sure. Go ahead, Sandy."

"We're working with DA O'Haire and the South Carolina folks. It seems they are trying to locate the drugs that were confiscated from Roger."

Every head at the table turned to look at her. "Seems the arrest happened in a small town and the drugs were transferred to their state bureau. I'm sure they'll turn up."

"Maybe they have."

All heads turned to Kevin.

He shrugged. "Could be what we found in the convertible—or at least part of the same batch."

We know that, Kevin. Why are you so edgy today? Quinn nodded. "Noted. Thanks, Kevin. Sandy. George, anything to report?"

"As you know, it's hard to get mental health records even when you know they exist. We strategized that the best angle to try and see if Marcia Fisher has mental health issues was to get DeAnn to talk with her."

"Did you?"

"We did. Kevin had DeAnn pulled out for a fake interview—and a break—and she's going to see what she can get."

"Thanks. Sam, do you have anything?"

"Nope. Following the information from South Carolina on the drugs. Nothing else."

"Any other information, comments, questions before I share what I've found?" Quinn looked around the table.

They spent the next fifteen minutes discussing the details of the information each had shared.

Quinn waited a few seconds after what seemed a final statement from George. "Anyone see any reason to talk further with Christopher?"

Sandy looked around the table. "Well, not really my issue, but if you release him, are you going to let him have the van they were in?"

Quinn shook her head in a decisive "No." She took a breath. "No, way. It's not registered to him and at this point even if I believe the equipment is his, we have no proof it is."

"I agree. Just asking."

"That's important. We don't want to miss anything. Feel free to jump in at any time. It sounds to me that we all agree there is risk in further interview with Marcia until the DA is ready to talk to her. Is that right?"

All heads nodded.

"Okay. It sounds like we're in agreement that the next step is to interview Roger Calhoun Young. I've waited to tell you what Chuck found and my further research on it. We needed to wrap up what we have at the moment. Once you see this information, I need everyone's focus on how we use it to interview Roger."

Quinn switched screens and brought up three small newspaper articles and waited while everyone read them.

After several minutes, Bill Michaels let out a slow whistle. "Your tech found these?"

"He found the one from Ohio. I found the one from Mexico and the second one from Ohio."

George said, "And none of this was in the FBI record?"

"Not yet." Quinn gave a quiet, simple response.

"I don't read Spanish. Would you translate, please?" Kevin turned slightly pink.

"Sorry. Should have asked." Quinn smiled at Kevin and then read them the article.

"Not to sound defensive," Bill looked around the table, "but unless a case is being actively worked, we often become the repository of information. But... you'd think that first article would have made the file."

"Only if there was a reason for it." Quinn smiled at him. "Thoughts on interview?"

Comments swirled around the table and Quinn captured them in bulleted notes on the screen.

"Anything else?" Quinn noticed Sam had been watching her. He winked.

"What's *your* idea, Quinn?" Kevin waited.

"Of course I've been thinking about this since Chuck gave it to me and you have just seen it. I think you've covered most of what I've been thinking. First, there are many pieces to this puzzle which belong in other jurisdictions. Our primary goal is to find out how Sonia and Phillip Young died, assuming he's the one in the bed, determine the source of the drugs and money in the convertible, and where it came from, as well as the convertible. Anything that might involve the sisters, or Robert Kemp Cramer, assuming he is found, will likely be federal in nature. Am I missing something?"

Several of them spoke at once.

"Sam?"

"I think you've figured out a key piece in all of this. Can I observe the interview?"

"No reason not to that I know of. Anyone else want to observe?"

All hands went up around the table except George, who she had already said would be her partner in the interview.

"Alright then." She looked at her watch. "I don't want Marcia going into the night worrying about whether she's safe. So, let's start with a short interview so we can tell her that the DA is working with the FBI on a plan."

"Sounds good."

"Yeah. Good idea."

"Makes sense."

"Quinn, DeAnn said she's fine to stay as long as we need her with Marcia."

"Thanks, Kevin. We'll have the matron let her know while we have Marcia out of the cell that she'll likely be there until tomorrow."

Kevin nodded.

"Sounds like we're all in agreement. Take a break. George and I will go talk with Marcia and then we'll plan on them bringing Roger into interview at six-fifteen. Please be at the Matron's desk by six so she can get you settled. Kevin will you make sure she knows there will be four of you in observation?"

"Yes, ma'am."

"Thanks for your time and continued work." Quinn stood.

Bill Michaels looked at his secure phone and read a text. "Quinn, may I see you a minute?"

"Sure. Thanks, folks."

The room emptied and Quinn shut the door. "What's up?"

"I need a minute to call the agents in Ohio."

"Sure. I'll step down the hall and be right back."

"10-4." He punched in a number.

Quinn opened the door and Bill motioned her into the room even though he was still on the phone. She heard the tail end of the conversation which he put on speaker. Her heart started racing.

"Good work, Agent. I'll see that your supervisor knows how much we appreciate the swift action. Good bye."

"Was that recap for my benefit?"

Bill smiled. "It sure was. Did you get it all?"

"I think so. They informed both women at the same time even though they live miles apart. Which one was so helpful?"

"Ann—the thirty year old."

"Were all three of the older children of Sonia and Anthony in foster care?"

"Seems so. Ann and Anthony, who she said was called Tony, for the longest."

"Did she know Tony had come to Tennessee?"

He shook his head. "Sounds like he got the worst of Anthony, Sr. That's why he was in foster care—lots of abuse."

"Do the sisters have the scarification?"

"Apparently the oldest does not. She seemed the most settled. She was adopted when she was two. Sonia gave her up willingly."

Quinn leaned on the table. "How is it that so many of these cases are like opening those Russian stacking dolls?"

"Because most folks who end up criminals come from pretty messed up homes."

"If they have a home…" she whispered.

"What's that?"

"If they have a home." She said more confidently. "No time now to discuss what a home is, but seems to me it's time to end the myth of the ideal family."

"Long overdue." Bill stood. "I'll let you get to your interview. Hope that information helps."

"Oh, yes. Big time." Quinn walked out and headed to her office to get her Yeti.

Interview

Quinn met George in the small office beside the Matron's office.

"Was there anything on the recording from the wire on DeAnn?"

"I asked the officer who took over the monitoring to give me an update. Seems the most Marcia will admit to is talking to a preacher when she was thirteen."

"About?"

"Why God would let someone like Uncle Bob control so many people."

"Interesting. Did she get an answer?"

"Apparently not one that satisfied her. She told DeAnn that was when she started skipping Sunday School and going to McDonald's with the other kids."

Quinn nodded. "Sounds like a teenager. Doesn't mean she doesn't have mental health issues. I think she does have resilience, though. She's managed to do what she's been directed to do and not get arrested."

"Yeah, let's hope we don't find out that there was something she did that was worse than trespassing."

"I'm confident the FBI and Peggy O'Haire will do some pretty thorough work before they give her immunity and a new identity." She took a sip of water. "Our job is to see what we can get out of Roger. Let's get Marcia settled for the night and then we're on it."

"Matron has her in Room One."

They walked down together.

"Good afternoon, Marcia." Quinn smiled at her.

"Afternoon."

Both Quinn and George pulled chairs up to the table. *I hope that makes her feel that we're here as a team to help her.*

George set the recorder on the table.

"This is Detective Isaacs of the Round City Police, in Interview Room One with…"

"Detective Marshall of the Round City Police," he looked at Marcia.

"Marcia Fisher."

"Marcia, you are still under your Miranda Warning, but I will repeat it if you wish."

"No need."

"Do you wish to have an attorney present?"

"No. I don't want anyone else present."

"The District Attorney and the FBI are working on a plan regarding your request for witness protection. As I told you, they will interview you…"

"You said the District Attorney, not the FBI."

"I'm sorry if I omitted that. The state of Tennessee does not have a witness protection program, so the FBI is the only agency which can offer you protection."

Marcia's head drooped. "Fat chance they will."

"Marcia, please look at me." Quinn kept her voice soft and even. "Thanks. Everything you can share of your own knowledge about Uncle Bob will be considered. I promise you." *Are you smart enough to read between the lines?*

"I guess we'll see."

"I also wanted to tell you that the woman in the room with you will likely be moved tomorrow. It may take another day before you meet with the DA and FBI. Do you prefer to be alone if she is moved?"

Marcia's shoulders slumped. "Guess I can't expect one of the nicest people I've known, besides Christopher, to stay in a jail cell because of my life circumstances." She looked up suddenly. "Is Christopher still here?"

Quinn made an instant decision to see what it might cause her to say. "He is."

"Honestly, he doesn't even know anything about Uncle Bob other than the fact that he had us go videotape land from the drones."

"You never told Christopher your fears?"

Marcia's eyes went wide. "Are you kidding? I only told you because I figured the best—heck the only—chance I have of getting away from the family is if you can help me."

"Just tell the DA and the FBI the truth and anything you can think of that will help them get Uncle Bob."

"Do you think they'll believe me when I tell them I was made to watch a murder when I was twelve?"

"Tell the truth and give as much detail as you can."

"I was sent pictures when I was in college to remind me to do whatever I was given to do."

"Do you have any of the pictures?"

She shook her head and a vacant look appeared in her eyes. "Never."

"Try to remember everything you were directed to do. The more information you can share, the better it will help."

"Help what? They'll never catch him."

"Why do you say that?"

"No one's seen him in years. Everything is by mail. You get a burner phone and receive texts, or get keys—like the ones to the van."

"How does he know where you are?"

"There is a check-in system. Speaking of which I must be close to the end of the seventy-two hours."

Quinn tried not to turn her head to George. *Oh, Marcia, the FBI will want to be in on that check-in.* She counted the hours they'd had her. *Fifty, give or take. Depends on when she had her last check in.*

"How did you pay for gas for van?" George watched Marcia.

"I was sent cash with the keys. It should be in the van."

"Did Christopher know you got the cash?"

"He may have figured out Uncle Bob sent it, but he'd just think it was to cover expenses and pay him. I had the key to the drawer it was in."

That explains the two thousand dollars in the drawer.

Quinn smiled at her. "Just remember, Marcia, the most important thing is to tell the DA and the FBI everything you can."

Marcia nodded her head without much enthusiasm. "Detective…" She looked at Quinn. "DeAnn made a stupid mistake because of a man. They got the watch back, so can't you help her get a deal?"

"I'm glad you're concerned for her. I'll pass the information along to the detective working her case." *Empathy. There's hope for you, Marcia.* "Anything else? Do you want to stay by yourself?"

"Yeah. I'll either survive this or I won't."

"This is Detective Isaacs ending interview with…"

"Marcia Fisher."

"Detective Marshall escorting Marcia Fisher to her cell." George stood and opened the door.

Quinn clicked the off button on the recorder. *Have you figured out, Marcia, that you're still being recorded?*

"Thanks, Detective. I apologize for being such a bitch at the beginning."

"Take care of yourself, Marcia. You have a lot of life ahead of you." Quinn smiled at her.

George took Marcia down the hall. Quinn stretched and then walked into the hall. She heard the door to the observation room open. Sandy Davis and Bill Michaels walked out.

"Hey, didn't know you were there."

"Concerned about that?" Michaels said.

She laughed softly. "Not at all. Just didn't occur to me you'd want to see this one. But it makes sense. Sorry not to have suggested it. Of course you'd want to see her in person—so to speak."

"I should have brought it up." Bill Michaels walked up beside her.

"Come on. Matron will have coffee and iced tea. I need to regroup with George for a minute and then we'll be ready at six-fifteen for Roger."

"Can't wait for that." Sandy kept pace with them.

Chapter 26

All experience is great providing you live through it.
Alice Neel

Interview Room Two

"Quinn, I'm glad we could be in Room Two. It's bigger."

"Yeah, with guards on this guy, it made more sense. Thanks for thinking of it. Ready?"

"Oh, I can't wait until he sees you walk in the room."

Should be interesting. She straightened her shoulders as George opened the door.

Roger Calhoun Young looked even thinner than when they arrested him Sunday night. He was seated at the table with ankle chains and his wrist cuffs connected at the waist. There were two guards standing behind him.

Either one of them could win a weightlifting competition. Quinn sat directly across from Roger and turned on the recorder. "This is a test." She stopped it and played it back.

She looked Roger in the eyes. "Good evening. This is Detective Isaacs of the Round City Police in Interview Room Two with…"

"Detective Marshall of the Round City Police and…" He nodded to the guards who each gave their names.

"We are here to interview…please state your name, legal address and date of birth." She stared at Roger.

"Well, hello there. I think we've met before."

"Please state your name, legal address, and date of birth."

He smirked. "Roger Calhoun Young. No fixed address." He gave his date of birth.

George wrote it down even though it matched what they had on file.

"Mr. Young, you have the right to remain silent...." Quinn completed the Miranda warning. "Do you understand these rights and responsibilities?"

"Yep."

"Do you wish to have an attorney present?"

He chuckled. "You slipped under the wire on your seventy-two hours to hold me. The day I need an attorney for a traffic violation will be the day...well, let's just leave it that I can take care of myself. No, I don't want an attorney."

"Very well. Mr. Young, you were arrested on a traffic violation for a broken and non-operable tail light, which in the state of Tennessee is illegal." She leaned in. "But, as I'm sure you know, you have an outstanding warrant in South Carolina on which we have you detained and can do so for up to thirty days—while the authorities there decide if they want to extradite you."

He glared at her.

"That, however, is not our problem here in Tennessee." She smiled.

"Think you're clever don't you? Acting all folksy in the park. Your buddy over there showing up at the Dew Drop Inn. Where's your third side kick? Does your real boyfriend know you were making out in the park with a cop?"

Quinn did not move a muscle on her face.

"No answer? Figures. So, sweetheart, why are we here? It isn't because of a broken tail light. Appears you have some questions."

"I do. Funny, your defective vehicle is registered to your Uncle Bob just like the convertible. I know you're disappointed you couldn't find Sonia." She opened the folder in front of her and took out a photograph of the "brand" on Sonia's hip. She turned it in front of him. "Recognize that?"

He didn't blink.

She took the picture of Sonia on the floor, turned it around and set it next to the other picture. "Maybe this one looks more familiar."

He didn't blink.

She took the picture of the male Young found in the bed. "Which of your relatives is this?" She placed it next to the one of Sonia.

He didn't blink.

"Maybe you know which of your relatives this is." She took the picture of the driver from the convertible.

George watched her carefully. *Way to go, Quinn. You are steady as a rock. You've got this.*

Quinn set the picture on top of the others. "What will Uncle Bob think of this relative?"

He didn't blink.

"Mr. Carter…" Quinn hesitated.

Roger Calhoun Young blinked and then rattled his chains. "Let me out of here."

"I'm sorry. Is there a problem, Mr. Young? I wanted to ask you a question about your Uncle Bob."

"I want you to stop talking." He spat the words out.

"I have the right to question you."

"I don't have to answer."

"No, you don't. You also have the right to an attorney. Do you want one?"

"No." Spit hit the table.

"Then I have another question, but first I need assistance from the guards." She looked up at the man she knew to be the senior guard.

"Please remove his hands from his waist. You can leave the wrists cuffed."

The two guards easily moved the chair back from the table and one leaned down to unlock his cuffed hands from the waist chain.

"Thank you." She nodded to the guards who stayed right by each arm of Roger Calhoun Young.

"*Señor* Young," she spoke in her flawless Spanish.

He glared at her.

"*Por favor, pon tus manos sobre la mesa.*"

He left his hands in his lap.

"It would be best if I didn't have to ask these guards to put your hands on the table."

He didn't move.

"Guards."

One on each side of him, they lifted his arms and put his hands on the table.

"Those very faint scars, Mr. Carter, are very well done. Would you like to tell me the story of finding your twin brother and the fishing trip to Mexico?"

The guards held his arms in place.

He didn't move or speak.

"Then the last question I have before I turn you over the FBI is this—do you know the penalty for perjury, Mr. Robert Kemp Carter?"

He didn't move or speak.

She smiled. "Doesn't really matter. It's the least of the charges you'll be facing." She nodded to the guards. "Gentlemen, since Mr. Carter seems unable to speak. You can return him to isolation. He'll remain there until the FBI and the state of South Carolina figure out whose case trumps the others." She held up her hand. "One minute. Señor Carter, "Tenemos una confesión de la cirujana en México." She smiled. *I don't usually lie, but I suspect the FBI will have that confession from the surgeon before it's all said and done.*

Roger Calhoun Young AKA Robert Kemp Carter sat stone-faced. "I'll get you, bitch."

"That's Detective Bitch to you. For the record, we'll add threatening a law enforcement officer." She sat back in her chair. "Oh, and Mr. Carter, before you go, you better believe if I can prove you killed Sonia Young and her son, there will be more charges. Get him out of here."

The guard reattached Carter's wrists to his waist and each took an arm and all but carried him out of the room.

Quinn clicked the button. She did not bother to sign off on the recorder—everything was on videotape and had been observed by the DA on video, and in the observation room an FBI agent, an agent of the SBI, a DEA agent, and Detective Millwood. She wasn't worried about it.

The agents were in the doorway when Quinn stood up. "He's all yours. But, I promise you if I can prove he killed Sonia and her son, you'll get those charges, too. See you upstairs then you all need to go home." She headed down the hall.

Conference Room

Quinn was already in the Conference Room when the agents and Detective Millwood walked in and sat down.

George was last through the door. "Sorry. I *had* to wash my hands."

Quinn laughed. "I need a shower."

Bill Michaels spoke first. "Good job, Quinn. On the research and the interview. Looks like we'll need those keys you found in the convertible."

Quinn turned to George. "Would you please see that the safety deposit box keys get transferred to the FBI?" Then she looked at Bill. "And, if it's appropriate at some point, we'd love to know 'the rest of the story on those keys.'"

"I'll share if I can."

The door to the conference room opened. They all stood as the Chief walked in.

"Sit. Sit. Good job everyone. Do your debrief and then I'll say what I have to say." She sat next to Quinn.

Each of the agents spoke to their on-going investigations and how they anticipated this would play out.

"Questions or comments?" Quinn looked around the table.

No one moved.

Chief Hansen straightened in her chair. "We're a small, rural police station which has had more than our share of crime already this year. We've lost a fellow officer and that leaves a mark on all of us—especially on the officer who defended him." She looked at Quinn. "While we will continue to try and find out who is responsible for the deaths of Sonia Young and her son, we've done our job here in Round City. Now the rest of you can sort out the details with the DA around Ms. Fisher and Mr. Carter. It is my understanding the DA is not bringing charges against Mr. Cox, but will send him on his way with a stiff warning. I appreciate the support of your agencies and each of you as individuals. We are always grateful for quality people who can put their nose to the grindstone and move a case along. Thank you for coming. Now go home—and for my folks, that's an order." She stood and left the room.

Quinn held up her hand. "Before you go, please accept my personal thanks for your help, your commitment to this case and I hope you are successful in solving all the other cases which appear to be attached to this man." She pushed her chair back. "When our Chief gives an order, we follow it." She stood.

They all clapped.

"Good job, Quinn."

"You cracked this case."

"Way to go."

Quinn held up her hand again. "Team work got us here. Glad to be part of it." She shook hands with each of them.

1211 Sunrise

Quinn backed into the driveway as the garage door opened. A smile spread across her face when she saw Billy's SUV—his, not his work SUV. She jumped out and slipped out of her shoes at the door.

Billy opened it and held his arms out. "Welcome home, Detective."

She leaned into him and he held her tight. He whispered in her ear. "I love you."

"I love you." Her head was resting on his shoulder. "Thank you for coming right away."

"Sheriff would have it no other way."

She pulled back. "Oh, no. Were you in a meeting when I sent the text?"

"No, but I'm on duty tonight. I called my sidekick and he was happy to come in and the Sheriff was all about it. So relax. Hungry?"

"Starved. I don't know what there is to eat in this house." Then she turned toward the counter. "Do I smell barbecue?"

"From The Corral. It was ready as soon as I walked to the side door."

"I want to tell you about today, but can I go shower and change before we eat?"

"You've got it. I'll get things ready. Nice night. Shall we sit on the back terrace?"

"Perfect. I'll have wine."

"My pleasure. Now go."

Quinn put her service weapon and badge in her safe and headed toward her bedroom. She was pulling her jacket off as she went.

Oh, love of my life, you will hear about tempting me like that. He turned to fix their plates.

Twenty minutes later she walked in the kitchen. She had on a pale-blue flowered caftan.

Billy whistled. "You look relaxed."

"I don't look anxious?"

"Not at all."

"Well, I am. I can't wait to tell you what happened." She had a big grin.

He took their plates out of the oven. "The coleslaw and drinks are on the table. Go." He nodded toward the French doors.

Quinn opened the doors and saw the flowers on the table. "Oh, Billy. They're lovely."

"Even I, a mere brown thumb gardener, can cut flowers and put them in a vase."

"They are beautiful, but all the more so that you thought of it. Before I tell you what happened, will you please help me remember to buy a bookcase?"

"Did this case produce volumes?" He squinted at her.

She laughed. "No, I have a friend who needs one. Now let me tell you what happened."

Billy held up his hand. He took his phone and sent a message. "Okay, there's an email in your inbox to buy a bookcase."

She laughed. "I could have done that, couldn't I?" She shook her head and lifted her wine glass. "Thanks. I love you."

He clinked his glass against hers. "I love you."

She told him the plan the team had come up with and how each agency followed up on their part in trying to put things together. Then she told him about the interrogation with Robert Kemp Carter. She smiled and took a sip of wine.

"Okay, I'm dying to know how you figured out he was Carter, but first is the Fisher woman going to get a break?"

"Not up to us. I suspect Peggy will hold her charges until she works out the details with the FBI."

"Maybe she doesn't need witness protection with him…that was stupid. She might have to testify."

"Bingo, ace detective." She laughed.

"So, how did you figure out he was Carter?"

"Chuck did a search in archived newspapers and found a story about the death of Robert Kemp Carter. It was a local story in a small town newspaper in Ohio. They were looking for his twin brother Roger Calhoun Young. Oh, and apparently, Roger studied Spanish in college." She grinned.

"Why didn't anyone find that before?"

"As Chuck said, not everything ends up in official legal databases."

"Well, good for him for being a sleuth."

"I took the information and started doing some digging myself. Based on their ages and the fact the paper said they were twins, I found identical twin boys in Ohio who had been abandoned and no family members could be found. They were adopted by two different families: the Youngs and the Carters." She took another sip of wine. "I just lucked across the piece in the Mexican paper about twin brothers from Ohio who had been fishing seventeen years ago and the boat capsized. Another fisherman tried to save them but one reportedly died on the way to the hospital."

"And? How did that play into it?"

"I assume Carter had it set up all along. It was a month before the piece in the Ohio paper saying Carter had died. It's also when he dropped off the radar of police. Coincidentally, it's also when Sonia Young moved to Tennessee. Anyway, I talked with some medical folks at the university and it's possible to graft skin from identical twins without rejection or immunosuppressants. So, I took a chance that Carter had his Roger Young's fingerprints transferred to him in a Mexican hospital."

"Did he?" Billy's eyes were wide.

"The FBI will figure it out for sure, but his fingers all have very pale scars that support the theory."

"Well done, Detective. Well done."

"Thanks, kind sir. I still don't know how the convertible played into it. I assume Tony Young—we learned from one of the sisters that's the name he used—was sent with it to have Sonia make a delivery. I honestly don't know and we may never know." Her secure phone buzzed.

"Isaacs." She listened without speaking. "Thanks, Doc. We'll see if we ever have true confessions from Mr. Carter."

"Have a good night, Quinn. Word in the building is that you earned it."

"We all did. You go home, now, too."

"I'm home. The SBI forensic tech called me. He thought we'd want to end the day with a ruling."

"Better than none. Thanks, Doc. The sisters will not likely claim the bodies. So, we'll deal with that tomorrow."

"Night, Quinn."

"Night, Doc."

Billy waited on her to finish.

"Official ruling on Sonia and son is murder/suicide."

"You think Carter did it?"

"I do. This, however, is a case of speculation that will lead nowhere. If he did, he is a master at staging a murder/suicide. That is the ruling we have by the ME. Maybe it will become the cold case I look at when I retire."

"Maybe. And, maybe you cut yourself some slack and celebrate the leadership you gave your team to get this far."

She smiled at him. "You are so good for me, Billy Williams. Have I ever told you that?"

"Once or twice. But, please don't stop."

She leaned in and kissed him.

"You have no idea how good you are for me, Quinn Isaacs."

She stood up and took his hand. "Then perhaps you could show me." She opened the French doors and headed straight for the bedroom.

About the Author

Jacque Jacobs earned her PhD from Southern Illinois University in 1982 and had a forty-five year career in education on five continents. She is a life-long reader and has always loved detective stories and spy novels. *The (Early) Morning Crime* is her ninth novel and the third in her second series: *Detective Quinn Isaacs.*

Jacque currently lives in Vero Beach, Florida, where she has lived a cumulative eighteen years—which is the longest she has lived anywhere in her life. She and her late husband, Dr. John F. Jacobs, worked in international universities and schools in Australia, Uruguay, Venezuela, Italy, Germany, Finland, the United Arab Emirates, and her most recent experience was in Salvador, Bahia, Brazil. They took advantage of the opportunity to travel extensively throughout those experiences and Jacque credits the opportunity to get to know people of different cultures in the development of her characters.

She hopes you enjoyed this book and invites comments to her at JEJLetters@gmail.com

Notes from the Author

While this novel, like all of my novels, is purely a figment of my imagination, it is important to me to make sure that details are as accurate as I can make them. When I state the charges for a specific crime, the information is as accurate as I can find based on the laws of the state of Tennessee where the story is set.

My doctoral studies and much of my professional experience is in leadership. The actions of Quinn as a leader come from my long experience leading teams, schools, and a university department. I have always believed that a leadership position requires you to build or strengthen the skills, knowledge, and confidence in the people you serve to lead whatever aspect of the work they do. It is my opinion that we will solve many more problems in our work and life if we work together as a team. It is fun to write Quinn's development in that arena.

Thank you for your interest in my writing.